Mr, Mrs, Freeman
P9-CSG-002
, Goshen
Ind.

The Wandering Heart

The Wandering Heart

by

NANCY J. SELL

ZONDERVAN PUBLISHING HOUSE
Grand Rapids Michigan

Library of Congress Catalog Card Number 66-18947

Printed in the United States of America

To My Children
Ruth, Janet and Danny

. . . . . and my sincere appreciation to my sister, Lucy Chapman, and her daughter, Judith, for their help and encouragement.

They wandered in the wilderness in a solitary way; they found no city to dwell in.

Ps. 107:4

The Wandering Heart

Chapter 1

THE OFFICE WAS silent except for the steady tap-tapping of one typewriter which, had it been a half-hour sooner, would have been a proverbial "drop in the bucket" of the daily humdrum of office routine. The lone typist glanced up at the large round clock, frowned, then hastily removed the letter she had been typing. She folded it carefully and quickly, and then slipped it into the envelope she had previously addressed. It was almost five-twenty-five, and if she hurried she might make the five-thirty bus. The light, misty rain which had started shortly after noon had turned into a downpour, and she was not anxious to wait until six for the next bus. She covered her typewriter and cleared the few scattered paper clips, pencils and erasers into the drawer with one hasty movement of her arm.

The young lady was the last one to leave except for Mr. Chapman who was still in his private office, and she was glad she did not have to make small talk with any of the other workers. With relief she had noticed Lawrence Spencer leaving with Dan Sanderford and Ben Reardon not more than five minutes ago. She did not care to remain here with any of them.

Snatching up her coat, she ran for the elevator, her high heels making a loud clicking sound as she left the carpeted floor of the office and ran down the tiled floor of the corridor. As she rounded the corner, she was dismayed to see the elevator door shut. She watched the indicator creep slowly down to "one." As it passed the "one" and continued its slow pace down to "B," she cursed aloud to herself.

"Got troubles, Amy?"

She was startled and just a little embarrassed as she whirled around, unaware that she was not alone. She had not heard the office door directly opposite the elevator open, nor had she heard the soft-soled approach of Dan Sanderford as he came up behind her. The arrow stopped at "B." Dan pushed the button. They waited in silence as it made its slow journey back up to the third floor where they waited. Amy mumbled something about missing her bus as they stepped into the empty cubicle. She hoped that would be the end of their conversation.

As she hurried across the main floor of the bank, she was glad no one stopped to talk to her. The many scattered desks on either side had only a few busy occupants, and they were anxious to go home. Dan had stopped at Lawrence Spencer's desk with some papers she had seen him carrying, and for this she was relieved too. She did not have to feel Larry's eyes boring through her as she made her way to the door. The lack of conversation in the elevator had made her slightly uncomfortable, and she was glad to be out in the air, wet though it was.

She held her purse over her head to protect her blonde curls somewhat from the weather as she hurried out the big revolving door of the First National Bank of New Hope. There was but one other building between her and the bus stop, and as she sighted her bus coming down the street, she decided to make a run for it. She did not see the woman, also hurrying, but in the opposite direction, her arms laden with packages of varied sizes and shapes. Amy felt like screaming at her as they collided head-on. She handed the woman the last bundle and murmured a "sorry" as she turned to see her bus pulling away from the curb. She stamped her foot and cursed again, this time in a much stronger fashion to fit the circumstances.

Amy stepped to the doorway of a dress shop and lighted a cigarette as she resigned herself to waiting. The weather was much too unpleasant to attempt any window shopping. To add to her annoyance, she saw Dan Sanderford come out of the bank. He stopped to purchase a newspaper from a little boy standing in the shelter of the bank's door, and as he stepped out onto the sidewalk, he put the newspaper over his head. He wore no hat.

Amy knew by his expression that he had sized up the situation, but why could he not let her wait in peace? She thought of going into the dress shop, but that would be too obvious. She disliked him immensely, but she did not want to be rude. *Ignorant* she thought described her impulse better. She wished she were on that bus—on her way home.

Dan had spoken to her, but in her preoccupation she was not quite certain what he had said. "That's life," she answered with an apparent lack of enthusiasm, certain Dan had said something about her predicament. She was surprised when he offered her a ride home in his car. She did not know he owned a car. She refused.

"I'd be glad to give you a lift, Amy. I have to go right out your way, and I'm sure it's not far off the beaten path—no further than you'd have to walk from the bus stop." She was about to refuse again, more emphatically, when he went on as if he had not heard her declination. "My car is right across the street." He walked away from her, expecting her to follow. She did.

He had a car all right, the latest model – shiny black, long and sleek. He guided it expertly onto the city street and in their general direction.

Dan Sanderford was a good-looking fellow. Amy became aware of this as she sat beside him, occasionally glancing his way. She had never thought of him as handsome before. In fact, she had never thought of him at all. He was some kind of a religious fanatic, and she had always been relieved that she had not had too much occasion to associate with him. He was a big fellow, built like a football player, with dark, straight hair, deep-set eyes, fine features – yes, he was handsome. And always well-dressed and apparently well-mannered from what she had unconsciously observed now and then as she had caught a glimpse of him behind his horn-rimmed glasses.

And now she noticed something else about him: his lack of annoyance at the slow-moving, almost motionless traffic. *But that isn't so surprising,* thought Amy. Dan had been the subject of many a snide remark since she had come to work at the bank about a year ago, shortly after he began his employment there. He had been teased and ridiculed about his religion, and she was sure he was the cause of much of the laughter which came from the men's lounge. Their derision never seemed to irritate him, to sway him from his convictions, whatever they were. Or if it did, he never showed any outward sign. Still, when they spoke to him, they respected him. Funny, she never realized that before.

She had been taken aback just a little when he had made his presence known at the elevator, but she did not know why. The foul language she had used was not uncommon around the office. Dan had shown no sign of disapproval, no evidence that he had heard her. She had never heard him use any profanity. It was probably against his religion. Perhaps that was the reason for the slight embarrassment she had felt.

During the ride she was quiet unless he spoke first.

"You'll be going on vacation soon, won't you, Amy?" The vacation list was posted in the downstairs corridor.

"Next week," she answered with little interest. "Friday. A whole week away from that place." She wondered if he noticed the sarcasm in the word *whole.* It was the practice of the bank to give one week of vacation to those who had been working up to two years. Three years' employment or more meant two weeks vacation.

"Made any plans?"

"My brother's wife gave birth to twins day before yesterday," she answered, sure he was just being polite. "I thought I'd run up Friday evening and see if I can be of any help. I'll probably stay the weekend, and if I'm in the way I'll just make my exit."

He thought she would surely be a big help, for twins must mean a great deal of work. And the polite conversation ended. Amy pointed out her house which was on the other side of the street. He went past it, turned around in a driveway, and pulled up in front of the house she had indicated.

"Real service," she said as she got out, forcing a smile that went no further than her lips.

"With a smile," he added.

"Much obliged," she said, slamming the car door. She ran up the steps and into the house.

Amy went directly to the room which had been her home for the past twelve months. She put her things away and changed into slacks, washed her face with cold water, then went to the kitchen. After making herself a sandwich and a cup of coffee, she took them to her room. Mrs. Martin had not come home yet, and Amy was glad she had made it back to her room without having to pass the time of day with the landlady. Mr. and Mrs. Martin lived here alone except for their one roomer, Amy, their children having married and moved away.

Amy was allowed to use the kitchen but ate most of her meals out so she would not be in the way. She did eat breakfast there every morning though, since she was up and on her way before they got out of bed. Breakfast consisted of a piece of toast and a cup of instant coffee. Life was terribly routine.

She ate her sandwich while she looked at a magazine she had picked up in the kitchen. It did not interest her, but it was something to do. She went back to the kitchen, washed her cup, saucer and plate. After putting them away, she went to the basement to wash some clothes, then put them over the line to dry. Mrs. Martin had a washer and dryer, but Amy would not use them for she insisted upon living completely apart from the couple.

It was seven o'clock by the time she had finished her few chores and returned to her room. She turned on the television and flopped in the big chair near the window. "How delightful," she mused with curled lip, "all my housework done and the evening before me to enjoy!"

She would not have had the luxury of a television set except that her brother, Dave, and his wife had insisted that she have it. They were concerned that she should be alone so much, so they had bestowed this "blessing" upon her for Christmas. Oh, she did not live in complete seclusion. She went out on an occasional date, but she was fed up with men.

When she first started working at the bank, she had liked her co-workers and had mixed freely with them. They had seemed to like her, too, and she had gone out on several dates with one or two of the boys.

Then came the office Christmas party. She should not have gone. She knew what could develop from such reckless gaiety, but surely her new friends were far above the typical stories she had heard. She went to the party. The smoke-filled room and the smell of liquor were not distasteful to her, nor were the suggestive stories being passed from group to group.

But as the evening wore on and the drinks had made their effect on all who were there, Amy began to wish she had not come. She had a drink or two herself, but she knew her limit; the others did not. The men did not seem to care that they had wives waiting for them at home, that they would go to these wives with lipstick smeared all over their shirt collars. And some of the girls who were so carelessly putting it there had husbands at home, too. Even the single ones didn't seem to care. Karen Winslow, whose desk had been next to Amy's for the past year, mumbled something about the party getting rough as Ben Reardon stopped her words and laughter with a number of kisses. They ended in a clinch. Karen was enjoying it, not concerned that Ben was one of the married men.

Amy was repelled. She headed for the cloakroom and reached the door just as Lawrence Spencer grabbed her arm and swung her around to face him. He pulled her into the dark room, and before she knew what was happening, he had his arms around her and was smothering her with wet kisses, his hot, stinking breath on her face and neck, holding her so tightly she could scarcely breathe. She recalled how this man had looked at her during working hours, pleased that he thought her attractive. Now he was repulsive. In the darkness of the cloakroom, she suddenly realized he had no intention of letting her go. She screamed, but if anyone heard her above the laughter and pleasant squeals of the other girls, they probably thought she was enjoying herself, too.

She put her arms around him, and he showed his pleasure by holding her tighter. Amy dug her fingernails into his skin, and with all the strength she could muster, she drew her fingers along his back, tearing both shirt and flesh. His grip was suddenly released and he cried out in pain. She fought to keep her balance and quickly brought her foot up to meet his shin before he could get hold of her again. He was in a drunken rage. Amy grabbed her coat and ran. The taxicab that was sitting at the curb carried her away just as Larry appeared at the door looking for her. From that time on, Amy kept to herself, not sure whether she was avoiding her associates or they were avoiding her.

Larry was not one to give up though. Sometimes he was bold as brass. "I'll get you yet," he had chuckled as he stuck his head into the office where she was working alone. Then he had sauntered off toward the elevator, singing at the top of his lungs, "Once in love with Amy, Always in love with Amy . . . " She had slammed her desk drawer shut with an oath. But other times he seemed almost shy in her presence, such as the day he had stood in the doorway, opened his mouth to say something, then snapped it shut like a clam. One never knew what he might do next. He was a problem. But Amy's real problems had been with her since way back when. They made these insignificant ones of New Hope less than trivial.

She had come to this Connecticut town looking for something, and she had not found it. She thought she had, but it had burst in her face like a beautiful, shimmering bubble.

When she had come to the conclusion that she must cut herself off from her old life, from her old associations, she had placed before her a map of Connecticut. With her eyes closed, without design, she would choose the town which fell under her fingertip. However, not too far from the one she had picked, she saw New Hope. That was it. That was what she needed: *new hope.* That would be her home.

Connecticut always had held an unusual fascination for her. She had not visited it before moving here, but the pictures she had seen as a schoolgirl back in her small home town in Delaware had kindled her desire to visit the quaint scenes in person: the lovely white churches on their dogwood-covered hillsides in spring; the heavily populated beaches and the diamond sparkled Sound in summer; the verdant countryside transformed into autumn's multi-colored flaming beauty; and the winter scenes with their seas of untouched virgin snow, guarded by the stately, faithful evergreens. She had not been disappointed.

She watched the television story, half interested, and was relieved when it was over. She looked at the program listings for seven-thirty and turned the set off. There was a program she would watch later if she did not fall asleep first.

Amy was depressed. She picked up the magazine which had fallen to the floor, but was no more interested in it now than she had been earlier. She thumbed through it, then flung it across the room in disgust. As she switched on her little radio and stretched across her bed, she wished she had something to do to keep her from thinking so much. She heard some lovely organ music and settled down to listen, trying to quiet her unpleasant thoughts. As someone started singing, she realized she had tuned in to a local church program.

Groaning, she reached up to change the station, but her hand stopped in mid-air as she listened.

"Once I was drifting aimlessly, I had no port in sight . . . ."

"The story of my life, she said to herself. "Aimless Amy, that's me." She laughed sardonically at the way the words went together.

The voice was lovely. The song was in a minor key, and the baritone voice hit each note as true as the one before. Amy listened, not as much interested in the words as she was in the music.

"The Master Pilot took the helm, His blessings never cease . . . ."

As the melody switched to the major key, her flesh tingled. The words had nice thoughts to them, too, but she wished they did not have to be so fanatical about it. Religion was all right, if only people did not have to carry it so far. Take Dan Sanderford, for instance. People would like him if he were not always preaching at them. Well, she was not sure just how much preaching he did, actually, since she spent very little time talking to him. At least he had not forced his religion on her.

Dave had religion, too, but she had seen almost nothing of her brother since he went away to college. She supposed he had found it there, she was not sure. She had never heard of anyone finding it at college before. But he met Joy there, and she had it too.

Not for me, thought Amy. *I've got enough problems to handle without getting mixed up in something like that.* Two girls she had known back home had become involved in some cult, and they had experienced terrible emotional problems before giving it up. *Not for me,* she silently reiterated.

But she wanted to hear the song, and she had let her thoughts distract her. She raised up on her elbows, chin in hand and stared at the radio, trying not to miss a note. She was sorry when it was over, and as she rolled over to change the station so that she might not have to listen to any preaching, she again stopped, motionless.

"Thank you, Dan," the deep voice was saying. "That was Dan Sanderford bringing us that lovely message in song. Dan will be back in a few minutes to give us a few words."

Amy sat up in stark amazement. She could not fathom the words she had heard. Dan Sanderford! The fellow everyone avoided. The fellow everyone ridiculed. The fellow who had left her at her door an hour or so ago. Not possible! She tossed her saucy curls in unbelief.

But her curiosity was aroused and she perched on the edge of her bed to listen to the rest of the program. The announcer had said that Dan would be back, and she wanted to hear what he had to say. She relaxed again, having recovered from her original shock, as she thought what a topic of conversation this would make at the office. Dan Sanderford!

At last she heard the man with the deep voice mention Dan's name again, and she listened, her attention undivided. It had occurred to her that there could be another man with the same name.

"Thank you, Roy," he was saying. It was the same Dan Sanderford. She held her breath until he finished speaking, then turned off the radio.

Later that night, as she lay in bed, she kept thinking about her life. She had no goal. Her life had no purpose. But she was not interested in Dan's religion.

Chapter 2

As Dan drove away from Amy's place, his thoughts were filled, for the most part, with events to take place that evening. He was late, but his mother would have dinner ready and waiting. He would have to shower and dress quickly to make it back to the station by seven-thirty.

He pulled up to the traffic light on the corner and opened the car window to let in some fresh air. He wished women did not smoke. It certainly did detract from appearances, in his estimation. But it was not out of place for Amy Archer, nor was the foul language he had heard from her lips back at the bank. What an unhappy girl she was! She did not seem to have many friends at work although he remembered a time when she seemed to be quite well-liked. She surely found favor in Spencer's eyes, but there was something strange about that situation. She avoided him as if he were poison. Larry Spencer was a wild one, so Dan could hardly blame any sensible girl for avoiding him. Likable sort though, without his stinking cigars.

Amy was efficient and apparently enjoyed her work, but she was not part of the "one happy family" Mr. Chapman often called them. Dan was not either, but not for the same reason. He wondered subconsciously what Amy's reason was. He wished he had been able to talk with her more freely, but even as he had tried, he sensed her wall of indifference to even the everyday pleasantries he had tried to exchange with her.

As he stepped on the accelerator and swung the car back onto Route One, the rain came in the open window, forcing him to shut it.

Ten minutes later, he turned into his own drive, left the car at the back door and ran up the steps, taking them two at a time, again holding the newspaper over his head. The delightful aroma of roast beef greeted him as he entered the kitchen, assuring him that dinner would soon be on the table.

"You're late, son," his mother's voice warned from the dining room. "Better eat before you change. It's all ready."

Dan put his damp suitcoat over the back of a chair and washed at the kitchen sink. His mother came in from the dining room just as his sister breezed in from the front hall. She never *came in;* she always breezed in, making sure everyone present was aware of it when she did.

Dan carved the meat while they dished up the vegetables. He was about to ask where his younger brother was when the door flew open again, the same one his sister had come through.

"Say, how about some food!" he demanded. "A guy could starve around here, and no one would care!"

Elaine smiled as she handed him the bowl of mashed potatoes and pinched his cheeks playfully. He was unable to defend himself. "How would you like a hot white face?" he asked sternly.

The three of them laughed while Paul obediently took the potatoes into the dining room. He was almost eighteen and had recently graduated from high school. He had played first string on the football team for two years, and it was a sad day when he had to leave it. He was a big fellow, his size being the only thing he and Dan had in common. Paul stood a full six foot four, one inch over his older brother and used that inch to lord it over Dan. He towered over his sister who was four years his senior. He loved to tease her.

They followed with the rest of the dinner, and after Mrs. Sanderford returned to the kitchen for the gravy, they bowed their heads while Dan returned thanks. He was the oldest and had assumed the responsibility as head of the household when his father died six years ago. Dan was seventeen then and he, too, was about to leave high school. The family was well-situated financially, so he had been able to go on to college without being a burden to his loved ones. They were very dear to him.

They talked of the events of the day, of the radio program and meeting they were going to that evening, but Dan ate hurriedly, with little conversation, so that he might be ready on time. He said he would have his dessert later.

He showered and shaved while the women cleaned up the dishes. He came down before they were done, smelling of after-shave lotion.

"Everybody ready? Let's go, Elaine. Come on, Paul, or we'll be late."

His sister put her arms around him impetuously and kissed him on the cheek. "Why do I have you for a brother?" she asked frowning.

"Why, I think you're pretty fortunate to have a nice brother like me!"

"That's just it," she said with mock sadness. "You're my brother!"

She made hasty steps toward the door to avoid the brotherly swat she was about to receive. Paul followed, but Dan waited for his mother. He opened the umbrella and took her arm as they went down the steps.

Paul had the car running. After putting his mother in the front seat, Dan went around to the driver's side and made Paul get out. He did so reluctantly and got into the back with his sister. "Boy, will I be glad when I get my license," he mumbled. He was waiting for his eighteenth birthday for that reason.

"Well, little brother," said Elaine, "I'm going to check your birth certificate when we get home. You're a menace . . . " His hand was over her mouth.

"Done?" he asked. She nodded, and he let her go.

" . . . to the other driv . . . "

He yelped loudly as a perfectly matched set of uppers and lowers sank into his fingers.

Dan and his mother were amused, but they rode in silence. He was glad the traffic was not as heavy as it had been after work. This Connecticut town was the crossroads for many routes, all of which met in the center of town.

Roy was briefing the group when they entered the studio, and his smile expressed his relief that they had made it in time. Roy, or Reverend Carlson, as most of the people called him, had the opening minutes of the program, during which Dan stood with his head bowed in prayer. As he prayed, he asked the Lord to use him through this song, not that he should receive any glory, but that someone might hear the message contained in it and come to know *Him*, "Whom to know aright is life eternal." He stepped to the microphone as Elaine played the introduction and he sang the song with the prayer still in his heart.

> Once I was drifting aimlessly, I had no port in sight,
> There was no sign to lead by day, no gleam to pierce the night.
> No captain on board to chart my course, no compass and no
> goal,
> I could not find a ray of hope to guide my fevered soul.

As he switched from the minor key to the major, his voice became very soft.

> The Master Pilot took the helm, His blessings never cease,
> He took away the stain of sin, He gave me perfect peace.

The rest of the song was in the major key, more fully expressing the peace and joy of having Christ as Saviour.

He led me to a harbor, the water was smooth and calm,
My life was placed in His great care, His touch was healing balm.
If you would trust this Saviour, too, He'll give you peace within,
He'll still the troubled waters, and take away your sin.

Dan sang the chorus again softly, expressively, pronouncing each word clearly. He was so concerned with the message of the song that he was completely unaware of the beauty of his voice. As he stepped back from the mike, Elaine smiled at him reassuringly.

The broadcast lasted a half hour. When it was over, they all hurried over to the church where the service was already under way.

It was late when they returned home, and Dan went directly to his room. He had no sooner shut the door when he heard a voice calling from the den at the foot of the stairs.

"Mother!" No answer. "Mother, come help me! I can't find Paul's birth certificate!"

There was a screech as two pairs of footsteps came thundering up the stairs. Paul managed to squeeze his foot into the bathroom door before Elaine shut it, dragged her out into the hall, and proceeded to spank her soundly. Dan knew if they were to get any sleep that night he would have to intervene. He went out into the hall and held Paul's arms in back of him while their sister freed herself from his grip and ran to her room. Dan released him and shook his finger in his face. "Go to bed, little brother!"

As he turned to go back to his room, Paul made a flying tackle at him, and the two of them crashed to the floor. Within a matter of minutes, Dan had overpowered his younger brother, pinned his shoulders to the floor, and made him say "uncle." Paul was shaking his fist when Dan closed the door to his room.

"You'll get yours, bully! Next time I'll – "

A pillow had come neatly across the hall, hitting him squarely in the face. It had come from the direction of his sister's room.

"See here, second little pig!" he shouted. As he slowly rose to his feet, he growled, "I'll huff, and I'll puff, and I'll blow your door down!"

Her door remained silent, motionless, and there was an unwritten law of the household that no bedroom door was to be opened except by the room's occupant.

"Okay, piggy. You'll get yours tomorrow, too!"

They were all relieved to hear Paul's bedroom door close, thankful that at last they could settle down for the night. A full five minutes elapsed before another door opened, silently and slowly. A curler-covered head popped out, followed by a pajama-clad figure, robe clutched loosely about her. She slipped across the hall without making a sound and reclaimed her pillow. As she returned to tiptoe back to the safety of her room, Paul rushed at her from the darkness of the bathroom. She was unable to suppress the piercing scream which escaped involuntarily from her lips.

The two of them were sitting on the floor, doubled over with laughter, when Louise Sanderford came out of her room and turned on the hall light. She could not contain herself. Her two youngest were at each other constantly, and this scene, or one similar to it, took place at regular intervals. She thoroughly enjoyed their antics.

"Really, Paul," she scolded, "we should settle down now. It's so late."

"Yes, Queen Mother," he said, bowing low from the waist, his hand outstretched in a royal gesture. "Lady Louise. I shall comply with your most reasonable request. Mother dear," he added when he saw her look of exasperation. He was about to disappear into his room when his sister called to him from her door.

"Oh Paul," she taunted, "you'd better study up on your nursery rhymes. It was the first little pig that got his house blown down. That's you!"

His slipper made a loud noise as it hit her door, the exact spot where she had been standing. He heard her giggle as he finally gave up. He was puzzled. Didn't the second little pig get his house blown down, too? He'd have to look it up.

Some time later, Louise Sanderford climbed between the crisp, white sheets of her bed. She smiled to herself as she thought of her two youngest offspring who delighted in "getting even" with each other. They kept a close count on the score too. There was no end to their capers. They were so much alike, this boy and girl. Light brown hair, twinkling blue eyes, quick wit, ready smile. It often had been said that these characteristics were inherent from their mother.

They had their individual problems though. This dear girl, whose heart had been aching for almost two years for her soldier boy, was putting up a good front, but her true feelings were let loose in the privacy of her own room. She had just entered her third year of college when Mark was sent to Europe, and although there was some talk of getting married before he left, it was decided best for all concerned if they waited until his return. Mark himself had made the final decision, and Louise loved him for it. He was scheduled to return the middle of September, and they were anxiously awaiting this important event.

Paul was a happy-go-lucky fellow, his main problem being the steady string of girl friends he seemed to acquire. They never troubled him though, so she wondered if the girls were not the ones who were ending up with broken hearts. Judith Barker was his latest interest, and probably the longest, their romance having lasted a good four weeks. Perhaps this is it, his mother mused.

But there had been other problems for Paul too.

There was that time almost three years ago. Oh, what a hard time he had put them through! He was an extremely well-developed, muscular boy of fifteen then, and could have passed for much older. After confiscating some money here and there around the house and putting it with some of his own, he had joined a group of boys in a dice game, one of those held regularly in the basement of an older boy's home. It was the first and last time Paul had been involved.

Dan had just come home from college for the summer, and through some quirk of fate, more properly defined as divine planning, Dan had been calling, by invitation, on the boy's sister. He had discovered Paul in the basement with the other boys, and had dragged him home by the ear. Louise could remember it all so clearly. Dan was out of the car in short order, dragged Paul out, and beat him unrelentingly, blow after powerful blow falling on his face, his jaw, into his ribs.

Louise knew that Dan must have good reason for punishing his brother thus. Mightn't one call it righteous indignation? Was it? Although she depended upon Dan more than she cared to admit, especially in the difficult task of keeping Paul in line, she disapproved of his method. Paul could have done nothing to deserve such chastisement.

But she did not know until later that same evening that Paul had dishonestly acquired the money he had been gambling away, and that the boys had broken into the father's liquor closet in the basement. Paul, anxious to prove that he was one of the crowd, had whole-heartedly entered the competition of who-can-drink-the-most-before-we-get-caught.

So although Louise had disapproved of Dan's method of chastening, she had been quick to perceive the results. And grateful. Paul had a broken, humbled spirit. That night he came to her room.

"I'm sorry, Mother," he choked. "I don't know what else to say."

"That's all that's necessary, dear." The tears were running down her own cheeks, for it had been a long time since Paul had come to her this way. He had been belligerent for so long. "I prayed that you would be sorry, and my prayers were answered."

"How do you know I won't do it again, Mother? Or something just as bad? Maybe worse? I mean, what good is being sorry? I really am. I didn't mean that I wasn't. But it doesn't prove anything for the future."

"There's only one answer to that Paul, and you know it as well as I. It's a Christ-centered life, a Christ-controlled life, a life given *to* Him and kept *by* Him. To depend upon yourself is only to fail time after time after time. But knowing it in your head doesn't save you. Do you know it in your heart, Paul?"

He was quiet. She got up, put on her robe, and turned on the reading lamp over her bed. He was sitting on the window seat.

"Did Dan tell you what happened?" he asked without looking at her.

"He told me. Why don't you tell me the rest? That is, if you want to." Her motherly intuition told her that Dan had not given her full details.

"Did he tell you we were drinking?"

She winced. "No, son," she said softly, "he didn't tell me that. I hope you didn't enjoy it."

"I didn't at first. Well, I didn't at all, but it sure made me feel high. That's not the worst part."

"Oh?" Her heart pounded against her ribs.

"The fellows were planning on getting some cigarettes after that game."

She breathed a sigh of relief, a sigh that expressed relief after being handed bitter medicine when expecting poison. "I guess I expected you to try that sooner or later too."

"Oh, I've tried it, and I can't say I like it, although the guys said they didn't the first time or two either. But these weren't ordinary weeds."

She shuddered. "Why are you telling me this, Paul?"

He looked up at her in surprise. "I don't know. I honestly don't know. I'm sorry if it upsets you, Mother." Some of the old contention crept back into his voice. "I don't know," he repeated.

"Did Dan know about this?"

"Yeah. He heard the guys talking before he latched onto me. That's why he was so mad. He sure surprised me. Made a big fool out of me, too."

"I'm glad he found you."

"I sure was burned up at him. I think I coulda licked him if I hadn't felt so sick all of a sudden. He sure packs a wallop!" He touched the mouse under his eye and drew his hand down along the gash on his cheek. There were other puffy bruises on his face and neck. "I must say, though, it took some of the other hurts out—the ones in here." He thumped a big fist on his chest.

Louise felt a measure of relief at his last remark. There had been very few embroilments between her boys over the years.

"Paul, what are you going to do?"

"What can I do?"

"You know what I mean. You are an unhappy boy, and you know it. If this happens again, or something worse as you said, it could wreck your life. I'm sure I don't have to impress you with the seriousness of the matter."

He stared at the floor. "I guess there's only one thing for me to do then, isn't there?" He glanced up at her as he went on. "I tried to kid you all along, but I wasn't fooling you, was I?"

"No, son, you weren't. But you weren't kidding yourself, either. I'm glad you know that. God can use you, Paul, but first you have to belong to Him."

Without answering, Paul got down on his knees by the window seat. Louise knelt beside him and put her small arm around his broad shoulder, and that night Paul settled things with his Maker. His face shone as he put his arms around her and embraced her in a crushing hug. She patted him on the back, trying not to groan under the pressure of his powerful muscles.

"What a bird-brain I've been. I'm sorry for hurting you and Dan this way. Lainey too. I guess she doesn't know what a louse she has for a brother. But things are going to be different now." Paul choked back a sob.

"I know they are, Paul. Why don't you go tell Dan? I'm sure he is anxious."

"I will, Mother. I want to. But first I want to tell you, I'm going to pay back every bit of that money."

"No, Paul, you're not."

"There's no use arguing about it, Mother. As soon as I can get a job, I'm going to pay it back."

"Paul, when our sins are washed away, we start out with a clean slate. Our debts are forgiven. I want you to start out that way too. Now go on, there's no use talking about it." She pushed him toward the door. He turned to her and opened his mouth. "Not one word," she warned.

"We'll see about that another time then. Think Dan will still be awake?" he asked.

She nodded through her tears, and he left. She smiled happily as she pulled the covers over her.

Each year as they got older, Louise felt less adequate to fulfill the needs of her fatherless children. What would she have done without Dan's help? It seemed now that he always had possessed a stability, a maturity which had been coming much more slowly to the other two.

But Dan's heart almost had been broken, too, by the same brazen hussy he had been calling on that day he had rescued Paul. Louise had made it a point never to interfere in her children's affairs, but she had trembled with fear upon learning of Dan's attraction to a girl who played with men's hearts and then cast them away as broken toys when they no longer delighted her. He had come mighty close to getting burned. That could just well be the reason he had developed an over-caution toward the opposite sex.

As Louise's thoughts turned to Dan, her happy smile was turned to one of contentment. She loved all her children dearly, but when Jonathan passed away six years ago, she had turned to Dan for strength. He was a serious-minded boy. Oh, not that he did not have his share of the lighter moments, but he could be depended upon when he was needed. He was like his father in every way. Straight dark hair, almost black; serious brown eyes with heavy lashes; deep cleft in his chin; the same tall, straight frame. *So much like Jonathan,* thought Louise.

The feeling of contentment, however, came not from the thoughts of Dan's resemblance to his father. Her mind went back to the night about three weeks previous when Dan had knocked on her door, softly, so as not to awaken her had she already fallen asleep. It was late.

"Come in, son." She had known it was Dan, had known of the spiritual battle being waged within him. Dan had a burden for the people of New Hope, especially the young folk. Paul's close brush with disaster had alerted her eldest child to the desperate needs of New Hope's youth. He was inspired with great things to be done for them through the church. But Dan also had a burden for the people of Japan. For some time he had been torn between his desire to remain with the work here and his desire to go to the field. He had been so impatient for the Lord to make plain His will.

"Mother, it's going to be Japan," he said as he sat on the edge of her bed.

She felt a twinge of pain at the thought of losing him, but she was certain he had not noticed in the semi-darkness. "Oh, Dan, I'm glad!" she exclaimed, patting his hand.

"There's no question about it now, Mother. And now that I'm sure, I'm anxious to get started."

He had told her of his plans to be self-supporting, and she had thought it a marvelous idea. When he went over to the parsonage the next evening to tell his good friend the news, however, Roy had discouraged him on this score.

"Dan," Roy had said, "the people will take more interest in you, pray for you more often, if they feel they are working with you. If you have money you want to give to missions, there are plenty of others you can help to support. That way you will be interested in them too!'' When Dan relayed these words of wisdom to his mother, she had immediately seen the truth in them.

Louise Sanderford and her elder son had talked long into the night, and she had rejoiced with him, prayed with him. His call to the mission field was another evidence of answered prayer.

But now, as she felt the power of sleep taking hold of her, there was only one thing about Dan's call to the field that troubled her. She wished he did not have to go alone.

Chapter 3

IT WAS A long weekend, and Amy's thoughts would not leave her alone. In her twenty years she had accomplished nothing, and she had no desire to. This fact disturbed her a great deal. Oh, she had known her life had no purpose before she had heard Dan sing about it. And she had come to the realization long before that horrible Christmas party. She had never frowned on drinking and having a good time, nor had the dirty jokes been offensive to her. The one and only thing to which she had been opposed was the looseness with which the married employees mingled with those who were not married, or with those who were married to someone else. Although she had not been out of place in that atmosphere, she knew what heartbreak could result from such loose morals.

If only she were going somewhere, had some reason for living. She had never considered doing away with herself, but now as she looked at her reflection in the mirror and brushed her short, blonde curls, she wondered if anyone would miss her if she did. She was discontent with her life, with her day-to-day existence, but most of all she was dissatisfied with Amy Archer.

Monday came at last, and with it a feeling of relief, a feeling that she could breathe again. She wanted to get back to work, to keep busy, for it was only then that she could feel she was not a complete blank. She kept active all day, not because she was conscientious, but because it helped to keep her troublesome thoughts in her subconscious.

She caught a glimpse of Dan occasionally, and each time she did, the fact that he could sing so magnificently came as a surprise to her. She could not picture him standing in front of a microphone with all the poise and self-control his voice had indicated. These attributes were true of him, to be sure, but she thought it must be quite a different matter being so confident with one's voice going out over the sound waves. At first she had been anxious to tell him that she had heard him, but as the day wore on, she decided it wasn't such a good idea, after all. He would probably think she was interested in his religion and use that as an opening for discussing it with her.

The day passed quickly, and as she took her coat from its hook, he happened by. She found herself talking to him, against her better judgment. "I heard you sing the other night, Dan. Sure was surprised to know you had such a good voice!"

"Why, thank you, Amy," he said as they walked to the elevator. "I'm glad you heard the program."

The ride down to the main floor was without comment. The elevator was crowded. He wondered, as they stepped out, whether he should press the matter further. She answered the question in his mind as they walked across the spacious main floor of the bank.

"But you don't believe all that stuff, do you, Dan?"

He prayed for guidance before he answered this cynical girl. "Yes, I do, Amy. There's nothing that means more to me, nothing that makes life more worth living. I'd like to tell you about it sometime." They had reached her corner, and Dan was still speaking. "Why don't I give you a lift? It's rather silly for you to spend carfare when we're going in the same direction."

She hesitated. "No sermons?"

"No sermons," he promised.

Dan told her as much as he could about the radio program, his church, his call to the mission field, without making the young lady feel he was preaching to her. He sensed that she was little interested in his words, anyway.

Amy again accepted the proffered ride the following evening. Once more Dan talked of the things dearest to his heart, making sure Amy did not feel he was giving her a sermon.

The next evening Dan had to work late. Amy left fifteen minutes before him. He was a little relieved, not that he minded giving her a ride, but tonight he had other plans, and he was in a hurry. As he crossed the street to his car, he was dismayed to see her standing beside it.

"Picking up any beggars tonight, Dan?" she asked with forced levity.

For a moment he hesitated, not knowing how to get around the situation gracefully. If he told her he was not going home, she would be embarrassed for her forwardness and he might never have the opportunity to talk to her again. She probably would not ride with him any more. He made a quick decision, and apparently undaunted, asked her a question which astonished her.

"Say, Amy, how would you like to go to a dinner!" He had

no sooner said it when he realized how it sounded, so he quickly added, "It's just a group of young people. No couples or anything like that!" He was not asking her for a date!

"You must be joking, Dan!"

"No. No, I'm not. I never joke." He was smiling.

She raised her hand in protest. "No. Really. Thanks anyway. I'd be a square peg in a round hole. I'll just wait for the next bus."

He refused to take no for an answer. "Look," he started all over again, "you wouldn't need to feel out of place. There'll be plenty of people there that I don't know either, young people from all over this part of the state. Come on, Amy, it'll do you good!" He opened the door, and she got in. He was a hard one to refuse.

"I hope I don't live to regret this, Dan Sanderford!" she said as they drove out of the parking lot. When they stopped in front of the church she *was* regretting it, but she was stuck. She had not darkened the door of a church since David was married. And she could not remember the time before that.

They went down to the basement where several long rows of tables had been set up. People were swarming everywhere. Dan had introduced her to a number of them when a lovely girl came rushing up to them.

"Hi, Danny," she bubbled, slipping her arm through his. "Glad you could make it," she said laughing.

"Hi, Elaine. Everything going okay? Elaine, this is Amy Archer. Would you take care of her while I go find Roy? Do you mind, Amy?" The truth of the matter was, he would rather have it appear that Amy had come with Elaine. It was an impulsive move, asking her to come.

"I sure will," Elaine replied. *Hmph,* she sniffed. *So this is the kind of tramp Danny is going to bring around for me to play nurse-maid to! Hardly your type, Danny,* she mused sarcastically. *Pretty little thing though, underneath all that veneer. Wish I had a putty knife—*But Elaine quickly replaced her mental eyebrows and slipped a cordial arm through the stranger's. Amy was none the wiser.

Amy liked this vibrant girl, her sparkling eyes, her endless chatter. Effervescent, that's what she was. Someone rang a bell, and every-one milled around the tables, finally getting situated satisfactorily. As they sat down, she noticed the beautiful diamond on Elaine's left hand, and when Dan came and sat between them at the place they had reserved for him, she could not help but observe what a hand-some couple they made. Strange, he had never mentioned being en-gaged. But had anyone ever been that much interested in him? She thought not.

She was impressed. These young people were having a marvelous time. Yet there were no shady stories being whispered about the tables; there was no liquor being served; there was no pretending. They were enjoying themselves.

Amy reached into her purse for her cigarettes when they had finished eating and the tables were being cleared, but as her hand closed over them, it came to her sharply that no one was smoking. She looked around for an ash tray, then closed her purse. Probably not allowed in the church, she surmised. Fire laws, no doubt.

What next? A young man stood up at what appeared to be the main table, and all those who could not see noisily rearranged their chairs. Amy groaned. Not a speech! That was not fair of Dan to being her here without warning her!

The man was announcing something, but Amy had not caught his words although she recognized the voice as the one she had heard over the radio. Not a bad looking fellow—not what the world would call handsome—medium height, blond hair, and glasses which gave him a rather distinguished appearance.

Three girls stood up to sing, their voices blending beautifully in three-part harmony. It was something about being wealthy beyond all measure when you had religion. How ridiculous! "Far better than gold or wealth untold are the riches of love in Christ Jesus," they sang. Absolutely ridiculous! But one thing Amy did appreciate was good music, and since they sang rather fast, she had to pay close attention to catch all the words. *They really mean it,* pondered the restless heart of Amy Archer.

She half-listened as Roy Carlson brought the message, but unbeknown to her, some of his words were being imprinted on her heart to be recalled in the not-too-distant future.

But now she was anxious for it to be over so she could get out of this place, out of this stifling atmosphere. Besides, she needed a smoke. She headed for the door as soon as it was over after telling Elaine she would wait for them in the car.

At last they were on their way home, Dan and Amy in the front seat with Elaine between them, Paul and his girl in the back. First stop was Judith's house.

"Sure will be glad when I get my license," mumbled Paul after seeing Judy to the door.

"But what good is a license without a car?" Elaine poked Dan with her elbow and winked at Amy in the light of the street lamp.

Amy was quiet until they reached her door although there had been no lull in the conversation. She thanked Dan kindly and went into the house. Of all the ridiculous affairs she had been railroaded into attending, this topped them all!

Dan put the car into the garage. When he strolled into the house, his mother and Paul were in the living room. Paul was sprawled all over the sofa. He had a glint in his eye.

"Say, Ichabod," he said, using a pet name from their childhood, "pretty nice tomatoes you're picking up these days! How come you never told us you had a flame?"

"Not bad, huh, Paul?" Dan returned. "Say, what'd you think of her?"

Paul looked thoughtful. "The only word I can think of right now is," he paused for effect, "WOW!"

Dan laughed. "Just taking care of the King's business though. Sorry to disappoint you." He gave his brother's arm a hard jab as he headed for the stairs.

"But who's to say the King's business can't be your business?" Paul retorted as Dan's big feet disappeared at the top of the stairs.

Dan slouched down in his big comfortable chair and, having removed his shoes, put his feet up on the bed, at the same time opening his Bible. Before starting to read, he lay his head back, closed his eyes, and smiled as he thought of Paul's remarks. "Wow is right, Paul," he mused. But Paul's biggest fault was turning any situation into sport, and he knew as well as Dan that this hard, caustic girl held no romantic interest for him. His only concern was for the condition of her heart.

He supposed some men would consider her beautiful. Glamorous, certainly. She was of average height, slender and rather shapely, although her clothes seemed to be much more conservative than those worn by some of the girls at the office. However that wasn't saying too much. Her high cheekbones and the heavy make-up she wore gave her the unnatural appearance of a painted doll. Her greatest asset, appearance-wise, was the crowning glory of her beautiful hair. But everything else about her was so artificial, he now wondered if she hadn't encouraged that too. She had straight white teeth and a captivating smile which she used selfishly. No, there was a time when it seemed spontaneous and natural, but for no apparent reason she had turned introvert. Perhaps that word was a little strong. He really did not know much about the girl.

A mighty young'un to be so hard-boiled, his thoughts went on. *I'll bet she's not even old enough to vote,* he mused paternally, hardly past the age himself. *Must not have much of a family. Or maybe they don't have much of a daughter.*

Again he smiled as he thought of Paul's favorite descriptive word for the opposite sex. Who in the world had ever thought of likening a girl to a tomato? There was no comparison whatsoever.

But he definitely was not interested in Amy Archer. She was not his type.

Chapter 4

IT WAS A beautiful early summer evening. Flowers were in full array and trees were proudly displaying their new green foliage. Children, free from the burden of coats which recently had been put in mothballs, exhilarated by the freedom bestowed upon them by the closing of school, were everywhere to be seen, jumping rope, roller skating, bicycling. Older folk were sitting on porches watching them, wishing they could join them while others were leaning over back fences talking, comparing the growth of their tomato plants, wondering if it would rain soon. But these pleasant scenes were mere flashing pictures in the far recesses of Amy's mind as she stared out the window.

She had looked forward to this vacation with no great anticipation. Yet it was good to get away from New Hope for a while, away from her paltry existence. She could not get away from herself, however, from her own thoughts as she sat in the plush seat of the train, watching life hurrying by as it carried her nearer to her destination.

Such a humiliating experience she had brought upon herself by practically forcing Dan Sanderford to take her to that fool supper! The next evening, she had purposely left work early and taken the bus home. But this evening, when he had seen her carrying her suitcase toward the elevator, he had insisted on taking her to the station.

"I won't put you out again, Dan," she had said.

"Not at all, Amy. I looked for you last night. I was going to give you a lift."

"I finished early."

She was sorry now that she had let him take her to the station. He was doing it out of friendliness, she was sure, for he seemed to be a gentleman in every sense of the word. He had carried her bag to the platform and was going to wait with her until her train came, but she had discouraged him.

"Really, Dan, I've inconvenienced you enough. Don't wait."

She had not wanted to be sociable and she supposed he had seen that, but she was trying not to like him and she knew she did not like his religion.

Religion! She hated the word! Why did people not know they were better off without it? Life was so much simpler that way. She wondered if Dan's religion were the same as Dave's. She knew her brother had converted their mother to his way of thinking before she died a little more than a year ago. It did not make much difference, but if it made people happier when they were dying, she supposed it was all right.

She had been very bitter when her mother died. She wanted to finish college, having completed her second year. But then everything was going wrong. Dave wanted her to go on, but she had refused to be a burden on him and his bride. It was then that she had moved to New Hope, expecting to make a new life for herself. She was not proud of the old one.

She remembered little about her father, very little except for the bitter arguments that took place constantly between him and her mother. He had left them when Amy was very young and she had never heard the real reason for his departure, but as she had come to maturity, she had reached the conclusion that another woman had been involved. There was no grief when they heard of his death a few years later.

As the train neared Ocean Point, Amy could see nothing but her despicable self. She viewed her image in her mental mirror and deplored the reflection of herself before she moved to New Hope; she despised the picture she knew must be in Lawrence Spencer's eyes, but she despised him too. She was a complete failure to everyone, but no more than she was to herself.

She stepped off the train, and as the small crowd thinned out, she saw her brother. They exchanged rather formal greetings although he tried to be warm against the cool exterior shell his sister had manufactured. They drove to his house, about a half-hour's ride, and the conversation was painful on Amy's part. Dave asked her about her work and the town in which she was living. He told her of his work and the small business he had set up with several other architects in his employ.

At last the ride was over, and Joy was making every effort to give Amy a warm welcome. She had a round happy face, big round eyes—in fact, everything about her was round. Amy hadn't remembered her sister-in-law as being quite so buxom.

She wished she had not come. Dave left the room, and Joy talked incessantly. "How was your trip?" and "Would you like a cold drink?" and "Would you like to rest a while?" Amy wished she would shut up.

Then Dave came in, carrying a little bundle in each arm and laid them in Amy's arms as she sat on the sofa. She had never been so close to newborn babies before.

"Oh, Dave," she exclaimed, "they're darling!" Her eyes were shining. "But aren't you afraid I might break them?"

Joy and Dave laughed, delighted over her unnecessary concern. The tension was broken, the wall was removed, and Amy was glad she had come.

She made herself useful, for Joy had her hands full and had not yet regained her strength. There were dishes to do, beds to make, diapers to wash, and Amy found herself enjoying the busyness, but she was happiest when she was allowed to care for her tiny nieces. Joy did most of that, so taken up she was with the new role of mother, but occasionally Amy was able to get her hands on Rachel or Rebecca—*Ray* and *Becky,* she heard Dave calling them. It was not long until the *Ray* became *Sunshine.*

Although she would not admit it, she wished this dream house were her own. She was a little girl again, playing house. It was a cozy little home and represented everything she wanted.

Amy had the afternoons pretty much to herself. The babies took long naps after they got their tummies full, and Joy took advantage of the quiet time to rest, herself. So each day, after making certain things were in order, Amy, clad in bathing suit and robe and equipped with towels and magazines, headed for the beach.

She had but to walk down an old road, and as she picked her way, she wondered for what purpose it had been made, if ever it were used any more. It was hard-packed and dry with now and then a rock jutting up to tear at some venturesome vehicle's tires. The ruts were deep, and, strangely, it brought to her mind a road sign she had seen as a young girl, traveling with what she now considered a semblance of a family. The sign read: "Choose your rut. You will be in it for twelve miles."

If only I were that sure of getting out of mine, she reflected. But it was not fair. She had not chosen her rut. It was there waiting for her.

The ocean was exciting, and just a glimpse of it washed her unpleasant thoughts away. She had heard the waves breaking on the shore in the quiet of the first night she had spent in Dave's house, but the next day, when she had explored the surrounding area, the view of the dunes, the white sand, the rolling, crashing surf had taken her breath away.

She had the whole beautiful beach to herself and was undisturbed by the tiny people-specks she could see perhaps a half-mile away. When she tired of reading, she lay back and listened to the music of the breakers as the ever-present breeze soothed her restless spirit. Sometimes she watched the sandpipers chase a retreating wave, then reverse the race as the wave turned and chased them. They scurried frantically to keep their feet dry as the water crept closer to their heels. It was a fruitless race, but they never gave up.

Then there were the sea gulls as they hovered overhead, quietly resting on the crest of a breeze or banding together as they discovered a passing fishing boat, loudly scolding as they followed it to its nearby harbor. Now and then a gull would drop a clam on the rocks, then swoop down and pick it up, repeating the procedure until the hard shell of the delicacy was broken.

Her brother's home was a wonderful place, and it had become a haven to her. It was so good to be needed.

She returned each day in plenty of time to get freshened up and start supper before Dave came home. The week had been flying by, and not once had she considered leaving. She had enjoyed being part of this household, and now that it was almost over, she was looking forward to her return to New Hope with the same feeling of utter desolation with which she had anticipated this trip to Ocean Point.

On Saturday, Dave joined his sister at the beach. She watched him walk toward her. David Archer was of medium height, thin and wiry. He had been a sickly child. She had forgotten that. He was healthy enough now, so either he had overcome his weaknesses or he had outgrown them. His hair was blond and curly like his sister's, and his receding hairline was made more pronounced by a high forehead. He kept his hair short, in a crewcut. Dave was dependable, reliable, the best kind of father and husband. One could not have stayed with them for a whole week without seeing that. His and Joy's relationship had an undefinable quality, a richness in the nuances which vitalized their contented existence. That was remarkable, considering his own unhappy childhood. Amy envied them.

"Dave, do you remember much about—" What should she say? Dad? Pop? Father? He had been none of these to her. "—our dad?" she finished lamely.

"A little. He wasn't such a bad guy, Amy. Course you don't remember him at all, do you?"

"I'm not sure. You know, sometimes it's hard to tell the difference between mental pictures drawn by memory and those drawn by hearsay. Know what I mean?"

He nodded. "I know exactly what you mean. But you know, even though we were always loyal to Mom, I think she must have been partly to blame for their troubles."

"What happened to make you think that? Did she ever tell you?"

"Never. She kept everything to herself. That's not good either.

She was happy at the end though. That meant an awful lot to me."

"I know."

"But we've been worried about you, being left alone and all."

"I'm making out fine," she lied.

"We'd like you to come live with us if you ever have a mind to."

"That's good of you."

"What ever happened to that fellow you went with back home, Amy? I kinda thought that was real serious."

She did not want to talk about him with her brother or anyone else. "Oh, that just—sort of—disintegrated—I guess."

"Todd Kenton. That was his name. What happened?"

"Kenyon," she corrected. "I left. Remember?"

They were quiet for some time, soaking up the sunshine, listening to the antiphony of the ocean. Amy rose up on her elbows and broke the spell.

"You don't approve of me, do you, Dave?"

"Of course I approve of you. Why do you say a nutty thing like that?" She had surprised him with this unexpected inquiry.

"Maybe I should have put it in a different way. You don't approve of some of the things I do."

"I'd be lying if I said I did."

"Well, thanks."

"For what?"

"For not preaching at me."

He was bewildered by this change in her attitude. He had expected a deluge of defenses, justifications for the things which she did, things which met with his disapproval. He smiled. "Maybe I would if I thought it would do any good." He thought a minute. "You will come to church tomorrow though, won't you!" She had refused the previous Sunday.

"I'll think about it."

"Are you sure, or have you already made up your mind?"

She laughed, and it was a good sound, a rarity. "My brother is not only diplomatic, but psychic as well. I was going to wash my hair to get all this salt out of it. I have to be back to work on Monday, you know."

"Wash it tonight. Let's go for a swim." He stood up as he spoke and reached for her hand. They raced to the water.

It was a sad time for all when she had to leave the next afternoon. She had come to love the two babies dearly, and the natural warmth that evolved from Dave and Joy had engulfed her in a feeling she had never before experienced.

As they neared town, Amy said to her brother, "Dave, you and

Joy have so much—your lovely home and family. Thank you for letting me come." She had not been sure what to expect before her arrival.

"We didn't *let* you come, Amy. We wanted you to come. And yes, I do have a lot, all I ever want, except a son some day, Lord willing. But one of these days you'll have something equally as grand. Just you wait and see."

Dave parked the car and they walked toward the group of people who were waiting for the same train.

"Oh, Dave, who would want a big *nothing* like me?" She saw the look that came over his face and laughed. "Don't worry," she said. "I'll find myself one of these days."

He stopped and put her suitcase on the rough wooden boards of the platform, taking hold of her shoulders as he spoke. "Don't wait too long, Amy. And don't depend too much upon yourself." There was no trace of humor in his voice, no smile on his lips.

She was puzzled as she felt the train lurch forward and turned to wave to her brother. If she could not depend upon herself to straighten out the mess of her life, upon whom could she depend? Certainly not Dave. He had enough burdens on his shoulders. She settled back as she went over his words and wondered if her life were worth the effort.

Day followed night, night followed day, and the respite her vacation had afforded from the boredom of her daily course made it more difficult for Amy than before. The glimpse she had had of a different way of life—the routine of a contented family—made her existence more unbearable than ever.

Dan Sanderford was taking her both ways to work now. It had come about quite accidentally as he happened by her bus stop and picked her up that first Monday morning she was back. Although she was beginning to think Dan wasn't such a bad fellow, there was one thing about this arrangement which she did not like. It meant she left later in the morning and returned earlier in the evening, thus causing her to spend more time in the emptiness of her room. Loneliness was her worst enemy these days.

The days of that first week back in New Hope were fleeting. The nights were interminable. As quitting time approached on Friday, she felt she would go stark raving mad if she had to spend another evening as she had spent the four previous ones. Again her benefactor came to the rescue.

He stopped by her desk as she typed the last letter, speaking as she slid the neatly folded sheet into the envelope. "Say, Amy, we're having a little get-together tonight. Should be lots of fun. Think you might be persuaded to come along?"

"What about your broadcast? This is Friday."

"We alternate with about six other churches. How about it?"

"I don't know." She was thinking as she answered. It would be better than spending the evening alone again. "If I did, it would only be so I wouldn't have to look at four bluish-green walls. Can I go under those conditions?"

He stood with his forefinger to his chin, his eyes to the ceiling as if in deep thought. "Hmmm. Let's see. Nope. We don't have any bluish-green walls. I'll pick you up at seven-thirty."

He was at her door at exactly seven-thirty, alone.

"Where's Elaine?"

"She's at the house helping Mother get things ready. Didn't I tell you this shindig is at my house? We have to run around and pick up Judy. That's Paul's girl, remember?" He followed his first question with another, not waiting for an answer.

Judith Barker appeared at the door as soon as Dan's car came into sight. She was a beautiful girl, tall and stately, slender and graceful. She had long, sandy colored hair which she had pulled back into a ponytail. She was all grace and charm, but yet to Amy she seemed shy and reserved.

They came to the extremity of the gaudy, brightly-lighted growth called business, and after proceeding a mile or so further, Dan guided the vehicle down a road which, had one not known was there, one might have missed altogether. They reached the crest of a hill, and there, on either side of them as they rode along, were lovely big homes set back on wide, rolling fields of green grass. Dan's house was on another street, a little road which connected two larger ones, and was the only house on Sanderford Lane.

They turned into the long, wide drive at the end of which stood a large stone house. The drive was bordered on either side by a thick column of junipers, and off to the right were clusters of white birch. Around the house, in militant neatness, were green shrubs, and although erect and perfect in order, they served to soften the ostentatious picture. Pretentious it was, and Amy felt out of place.

They entered the spacious front hall, and Judy went right through to the kitchen. There immediately appeared at the same door another woman who welcomed Amy warmly as she approached.

"Amy, this is my mother. Mother, Amy Archer."

"We're so glad you were able to come, Amy."

She was a young looking woman with the same glowing expression Amy had seen on Elaine's face.

"Can I be of any help?" she asked hesitantly.

"No, but why don't you come sit in the kitchen while we finish up?" None of the other guests had arrived yet.

Amy followed Mrs. Sanderford, and as they entered the big homey kitchen, she saw that Judy already had made herself useful by drying dishes. She heard Elaine's voice as they came through the door.

"Paul, you keep your fingers out!"

"You may be able to boss Dan around," he retorted defiantly as he stuck his forefinger into the frosting and ran it around the inside of the bowl, "but not me!" He touched his sticky pink finger to the end of her nose, matters to be made worse by Elaine herself as she wiped it off with the back of her hand, smearing it across her cheek. She took the wide spatula she had been using to ice the cake and drew it across the back of his hand as he reached to get another fingerful, leaving a messy glob of it in its path.

"Now you're looking for trouble, miss!" he roared.

But his mother came to Elaine's rescue before he was able to give it back to her. "Paul, why don't you go get ready?" she asked, pushing him toward the door. "And besides, she doesn't boss Dan around."

"No, come to think of it, I guess you're right. She gets her own way without bossing him!"

Amy was amused. She had seen enough of this young man the night of the supper to know that he was the life of the party, that things started popping when he came in. But she had not known he was Dan's brother until they were in the car, on their way home.

Dan stuck his head in the door. "Come on, you guys, if you want a place to sit. Just about everyone is here."

They went through the dining room, and Amy's eyes widened with awe as she caught sight of the spacious living room with its wall-to-wall carpeting, huge windows with draperies that touched the floor, big stone fireplace, grand piano. She had never in all her life been in such an elegant home. Yet, contrary to what she had been thinking outside, it felt warm and "lived-in."

There was ample room for the forty or more young people who had already made themselves at home. Those who could not find chairs sat on the floor.

The program was well-planned. The thoughts which originated from the minds of these young people were very imaginative. They portrayed a television program, and as each one came out to be interviewed and tell a sad story, hoping to be recipient of huge prizes, the audience roared with laughter.

There were the inevitable commercials too. Amy thought they were the funniest advertisements she had ever seen. One young man advertised pills which one could take just before a test and not have to study. But of course one had to take the right pill for the particular test one was taking! Then a young lady gave a long spiel on "sicknin' cigarettes" which guaranteed to be satisfying if one lived long enough to find out. Near the end of her talk, a young man came out with a long white candle in his mouth, and after she held a match to it, he proceeded to choke vigorously, then fell to the floor.

But the high point of the show was when "Mrs. McCavity" was introduced and Paul entered, expensively attired in women's clothing, complete with fur piece and large flowered hat. His lips and eyes had been exaggerated with an abundance of make-up, and he had acquired a large, well-proportioned figure, made more ridiculous by his own enormous size. In a high-pitched voice, Mrs. McCavity related a heartbreaking story of a husband who had deserted her, of her five hungry children who had no warm coats for the coming winter. And to top it all off, they needed an unbelievable amount of dental work.

It was so hilarious that the Master of Ceremonies gave up the interview, and, doubled over with laughter, was hardly able to stay on his chair. Through all this Paul's face remained expressionless, but pandemonium broke loose when Mrs. McCavity turned to the audience with a big, ugly grin, her mouth devoid of any teeth save one or two, here and there.

The end of his jeremiad was the signal for Judy to make her appearance. She did so attired in a man's suit many times too large for her, rushing in with five toothless, crying "children" following her. After hitting the Master of Ceremonies over the head with an umbrella, "his" wife was dragged out by "her" ear. The place was in an uproar.

Amy became as one of them as they delighted in this comic scene, forgetting that she had considered herself an outsider. She experienced at that moment a desire to belong, to be a part of them in their happiness, not as much in the superfluous as in the deep gratification of purpose she knew them to possess.

Mrs. Sanderford stood in the archway for several minutes before they settled down enough for her to speak, and then invited them into the dining room where a delectable array of canapés, cakes and cookies, coffee and tea was spread across the table. Someone offered a short prayer. After forming a line, they all "dug in" at Paul's invitation.

It was a new experience to Amy, and, to her bewilderment, she was enjoying it to the fullest. Elaine stayed near her most of the evening, but it was unnecessary. The genuine warmth which generated from the young people gave her complete confidence in their sincerity.

They had something the likes of which could not be wrought by human hands. Amy wished she knew what it was.

"Paul, wherever did you get clothes big enough for you?" she found herself asking Dan's brother. They were near the end of the line, and except for Dan, Judy, and a few others, the rest had returned to the living room with their food.

"Oh, we have a big trunk full upstairs in the attic, an accumulation of twenty years or so. We used to wear them to costume parties."

"What do you mean, 'used to,' Paul? You should have seen him last year at the young people's Halloween party, Amy." Dan spoke to her from across the table where he was filling his plate. "He was a little curly-headed girl with a big, red lollipop!"

"I wouldn't talk if I were you, Dan." Then turning to Amy, Paul said, "He was my nanny!" Everyone joined in the laughter at this comical picture. "Remember the look on the face of that cop who stopped us on the way to the party, Dan? He couldn't believe you weren't an Amazon!"

"I remember. But he wanted to take *you* home to play with his four-year-old boy!"

"I wish I could have seen you. But I'm sure you're putting me on!" laughed Amy, addressing them both.

Dan went on. "But Lainey took the cake! She got down on the floor in the back of the car so he wouldn't see her, and she broke half the balloons she had stuffed in her clothes to make her fat. That poor fellow thought someone was shooting at him!" Dan laughed heartily at the remembrance of this episode.

They returned to the living room with their food. Some were on their way back for seconds after Mrs. Sanderford had warned that they had to eat every last bite. They were very obliging, and while a few were lingering over their coffee, Dan stood in front of the fireplace, the spot that had been their "stage," open Bible in hand, and waited for quietness as he put on his horn-rimmed glasses.

For a fleeting moment, Amy was annoyed that this delightful time had to be spoiled by something to which she was so violently opposed, but the pervading influence of the occasion had been as a tranquilizer to her belligerent heart. She found herself listening, drinking in every word. She became unconscious of the people about her, the surroundings, the messenger. She was oblivious to everything but the words being spoken to her hungry, yearning heart.

Dan's message was short, and she wanted to hear more. She wanted to question him when he took her home, but although she was not a shy person, she hesitated about this thing that was so new to her.

Paul walked Judy to the door, and they tried not to be too observant when he stopped her at the door and kissed her good night.

"My little brother is getting brave!"

"He's quite a guy, Dan." Amy was solemn. "I really enjoyed that tonight."

"I'm sure glad to hear that, Amy. But I was hoping it might be more than a good time to you."

An exuberant Paul opened the door. "Move over, Amy!" he exclaimed. "I can't sit in the back all by myself after *that!*"

"Finally got up enough nerve, huh, Paul?"

"'Bout time, don't you think, Dan?"

Amy's amusement at the two brothers, especially Paul whose apparent self-confidence all but disappeared when he was found alone in the presence of his heart's desire, was overshadowed by the words she was hearing over and over within. The Holy Spirit was talking to her in a still, small voice, and she had done all but ask the Saviour in.

Chapter 5

"For I am not ashamed of the gospel of Christ, for it is the power of God unto salvation to every one that believeth." Dan had quoted this from the little Bible, not actually reading the words.

Amy lay in her bed, trying to recall the passage word for word. No, he certainly was not ashamed of this Gospel, this Word of God. This Christ who was a complete stranger to her. But it was the latter part of the verse that was of her greatest concern, "to every one that believeth." He had emphasized that. It meant that whoever believed in the Christ of which he spoke might have this salvation which He, Christ, had provided through the shedding of His own blood. Dan had said that anyone might have it. It was there for the taking.

"We must become nothing before we can become something. It is only when we stand before the Lord as *nothing,* stripped of our own self-righteousness, that He can mold us as a potter molds clay and form us into *something* fit for the Master's use. But we must first accept this free gift of salvation which the Lord supplied by giving His body as a living sacrifice. 'For without the shedding of blood there is no remission . . . .'" he had also quoted.

Amy pondered these words as she stared up at the dark ceiling. As far as becoming nothing, that would be no problem for her. That already was one of her most outstanding characteristics. She wanted to become something. Something for Him. She wanted with all her heart to believe, to have this Saviour as her own. Dan had said nothing about being baptized, nothing about kneeling at an altar. Only that one had to believe. Could it possibly be so simple? That was unreasonable.

She made a momentous decision as she lay there in the dark. She was certain she could find that church to which Dan had taken her for that dinner, and she would go that very Sunday to find out more about this amazing thing she had been hearing.

But Saturday morning, as Amy made her bed and tidied up her room, the spark that had been ready to burst into flame the night before had all but died. How could she be so gullible, to think she wanted this religion, this foolishness? Hadn't she made up her mind long ago that she would never get mixed up in such things? She wanted no part in them and was irritated that she had allowed herself to be taken in by the tenor of the evening. The program had been delightful, true. But if she could not enjoy their frivolity without becoming involved in their fanaticism, then she would have to sever any friendly relations which might already have been established.

"Yes, foolishness! That's what it is!" she said aloud, glad she had nipped it in the bud.

But suddenly she stopped what she was doing and sat down as if listening, a look of consternation wrinkling her brow. *"The preaching of the cross is to them that perish foolishness."* She heard the deep voice, just as if the nice looking man with the rimless glasses was right there in the room with her. *Foolishness — to them that perish . . . . . to them that perish . . . . .* Amy could not tear herself away from the words. She said it aloud. "The preaching of the cross is to them that perish foolishness . . . . . " And again she heard the deep voice as it completed it, "*. . . but unto us which are saved it is the power of God.*" The word *us* had a particular emphasis, which fact troubled her all the more, for it did not include her. *Them that perish . . . . .* That included her.

It was a warm Sunday morning as Amy, dressed in an attractive beige linen dress, white high heel shoes, and white hat, entered the lovely church where the service was just beginning. She took a seat in the back and listened, searched, weighed every word, and was left wanting. The congregation stood to sing the last hymn, and she slipped out, not wanting Dan to feel obligated to take her home.

She was filled with disappointment as she walked the mile or so home. She had been so sure she would find the answers to the perplexities that crowded her being. She supposed the missionary speaker was of interest to those who knew him and knew of his work, but it had been an ungratifying experience to her. His subject had been, "Go ye into all the world and preach the gospel," — a message that could not possibly interest her. The one and only part of the service she had enjoyed was the solo Dan had sung, something to do with the message that had been preached. It was a touching thing, considering that he was going into the same kind of work. And my! Didn't he have a magnificent voice!

She walked along, trying to stay where it was shaded, one thought leading to another just as one foot followed the other along the hot pavement. She wondered about Dan, how a young man with so many friends, such a lovely home and family, everything he could desire, could forfeit all of it to go to the mission field. Wasn't he accomplishing a great deal here? Why did he deem it necessary to go preach in some remote place where he surely would not be appreciated? He would not be working at the bank much longer now. He would be leaving to go visit a lot of other churches to raise his support and to get to know the people who would be supporting him. This puzzled Amy, too, as she walked along. His family was obviously of considerable affluence, and he certainly was able to support himself.

He was a fine specimen of manhood. Strange that she had ever thought otherwise. The girls flocked about him, hoping to be the object of his interest. But he was a master at repartee and treated each one with the same warm, sometimes aloof, friendliness. Thus, each one hopefully pretended she was the only one who claimed his affection. Amy had taken all this in just the few times she had been with him socially. It was mighty peculiar Elaine did not object.

But she cast off all these immaterial things, deciding they did not really matter, if only she could find the answers to the soul-searching questions.

The depressing afternoon which she spent in her room brought Amy to the depths of despair. It was too hot to go out walking, and besides, where could she go? She sat by the open window and put her head down on her arm. Her unhappy life marched before her in a parade of unfortunate experiences; an unusual parade for there were no fanfares, no exciting music, no waving flags, no cheering. When it was over there was no applause. There was no feeling of exuberance. Just a void. A let-down. The crowd that had stood by and watched so quietly was suddenly gone, and she stood on the street alone and lonely with no place to go. She looked about for someone to ask, but there was no one to be found.

She had wanted this Saviour who could make her life worth living again; she had looked for Him, but what now? Where did she go from here?

"The preaching of the cross is to them that perish foolishness, but unto us which are saved it is the power of God."

" . . . . unto us which are saved . . . ." Did that not mean those who believed? Anyone who believed was saved according to all she had been hearing. In other words, God had provided this salvation through Christ and His death on the cross. But why was the preaching of it foolishness to anyone who did not believe? But it was to her. Or at least it had been before she had given it serious thought.

"To every one that believeth . . ." and then, ". . . unto us which are saved – the power of God," the still, small voice whispered just before she dropped off to sleep.

Amy sat dazed as she tried to determine what had aroused her from an unpleasant nap. Her joints ached and her hand was full of pins and needles from her uncomfortable position. She had a big red circle on her forehead where it had rested on her arm. She rubbed her eyes, trying to remove the fogginess from them when someone knocked on her door. That was it. Someone had been knocking. She jumped up, shaking the rest of the cobwebs away as she opened the door.

"Oh, Amy, I'm sorry. I didn't know you were resting. Someone is here to see you," Mr. Martin explained. "A young lady," he added, grinning broadly as he tried to tease the disinterested girl.

Amy was fully awake now, and as she went down the stairs, she was surprised to see Elaine standing in the front hall.

"We came to take you to church, Amy," Elaine said before she had a chance to speak. "I'm glad to see you're all ready! You will come, won't you?"

"I can't go like this. I'm so rumpled!" She looked down at her lovely, wrinkled dress. "Come on up with me while I make a quick change." Elaine followed her up the stairs. "I'm glad you came, Elaine. I was pretty sick of myself. Did you know I went to church this morning?" She had taken off her dress and put a clean one on the bed.

"Dan saw you when he sang."

"He made it sound so simple the other night, and I was hoping I might find out a little more about it."

"It is simple, Amy," Elaine bubbled enthusiastically. "If there were anything we could do to earn our own salvation, then Christ's death on the cross would have been in vain!" She zipped up the back of Amy's melon-colored cotton as she spoke. "'Not by works of righteousness which we have done, but according to his mercy he saved us.'"

"You mean then it's true? That all I have to do is believe?" She did not wait for an answer. "Then I believe! He's my Saviour, too! Did you hear that, Elaine? I believe!" She was unable to hold back the tears as she came to the full realization of it.

"I'm so glad, Amy," Elaine said softly, putting her arms around her. There were tears in Elaine's eyes too. "We've been praying for you."

They knelt briefly to thank the Lord for the miracle, then hurried down to the first floor.

"I've never known people like you, Elaine," Amy said as she opened the front door, her heart overflowing with gratitude. "You, Dan, – all of you!"

"Don't give *us* the credit!" Elaine exclaimed, giving her new friend a quick hug.

Dan was watching them as they descended the steps. "Say, girls, we're going to be late," he scolded. "Well," he brightened, "don't we look pleased with ourselves!"

"We are, dear," murmured Elaine, squeezing his arm as she slid over close to him to make room for Amy in the front seat.

Dan did not say any more, but he thanked the Lord for the soul just born into the heavenly family.

Chapter 6

"WELL, LOOK WHO'S all aglow, girls! What's with you, Amy? Got a new beau? Better hang onto him, but watch those fingernails!" Karen Winslow was being cruel.

"No, better than that, Karen. A whole new way of life."

"Oh, heavens! She must have got religion over the weekend! Imagine that!"

Amy looked at Karen, and for one brief moment she was at a loss for words. Her eyes went past the girl, however, and there in her line of vision was Dan, standing straight and tall, several desks away. He was trying to look busy, but he was watching her expectantly. As their eyes met, he smiled and winked at her, giving her the courage she needed.

"Not religion, Karen. A Saviour. He came into my heart and gave me a reason for living." She kept her eyes on the girl as she spoke, unflinching under the cynicism. "For the first time in my life, I've found happiness, and I'd like to tell you about it."

"No, *thank you!*" she exclaimed, walking away. "I live in complete bliss just the way I am!"

Amy suppressed a desire to link the word Karen had used with "ignorance," knowing it would serve only to widen the breach between them.

Karen had a natural gift for attracting the opposite sex, and the well-knowing members of it were drawn to her as bees to honey. She was extremely conscious of this ability and thoroughly enjoyed the attention it brought her. This fact was evidenced in the encouragement she added to the art: the long fluttering lashes which she automatically set in motion when some desirable male was near; the scarlet, bow-shaped mouth she coyly puckered when pretending hurt; the clothes she wore to emphasize her physical charm. Yes, Karen was in a world all her own, and she was in complete bliss, as she said, as long as there was a sufficient supply of males in orbit around her.

Karen did not like Amy, and although the feelings were mutual, Amy did not know why. It was more than that party, she knew, for Karen had given her the cold shoulder long before that.

Amy was on her way out to lunch when Dan came out of his office as she passed his door. "How's it going, Amy?"

"It isn't easy, Dan."

"Anything that's worthwhile isn't usually easy."

"I know that, and I'm enjoying the challenge. And thanks."

"You're welcome. For what?"

"The moral support."

He smiled and leaned against the door jamb, crossed his legs and put his hands in his pockets. "Say, Amy, I'm supposed to bring you home for supper tonight. They said I wouldn't get any if you weren't with me, so *please* don't let me down."

"I don't think it would hurt you to miss a meal, but I'd love to come, Dan. And thanks again. I'll see you later." She was delighted. This family was beginning to mean a great deal to her, and she enjoyed every minute she was able to spend with them.

Right after lunch, Amy saw Karen heading her way again, and she mentally prepared herself for another deluge of caustic remarks.

"Amy, I shouldn't have talked to you the way I did this morning. You haven't looked so cheerful in a long time, and I'm really glad you have something that makes you happy. Just don't try to rub any of it off on me." Karen gave her a little smile and turned on her heel.

"Thanks, Karen." Amy was sincere.

The afternoon had wings. Amy could not believe it when Dan came over to her desk to see if she were ready to leave.

"Say," he exclaimed, "if you're that anxious to work, maybe I could see about bringing your supper back to you!" She promptly started putting things away. "Finish what you're doing. I have to stop downstairs with some reports anyway. I'll meet you at the door."

He was at the door when she stepped out of the elevator. They walked to the car in silence. She waited until they were out of the parking lot and on their way before she spoke.

"Dan, did you know that Karen came to me and apologized this afternoon? Well, she didn't actually say she was sorry, but she's glad I'm happy—as long as I don't try to influence her."

"Good. That could be an opening, you know."

"I hope so. I just hope I can find the right words when I need them."

"The Lord will supply them."

It was quiet for a few minutes as they thought about the happenings of the morning and the preceding evening.

"Do any of your young people smoke, Dan?" Amy asked out of the clear blue sky.

"Some do, Amy. Why do you ask?"

"I had a feeling it would be out of place if I did, at both the supper and the party the other night."

"I'm certain it would never keep anyone out of heaven."

"It's kind of a hard thing to stop."

"I suppose so. It's really something you have to decide for yourself—between you and the Lord."

"What reason would you give against it, Dan? I mean aside from the fact that maybe you just don't like it?"

"'Ye are not your own. For ye are bought with a price: therefore glorify God in your body, and in your spirit, which are God's." Dan was thoughtful for a moment, wondering about her silence, yet confident the Holy Spirit had already begun His work in her heart. "First Corinthians 6:19, 20. Read it over later. Course that covers a great many things. Not just smoking."

"That's a good answer. I don't know whether to thank you or not."

When they turned into his drive, Amy noticed another car near the back of the house, a small foreign one.

"It looks like you have other company."

"No, that's my sister's car."

"Your sister's?"

"Yes, she's fixing supper tonight. That's why she was so anxious for you to come." He was opening the car door for her.

"Dan, I didn't know you had a sister."

He looked at her in amazement. "Of course you did, Amy," he said laughing. "Elaine's been with you almost every time I have!"

"Elaine?" The pieces began to fall into place. "Oh, Dan, please don't laugh!" They got the picture simultaneously and laughed together as they went up the back steps. "Don't tell anyone, Dan."

But he could not keep it to himself, and as soon as they entered the big kitchen, he had to tell his mother and sister who were busily putting the finishing touches on the meal. Amy felt foolish, but she joined them in their amusement. Better to be laughed *with* than *at*. Dan left her there with the two women.

"Then who is the lucky man, Elaine?"

"First Lieutenant Mark Walter Abrahamson. And soon to be *Mister* Mark Walter Abrahamson," she said proudly. "Wait. I'll get his picture."

Elaine left, and Mrs. Sanderford put her arm around Amy's shoulder. "Welcome to the fold, Amy. We were praying for you."

Amy put her arm around the woman's waist. "I know. Elaine told me, and I'm so happy about it all. I love you all for it."

Elaine was back with the large portrait and proudly displayed it to the newcomer. He was a good-looking boy, rugged features, dark curly hair. Amy's admiration was genuine. "You're a very fortunate girl, Elaine. I'm anxious to meet him."

Paul appeared from nowhere and started poking his fingers into the food. Dan came in dressed in sport clothes, and they proceeded to the dining room.

During the meal, Amy told them about her brother and his family, about the depressing afternoon she had endured before it had turned into a victorious one, about the song which had increased her dissatisfaction with herself.

They talked about Elaine's forthcoming marriage, about events to take place in the nearer future, and about the plans for the evening. Amy was surprised to learn that the Sanderfords owned a speedboat. They were avid boatsmen.

"Didn't Dan tell you to bring your swimming togs, Amy? I knew I should have called you. Men!" Elaine scolded him with a wilting glance.

Amy helped Elaine and her mother clear the table as Dan and Paul went into the living room. It was quiet on that front.

"You really don't have to help, Amy."

"But I *want* to, Mrs. Sanderford. You don't know what a pleasure this is!"

"You have to be kidding, Amy. Since when is doing dishes a pleasure?" These were Elaine's sentiments.

"Since right now. At least for me."

The three of them were finishing up the pots and pans when they heard a terrible crash. Amy looked at the other two in alarm.

"It's nothing to worry about, Amy. Come here." Elaine walked to the door which led to the dining room, and Amy followed, puzzled. Elaine pointed through to the living room where Paul and Dan were, on the floor. "It's just my little brothers. The one who loses has to say 'uncle' before he can get up. It's always Paul, although he puts up a pretty good fight. I guess they enjoy it, but I think the real reason they do it is so they don't get soft."

"They're both so big," Amy said as they went back to their work, "it's a wonder they don't break something!"

Mrs. Sanderford turned to look at her. "Yes, I always was glad we had a big house, especially when I realized those two would never stop growing. But it's going to be awfully quiet around here when Dan goes. And Paul will be leaving for college too." Her voice evidenced more pride than disappointment.

"And you'll be getting married before long," commented Amy to Elaine, thinking of the older woman being left alone.

"Yes, but we're going to be staying here for a while, at least until Mark decides what he wants to do, where he wants to go."

Amy thought this wise and wondered if it had not been planned this way so the lovely mother would not suddenly be left alone.

"Say, ladies, almost ready?" Paul was dressed in bathing trunks and was carrying a pair of skis.

"Amy, I'll personally take upon myself the responsibility of teaching you how to ski."

"Oh, Amy, you mustn't let this opportunity slip by!" his sister exclaimed with forced sarcasm. "This talented artist doesn't frequently offer his services to us less fortunate beings!"

"I'll just watch," laughed Amy.

"You're coming, aren't you, Mother? I just called Judy, and we're going to pick her up on the way."

"Are you going to teach her to water ski too?" asked Dan who had come in just in time to hear his remarks to Amy. "Or did you have something else in mind?"

Paul whirled on his brother and gave him a right hook just above the belt.

"Children must play. Come on, Amy. I have a suit you can wear. It's really lots of fun."

"All right," Dan said after Judy got in, "let's take a vote. Long Island Sound, or Lantern Lake?"

After each had expressed his opinion and had more or less decided on the Sound, they turned to Amy who had not put in her vote. "I'm with you all the way. I love the salt water. Is it too far though?"

"No, we're about half-way between."

And it *was* fun. Amy thrilled to the feeling of speed, the wind pulling her taut against the towline. It was exhilarating. The sting she felt along the side of her body as she hit the water was hardly noticeable.

Elaine and Judy each had a turn, then Elaine took the helm and her brothers dove into the water. They made a wide, sweeping circle, each of the boys on a slalom ski with separate ropes.

It was a delightful evening, one such as Amy had never known. After a beautiful sunset, she was sorry to see they were heading back toward the dock. Dan cut the motor some distance from shore, however, and Paul threw out the anchor, causing a good splash which soaked his mother.

"Sorry. But I told you to wear your bathing suit!" He sat down close to Judy, encircling her in his arm as he shouted, "Turn on the moonlight!" She blushed profusely.

They talked for a long time. Although most of the names mentioned were foreign to Amy, she was content to stay as long as they were led to do so. She listened to the chatter which seemed to be echoed in the sounds of the night, felt the cool water as she dangled her hand over the side of the boat, and rejoiced in the fellowship her new-found faith afforded her.

Much later, as they again piled into Dan's car, he voiced a suggestion the subject of which was furthest from their minds, except for perhaps his own and Paul's.

"Anyone for milkshakes?"

"Always hungry, aren't you? I guess you didn't like my supper, did you?" questioned Elaine with a glint in her eye.

"Sure I did. But we just worked it off. I'm hungry again."

"Not 'again.' Yet. Well, then, let's go back to the house and fix them."

"You're a fine one. I offer to treat you and you insist on going home!"

"I appreciate your generosity, but Amy has to change into her own clothes, so we might as well go back to the house. We'll take a rain check on the milkshakes though, won't we, Amy?"

"Good idea. But I don't believe I could eat a thing after that dinner."

"At least someone liked my cooking," sniffed Elaine.

They had their refreshments, and the wonderful time was over. The clock on the kitchen wall warned them of the hour.

"Thank you *all* for a very wonderful evening," Amy said, her heart full of appreciation. "And thank you for all you have done for me!"

"We want you to come any time, Amy," Mrs. Sanderford called to her as she and the rest of the young people climbed back into the car.

Chapter 7

"THEREFORE IF ANY man be in Christ, he is a new creature: old things are passed away; behold, all things are become new."

Dan had thought of this verse from Second Corinthians several times a day, every day for the past four weeks. He thought of it now as he caught a glimpse of Amy, her eyes bright with excitement, talking with Karen Winslow.

Amy was a new creation, and her whole personality had made a complete transition. True, her outward appearance had not changed drastically. The heavy make-up she had worn had not disappeared completely, but the conservative amount she now wore gave her a soft, natural look, a look that made her glow. Her real beauty, however, came from within, from a heart that had been washed pure with the precious blood of the Lord Jesus Christ.

Dan had talked to Roy Carlson and his wife about her, asked them if they would take her under their wing, but now he wondered if it had been necessary. He marveled at her new vitality, her new determination of spirit. Still, she was a "babe in Christ" and might need a little undergirding once in a while.

His service to the bank was to terminate in just a week – next Friday. He was anxious to get started on his tour of the various churches, but he had a feeling of defeat that he had been unable to accomplish more here. He had something to talk over with Amy concerning one of their fellow employees, but he would wait until things were a bit more quiet. Perhaps at lunch time. As a rule she did not go out to eat with the other girls.

"How's it going, Amy?" It was not the first time he had asked her that.

"Looking up, Dan. I really think Karen is interested even though she tries to appear indifferent. She's not such a bad person when she's alone."

"Bless you, Amy, but watch her. I've known her a long time.

I'm glad you're here to carry on. I wish I could have done more."

"I wish you didn't have to leave, Dan. You've been my moral support."

"That's not true. Well, maybe the first time, but after that you were on your own. You're doing fine."

"But I am going to miss you."

"It's nice to be missed." He smiled. "I wanted to talk to you about that—my leaving, I mean. Amy, I've been talking to one of the fellows, and I think I finally got through to him. I wondered if you would talk to him when you have the chance."

"I'm not very eloquent, Dan, but I'll do my best. Who is he?"

"That's all we can be expected to do. He's Larry Spencer."

"No."

She answered too quickly, too emphatically, and she was aware of it as soon as the one word was out. He stood up, puzzled over her reaction. She certainly had had no inhibitions whatsoever about witnessing, and this unusual attitude was incongruous to her recent willingness to serve the Lord.

"All right, Amy."

"I—I'm sorry, Dan," she stammered, "but I can't. You'll just have to pray that you'll see results before you leave. I'm sorry," she reiterated.

"I'll do that, Amy. But you'll pray, too, won't you?"

She nodded assent, but the whole matter had struck a dissonant chord.

To add to her discomfort, Karen, just returning from lunch and flanked on either side by several of her female cohorts, was heading her way. Karen was a hypocrite, a chameleon whose colors changed to suit her surroundings. They pretended to be heading toward their leader's desk, but Karen stopped in fake amazement and looked at Amy.

"So. Now we know, Amy. All this religious business! It was all a big act—a big play for that scrumptious Dan Sanderford!" The girls joined her in her enthusiasm. Amy heard such remarks as, "We've got your number now!" and "I'll bet she'll never make the grade with him!"

Her face turned red with embarrassment. She needed encouragement but she prayed with all her heart that Dan had not heard these unkind, unwarranted remarks.

"You don't understand, girls—Karen—"

"We sure do!" Karen was despicable. "You really had us fooled, Amy, but better stick to you-know-who. He's much more your type!"

The one male Karen wanted most to conquer seemed unaffected by her female charm. For that reason, that alone, she had taken upon herself the very enjoyable task of harassing Amy, breaking her down piece by piece, antagonizing her until she eventually would strike back with equal vengeance. So far she had been unsuccessful.

Amy's face turned from an embarrassed crimson to an enraged scarlet. "I'd be careful if I were you, Karen Winslow." She stood up and stared at the girl, her blue eyes flashing. "Your jealousy is showing!"

It was fuel to the young lady's already smoldering fire. She laughed loudly, forcing sarcasm into her very breath. "Well, if that isn't one for the books! Me, jealous! Ha! If I ever lack for male companions, Amy, I'll let you know. Maybe you'll lend me one of yours! Or maybe there's some guy back where you came from! Better give us the low-down sometime!" They went their way, laughing loudly together.

Amy clenched her teeth. Her day was ruined, and the afternoon was misery. She made sure she did not walk out with Dan at the close of the day. He was sitting in his car, waiting at the curb, when she came out the front door of the bank. He had always waited inside.

"Don't let them get you down, Amy," he said as they turned the corner.

So he *had* heard. She flushed. "She was hateful, Dan. I didn't know what to do."

"You know, you did just what she wanted you to do."

She looked at him in surprise. "Why, I never thought of that, Dan. I do believe you're right!"

"She's a hard-hearted girl, Amy, and she'll go to any length to hurt someone if she gets it into her head to do so."

"I know that. It just never occurred to me—Thanks again for your help."

With the weekend coming on, Amy found it comparatively easy to put aside Dan's problem with her own: her dislike of Larry Spencer, Karen's acerbities, and the troublesome memory of one who forced aside all other thought, Todd Kenyon.

The weekends were now a time of special blessing to her, not only because of the regular church services, but also because of the extra time she was able to spend with her new friends. Their activities and those of the church continued one right after the other, and Amy was included in all of them.

She and Elaine had become fast friends, and either Elaine or her mother had called Amy every Saturday for the past month, usually to go shopping. They always arrived back at the big stone house for lunch.

So, Dan and his problems, Karen and her verbal lashings, became insignificant in her anticipation of her shopping date for the following day.

Amy was waiting on the sidewalk in front of her house when Elaine and her mother drove up in Elaine's little car. By the time they finished the necessary shopping in town, the sky was growing overcast, so they hurried at the supermarket where they stopped for the week's supply of groceries. Amy helped carry the packages into the house and also helped Elaine put them away.

"We sure needed some manpower today," puffed Elaine as she brought in the last bag and deposited it on a chair.

"Where is your manpower?"

"Paul is on a picnic with Judy and her family. Dan is on a bike ride with the junior boys."

"Not such a good day for either of them."

"Those boys will suffer through it, believe me. Even if a hurricane comes up! They've anxiously been waiting for this one last outing with Dan, and there probably won't be too many chances for them after next week. So let's hope the rain holds off."

They finished putting the groceries away, and Amy was about to sit down when Elaine grabbed her by the hand. "Oh, no you don't! Come on. I want to show you some of my prize possessions."

Elaine's room was lovely. It was like a picture with its soft, pink walls, deep rose carpeting, and fluffy white curtains which reflected the light from the windows. The bedspread was white with a pink dust ruffle to match the walls. The room was bright and exciting, sweet and simple, like the girl herself.

They sat on the floor in front of the hope chest. Elaine took each piece out, one by one, to show Amy. Most of the things she exhibited were new, but a few of them were heirlooms—a hand-crocheted tablecloth, sterling silver candlesticks. She handled these fondly, and Amy could see they meant a great deal to her. Mrs. Sanderford came in and sat on the floor with them.

"These were my grandmother's, Amy. She made the tablecloth. That lovely crystal set belonged to my husband's mother. She wanted Elaine to have it."

Elaine was in the closet pulling things out, and when she was done, she had a huge pile of boxes and bags on her bed. She bubbled over with enthusiasm with each article she took out, and during the whole process her main topic for discussion was Mark. She proudly displayed her trousseau, pointing out each detail as she held things in front of her to give the appropriate effect.

"Mother made these for me!"

"They're lovely!" exclaimed Amy. She turned to the other woman. "Mrs. Sanderford, they're just beautiful! Why, you're an artist. You should go into the dressmaking business!"

Louise Sanderford's face beamed. "Thank you, Amy. I really

did consider it when I was younger, but I knew if I *had* to sew I wouldn't enjoy it."

"You have a remarkable mother, Elaine."

"And would you believe it? She absolutely refused to teach me how to sew." Elaine had a hurt look on her face which caused Amy to look questioningly at her mother.

"Don't you believe her. She didn't even want to learn how to sew on a button. I finally gave up!"

"The truth of the matter is, she was afraid the bad fairy would come and make me prick my finger." They giggled like three little girls.

"I'll bet she was afraid Mark wouldn't wait for you, and then she'd be stuck with you," Amy teased.

"She doesn't know what a prize she's losing then," Elaine returned, giving her mother a bear hug. "Like to know something, Amy? Mother's making my wedding gown too."

"You're such a fortunate girl. I wish I could see it."

"That's not allowed," the bride-to-be told her, shaking her finger.

"You'll just have to wait until the wedding, Amy," Mrs. Sanderford offered.

"Now, Mother, what makes you think I'm going to invite her?"

Amy was taken aback. "Oh—" she started. "Oh, I'll come anyway!" Their laughter was a tonic to her, this lovely lady with the twinkling eyes, her daughter who was so much like her. Mrs. Sanderford had a youthful appearance and manner that made one forget there was any difference in age, and she easily fit in with any plans her children made.

"We look about the same size, Elaine. Maybe someday I'll borrow it."

"Good idea. That is if Mother takes care of it when she uses it again." There was no end to this girl's teasing, but Amy was beginning to recognize the twinkle which inevitably appeared in her eyes at such times.

"I'll probably never use it either, so don't save it for me."

"That's what they all say. You'll see."

The three of them were putting the treasures back into the cedar chest when Elaine looked up in surprise.

"Oh, hi, Danny! Eavesdropping again?"

He was standing in the doorway, leaning against the jamb, legs crossed, hands in his pockets—his usual stance. He was enjoying all the chatter.

"How about some food for a growing boy?"

"Oh, please don't grow any more," his mother begged with her hands clasped in front of her. "We can't figure out *now* whether to cut some off the bottom or the top!"

He started to leave, chuckling, when his sister called to him. "What happened to your hike, Danny?"

He came into the room, put his arm around her shoulder, and led her to the window. "See that stuff splashing against the other side of the window? They call it rain."

"Oh." She looked at him with a blank expression. "I thought it was liquid air."

"Whatever it is, it's wet," he said as he left the room.

"You're chicken!" she called after him.

He bounded down the stairs, cackling loudly as he went. Mrs. Sanderford followed him to start lunch while the two younger girls finished putting the things away.

"I envy you, Elaine," Amy said seriously, her brow furrowed in deep thought. "A wonderful family, all these lovely things, your wedding plans. What more could a girl want?"

"One of these days, Amy, you'll be doing this very same thing yourself. Mark my words. And I'm going to find someone for you, even if I have to sic Paul on you!" She almost said Dan. Better not give this young lady any ideas!

Amy laughed. "I'm quite sure Judy wouldn't go along with that, but I'll just bet life would be very interesting with him around all the time!"

"Isn't Judy a lovely girl? Paul is really gone on her."

"If I ever do get married, it will have to be to someone who doesn't work in an office. So he won't have to go to their parties," she answered the other girl's questioning glance. "I'll tell you about it some day."

Elaine abruptly changed the subject. "Amy, I want you to be one of my bridesmaids. Please don't say no, Amy, Mother and I have already talked it over and she says we can get the material next week, and I'm going to help her make your gown and you can help too, and I really do know how to sew, Amy, Mother made me learn 'cause she said she wasn't going to sew Mark's buttons on or mend his socks and Amy, I love you dearly so please don't say no!" This all in one breath.

Amy was astonished. "You can't mean—"

"But I do, Amy. You *must* say you will."

Amy had tears in her eyes. "I'd consider it an honor, Elaine. But you must have a lot of other friends—"

"Most of my real close friends from school have married and moved away. Patty Marshall, well, now she's Patty Anderson—and she's the girl who's going to be my matron of honor—anyway, she moved to Flint after she got married. We sent her the material and she's making her own gown, so she won't be coming till the day before the wedding. And my cousin, Robin, is going to be my other bridesmaid. And there's no one I'd rather have than you!"

"I'd love to, Elaine," Amy said, deeply touched. "I'm just so thrilled you asked me."

"Now Mother said we can run down to New York next Saturday and get the material, and then by the following week it should be ready for fitting. Robin is coming that Saturday, too, so it should work out perfectly. She lives in New Jersey. Oh, I'm so glad, Amy!" Elaine could not stand still.

"Soup's on!" Dan called up the stairs.

They chattered all through the meal, mostly about Mark's return and the wedding, also about Dan's upset plans of the morning. He thought they might get together yet for a hike since they had well over a month before school started, and he would be home off and on during that time.

When Elaine took Amy home late that afternoon, they equaled each other in their excitement. They had almost reached Amy's house when she turned to her new friend, her heart full to the brim.

"Elaine, I can't get over the wonder of all that's happened to me. I was about to give up, call it quits, and then, overnight, a miraculous thing took place that made me so happy I thought I couldn't take any more. But everyday it gets better."

"I'm happy for you, too, Amy. We think you're pretty swell."

Sunday flew by with its multitude of activities—there was always so much to be done. And Monday came all too soon with its wealth of problems.

Amy opened her typewriter, and before she plunged into the activities of the morning, she found herself thinking about Dan's concern for Larry Spencer. She did not want Dan to know—he could not possibly know of her unpleasant association with this man or he would not have asked her to take this responsibility. She was not even certain she could pray for Larry. She had not spoken to him once in the past seven months, could not because of the contempt she felt for him.

But as she looked at herself in the light of her new experiences, she wondered if she were not just as much to blame for what had happened. Her presence had indicated her approval. But no matter how much of the blame she tried to put upon herself, it did not alter the low opinion she had of Lawrence Spencer.

It troubled her all week, especially since the days were slipping by and Dan had not mentioned it again. She so hoped that he would have some good news to give her before he left, or at least relieve her of the responsibility he had put so lightly upon her shoulders.

Friday came, and with it a knowledge that she must question Dan about it. When she stepped out of the elevator after lunch, however, she came face to face with the problem himself, the corridor being empty except for the two of them. She was going to hurry on by when he stopped her.

"Amy—" His voice spoke a question rather than a statement. She stopped but did not turn. "Got a minute?"

He had red hair, probably more on the strawberry-blonde, a few freckles here and there, and a dimple in each cheek when he smiled. The dimples gave him a boyish appearance. He was trying to smile now, but there were no dimples. He was rather stocky and stood only four or five inches taller than Amy.

She did not answer. She refused to look at him.

He went on, not needing an answer. "Dan tells me you believe in this religion he's been telling me about. I was hoping maybe—you know, since he's leaving and all—" It was not easy for him either.

"I'm sorry, *Mister* Spencer."

Amy looked for her moral support, but he was nowhere in sight. She was at a loss for words when his advice of some weeks ago came to her. *The Lord will supply the words, Amy.* A wordless prayer went up from her heart. Her facial expression softened along with her voice.

"I'd be glad to help you, Larry, but I don't know much about it myself yet. I only know the Lord Jesus Christ came into my heart and made my life worth living again."

Suddenly Dan was there with his arm around Larry's shoulders. He smiled at her and winked.

"Was there any particular matter you had in mind, Larry?" Her voice was controlled, her words sincere. Amy was growing in grace.

Chapter 8

LARRY SPENCER WALKED the several blocks to the apartment house where he lived. He took the key from his pocket as he stepped from the elevator at the eighth floor, walked the dozen or so steps to his door, and unlocked it. Each motion was a product of habit. He entered his lush quarters. At this point, his general procedure changed.

Each day when he arrived home from work, if he had not stopped to eat on the way, he would fix himself something which he called supper. Then, after his repast, if his utensils were running low, he would wash the dishes. This only happened about once a week, however. Much too often, he thought. After eating, if he did not have a date for the evening, he usually read or watched television until all hours of the night. Occasionally he would go out bowling with some of the fellows who lived in the same building. Saturdays he almost always went golfing, usually with Tracey Manning or Dianne Blake.

But that kitchen. He would have to speak to the maid about it and see if she would clean it up now and then if he paid her a little extra. These thoughts flashed through his mind as he held the phone to his ear and glanced out into the messy kitchenette. He did not care about the mess, really, since the eyesore was usually visible to no one else, but it *was* an unpleasant sight.

He spoke to the man at the garage and asked to have his car brought around to the front door in an hour. This was the point where his daily routine changed. He had a dinner date this evening with a young lady he had taken out many times, a very beautiful, wealthy socialite. Up until today he had been looking forward to this evening with a great deal of anticipation. She was delightful company besides being well-heeled, and if ever he seriously considered becoming involved in the estate of matrimony, he might put her at the top of his list. But these considerations had been prominent in his mind before this day—this eventful day when he had been able to talk to Amy.

Larry thought of Amy as he dressed for the evening, thought of the way she had affected his life, disturbing his aplomb. In fact, she and Dan Sanderford had each upset, in an entirely different manner, his egotistical, well-planned future.

Larry Spencer was a precocious young man. He had come along a difficult way and had acquired a wealth of knowledge and experience from the school of hard knocks. It was through this medium he had learned to take what he wanted the first time opportunity made its appearance at his door. The world lived by this criterion, so it was in his best interest to do the same. By exercising this principle, he had been able to elevate himself to the position he now held. Just a few short months ago he had been promoted to head teller, and now he was certain another promotion was imminent. It did not concern him that he had forced his way, that he might have left others choking in his dust. In spite of this fact, he was well-liked, for on the surface he was a buffoon, a jolly-good-fellow. He was charming.

He had been comparatively content with his job, his surroundings, until Dan had made his appearance. They worked in close association, and Larry liked him. Dan was astute, reliable, and as straightforward as a person could be. Larry perceived that his colleague's manner of progression certainly was more forthright than his own.

But Dan could well afford these attributes, for, in contrast to Larry's circumstances, he had had his worldly possessions handed to him on the much-coveted silver platter.

Occasionally Larry became sick up to his ears of Dan's holiness. If there was anything he could not abide, it was such a holier-than-thou kind of person.

"You can go— "

"Save it, Spencer," Dan had said firmly, severity creasing the corners of his eyes and lips. Then, just as quickly, seeing the red creep into Larry's face and neck as the anger flashed in his eyes, Dan's own expression had softened as his mouth widened in a grin. "It'll keep. Save it for later." It had eased the tension.

Larry's irritation had subsided time and again under Dan's tactfulness. Dan Sanderford was no sis. He was strictly a man's man. From thence Larry had endeavored to curb his vile tongue in the presence of such godliness. "Tar and molasses" was usually the extent of his cursing in Dan's company although once in a while, to prove he was not getting religious, he allowed himself, for convenience, to forget his present company. He had a vocabulary that did not lack for descriptive phrases. *Tar and molasses* replaced a much stronger utterance, though he failed to elaborate on what it substituted.

Initially Larry had not minded Dan's continuous reference to his beliefs. He had long since steeled himself against the influence of the Almighty. But the Word of God was making its effect on him, gradually and quietly, and against his will. Larry's wall of indifference was being destroyed, piece by piece, inch by inch.

He had been under Dan's influence for about a year now, but he actually had not been listening to the verses quoted or the remarks concerning them, for they were not new to him. He knew them all. Many times he had to restrain himself from quoting them back to Dan, or from finishing them before Dan had a chance. That would stop his preaching at him! But if Dan knew of his knowledge of the Bible, he might become curious. The truth was, Larry's father was, and had been for many years, a circuit preacher in the hills of Pennsylvania. This was a well-guarded secret which he avowed would never become public information.

God's Word had been an important part of Larry's life as a child, but he felt he had had an overdose and he had rebelled. Unable to take any more and lightly referring to himself as the prodigal son, the black sheep, he had left home. So, fresh out of high school, worldly-wise and conscience-free, he had left, breaking the hearts of his parents and thumbing his nose at God.

That was a decade ago. For the first four years he had had no contact with his family whatsoever. After serving two years in the army, he had worked his own way through business school. The recollection of those difficult years was a booster in his determination to reach the top. He had achieved good grades with little effort, the one and only thing that had ever come easy for him, which fact made his studying almost effortless. Thus, upon completion of his business course, finding satisfactory employment had proved to be no great difficulty.

As he finished shaving and began combing his red hair, Larry thought again of the verse Dan had quoted to him that day, a verse he had quoted to him on a number of occasions.

"For scarcely for a righteous man will one die, yet peradventure for a good man some would even dare to die. But God commendeth His love toward us, in that, while we were yet sinners, Christ died for us." Larry knew it as well as he knew his own name.

He did not care how much Dan talked *about* eternal life, *about* Christ and the necessity of a personal acceptance of him as Saviour. He did not care how much he talked *about* the Bible. If only he would not quote verses *from* it. It was almost as if God Himself were speaking out to him and pointing an accusing finger at him. Larry also knew the verse about God's Word not returning unto Him void. It was a piercing sword and it left him speechless, without argument, unprotected by this fort he had constructed about himself.

"Except a man be born again he cannot see the kingdom of God."

This verse from the third chapter of the gospel of John was not new to him either. It did not speak of mysterious witchcraft. It did not speak of some sort of hokey-pokey. And Larry did not find it necessary to ask as did Nicodemus in the next verse, "How can a man be born when he is old?"

No, not witchcraft. But time and again Larry had scoffed at his parents, at their humble beliefs, telling them they were behind the times, that people, sensible people had tossed these foolish beliefs out the window ages ago. Why, nobody, but nobody believed the Bible literally any more. It was antiquated and out of date, full of mistakes and contradictions. He was glad he had relieved himself of their weird influence, the influence itself seeming to him as witchcraft.

But there *were* people, sensible people, who still believed God's Word, who accepted it as the infallible Book, divinely inspired by God, and who considered the Bible as the only rule for life and living.

"Ye must be born again."

He could see his father's face as his earnest voice reached out to his people and their sincere faces as they drank in God's Word.

"Except a man be born again he cannot see the kingdom of God."

A regeneration. That's what this verse spoke of. As he was born of fleshly parents, he became a fleshly being. He was a sinful being, unfit to be looked upon by a just God. And just as it was necessary to experience a physical birth to belong to human parents, it was necessary to experience a new birth to become a child of God.

"Except a man be born of water and of the Spirit, he cannot enter the kingdom of God," was the answer Jesus had given to Nicodemus. "That which is born of the flesh is flesh; and that which is born of the Spirit is spirit. Marvel not that I said unto thee, Ye must be born again."

"Ye *must* be born again." Not, "If you would like to," or "If it conveniently suits you," or "If you feel a stirring in your heart." But "Ye MUST be born again." There was no other way.

If only he could go that way and still hold onto things he enjoyed so much, things that always gave him "kicks." To give them up, that would be asking too much. Of course no one had told him he would have to give anything up, but Larry had walked so closely to the Christian life, riding the fence as it were, that he knew what things mixed and what did not.

Take liquor, for instance. He could drink more hooch and hold it better than anyone he knew. And it made him feel so self-sufficient, so daring, so absolutely desirable—and desiring.

Too bad it didn't affect Amy that way. Too bad, indeed. She was his world to conquer. She was Amy Archer and she had been created for him.

And she was an independent little customer. He would tame her. Not that he did not need some taming himself, but as far as Amy was concerned, he was putty.

Larry was driving through the city streets as his thoughts again turned to Amy. He had admired her from the very first day he had laid eyes on her, and he thought she had shared his interest. The pleasure she had registered as a result of his attentiveness was not a product of his imagination, he was sure. She was the main cause of his discomposure. At first he had been enraged by her opposition to his advances, then puzzled. It gave him reason to wonder if her rebellion was caused by high moral standards, or perhaps something deeper. Oh, he knew many girls who professed no religious standing whose moral standards were far higher than his own. But this particular female had seemed to welcome his approving glances.

He had taken her out once or twice before that eventful evening at Christmastime when she had unquestioningly conveyed the message to him that she was untouchable. On one of those dates prior to that party, he had parked down a lonely road, ignoring her protests. She had become completely rebellious. He had taken much more cooperative girls down lover's lane, but Amy's standoffishness had served to kindle his determination to conquer.

Would his interest have remained so alert had she yielded? That was questionable. "Easy come, easy go," he had always contended. But she was Amy. He wanted her.

When Dan had first told him of Amy's conversion, he knew that the rift between them had widened considerably, for he had no intention of getting involved in just the thing he had sought to leave behind, no, not even for this pretty miss. So he decided to bide his time, hoping her enthusiasm would burn itself out. Then he would make an attempt to reconciliate himself to her.

He pulled up in front of the brownstone mansion, wishing as he rang the bell that he were calling for Amy instead of this scatter-brained little butterfly with all her riches.

Although his intentions toward Amy had not been honorable, his interest in her was genuine. He wanted her for his very own. It was an unmitigated notion, for no other woman had made him seriously consider giving up the blissful estate of bachelorhood. He would relinquish it willingly for her. This fact had become more apparent than ever this afternoon when he had talked to her, asking her questions he had not needed to ask.

Her name haunted him.

Larry dropped his freshly lighted cigarette to the step and ground it out with the heel of his highly-polished black shoe, coughing vigorously as he did so. Everything was tasteless lately.

He rang the doorbell again, louder and longer this time, to express his annoyance with the maid, his impatience with his date.

Larry was dissatisfied with everything.

He knew he was a sinner in need of a Saviour. He knew God had provided man with a choice, a free will to choose or reject. "He that is not for me is against me," said the Almighty. And Larry had come to the place where he must *make* the choice. The patient witnessing of his associate, Dan, had humbled his supercilious ego.

His whole status had altered. Larry was miserable. He was *not* self-sufficient. The conflict within him was eating his insides away. It did not take a man to go along with the crowd. He knew it. He had known it ten years ago when he left home. Any boneless jellyfish could go along with the crowd. That took no backbone. It took a man to stand up for what he believed.

The things which had been his very life-blood had turned sour; his aspirations had become insipid. The choice belonged to Lawrence Spencer and to no one else. He would have to answer for no one but himself. The choice was his, and choose he must.

Chapter 9

AMY SAT AT the piano and thumbed through several song books. She was waiting for her final fitting, but Mrs. Sanderford had run into a minor problem with Robin's gown, so she had excused herself with the understanding that they would call her when they were ready for her.

It was two weeks since she had seen Dan and she missed him, especially at the office. It had seemed like a wilderness to her at first, but it was not long until she realized that she *was* able to work independently, that she *was* able to stand on her own.

On an impulse, she had asked Larry to come out to church that following Sunday, a move that had surprised even her. The fact that she had found the grace to talk with him at all had been amazing to her. It was good to have that bitter feeling removed, the bad taste gone.

She started picking out the notes of the song for which she had been looking and wished she had paid better attention during the few music lessons she had been privileged to take.

"Hello, Amy."

She looked up in surprise. "Well! Hi, Dan! I didn't know you were home."

He stood just inside the doorway. He was dressed in gray slacks and a black pullover sweater. The white collar of his shirt was open at the neck. He wore no shoes. He held a big sandwich in one hand and a glass of milk in the other while he tried to keep a book from slipping out from under his arm. He was wearing his horn-rimmed glasses and looked like a studious boy who found eating a better pastime than studying.

"I'll be making fairly short trips until after the wedding since I have a lot of territory to cover in this part of the country. I will be going south on Monday though. Probably as far as Virginia. Maybe North Carolina. Be gone about two weeks." He walked over to the grand piano and leaned on it, holding his sandwich out to her. "Want a bite?"

"No, thanks."

"I'll go make you one." He started to leave.

"No, really."

"You don't like tuna fish."

"No. I mean yes, but I'm not hungry. You and your cousin surely do look alike, Dan. She resembles you more than Elaine or Paul do. She's a beautiful girl."

"Robin? She takes after her father. He and my dad were brothers."

"He was very handsome. I saw his picture in your mother's room."

"I wish you had known him, Amy. He was a fine person. The finest. This place was like a tomb after he died."

She could not imagine this home resembling anything so empty and cold.

"But hey! Thanks for the compliment!"

"I didn't mean to be complimentary," she quickly retorted. "Your mother is a dear, too, Dan. You couldn't have gone wrong taking after either one of your parents. You surely must have taken after someone else."

"Touché!" Dan exclaimed. "I asked for that. Mother is a gem, isn't she, Amy? But getting back to Robin, she needs a lot of prayer. She's practically engaged to a fellow who doesn't believe as we do—as she does. In fact, he isn't of the same faith. He's a real nice guy. Everyone likes him. But if she marries him, she'll be in for nothing but trouble."

"Well, if she loves him and marries him, don't you think he'll—"

"It doesn't work that way. If her faith isn't enough to keep her from marrying him, then it won't be enough to influence him after marriage. I've seen it happen to too many Christian fellows and girls. It makes for a lot of misery."

Everything he said sounded reasonable. It made her dreadfully uncomfortable. She changed the subject abruptly.

"Dan, the next time you're asked to sing, would you sing this?" She pointed to the song she had been trying to play. "I'd love to hear it again."

"Are you asking me now?"

"Um hum."

"Then I'll sing it now." He put his food on the dining room table and came back to the piano.

The late afternoon sun flickered in the quiet of the large room making the use of artificial lighting unnecessary. It made a halo of light around the young lady as she sat by the piano. She was arrayed in layer upon layer of silk organza and nylon tulle, a shade of blue that matched her eyes.

Dan became aware of that fact as he stood in back of her. He put one stockinged foot on the bench beside her. "Why don't you sing it with me?" She looked up at him when he spoke, and this was when he became conscious of the color of her eyes. He had never noticed how blue they were.

She was laughing, and the sound was music in itself. "I have enough trouble trying to play it!"

He sang the first verse, and as he went into the chorus, Amy felt a chill run up her spine. He sang the first few notes of the second verse, then stopped.

"No, the second is in G-Major. Same as the chorus."

"Oh, I see. Of course." She started playing again, and as before, she thrilled to the words and music. "That's beautiful. You have a magnificent voice, Dan." *And what a shame to waste it in some far away place where it won't be appreciated,* her thoughts raced ahead of her.

"Thank you, Amy. That song means a lot to you, doesn't it?" he asked in an effort to change the subject. His voice was merely a gift God had bestowed upon him for His own use, a gift which could be reclaimed if it were not used for His own glory.

"It certainly does. I'll always love it, I guess because it's so true. I want to thank you for what you did for me."

"Not I, Amy. Just thank the Lord. You've come a long way in the last few months."

"You'll never know how far, Dan." *Never, never, never.* "But can't I thank you too? I was searching for something—I didn't know what. And if it hadn't been for you—"

"If it will make you feel better," he said laughing.

"My life was so empty and useless. Why, I could have dropped off the face of the earth and never been missed. And now, suddenly life is so full. I have so many new friends, and there's so much to do all the time. This is the first time in my life I've known what real happiness is."

Dan, with his foot on the bench beside her, put his elbow on his knee, his chin in his hand. "My cup runneth over," he said as his mouth widened in a soft smile.

Excitement sparkled from her eyes as she looked up at him. She was beautiful in the flickering shadows of the late afternoon. The coarse, imitation exterior was gone, and she had emerged the sweet natural creation that she was.

Just beautiful, he thought.

Dan let out a war whoop that shook the rafters. "Ya-ah-ah-hoo-oo!" He did a somersault across his bed and landed upright on both feet. He grinned sheepishly as he turned to see Paul staring at him from the doorway.

"Must be a skirt," Paul mumbled to himself. "A guy just doesn't flip like that unless it's over a dame."

Dan looked like the proverbial cat that bit off more than it could chew.

"Ugh!" Paul's innards reacted unpleasantly to the force of Dan's fist. "Uncle! Uncle!" he finally yelled. "Ya big lummox!"

"Get lost!" Dan snarled over his shoulder before he shut his brother out of his room.

"Whoizshe? Whoizshe?" Paul fairly screamed.

"For me to know and you to find out," he shouted at the rumpus on the other side of the door.

I am in love, Dan said to himself, his eyes widening in amazement. *I, Dan Sanderford, am in love with the sweetest tomato in the world.*

Chapter 10

It was the last Saturday in August. The hot, sultry summer which Amy had dreaded had turned into a pleasant, fruitful one, and it had passed quickly. Today was the grand finale to it all, the Sunday school picnic. It was actually a church picnic sponsored by the Sunday school, for just about everyone was in attendance. Everyone became a child for that day.

Amy especially anticipated these outings, these times of fellowship, for no matter what the affair, it was always closed with a time of devotion. Her spiritual growth had been remarkable because of such devotions.

The picnic had been scheduled for the previous Saturday, but to the disappointment of all, it had been postponed because of rain. The disappointment of the Sanderford family was turned to delight at the postponement, however, when, in the wee small hours of the morning of this last Saturday in August, the elder son and brother returned home unexpectedly. He had driven straight through the night before in order to be with his family for the weekend.

Paul, Judy, and a few other young people had driven up to the state park early in the morning to reserve tables for the crowd. When the Sanderfords, with Amy, arrived late in the morning, they had them arranged in a large circle.

Most of the people had arrived, many of whom Amy had not met. Someone started games for the children, and she helped, but she was content to sit and watch the proceedings thankful she had become a part of them.

The men had wrestling matches, and of course each spectator cheered for his or her choice, usually a member of the same family. Through the process of elimination, Dan and Paul were the last ones in the competition.

"Which one are you rooting for, Lainey?" She had adopted the pet name the boys had for their sister.

"It wouldn't matter much, Amy," she laughed. "There's really no question who the winner will be."

The boys got up and brushed the grass and dirt from their blue jeans as the winner was cheered.

"Say, Dan, you could be big-hearted and let me win once in a while. I'm developing an inferiority complex, you know."

"Fat chance of that. Besides, I'm just trying to keep you from getting conceited."

"Well, look who's talking about having a swelled head!" With that, he threw Dan over his shoulder and headed for the water while the older, his arms flailing about, pounded the younger on the seat. Both of them, fully dressed, were soaked. They decided to change and go for a swim before lunch.

The women were setting the tables and fixing the food and could not be persuaded to join them until lunch was out of the way. Roy Carlson and Larry, who had just arrived, went with them.

Elaine was the first to notice something suspicious in the offing when they returned. The simpleton expression on their faces was not for nought.

"Now what are you boys up to?" she asked.

"And what makes you think we're up to something?" Paul put his nose to hers in defiance.

"Because you're always up to something," she retorted, not moving from his cross-eyed stare. "I recognize the symptoms."

"Well, don't be so nosy. And don't be such a wet blanket."

There was no need for him to warn her. She had never been guilty of either of the things of which he was accusing her.

Larry sat at the end of the table which Amy was setting. She had listened to the conversation in half-amusement, but had not been conscious of anything being amiss.

When Dan was sure he had her attention, he casually walked over to where Larry was sitting.

"Say, Larry," in mock concern, "those are some pretty good scars you have on your back!" He inspected them closely, running his forefinger along the red streaks on Larry's back.

Paul and Roy, curious, sauntered over and sympathetically agreed with Dan.

"Boy, I should say, Larry!" Roy exclaimed.

"Somebody horsewhip you?" asked Paul.

The four of them roared with laughter. They were most pleased with themselves. Their little joke was a success. But they were unable to bask in Amy's confusion. She was on her way to the pump to get water for the coffee.

When she returned they were in the water, so she was spared

the agony of having to face them right away. Although the incident was not mentioned again, she did not miss the twinkle which occasionally appeared in Larry's or Dan's eyes. She had not wanted them to know, certain that their disapproval of her actions would alienate her from them. Much to her wonder, there had been no criticism of her in their exploits. Nor had there been any criticism of Larry. All this was bewildering. Perhaps some day she would understand.

It was obvious that her enthusiasm for the occasion had lost its fervor although she tried to be cheerful lest she spoil someone else's fun.

After the remains of the fried chicken, potato chips and salads were put away, Amy, Elaine, Mrs. Sanderford and some of the other ladies donned their bathing suits and spent a good part of the afternoon in the water. They sat around the small beach on blankets and chatted the rest of the afternoon away.

Suppertime came all too soon, and after a strenuous day the smell of hamburgers, hot dogs, and coffee which the women had started drew the men and children magnetically to the tables. The food never had tasted so delicious, made so much more appealing by the invigorating great outdoors.

The picnic was over after a time of singing and devotions. It was a perfect ending to a glorious day.

Amy insisted on staying at the Sanderford home long enough to help clean up the picnic mess. They were busily washing jugs and silverware, and putting baskets and food away when Elaine, noted for her frankness, asked something which Amy was certain would come up sooner or later.

"Amy, what do you know about those marks on Larry's back?"

Amy explained as briefly as possible the reason for the little act the boys had put on for her benefit. If she did not tell them, she knew Paul or Dan would.

"I never dreamed I had left such lasting marks on him. I sure hope they'll fade. But I was hoping you'd never hear about it."

"He probably deserved it," consoled Mrs. Sanderford.

"No more than I. But I'd rather not talk about it, if you don't mind."

"Then the subject is closed forever. Amy, if you're not too tired, why don't you stay a while and help us get this invitation list straightened out! Then maybe we could start addressing some of the envelopes."

Mark was due home in less than three weeks. His last letter gave September twelfth as a tentative date, and Elaine would explode if she had to sit still. She had not received any mail from him in several days, which fact helped to increase her tension.

The wedding date was not tentative, however. It was boldly

imprinted on the invitations, "October Twentieth." Elaine and her mother wanted to get as many things as possible out of the way before Mark came home, and item one was the wedding invitations. There would be another million things to do after Mark's return. So the three women settled themselves at the dining room table, before them a profusion of papers, pencils and envelopes.

Paul and Judy came in. He had celebrated his birthday the week before and had promptly obtained his driver's license. He had just taken Judy's family home and helped with the cleaning up of their picnic supplies.

Judith Barker was a lovely girl. The discomfort Amy had felt in her presence melted away when she realized that Judy's coolness toward her had only been an outgrowth of her shyness. She seemed to be withdrawn until she overcame this shyness, and this she was able to do only after she became well-acquainted with a person.

Paul had eyes for no one else now. After being assured there was nothing they could do to help, he led her into the living room and sat close to her on the sofa. He put his arm around her as they looked at one of Elaine's bridal books, Paul hoping it would give Judy some helpful suggestions. From the sound of their muted conversation, they were not altogether interested in Elaine's wedding plans.

Dan sat in the big overstuffed chair, or rather he sprawled in it, reading the newspaper. When Amy occasionally glanced into the quiet living room, she found it somewhat disconcerting to discover that he was not looking at the newspaper at all.

"You got quite a sunburn today, Amy. Better put something on it before you go home."

He was easing her loss of equanimity, but she did not believe the sunburn was of consequential interest to him. He was reveling in his little sport back at the picnic grounds, she supposed. Elaine and her mother were busy with their work and had not as much as looked up from it.

Paul got up suddenly, silently, and walked over to the front window. "Say," he said pensively, "looks like the United States Army coming up our driveway."

His mother scolded him. "That's nothing to joke about at a time like this, Paul."

"Okay." He shrugged his shoulders. "Then the United States Army *isn't* coming up our driveway. But it's going to be coming up our front steps any minute." He tried to sound indifferent, but he could not suppress the excitement in his voice.

Elaine's face was drained of any color as she looked at her brother. She ran to the front door while they crowded around the windows. She made it to the porch where she froze, her legs unable to carry her any further. Unbelief was written across her face.

Amy recognized the lone soldier in the dusk of the early evening as the one in Elaine's picture. He broke into a run when he saw his beloved and took the steps two at a time, hardly touching any of them. He threw down his khaki bag as his arms went around her. She was holding so tightly to him he had to draw her head back to kiss her, a kiss which was the ablution of two years of heartache and loneliness.

Then Dan, Paul, and their mother were there on the porch, Dan pumped Mark's hand while Paul pummelled him on the back. Mrs. Sanderford was trying to get close enough to kiss him. Elaine's face was buried in the roughness of his uniform.

They walked to the door as one body, all talking at once except for Mark and Elaine who had not spoken a word. The two boys and their mother returned to the living room as Mark stopped in the front hall, took a clean hanky from his pocket, and wiped the tears from his sweetheart's face, then blew his nose. It was quiet as he kissed her again. The five occupants of the living room could not take their eyes from the tender scene before them.

Some minutes elapsed before the two of them joined the rest of the group. Elaine proudly introduced Mark to Judy and Amy as she clung to his hand. Suddenly everyone was talking again.

It *had* been a glorious day!

Chapter 11

DAN PUSHED THE perspiration back from his tanned forehead into his rumpled black hair. His bare chest glistened with beads of dirty sweat, and his bare legs and feet below his Bermuda shorts were wet with dirty, soapy water.

Though the first two weeks of September had passed, it was still summer and it was still hot.

He plunged the sponge back into the hot water and let it dribble messily the foot or so between the pail and his car. He was to be off again tomorrow afternoon, for over a month this time, and he thought he might as least start with a clean car.

"Would you like some help, son?"

He turned to grin at his mother. "Nope. Thanks just the same. You know ladies don't wash cars."

"You're much too gallant, Dan." Yet she would not change him a whit. "Neither do gentlemen, for that matter."

"Only gentlemen with dirty cars." He grinned again. "What's really on your mind?"

Sometimes, when he grinned like that, it was hard to believe the years had gone so quickly, that he was not still her little boy. Could it not have been just yesterday, or maybe just last year that she had stood at the kitchen door with a yardstick in her hand, waiting to administer the promised punishment to her little three-year-old? He had been forbidden to cross the fields to play with a neighbor boy unless he obtained permission first. Three days in a row he had ventured off, and three days in a row he had ambled home, knowing just what awaited him as soon as he arrived. She could vividly remember the sharp pain in her mother-heart as the little fellow trudged up the back steps and stood before her, looking up at his beloved mother with adoration in his eyes. In his dirty hand he had clutched a bedraggled bouquet of buttercups, daisies, and dandelions which drooped over his hot little hand, forming a wreath about it. Had any spanking ever hurt *her* more than that one had?

Twenty years ago! Where had they gone?

Dan had returned to his work. Louise brought herself back to the situation at hand, casting a quick glance down the long driveway toward the street.

"I'll tell you, son. Amy is coming here today, and I just wish there were some way to get her away for a while. She's been working so hard, and she really needs some time to relax. And then, too, Bea is coming today, so Amy really need not help." Bea was the Negro girl who came in to work for the Sanderfords once a week, more often for special occasions. "I do appreciate Amy's help, but I think she's been going at it too hard."

"She has been a little trouper, hasn't she?" Dan went on slopping water.

"It's such a lovely day. If it wouldn't disrupt any of your plans, why don't you see if you can get her to go somewhere? Maybe out in the boat for a while?"

"That's a great idea, Mother." He tried to sound casual. "Splendid, I'd say. I only wish I had thought of it myself. But I hardly dreamed you'd let up on that whip you've been holding over her these past few weeks!"

"Oh, go on with you!"

He could think of nothing more pleasant than spending the afternoon on the water with Amy.

"Suppose I pack a lunch for you?"

"Better wait and see what Amy has to say first. It would save a lot of bother if we just bought something though. You've been going at it pretty hard yourself."

"Well, let me know then. I'll be glad to fix something for you," she called over her shoulder as she headed for the house.

"You spoil us!"

A day alone with Amy. She just had to agree. Would he be able to tell her? Would he be able to convey the message to her without actually telling her? It did not matter either way. Somehow he would let her know, and at the right time.

Even while he was thinking it, Elaine's car appeared.

Amy's heart gave a queer little lurch as the scene in the drive came into view. *How ridiculous,* she thought. *I scarcely know the man, yet more and more I find myself acting like a silly schoolgirl.*

She could not help but be delighted over Dan's suggestion, although she felt a sense of guilt in so easily deserting the activities she had come to take part in.

"Let me help you wash the car then."

"You're trying to defeat our purpose. I'm almost done. And

besides, Mother and I have just been through that. Ladies don't wash cars."

"Ladies who are anxious to go out boating do."

With that, she grabbed the hose which Dan had just turned on at the house. He came toward her with the intention of relieving her of it, but she turned the long, straight stream of water directly on him, fully expecting to get the worst end of the deal. In the distorted picture made by splashing water, she could see a big wide grin.

"Terrific!" he shouted. "Feels great!" She turned the nozzle toward the car. "But you'll be sorry anyway!" he added.

"Don't be so sure," she laughed. "It's not too late for swimming, is it, Dan? I know it's plenty hot here, but it might not be on the water."

"We can go to the lake then. It's always warmer there than on the salt water."

"Good. Can we take the skis? I'd like to try them again." She hoped she did not sound too anxious.

"You betcha. Why don't you go get ready while I finish up here. Have to hitch up the trailer too."

"Isn't there something I can do to help?"

"No. And if you're anything like Elaine, I'll still be ready first."

"Is that so! Well, we'll just have to see about that!" Amy started for the house. It had been decided that she would borrow Elaine's suit again to save a trip back to town.

Paul emerged from the back door. From the looks of his attire, it was apparent that he had made plans along the same lines. Dan's heart sank.

"Oh, say, Dan," Paul said, disappointed, too, to see his brother hitching up the boat trailer, "I didn't know you were planning on using the boat today."

"I don't recall your mentioning it either." Dan grinned at him, but it was obvious he was not about to abandon ship so easily. Each possessed a stubborn streak which he was able to exercise without so much as a cross word between them, and without a frown. Something usually gave before the harsh words.

"Judy and I were going to have one last fling before we have to leave for school— "

"Why don't we all go together?" It was Amy's suggestion. Dan felt like choking her. "I think it would be lots more fun. That is, if you don't mind intruders, Paul."

Dan tried to cover his disappointment. "Sure, sport. Let's do that."

Paul brightened. Half a loaf was better than none. "Well, I guess that's the sensible solution, isn't it? How soon, Ichabod?"

"Ten minutes."

"What about supper? You weren't planning on getting back, were you?"

"Mother said she would fix stuff, but I thought it would save a lot of fuss if we stopped at the state park for hot dogs or something of the sort. Suit you?"

"Oh, sure. No mess to clean up either."

"And since when did you worry about that?" Dan asked as he went up the back steps. Amy had already disappeared.

"I'm going for Judy," Paul shouted, much louder than was necessary. "Tell Elaine I'm taking her car for a few minutes."

Five minutes later Amy appeared, noticing with satisfaction and a certain amount of I-told-you-so that Dan was not yet in sight. Her heart skipped a beat as she looked forward to a pleasant afternoon. She must be careful not to get any silly notions.

She walked slowly to the car, but turned quickly as, simultaneously, a variety of sounds reached her ears. There was Elaine's car coming up the drive, the squeaking of the rusty faucet, rushing water, and, from the same direction as the latter two, a loud horselaugh. The timing was perfect.

Amy screamed, then choked on a mouthful of water. "Dan Sanderford," she gasped, "that was a dirty trick!" She was trying desperately not to laugh. "I'll get you back for this!" she sputtered.

"You already did!" he roared. "I was getting *you* back, remember?"

"Well, it's your nice clean car that's going to get soaked!"

"Won't hurt it a bit," he assured her, still laughing.

It's worth it, thought Amy, just to hear him laugh like that.

They reached the lake within a half-hour. Ten minutes later, Paul and Dan had the boat launched in spite of the heckling they received from the two spectators. They were enjoying it though they would be the last to admit it. The atmosphere for the afternoon had been established, and it continued right up until evening when they pulled into the state park for supper.

Paul threw the anchor over, and they swam the thirty feet or so into shore. The park was almost empty. It was not only late in the day, but also late in the season.

"You folks made it just in the nick of time," the jovial little man in the refreshment stand told them. "Five or ten minutes later and this place would've been locked up tighter than a drum." The twinkle in his eyes and the grin that almost covered his fat pink face told them that he more than welcomed a little late company. "What'll it be, folks?" he asked. "Got some nice hot hot dogs here. Give 'em to ya fer half price since I was gonna take 'em home to ma dog anyways. How 'bout it?"

"Sure can't pass up a bargain like that now, can we? As long as we can't treat the ladies to filet mignon, huh, Paul?" bantered Dan. "I'd say let's have hot dogs. How about it, Amy?"

"I'd say sure enough."

"I'd say let's hold out for filet mignon, but I'm starved!" Paul thundered, banging his fist down on the counter.

"Four hot dogs, comin' right up!" the little man shouted, trying to match Paul for loudness.

"That's enough for me. How many for you, Dan?"

"Sorry, shrimp," the man advised Paul, "unless you want your friend and the ladies here to go hungry— "

"Friend!" Paul shrieked in a high squeaky voice. "Friend," he repeated in a normal tone. "He's not my friend. He's my brother. You don't think I'd *pick* a friend like him, do you?"

The man ignored him. "Only got, let's see," he said as he opened the box-like refrigerator, "four cooked, and one, two, three, four more to put on. Eight left altogether."

"Well, put 'em on, man! Whatcha waitin' for?" scolded Paul.

"I feel sorry for that poor little wife of yours— "

"Come on with those weiners, man. And she isn't my wife! Do you think I'm nuts?" The man turned and opened his mouth, but Paul raised a protesting hand. "Okay, okay, don't rub it in. How about tendin' to business here, huh?"

The man put the fresh hot dogs on the grill and handed them each a cooked one. "If you're so all-fired starvin', son, why didn'tcha bring some ge-dunk with ya?" His eyes twinkled all the while he talked, and he fit in perfectly with the atmosphere of the day.

"Well, you can just betcha I woulda if I'd a known you'd be so all-fired slow!" Paul took a big bite. "You know, Sam, you'd be rich if you'd tend more to business and less to gassin'. Know that, don't you?"

"Say, sonny," he said, leaning over the counter and scrutinizing Paul, "weren't you here last week? Sure, and it was you here with that cute little redhead." He scratched his chin, then followed the itch around to the back of his neck. "Sure enough, 'twas. Last Saturday. And her name was, let's see," he scratched his itching chin again. He looked at the girls, then casually at Dan and quickly caught the name Dan mouthed. "Let's see," he repeated slowly, thoughtfully, "her name was Shirley, I think. Leastwise it sounded like that. Now let me see. Shirley—Shirley— " He scratched his brain for a last name, then caught Dan's glance again. "Sure enough. It was Shirley Cooper. Wasn't it? Or was it Hooper? No, it was Coop— "

"What yo tryin' to do there, little man?" Paul stood with his mouth agape, looking from one to the other, then back to the man.

"What you trying to do, get me inta trouble or somethin'?" Paul squeaked. "What you tryin' to do? I wasn't here last Saturday, and you know it. Fact is, I haven't been here since our Sunday school picnic two weeks ago, no three — "

"Well, now," he drawled, "could be I had the wrong week — "

"Wrong week! Wrong year, too, huh? And maybe the wrong boy, how about it?"

Dan guffawed loudly and slapped Paul on the back. "Be sure your sin will find you out, Paul. You should have known better than to come sneaking up here last — "

"Not you too!" he shrieked. "C'mon, Dan, you know I — Judy, you don't believe all that garbage, do you? Now, Judy, you know I told you — " She turned her back on him and bit into her hot dog. "See now, man, look at all the trouble you're making, and what'd I ever do to you?" Paul was desperate. "Amy, *you* believe me, now don't you?"

A cloud of doubt creased her brow. "Well — I just — don't — know, Paul. I'd like to, but it sure looks as if all the evidence is piling up against you."

Paul groaned.

"Come on, Amy," said Dan, still chuckling, "let's go sit at a table. I'll come back for the root beer."

"Let's take a walk down that trail," Paul suggested to Judy after they finished their meal. She silently agreed with a wink in Amy's direction.

"Hey, Paul," Dan shouted when they were some distance away, "don't you think you ought to have a chaperone? I'd be glad to — "

"You want a fat upper lip? Besides, she carries her own. A ruler."

"Still twelve inches?"

"Naw. Down to six now." Judy took one step further to the right of him. He glared at her.

Dan and Amy sat at the outside of the picnic table and watched the boats as they drifted in the late evening sun. Even the ones under power seemed to be taking their time, trying to stretch the remaining minutes of daylight into hours. It was hard to believe there was a busy, bustling world beyond.

"It's nice here."

"Lovely. When will you be leaving, Dan?"

"I don't know yet. We thought probably early spring, by May, anyway. But things have been shaping up pretty fast. It's hard to tell yet though. Why?"

"Just wondering. Your family is going to miss you. Everyone will."

"You?" he asked hopefully.

"Of course," she quickly answered, then flushed.

"Have you any plans, Amy? I mean have you thought at all about going back to where you came from? Delaware, wasn't it?"

"There's nothing there for me. No family whatsoever. Oh, I have some cousins, but I'm not so sure I'd know them if I bumped into them on the street. My brother, Dave, is the only family I have. I guess that's why I've made such a pest of myself with your family."

"You've done no such thing! Mother would have a fit if she heard you talking like that!"

"I hope you're right," she smiled. "But I guess I'll stay right in New Hope. My brother has asked me to come up there, many times, but I do like New Hope, and I seem to be able to manage quite well on what I make. Some day he may talk me into coming up there to stay, but now that I have so many new friends, I'm quite content."

Neither spoke for a few minutes.

"I suppose you'll be married by the time I come home," Dan ventured.

She laughed. "Hardly. Maybe you too. But who — whom would I marry?"

"Well, seems to me I've seen some pretty interested glances being sent your way."

"And by whom, pray tell? How can I catch him if I don't know he's chasing me?"

Dan answered by singing a little ditty she had never heard before. "A crop of red hair and a freckled nose, he carries a dimple where e'er he goes."

"And what is that supposed to mean?" Why did she have to blush so easily?

"Whatever you'd like it to mean."

"In that case, nothing."

He couldn't have wished for a more satisfying answer.

"Say, Amy, I owe you a milk shake. How about it?"

"You're kidding, Dan. Where do you put it all?"

"I told you I never kid." He patted his hard stomach and belched in an ungentlemanly fashion, doing a poor job of concealing it. "Plenty of room there yet."

"Not for me, thanks. Too many calories."

"On you they look good."

"*Reverend* Sanderford! I'm surprised at you!" She colored profusely.

He laughed uproariously. "Reverends *are* human, you know." In a confidential tone, he added, "But I'm not a Reverend yet anyway."

He grinned, leaned heavily on his knees with both hands as if needing an extra boost, and stood up.

Seriously, Amy asked, "Will you be? I mean, is it necessary to be a missionary?"

"Not necessary, but sometimes it helps. I expect to be ordained before I go though."

"Not if I tell on you."

"But you won't. I'll tell my mother you made eyes at me, and she won't let you in the house any more."

"You win. I won't if you won't. But only because I'm afraid your mother would take your word above mine. Is it a deal?"

"Okay, it's a deal. You squeal, I squeal. How about the shake?"

She gave her head a rapid little nod in the negative, and he walked back toward the refreshment stand. He returned with two shakes.

"Thought you might have changed your mind. It's supposed to be par for the course, you know. For women, that is."

"Oh, you! You know that's not true. Not always, anyway. It's not that we change our minds so easily. It's just that we have a hard time making them up in the first place! But I can't drink that, Dan. Not all of it!"

"Drink what you want then and I'll finish it. See, I'm not hard to get along with." *I'm really not, Amy,* he thought. *And I could get along just fine with you.*

He wanted to say so much more to her. She was so sweet, so delightful – everything a woman should be. And beside her he felt like such a clumsy ox. He was tongue-tied and idiotic.

But suddenly it was enough just being here with her.

Paul and Judy appeared at the beginning of the trail where they had disappeared and sauntered along hand in hand.

"Looks as if he convinced her."

Amy giggled. "That *was* a mean trick, you know. I wonder if she explained it to him."

"He had it coming. You can't imagine some of the tricks he pulls. I doubt if she told him though. It's like Judy to make him squirm a little."

"Smart girl."

"Oh, now you wouldn't make a fellow squirm like that, would you, Amy?"

"Just depends who he was and how much I liked him!" she returned.

"How about me?"

She blushed again and turned to watch the two coming toward them. "Why, you don't squirm, do you, Dan?" She laughed nervously. "Besides, you're taking an awful lot for granted."

He was stretched out with his legs crossed, his elbows in back of him on the table. "I never had any reason to think you *disliked* me, if that's what that remark was supposed to mean." If only the conversation had taken this turn before the other two had come back.

"I never let on. Hated to hurt your feelings. I'll just keep on pretending, if you like."

Paul and Judy were within earshot. Paul broke into a run. He grabbed one of Dan's outstretched feet with both hands. In order to keep from being dragged onto the ground, Dan jumped up and followed him, clumsily hopping about on his free foot. Amy quickly rescued the splashing drink, and with that, Dan managed to get his hands around his brother's neck. It was awkward cavorting for a few minutes, but they finally thudded to the ground in a cloud of dust.

"Uncle a'ready!" shouted Paul, scarcely able to get it out midst his laughter. "One of these days," he threatened, getting to his feet. "One of these days, just wait and see. And just wait until you come home the first time, brother! After four years you'll be as soft as a marshmallow!"

"You hope!"

"Much as I hate to suggest it," said Paul, brushing some of the loose dirt from him. "I suppose we shouldawta get on our way, huh? Sure has been a nice day."

"Well, it's back to the water then, children," offered Dan. He was reluctant to leave, and it was apparent.

"Can't you bring the boat in closer, Paul?" wheedled Judy. "I don't want to get wet again. Please?" she pleaded.

"So solly. No can do. Tell you what, fair maid. You stand on my shoulders and I'll walk you to the boat. You won't get more than your pretty little – " he paused and rolled his eyes, " – tootsies wet."

Judith ignored the insinuation and stood on the picnic table. She stepped from there onto Paul's broad shoulders. He firmly grasped her ankles to steady her and proceeded carefully to the water.

"So long, friend," he called to the man who was just closing up shop and interestedly looking at a gospel tract Dan had given to him. He waved to them, then watched in amusement.

The water came up to Paul's chin, up to his nose, and still he went until he was completely submerged. They had almost reached the boat when – kersplash! Judy went down, and Paul's head popped up. He tossed his hair back from his forehead and tried to look apologetic as she reached the boat and turned to face him.

"You – you – you – " she sputtered. "I'll never speak to you again! *Never!*" She lithely swung herself up the ladder with Paul humbly following.

"May I give you a lift, Amy?" Dan asked. They were still standing on the beach where they had watched the proceedings.

"Race you to the boat!" she exclaimed, diving into the water. In spite of her head start, he was standing in the boat when she reached it. He put his hand down to assist her, but she ignored it. She had been avoiding his touch all afternoon.

Paul was still apologizing to Judy. "You know I was only trying to have a little fun."

"I'm not so sure you weren't here last week with Shirley Hooper – "

"Cooper," he corrected.

"You just can't be trusted, Paul Sanderford. Well, maybe *she* trusts you. And for your information, I don't *care* what her last name is."

"Come on, Judy. Don't spoil such a nice day – "

"Oh, so now I'm spoiling it. You can just go peddle your wares somewhere else. Men!" she muttered in exasperation.

"I was only kidding – "

"Well, I guess you know I'm not!" She turned her back on him again, which move proved to be a mistake on her part. Paul picked her up and held her over the side of the boat, hoping, among other things, that she would cling to him and beg him not to let her go. Instead, she folded her arms, crossed her legs, and closed her eyes, assuming a completely disinterested opinion of the whole situation.

Paul looked at Dan as if for some brotherly advice but quickly reclaimed control of the situation and planted a hard, possessive kiss on her pretty mouth.

Judith came to life. Her hand struck a cracking blow to his cheek. With that, Paul released his grip. Judith was in the water again.

"C'mon, Dan, let's leave her here!" Paul stormed as soon as she had bobbed to the surface. "She's not worth taking back!"

But by the time he had reached the motor, Judy was back in the boat. She gracefully maneuvered herself to the bow and sat with her back toward Paul. She ignored him during the trip back.

The sympathetic heart of Amy was filled to overflowing, but for which one, she could not decide. If she had known what to do, she would have been willing to patch things up between them. Dan noticed her concern, and with a multitude of gesticulations, both facial and manual, tried to put her at her ease. Each time Paul looked his way, Dan automatically became deadpan again, his hands falling motionless to his lap.

Amy burst out laughing. It was contagious, and Dan joined in.

For a brief moment, the exact one Judy chose to look back at them, Paul broke out too. Her cold shoulder became a block of ice.

"You're not really mad, are you, Judy?" Amy asked when the boys were taking the boat out of the water. "I don't see how you can stay mad at him. Although I agree, you do have good reason," she tactfully added.

"Not too, Amy, but don't tell him."

"I won't," she conspired with a smile.

During the ride back to New Hope, Judy slid into the furthest corner of the back seat while Paul sprawled all over the rest of it. Judy talked to Dan and Amy, and Paul talked to Dan and Amy, but nary a word did either say to the other.

After changing, Amy joined Judy in the kitchen to await the boys. Dan came down first, reeking of after-shave lotion and obviously minus the all-day acquirement of stubble from his face.

"Paul's coming right down. Let's go wait in the car."

They had no sooner seated themselves in the car when Paul appeared at the door. Judy reached over and locked the car doors. It took Paul no time at all to realize what had taken place. With a most graceful sprint, he landed on the hood of the car, leaned back nonchalantly against the windshield and crossed his arms and legs.

Dan let the car coast slowly down the drive. Just before reaching the street, he quickly jammed his foot on the brake pedal. Paul went sailing off the front and landed upright on both feet. As soon as he recovered his balance, he turned around and defiantly leaned on the hood, rested his chin in his hands, and stared at them. They were in an uproar, even Judy. All, that is, but Paul.

"How can he keep such a straight face?" asked Amy.

"Watch this," Dan told them. He leaned heavily on the horn.

Paul leaped three feet into the air, a confusion of long arms and legs, and exhibited a large, cavernous mouth.

"My word!" roared Dan. "I do believe I saw his ingrown toenails!"

Just as quickly, Paul resumed his original position, all sign of humor removed from his face. He stared blankly at the three inside the car.

"Okay, brother, we give," Dan called to him. "Come on, Paul," he called again, opening the window, "the hour getteth late." He blew the horn again. Paul leaped, ran to Dan's open window, reached in to unlock the door, and climbed in.

"Say, Dan," said Paul as they stopped in front of Judy's house, "be a good little boy and pick me up on the way back." He was firmly holding Judy's hand to keep her from escaping. He gave Dan's head a hard push with his elbow as he got out. "Right-o?"

"Could be arranged," Dan answered, encouraged. "Don't be too hard on him, Judy. He'll grow up one of these days."

Paul whirled on him, but the car had already moved away from the curb.

"It really has been a grand day, Dan."

"We'll have to do it again sometime."

"Wouldn't that be fun! But when? The weather will soon be too cold, and then you'll be leaving."

"Maybe we'll get in another outing before the weather gets too chilly. But if not, we'll have to take a rain check on it, okay?"

"Sure," she laughed.

"Let's say the first fair Saturday of my first furlough." They both laughed again. There was a close companionship borne of a warm, carefree afternoon.

"How about coming in for a cup of coffee, Dan? We didn't have any, and I missed it. I'm really good at making instant coffee! That is, if it isn't too late," she added almost apologetically, offering him an out.

"Is it?"

"That's up to you. I made a cake last night with my own two little hands—and Mrs. Martin's help—if that's any temptation to you! I'm right proud of my achievements in that line."

"Ho ho! Now I'll tell my mother you're trying to tempt me! Tch, tch, tch! What will she say?" But he was getting out of the car.

"Just give me a sliver, Amy," he said as he seated himself at the kitchen table. She cut into the beautiful cake. "Make it a big one though."

She laughed as she put it on the plate. "I wondered. It's not like you to turn down food, no matter how undesirable it might appear."

"Well now, this looks mighty fine. Mmmm. Tastes mighty fine, too. Make some man a fair wife some day, I can see." Now was the time, if he could just keep the conversation going this way.

"Maybe fair," she half-heartedly agreed. "Dan," she said, suddenly serious, "I'm glad you came in. I'd like to ask you something."

"No, I'm not taken."

She smiled, but she could feel the color rising again. "Be serious."

"I'm serious," he said, frowning.

"I didn't say angry!" She smiled at him again, and the frown disappeared. "You know Karen Winslow has been giving me a hard time. In fact, she has always given me a hard time."

"Yes, I noticed. She's got something stuck in her crop, hasn't she?"

"Apparently. But I don't know what it could be. I guess she

just dislikes me, although I don't remember ever doing anything to make her feel that way."

"Some people don't need anything. They just have to have someone to heckle. She's like that."

"Well, I've been praying for her— "

"Did you tell her? She might be furious." His eyes twinkled again.

"Dan, please be serious. No, I haven't told her, but I might sometime. What I wanted to ask you is this: do I have the right to pray for her? We're supposed to pray 'in His will,' but how are we supposed to know just what His will is? I mean, how can we know we *are* praying in His will?"

Dan was serious. "We don't always know what His will is, Amy, but we can pray that His will might be done. And 'if it be Thy will' may such and such be done. But when it comes to praying for a person's salvation, I believe we have the right to pray for anyone."

"And what do you base that on?" she asked. "Is there something in the Bible?"

"Smart girl. Never take a person's word for it. God's Word is the final authority. Do you have your Bible? I'll show you."

When she returned with it, Dan turned to Second Peter, third chapter, ninth verse. "See here. The last part of the verse—'God is not willing that any should perish, but that all should come to repentance.' It's my firm belief, on the basis of this verse, that we have the right to pray for any person's salvation, and in so doing we know we are praying 'in His will.'"

"Yes, I think that's very clear too. I'm going to mark that verse, Dan, and I hope some day I'll know my Bible as well as you do. You know right where to turn for everything, and I have to hunt and hunt. I am improving, though, so maybe there's hope!"

"The more you read it, the better you know it, Amy. That's the only way. You're doing fine. I'm proud of you!" He drained his coffee cup. "The Lord has a will for our lives, too, Amy. Have you thought about it, or prayed about it?" Dan asked, making another effort. "Did you ever think, maybe He wants *you* to go to the mission field too!"

"That's the last place He'd send me!" Amy quickly replied, lightly laughing. "And I'm sure glad of that!"

Dan felt deflated. "I really must be going now. Your cake was delicious, and next time you make one, I hope you'll invite me again!"

"I'll do that, and thank you, Dan. For your help, I mean. And of course for the nice compliment too. It isn't often I get such flattery, so you can be sure I'll do that." She walked to the porch with him. "Good night, Dan."

He resisted a strong impulse to lean over and gently touch her lips. He started to speak, then turned to leave. *That's the last place He'd send me!* "Good night, Amy." He hurried away.

Paul stood up when he saw Dan turn into the Barker driveway. A few minutes elapsed before he left her standing on the porch. He waved to her as he got into the car.

"All fixed up again, huh, Paul?"

"Oh, sure." They went several blocks without speaking. Then Paul broke the silence. "Say, Dan, how do you suppose that old codger knew about Shirley Cooper? Sure is a funny one, isn't it?"

"It sure is," Dan agreed, thoroughly puzzled.

"Boy, that Amy sure is a looker, isn't she? Now that she doesn't wear so much war paint. Course she was a knock-out before too. Too bad she's so old. Must be almost as old as you."

"Well, say, thanks. You're not that far behind, you know. I'd say she must be twenty. Yes, I think Elaine did say that. A little ancient for you, anyway."

"I'll say!"

"Getting pretty serious with you and Judy, isn't it?"

"Never can tell. Say, Dan, I sure hope we didn't spoil your plans for today. I had no idea—"

"Naw. Course you didn't. You know it scares me silly to be alone with a girl anyway."

"Yeah," Paul said, grinning, "me too."

Chapter 12

DURING THE WEEKS following, Amy spent every available minute at the big stone house. There was much to be accomplished and it seemed not nearly enough time to do it all. Elaine had become virtually unconscious since Mark's return and had to be reminded constantly of things which required her attention. Mark's home was in Maine, however, so his time was divided between his family and Elaine. His weekends were spent in New Hope. During his absence, Elaine was able to buckle down and make herself somewhat useful.

Paul and Judy had gone to a college upstate, and Dan was away most of the time, both of the boys having to leave at a time when they were most needed.

Amy had become indispensable to their mother, or Aunt Louise, as she had been requested to call her. That had come about the Saturday Robin came for her fitting.

Amy, too, was in something of a trance. Much as she hated to admit it, it was not because of the wedding plans. Not entirely. She had been in ecstasy since that outing at the lake with Paul, Dan and Judy. She had lived it over many times, and especially those few minutes back in the Martin's kitchen. It was the first and only entertaining she had ever done, and the fact that it was Dan she had entertained was not frightening. Being with him had seemed, at the time, to be the most natural thing in the world. Now it frightened her.

But she was deeply engrossed in wedding preparations and loving every minute of it.

It was not only the wedding preparations which were time consuming. There were showers for Elaine, stag parties for Mark, and combination affairs for both of them. Amy was in the middle of everything, fixing food, doing dishes, helping with correspondence. There was no end. Sometimes she wished there never would be.

The evening before the big day, people arrived in droves – relatives, close friends of the family, messengers with gifts—a constant stream to and from. By prearrangement, many of the guests were staying at the house, many more were being accommodated by local friends, but the majority had to find lodging elsewhere, sorry they had neglected to R.S.V.P.

Elaine had planned for Amy to spend the night with her, but her Grandmother Sanderford arrived unexpectedly that night. Amy graciously insisted that she return to her own place that the grandmother might have a place to stay without having to go to a motel.

Paul and Judy arrived late that night, just in time to take Amy home. Dan had not yet returned, giving her cause to be concerned. Aunt Louise and Elaine had not been able to conceal their anxiety.

The next morning when she was called to the phone, however, she was not too surprised to hear Dan's voice at the other end.

"Hello, Amy. I'll come pick you up any time you're ready."

"Oh, Dan. I'm glad you're home."

"Nothing could keep me away today. You weren't worried, were you?" he asked hopefully.

"Well, I wasn't the only one. Give me a half-hour, Dan, and I promise not to keep you waiting."

He was about to ring the doorbell when she opened the door and stepped out.

"Well, aren't we punctual," she said laughing. "Oh, I'm so glad it's such a beautiful day. The sky always looks so blue in October, and the clouds so white against it!"

He smiled down at her as he opened the car door. Her almost-childish excitement amused him. He got in the other side and slid behind the wheel, taking just enough time for her to regain her composure.

"What time did you get in?"

"About one o'clock. Had trouble finding an empty bed too."

"Where did you sleep, in the car?" she asked laughing.

"Well, I thought I might have to, but Paul was sleeping soundly, so I moved him into the bathtub and slept in his bed."

She laughed again. "I might believe you if I thought he would fit."

"No, I just pushed him over. He got up pretty early this morning, so I managed to get a couple of hours' sleep."

"How's Elaine this morning?"

"Cool, calm and collected. She shocked us all considering the state she's been in the last couple of months."

The house was surprisingly quiet when they entered. The guests had wisely made themselves scarce, and Paul had gone over to the parsonage where Mark was staying with his parents and brother, the best man. Mrs. Sanderford was glad to have her younger son out of the way. He had taken over where Elaine had left off, more nervous than a mother hen.

Some kind folk had sent over salads and cold meats for lunch, but no one seemed to be the least interested in food. They went through the motions of eating from sheer force of habit.

After lunch, while Dan made an effort to help Bea tidy up the kitchen, the five ladies, Elaine, her mother, Robin, Patty, and Amy retired to Elaine's room.

Barbie, the flower girl, was the adorable five-year-old daughter of Pastor and Mrs. Carlson. She had looked forward to this day with increasing excitement. She had her Daddy's blonde curls, a little round face with a turned-up nose, and a few freckles scattered across her nose and cheeks.

Dan had teased her during lunch, insisting that she had been sunburned through a colander. She pretended to be angry with him, but everyone knew it was an act. She idolized him, hugging and kissing him every chance she got. She tried to rumple his hair, but he grabbed her around the waist and sat her on top of the refrigerator until she promised to be good. It was not long until she came scampering up the stairs, her stubbornness giving out when she realized she might miss some of these preparations for which she had waited so long.

Elaine was ready first. She had obediently followed their every command while all five of them collaborated. They took out her curlers and primped and fussed over her until she looked as if she had stepped out of one of her bridal books.

They helped each other, but scolded every time Elaine tried to do something to assist. Barbie looked like a life-size doll, and each one of them had to take a turn at hugging her.

"I wish Mommy put curlers in *my* hair," she exclaimed with her lips pursed.

"Don't you want to be like Amy, Barbie?" Elaine scolded. "You and Amy have the prettiest hair of all 'cause God gave you your curls." Barbie looked at Amy's beautiful hair and was satisfied.

Dan appeared in the doorway. Amy suppressed a gasp as she saw him standing there in his tuxedo, tall, and oh, so handsome!

Barbie, a bundle of pink fluff, her dress a duplicate in miniature of Patty's, ran to him and jumped into his arms. He had to hug her too.

"Say, Barb, how'd you like to go to Japan with me!"

Her face beamed. "I was *wishing* you'd ask me, Dan. But we'll have to get married first, won't we? Then I'll be the bride!" She giggled with delight as she put her arms around his neck and planted a kiss on his cheek.

"We'll have to wait until you grow a little more, I guess," he added cautiously, not expecting such enthusiastic agreement. "Your mommy and daddy wouldn't let me take you away from them anyway. But I'll bet you won't wait for me. Why, you have so many boy friends!"

"I know," she agreed pensively. "But why don't you have any girl friends?"

Dan felt the color creep up the back of his neck, and he shifted uneasily. "'Cause I just love you!" *And besides, Barb,* his mental voice went on, *I'm scared silly of them! All but you and—Amy.* He cast a glance in her direction, and their eyes met briefly. It was time to talk about something else. "Now, little miss," he scolded the five-year-old, "if you don't sit still and stay pretty, I'm going to put you back on top of the refrigerator until it's time to go." He put her down.

"I'll be good," she promised as she covered his big hand with kisses.

"Say, it's about time we were on our way," he exclaimed, looking at his watch. "Everyone ready?"

"Danny, don't you know it's not right for a bride to be on time for her wedding?"

"So I've heard. But are you sure you're worth waiting for?" he teased.

"He waited for two years. I don't think he'll mind waiting a few more minutes."

"Well, that's open for debate. C'mon, Barb, let's get out of their way. Then maybe they'll get a wiggle on."

Mrs. Sanderford was lovely, a gracious lady. She was always well-dressed, the picture of fashion. Yet there was nothing in her manner to suggest overbearance. She carried her wealth with extreme indifference, and it gave one the impression that without it she would be the same charming lady. She was happy over this union which was about to take place.

Paul and Raymond, Mark's friend, led the procession and stood next to Mark and his brother, John. Amy was next, followed by Robin, then Patty. Barbie walked down the aisle after the matron of honor and did everything explicitly. But when she got to the altar, she unceremoniously looked up and said, "Hi, Daddy!" to Reverend Carlson who was standing in the pulpit, trying to look very formal.

Everyone smiled, some even snickered, but the incident passed quickly, for the bride was coming down the aisle and all eyes were on her. Her hand rested on Dan's arm and her eyes were downcast until she had almost reached Mark. When their eyes met, a volume of unspoken words passed between them.

When it came time to give the bride away, Dan took his sister's hand and placed it on Mark's arm, then stepped back to his place beside his mother.

The couple knelt at the altar while the soprano soloist sang the lovely hymn, "Saviour, Like a Shepherd Lead Us." It was an appropriate song, for these two dear ones had sought His leading every step of the way.

The rings were exchanged, and Mark and Elaine were pronounced husband and wife. The young man kissed his bride. With one big sigh, the audience started breathing again.

The reception was held at the Sanderford home, and when the bridal party arrived after having pictures taken at the photographer's studio, the guests had already congregated. It was a joyful occasion, and everything had gone perfectly.

The newlyweds left in the early evening, slipping out unobserved with the assistance of Dan, Raymond and John. Paul did everything he could to hinder.

Amy was sorry when it was over. She looked tired when Dan took her home late that night.

"It was a wonderful day, Dan. A perfect wedding."

"It was. They certainly were meant for each other." He walked to the door with her, trying to keep her with him a little longer. "Amy, did you hear? I'll be leaving two days after Christmas."

She was so full of wedding that his words did not immediately register. Then the import of the statement struck her, like the verification of the end of the world.

"I'm sorry, Dan. But I guess you're not."

"No, I'm anxious to get started. I had expected to be around another four months or so, but the arrangements were made very quickly. It's going to be a long stretch, but I guess the hardest part will be saying good-by."

When she reached the door, she opened it without hesitating and stepped inside. "Good night, Dan."

"Thanks for all your help, Amy. I don't know how we would have made out without you."

"No thanks necessary, Dan. Good night."

She was gone. He did not want her to leave so quickly. He had so many things he wanted to say to her. But she was gone.

His eyes had been on her almost all day as he thought about the things he wanted to tell her, phrasing and re-phrasing until they sounded the way they should. His heart had beat faster every time he had stood close to her, every time their eyes had met or he had been able to watch her, unobserved. She had bubbled over with the excitement of the occasion, and his pulse had quickened each time she had spoken to him or had smiled at him. No other woman had affected him this way, and he wanted to tell her. But now she was gone.

Perhaps it was better this way.

Chapter 13

A LARGE CROWD had gathered at the International Airport. There were aunts, uncles, cousins, friends, and many, many people from the local church. They covered a wide range of ages, and there were plenty of young people with whom Dan had grown up. Many of the older ones had known him since he was a little lad and had watched him grow into this fine spiritual giant whose life had been set apart for full-time service for the Lord. This parting would have been a time of sadness had it not been for the knowledge of this consecration.

Dan gave his brother a hard right to the arm as he passed in front of him, but Paul did not return the compliment, nor did he as much as smile. Dan let the matter drop. He could see his brother was having a difficult time.

Periodically he found himself scanning the large group, looking, hoping. Elaine was standing close to him and spoke in a voice meant only for him to hear.

"She didn't come, Danny."

"Who?"

"Oh, I thought you were looking for someone." She did not say any more.

Dan was pensive for a moment. "Why didn't she come, Lainey?"

"Who?" He was not amused, nor had she expected him to be under the circumstances. "She didn't say," she hastened to add.

"Did she tell you she wasn't coming?"

"She said she might not."

"Why didn't you tell me?"

"I wasn't sure you— " her voice trailed off. "Why didn't you tell *her?*"

"Tell her what?"

"Nothing. I just thought— "

Neither spoke but smiled and nodded graciously to the many friends who were buzzing about them.

"You thought right," Dan mumbled after a long pause.

"Then why didn't you tell her?"

"I couldn't. She doesn't feel the same way—about me *or* my calling." He turned in politeness to speak to someone else, but immediately turned his attention back to his sister.

"Then you should have asked her how she felt." Elaine spoke, and she believed everyone should be as open as she herself was.

"Do you know?"

"She didn't say."

"Neither did I."

"Not in so many words."

Their discussion was interrupted again, but time was of the essence. This matter must be settled now, to a degree.

"Does anyone else know?" Dan asked as soon as he was able to turn his attention back to Elaine.

"I think not."

"Then let's keep it that way."

"I'll keep you posted, Danny."

"I'd appreciate that."

"I wish she were going with you," Elaine choked.

"So do I."

Dan's fellow passengers were boarding the plane, so the time for conversation was over. They bowed their heads while Reverend Carlson asked the Lord's blessing on Dan, not only for a safe trip, but also for his fruitful service at his journey's end.

Though it was an occasion for rejoicing, the tearful and heartbreaking good-bys were a sharp reminder of the long separation ahead. Dan shook hands all around and lastly embraced his mother and sister, both at once. They tried to keep back the inevitable tears for his sake. He shook hands with Paul again, then slapped his brother on the shoulder. Paul was unable to speak.

With that Dan left them, not turning to look back until he was seated on the plane where they could not see his own anguish. He watched from the little window as the plane slowly moved away, straining, hoping to see—just perchance—

But there was no sign of the lovely girl who had stolen his heart away. He had so wanted to see her again. He had been foolish to hope. Why, a girl like Amy could have the pick of the crop. And she should have taken time to see him off, mere acquaintance that he was! He had hoped to be more than that to her. Perhaps it was better this way. He kept telling himself that.

At this very same moment, on a train speeding toward New Hope, sat Amy Archer. She tried to interest herself in the magazine she had bought in the station, in the flashing scenery outside the window, in the scores of people who occupied the same car with her, but somehow, in all that would have ordinarily interested her, something was lacking. She knew what it was. When she got back to New Hope he would be gone. She missed him. True, he had not been around much these last few months, but there were always those wonderful times when he had made unexpected appearances.

She had become increasingly aware of the fact that the more time she spent with this dark-haired, brown-eyed young man, the more she wanted to be with him. That would never do. She was not about to admit her feelings, not even to herself. Not in voluntary word or thought. Besides, Dan could not possibly be interested in her anyway. And if by some miracle he ever were, it would be an unrequited love. She could never return it.

Elaine had begged her to go to the airport to bid farewell with the others, and she had wanted to go. But she had purposely stayed in Ocean Point after the holidays, refusing to listen to her heart. She had steeled herself and had remained away from the scene that she might not be tempted. She wanted so much to see him again, if only to say good-by.

Did Larry Spencer go to the airport? she wondered. He and Dan were good friends now. In fact, they had always seemed to be something more than business acquaintances, but since Larry's conversion they seemed to have a lot in common. But then the Sanderfords were everybody's friends. And so was Larry, for that matter.

He certainly had been attentive lately. Trying to make up for his misbehavior to her, no doubt. But inevitably she felt herself withdraw in his presence. She couldn't help it. Nor could she look him straight in the eye. And when occasionally she did so accidentally, she knew she was blushing profusely. And knowing it only made the color deeper.

He surely was a fine fellow though, a lot of fun. Did he ever take anything seriously? Hardly ever. But he was honestly and truly born again. Such drastic changes could not occur in a person simply by his turning over a new leaf or by pledging himself to finer things. He had been redeemed by the precious blood of the Lamb.

Dan thought a lot of Larry. Dan. Why did she have to think of him again? He must be miles away by this time. Certainly was hard on the family having him leave like that. By no means easy for Dan either.

Oh, to have had a family like that! She would have been an entirely different person, undoubtedly. But that was fate. No, she must not think that way any more. God planned everything. He left nothing to chance.

If that were the case though, why had He let her make such a mess of things for herself? If only she could talk it over with someone, find out if there were an explanation for it.

At times she was able almost to forget—almost. But how did one go about forgetting? Was it right to forget when one had snuffed out a life—a life that God had created?

Todd Kenyon, I hate you! I wish to high heaven I had never known you! She shuddered as she slid down further in the seat.

Then, having previously learned a hard lesson on how to cope with difficult matters, Amy set about to occupy herself with immediate problems, putting the impossibility of Dan and his life completely from her mind.

Chapter 14

THE AUSPICIOUS WINSLOW estate was threaded by a long, winding driveway which was encased from beginning to end in well-groomed rhododendrons, each perfectly matched in color and shape to the one next to it. At the street end of the drive was an iron gate. Attached to it was a high iron fence which started at one side of the gate and continued its long uninterrupted journey until it reached the other side of the gate. There was another gate somewhere at the back of the property, but its lack of use was reason enough to forget its existence.

Karen Winslow sped through the gate and up the long drive at breakneck speed, as if some supernatural force had put demons on her tail. She came to a dusty, skidding halt at the front of the white house. Tony had told her time after time not to bring her car to a halt that way. "It takes an inch of rubber off your tires every time you do that, Karen, baby." So, it took an inch of rubber off. So, she would get new tires when there were no more inches left.

She went up the wide stone steps, into the spacious, thickly-carpeted hall, and up the staircase in the center of it. The house itself was a relic of the Civil War, but it had been redecorated and remodeled many times since to keep up with the changing times.

When Karen reached her bedroom, she hastily peeled off her clothes, throwing them on her bed as she did so, then wriggled into a skimpy swim suit.

"Hello, Nora, my love," she said, patting the peroxide coiffure. It gracefully topped a long and slender swim-suited body. Several feet from where she reclined was a large sky-blue pool, filled to the brim with glistening, inviting water. "How's the lovely loafing lady?"

There was a twinge of sarcasm in Karen's voice which was noticed but ignored. "Oh, you're home. I thought I heard your car." Nora looked up from the book she was reading. "You know what Anthony said about stopping your—"

"I know, I know," Karen retorted with annoyance in her voice. "Tony talks too much." She sat on the grass. "When will he be home?"

"About seven, I think. At least I told Myra to have dinner ready at seven-thirty. Why?"

"I need some money."

"Didn't you get paid?"

"I gave it back and told them they needed it more than I did. Come on, Nora. You know that's peanuts."

"Your father wanted you to have the responsibility of a job, love. It doesn't make sense if you're going to keep coming to him for money."

"Nora, do you honestly think it makes sense anyway? Tony's got—"

"Karen, I don't mind your calling your father by his first name, but I would appreciate it if you would call him Anthony."

"Why? Lorelei called him Tony. Why shouldn't I? Don't be stuffy, Nora." She spoke of her mother, Anthony Winslow's first wife.

"Maybe that's why." She smiled knowingly. "Anyway, it bothers him to think of your being lazy. Something about idle hands getting into trouble. You know?

"I know. He's a stuffed shirt too."

"Meaning I am?"

"Sometimes." Karen pinched a bare toe. She liked her stepmother. There was not more than ten years' difference in their ages, and they got along famously.

"He isn't anything of the kind."

"Oh, I know. He's a doll. But what about you?"

"What about me?"

"You're lazy. He doesn't seem to mind that."

Nora Winslow grinned sheepishly and went back to her book, pretending to be engrossed in it. "That's different."

"It sure is!" Karen retorted.

The other woman put her book down again. "You really have liked it, haven't you? I mean, you've made a lot of friends down there. Maybe you'll find yourself a rich husband. Then you'll be able to loaf too."

"At the bank?" Karen shrieked. "You're quite humorous today, Nora. But if I find one, I'll know how to trap him. I took lessons from you."

The remark was ignored. "There must be *some* husband material down there."

"The president's well-padded. But not only financially. Besides, he's stuffy too. And married."

"So is Ben."

"Was," she corrected. She herself had helped that situation. "Ben's just a fill-in."

"You've got a hard heart, girl."

"It helps. Not so likely to get hurt."

"Don't count on it."

"Look at miss crisp, cool and comfortable talking!"

"I didn't come by it easily, love. You mean that's all?"

"Heavens, no!" Karen shrieked again.

"What's wrong with the rest?"

"Nothing really, I guess. Some of them anyway."

"Come on, girl, give. Who's the real thorn in the flesh?" Nora received a blank look. "There's someone down there keeping your interest in banking alive. You can't tell me— "

"Then I won't."

"Then don't." Disinterested, Nora picked up her book. "Why don't you go for a swim and let me get back to this! I've read one paragraph over three times." She slid down in the chaise lounge.

"Then read it four!" Karen grabbed the book in question and flung it forcefully toward the bushes as she dove into the clear water.

Nora cursed in a very unladylike fashion and painfully eased herself from her comfortable position to retrieve her precious book.

"That was a dirty trick, Kar," she reprimanded as the young lady stretched herself out in the late afternoon sun.

"I know. I'd hate for you to get *too* lazy. His name is Larry."

"Whose name is Larry?" Nora asked without looking up.

"The thorn in my flesh."

"Why?"

"Why what?"

"Why is he a thorn in your flesh?"

"Because he has another thorn in his."

"I get it," said the older woman, now more than mildly interested. "When you get what you want, you don't want it. So, therefore, what you can't get, you have to have. Right?"

"It's more than that," Karen answered with a frown. "She's really got him hooked though. Hook, line and sinker."

"And Karen Winslow can't bear to be a loser."

"Do you know the Sanderfords, Nora?" Karen asked, deliberately changing the subject. Nora shook her head. "They live in that real elegant place we passed that day last week when we went to pick up Tony. Remember, I said it reminded me of a mausoleum? Only it doesn't, really. It's quite fascinating. I was in it once. I went to school with the Sanderford girl, Elaine, and since she and I were real chummy for a while, I got invited to her sixteenth birthday party. You see, her brother was a senior when we were juniors, and the star football hero of New Hope High. In fact, he was the big hero for three years running. He was a real bone-crusher. Broke a couple of legs and about four arms—"

"How many did he have?"

"What? Oh, not his own, dope. He sure was a different guy when he got off the football field. Not pushy at all. Well, this brother used to work at the bank. Work! Pooh!" Karen sneered eloquently. "Work! He had a position! Anyway, he's a real drooly."

"Interested?"

"Patience, love. As I was saying, he's the reason for the phrase, 'tall, dark, and handsome!' Tres magnifique! I'm not kidding, Nora. When he looks at you with those big brown eyes, brother, you know it. Ooh la la! It really made me uncomfortable though, much as I hate to admit it."

"Sounds like some boy. Interested?"

"And how! No, I'm not interested. I could have gone for him except that he's already married—to a religion. Can you imagine?" Her voice reached a high pitch. "He's gone to Japan as a missionary. Isn't that quaint? It's really pathetic though. Such a loss to American womanhood. But anyway, you made me get ahead of myself. I was telling you about the sixteenth birthday party. You see, Elaine and I sat next to each other in Biology class since there weren't any T's, U's, or V's, so I managed to get quite chummy with her. Because of her brother, of course."

"Assumed."

"This Elaine was really a sweet kid, I must admit. Spoiled but sweet."

"You were spoiled and sweet yourself once, so I've heard."

"I know. Now I'm just spoiled. Don't interrupt. Well, that was the one and only time I was ever in their house. Can you imagine, Nora," she said, rolling over on her side to catch the other's reaction, "they actually *prayed* before they ate the cake and ice cream!" Karen's voice was a loud-pitched scream again, and she laughed scoffingly. "Isn't that a panic!"

"I don't think it's funny, Karen."

She looked at her stepmother in amazement. "Come off it, Nora. Where's your sense of humor?"

"Where it belongs. I mean it. I think—"

"I heard you," Karen snapped, cutting her off angrily. "You disappoint me."

"Sorry. But what's all this got to do with the real lover-boy?"

"Well, that's when I decided this Danny boy wasn't for me. He's a hard nut to crack anyway. He's immune to feminine charm."

"But why are you telling me all this if you're not interested?"

"Oh, yes. Well, Amy — " Karen caught the question in Nora's glance. "The thorn's thorn. Amy Archer. Isn't that sweet? Amy got this religion from Dan, and believe me, she could have had him. And without half trying. That's what I was counting on to get her out of the way. But the dumb bunny actually let him get through her fingers."

"There are some girls who wait to be chased, you know. Maybe she didn't like him."

"That's rare!" Karen scoffed. "You've never seen him. They're good friends, but she claims that's all there is to it."

"So now she's got your Larry. Leave them alone, Karen. Maybe it's true love."

Karen sat up and grinned wickedly. "And how would you define true love?"

"Contrary to whatever you think, I love your father."

The younger girl's expression remained the same. "I'm aware of that. And why shouldn't you?" She fell back and closed her eyes. "The situation isn't quite like that though. It's all one-sided."

"Is he rich?"

"Hmmm — " Karen was thoughtful. "Doesn't seem so. He lives in the Stuyvesant Arms. That's the swankiest apartment house in town. But I think whatever he has, it must be all of his own making."

"Handsome?"

Karen sighed. "No. Adorable. Red hair, freckles, short and dumpy. The opposite of tall, dark and handsome."

"Must be quite a boy, pet, to upset your ego this way. Not even handsome nor in the upper income bracket."

"He's quite a boy," Karen agreed lazily. *Much too much to waste on Miss Amy Archer.*

"Any plans?"

"I'm working on it. It'll take a little time. Oh, hi, Tone," she greeted, opening her eyes drowsily. Nora sat up.

"How are the only two women in my life?" he greeted cheerfully. Anthony Winslow was thin, debonair, and distinguished looking with streaks of gray in his thick brown hair.

"Pampered," his wife answered. "And just remember, three's a crowd!"

"And pretty," he added as he kissed her.

"Overworked and underpaid," added Karen sarcastically.

"She's enjoying it, Anthony. Don't let her tell you otherwise."

"How much do you need, Karen?"

"How much have you got?"

"I'll make out a check in the morning."

"How about tonight? I won't see you in the morning and you might forget. I have oodles of shopping to do."

"Remind me after dinner."

"I'd scold you, Anthony, but I'm afraid I might get left too."

"Not a chance."

"You're early tonight."

"Mind?"

"You know better," she said as they strolled arm in arm toward the house.

Anthony Winslow worked hard. He had worked hard all his life. Wealth was one of his attributes of recent years, and Anthony knew the value of work. He was determined that his daughter would not be spoiled rotten by the absence of it and the presence of everything she wanted. True, he handed her just about everything she wanted, but only if she were willing to put her hand to the plow, also.

Nora Cartlane had been good for Anthony Winslow. Karen knew it. She had known it the moment she had laid eyes on her three years ago. Lorelei had been gone eighteen months. A year and a half Anthony had mourned. Then he met Nora. It was she alone who had put the smile back on his lips. A good belly-laugh had been a long time in coming, but nevertheless, that had eventually been replaced too.

Her stepmother was more like a sister to Karen, a sister she had always wanted. They shared their secrets and occasionally their clothes. The fact that Nora was sometimes a bit more conservative than Karen did not bother the younger girl at all. She patiently listened, but if she did not care for what she heard, she promptly forgot it.

Yes, I have plans, Nora, dear. But I'm not even telling you. If Amy doesn't bend under the weight soon, well, I'll just have to use more drastic measures. I've been too long-suffering. What is my next move? I know of a man, Nora. A man named Todd Kenyon. He might be the answer. But not just yet.

Karen had a juicy tidbit she was saving in her little bag of tricks.

Chapter 15

THE BACK DOOR slammed shut. Paul was home. He liked to make sure everyone knew it. He had arrived several days ago for Christmas vacation, and this evening he was going back for Judy who had been unable to leave at the same time. He was anxious to get started. He did not like to be away from her for so long. Fifty miles was too far. Fifteen blocks was too far.

"When do we eat?"

"Soon. Elaine is going to pick up Amy in a few minutes." Louise Sanderford inspected the tablecloth she was about to spread over the table, then rolled it into a ball. "Put this in the hamper, son." She took a fresh linen cloth from the buffet drawer.

"Don't you ever think of anything besides your stomach?" asked his sister.

"Sure. That's why I'm anxious to eat!" he retorted. "Say, speaking of Amy. Before Dan left, I kinda got the idea he was sweet on her. Can you imagine old Ichabod finally getting bit?"

Two years Dan had been gone, and no one knew it better than Paul. He had been sick with emptiness for a long time after, but he had tried not to let on. Going off to school had not helped either, since a fresh wave of emptiness came over him with each homecoming. He had no business getting weak when it must be so much harder on Dan. It was plenty rough on these ladies, too, mused Paul. Life sure got tough as you got older.

"Whatever made you think that?"

"Search me." He pinched his sister's nose rather hard. The roguish twinkle in her eye was a constant invitation to her brother, and sometimes her husband, to pinch or deface her in one way or another. "Too bad he's not here to stake his claim!" he added as he headed for the stairs.

Each one of the family was outspoken in his own way: Paul, facetiously so; Elaine in her extremely frank manner; and Dan, tactfully. Dan had once been openly frank like his sister, sometimes to the point of bluntness, but he had learned it was to his own benefit as well as that of others, to use diplomacy. Their mother was perhaps the most reserved of all. She disliked harboring any hidden sentiments but often held her peace for the sake of someone's feelings.

Two years! How Louise missed her eldest child! They had shared so many wonderful Christmas holidays in this house, and now this second one Dan would be away would be no easier than the first. She had thought it would, but now she missed him more than ever. However, they had so much to be thankful for: safe-keeping through another year; Dan's fruitful ministry on the field; the new little life being entrusted to the care of Mark and Elaine, still months away. God had blessed them abundantly.

"I'm going now, Mother. I'll do that when I come back." Elaine referred to the partly set table.

"Elaine, please. I wish you'd keep out of Amy's affairs." She was disturbed by her daughter's determination to help Amy. What disturbed her more was what she thought might be Amy's reaction. Elaine was much too frank for her own good.

"Now, Mother, I think she *needs* someone to talk to her. I mean, since she lives alone—no family and all."

"You may be right, dear, but you're not her mother and she may resent your interfering."

"I'll be gentle. After all, she's a big girl." *And you may not know it, dear Mother, but what I'm really doing is looking out for big brother's interests. You heard Paul say it. He's not here to stake his own claim.* Elaine's thoughts raced on. *I can't sit back and—*

"Big girls get hurt, too, dear."

So do big boys. Aloud, she said, "That's why I'm going to talk to her. I'll be back soon, sweetie."

Amy was watching from inside the front door, and she stepped out into the cold air as soon as she saw Elaine's car turn the corner.

Oh, Amy, Elaine said to herself, *if I could only tell you what I really want to. Two years Danny's been pining for you, and you hardly know he exists. He's just the grandest, the best. How could you, Amy! He loves you, and men like Danny don't fall easily. They're once-in-a-lifetime people.* Elaine pulled up to the curb and watched her friend descend the steps. Such a sweet, delicate face. And that figure! It was enough to make other girls green, but either Amy carried it well or she was not completely aware of her physical blessings.

Elaine thought of her own slender shape and how it was being affected by the ever-so-slow growth of the new life she and Mark had created. Others had not noticed yet, but she could tell as she buttoned her slim skirts and held her breath until she got them fastened. And that miracle of life inside her. It had assured her last night of its reality as she became aware of a flutter of movement. At first she had not been certain, but she had felt it again this morning.

"Hi, Lainey!" Amy greeted cheerfully as her mouth curved into a full smile, showing her straight white teeth. "How you feeling?"

"Hi, yourself. Much better, thanks."

"I do believe it will snow," Amy said, wrinkling her nose in disapproval.

"I do believe you're right."

"I hope not. Larry and I were going up to Glendon tomorrow night. According to the reports, we're likely to get quite a storm."

Elaine was silent. She did not speak until they were off the main highway. "You and Larry are getting to be quite a twosome."

"Oh, sort of. He's quite a guy. Have you ever seen such a complete change in a person?"

"Um hum."

"Who?"

"You."

Amy nodded in agreement. "You're right there."

"You like him pretty well, don't you?" She was afraid to ask.

"He's wonderful company. We're just good friends though. Why do you ask?"

"He's in love with you, Amy." Elaine turned the car into the drive, glad she did not have to look at the other girl.

"Of course he's not!" Amy exclaimed. It was ridiculous. She got out and waited for Elaine to come around the back of the car. "Why, he and I – "

"Amy." Elaine had a way of commanding attention. "I think you'd better take a good look at the situation. Larry's in love with you. He hasn't so much as looked at another girl in months. If you feel the same way about him, well, then okay. But if not – "

"Why, I never even thought of him in that way." Yet she knew it was true.

Mark poked his head out from under his car. "She's right, Amy." Elaine cast him a grateful glance. He left his work and joined them as they reached the steps. He put a smudge of grease on his wife's chin as she tried to duck his blackened hand. "Larry melts every time you get near him, Amy," he added.

She was annoyed. Mark left to get cleaned up, and she felt more at ease. "Now if Larry felt that way about me, wouldn't I be the first to notice? I mean, I'm with him at work everyday. And he's never given me any reason to think – "

"Maybe that's it, Amy." Aunt Louise turned from the sink where she was busily washing salad greens. She spoke kindly, and her words were soothing to Amy's irritation. "You've been so close to him you haven't really been able to see him—in the right perspective."

Amy was still, pensive. Her chagrin had vanished although she felt Elaine spent too much time minding other people's business. "I think you're all wrong." But she had not convinced herself.

"I hope I haven't spoken out of turn, Amy." Elaine's eyes and voice softened also, putting them nearer to old terms. "It's just that I hate to see either of you get hurt."

"It's all right, Elaine. I appreciate your concern." Amy was still dubious. She laughed hesitantly. "It's strange. I just hadn't considered him as a potential husband."

Elaine excused herself and went upstairs to lay out Mark's clean clothing.

"Sit down a minute, Amy." The older woman dried her hands on her apron and sat opposite her. "If you're *not* interested, don't you think you should break it off now? I think in the long run it would be much easier on Larry that way." There was nothing presumptious in her advice.

Amy was glad to have such an understanding friend. "I guess you must be right. But he's such a good friend, and we've had such grand times together. It seems almost cruel to do that."

"Maybe it does. But not nearly as much as if you encourage him. You'll be building him up for a let down."

Amy thought about it as she traced her finger along the design in the kitchen table. "We're supposed to go to a cantata up in Glendon tomorrow night. I'll try to tell him then. It's going to be a hard thing to explain, especially since I'm not convinced myself."

"You probably think it's none of my business—"

"Oh, but I don't feel that way at all, Aunt Louise. I really do appreciate all the help you've given me."

"Well, we think an awful lot of you, Amy, so I feel I should express my opinion, especially since Elaine has been so outspoken." She was almost apologetic. "If I were you, I'd break that date with him. The more you see him, the harder it will be. If you love him, too, then that's different, but—"

"Thanks, Aunt Louise. I'd have been lost without you these past two—no, two and a half years. I don't know what I would have done without you. And I mean that. Do you know, it's been just that long since I first met you? I've been so busy, I don't know where the time has gone."

"It always passes quickly when we're busy and happy with what we're doing." Louise was thinking of the loneliness she had had to overcome herself, how she had been able to do it by keeping herself occupied.

Amy smiled and patted her hand. Elaine and Mark were coming down and she wanted to close the original subject. "And I really do thank you for your advice."

Mrs. Sanderford went back to the sink while Amy busied herself by putting ice into the crystal glasses which had been set out.

Paul came in. "Well, I'm sure glad you're here, Amy. It's getting late. And you know what else it's?"

"No," replied his sister. "What else is it it's, Fritz?"

"It's starting to snow. I've got to get started pretty quick – before Judy calls and tells me not to come."

"Well, I'm glad to see Judy's better equipped with brains than you. Every marriage needs a good stabilizing force – "

"Watch your lip there, kiddo. Besides, I'm still sore at you. Imagine, making a grandmother out of my dear little mother. Why, she hardly looks old enough to be a mother, let alone a grandmother!" He put his arm around his mother to comfort her. "Mark's going to have to get out that old rocking chair that's in the basement and get it fixed. Poor little mother," he consoled.

"Well, Paul," Mark said, putting his arm around Paul's shoulder and confiding in a fatherly tone, "there comes a time in every boy's life when he has to grow up."

Paul stormed into the dining room. "Let's eat!"

Larry's car turned into Amy's street almost as if of its own accord, as if it knew the will of its master without his controlling hand.

There was an abundant accumulation of snow which had fallen the previous night, and although it was still early evening, the slow-rising moon gave the surroundings an ethereal luster. A combination of that and the crisp, frosty air gave Larry an exuberance, a lightness of heart that almost reached the point of giddiness. He reveled in this atmosphere which had a way of clearing one's thoughts, giving one a renewed impression of old things, just as the purity of the snow gave the familiar environment an entirely different aspect. Yet the old was there, sure and secure.

The main highways were free of most of the snow, having been plowed even before it had stopped falling, and plowed again. The constant churning of tires and skid chains had removed all but a dirty mixture of sand and snow from these roads. But the side streets, though plowed, were hard-packed with a thick coat which, in the pale glowing light of the slow-rising moon, gave him the feeling he was in a great white tunnel. The heavy-laden trees overhead formed the roof.

Larry left the motor running so the inside of the car would stay warm. He rang the bell, and while he waited he breathed deeply of the invigorating air, nostalgically remembering the way he used to do the very same thing as a little boy. Only then he wished he could store some of it away to use in the hot dryness of summer.

He was enthused about this evening with Amy. It would be their last until after the holidays. He would see her again before they went their separate ways for Christmas, but not alone. In a few days she would be going to her brother's in Massachusetts, and he would be going in the opposite direction – home.

Home. It was a good word. Had such a good sound to it. He had great anticipation for this, too, although he wished he and Amy could be together for this most enjoyable time of year.

When he had finally come to his senses, a wanderer truly come home, there was great rejoicing. The angels could not have outdone the Spencer family of Farmingtown, Pennsylvania on that score. The very night he settled things with God, he called his parents to tell them the good news. There were tears of joy for all concerned. Their prayers of ten long years had been answered.

He had gone home shortly after, the first time in those ten years, and, as at the return of the Prodigal Son when his time of riotous living was over, the fatted calf was killed and there was great feasting. His three older brothers and two younger sisters, all married and with families of their own, had been there too. The family circle, broken for so long, was at last complete. What a project it had been, getting to know all his nieces and nephews, all of whom he had never seen save the three oldest.

With Amy's help, Larry had recently finished his Christmas shopping for this large family. They had had a marvelous time doing it together. She had helped check off the many names on his list, then double-checked them as she put the finishing touches on the wrappings. She had insisted on re-doing some that he had done, and he had willingly submitted, just for the sake of watching her do them over. They did look rather dilapidated alongside hers. She was such delightful company. The festive decorations, the jolly fat man in the red suit, the Salvation Army lady ringing her bell on the corner – all symbols of the season – had contributed to their gaiety, their unexpressed desire to recapture their childhood.

Mrs. Martin opened the door and shivered as the cold air reached her. Larry stepped in quickly and shut it behind him. He unbuttoned his overcoat, revealing a bright red tie. He assured the lady that it was only to be in keeping with the season. She laughingly advised him that green would go better with his hair.

Mrs. Martin liked Larry. Although she was not in accordance

with the prospect of losing Amy, she was of the opinion that they were perfectly suited to each other. She had never tried to conceal her opinion.

Amy came down the stairs, and Larry watched her every step, not concerned that he was staring, perhaps making her feel uncomfortable. She was the perfection of feminine pulchritude, and he had never seen perfection more perfect. She was dressed in a red wool sheath. Around her neck she wore the crystal necklace he had given her. It sparkled with a million tiny lights as it transmitted the hues of the various surroundings with her every movement.

He had picked the necklace out that day and had it delivered. He had chosen to do it this way that she might be spared the embarrassment of refusing it in his presence if she did not wish to accept it. He was glad she was wearing it.

She handed him her coat which she had carried over her arm, then put a fluffy white scarf around her neck. He held her coat for her.

"I never saw this coat before." He needed something to say, and at the moment this seemed most logical.

"Christmas present," she said, smiling at him.

"Oh?"

"From me to me," she explained as they went out into the clear night air.

He took her arm as they went down the steps, for the recent snowfall had left some slippery spots. Her nearness made his head spin.

A half-hour later they entered the warm church. They had not been seated more than five minutes when the lights went out. Candelabrum containing seven candles at the front of the church was the sole source of illumination. There was a hushed reverence as the robed choir proceeded down the center aisle, each member bearing a tall white candle. Each candle was placed at a vantage point around the choir loft. The organist played a Christmas hymn for the processional while the choir hummed the beautiful notes.

It was lovely. Amy and Larry settled down to enjoy the cantata. He reached for her hand, a thing he had never done, and for one brief moment he sensed a withdrawal, a hesitancy in her movement. Then she relaxed again, and he covered her small hand with his other. Several minutes passed before he looked her way. When he did, she spontaneously met his glance with a smile, but just for one brief second. He knew, even in this almost dark auditorium, that the color had rushed to her cheeks. And in a way, he was glad.

Winning Amy's confidence back had been a long, drawn-out process. True, they had been good friends for almost two years now, but he had never made the slightest advance toward her, being convinced she would cringe from his touch. In fact, the gift he had so recently given her had been, he was sure, the first outward sign of his feeling for her, and he had been extremely hesitant about the whole matter. She had accepted it graciously; she had accepted his hand. Larry's head went spinning again.

They stopped for some refreshments on the way home. All too soon they were back at Amy's door. Larry had been tongue-tied the entire evening.

"It was a wonderful evening, Larry. The cantata was lovely. Thank you for taking me." They stood on the porch, and she reached for the door.

"The pleasure was all mine. I wish it were just beginning, Amy." He casually leaned against the door in an effort to delay her. "Amy, can we talk?" he asked softly.

She hesitated, her hand still on the doorknob. Larry moved, and without answering, Amy opened the door and walked through the dimly-lit hall, put her coat over the newel post, and went into the dark living room.

He followed her, uncertain at first just what her actions had indicated. She reached for the small lamp next to the sofa, but he stopped her and not a moment too soon.

"I can talk better in the dark." The light from the hall he thought was more than sufficient.

She sat on the arm of the big overstuffed chair. This new, strange quietness of hers made communication much more difficult than it already was.

"Amy— " He did not look at her. He was at a loss for words, her attitude contributing greatly to his uneasiness. Perhaps he should have waited, not been so hasty. "Amy," he started again, gently, softly. But suddenly he blurted out words he had not intended to say at all. "Have you forgiven me for—well, you know what I mean. Have you, Amy?" He looked at her now, and the scarlet from her dress seemed to creep into her neck and face.

She put her hands to her cheeks. "Of course, Larry." She looked away. "But if that's what you wanted to talk about, I'd rather not."

"No. No, it isn't. I want to forget it, too, but I'm glad you have. I had to find out for sure because, well— " He ran his fingers through his hair, then along the back of the chair. He wished he did not sound so ignorant. "I guess you know how I feel about you, Amy," he said, running his fingers through his hair again. He stood in front of her, very close.

"I didn't." She was afraid to look at him. She could feel his steady gaze. She wanted to say, "I didn't until Elaine told me."

"You should have, Amy. I've told you a million times." Her

eyes met his with a question. But before she could put it into words, he went on, at the same time taking her hands and drawing her to her feet. "You never heard me because the words were inside. Every time I saw you—sometimes I knew you were near before I saw you. And every time I heard your voice. The words couldn't come out. Not before I knew for sure—"

"Larry—" Her voice was void of any expression, and her throat was parched. "Please—" Again she looked away.

"I guess I should have known." His face was crestfallen, and bitter disappointment was written across it.

Amy walked to the window and, away from his gaze, unclasped the lovely crystal necklace. It was quiet. Finally he followed her and stood behind her as she looked out the window at his car, so lonely in the moonlight.

"You're a wonderful guy, Larry." She turned to face him and reached her closed hand out to him. His hands remained in his pockets.

"Is it hopeless, Amy?" he asked quietly. "I mean, is there any chance?" Again he was at a loss for words.

She hesitated before she answered, but her hand was still stretched out toward him. "I like you an awful lot, Larry, and I like being with you. So how can I say there's no hope? I just don't know. I'm not sure how I feel, but I didn't mean to encourage you. I guess I haven't been fair."

"I didn't ask for anything in return for friendship." He covered her closed hand with his own as he spoke, then stepped closer to her. "I was hoping you liked these."

"They're beautiful."

"There were no strings attached." He took them from her and fastened them around her neck. Putting his forefinger under her chin, he gently, firmly tilted her head back until she had no choice but to look full into his face. He was so close. Ever so gently he touched his lips to hers. She did not return his kiss, nor did she turn away.

"Good night, Amy." He put his coat on, stopped to look back at her briefly, and was gone.

Amy scarcely breathed until she heard the noise from the car blend into the night. She heard and was troubled. She had not moved from the spot where he had left her, watching as he slowly descended the steps, his shoulders drooping in dejection. She watched him as he got into his automobile, heard the muffled thud as he slammed the door with extra firmness. He tried to start the car several times, and when it finally took hold, the motor raced violently. The wheels spun in the snow as he floored the accelerator, and the persistence of it made Amy uncomfortable. He released the pressure, paused a long moment, then started again, slowly and smoothly. As the vehicle gained momentum, Larry's foot became dead weight on the gas pedal again, and she heard him race down the street.

He had been hurt, but what was the real cause of his reaction? Was it annoyance? Anger? Perhaps both? She wished she knew. She had valued his friendship, but where did it go from here? It could not possibly remain the same. It would have to go either one way or the other. She knew Larry that well.

She collapsed on the sofa and curled up with her head resting back on a small pillow. The darkness was soothing, softening the harshness of the objects about her, covering the tiny flaws of the sofa, the spot on the carpet, the roughness of the wallpaper. The Martins were always talking about redecorating, but inevitably the move was pre-empted by something more important.

Amy had been so filled with self-pity before she had come to know the Lord that she had been unaware of the friends she had in the persons of Mr. and Mrs. Martin. Primarily, they had taken her in as a roomer to satisfy their hunger for the sounds of young people in the house. They needed someone to fill the empty places left by their children. She had failed miserably in this respect, but with higher goals in sight, she had set about to make up for the wrong she had done them. Their home had become hers.

If only she could stay here and not have to face the reality of daylight.

"If you don't love him, end it right away. Before someone gets hurt." Aunt Louise had been so right, but the warning had not come soon enough. Amy had thought of her words many times since leaving the Sanderford home the evening before, but unrelentingly the question came back, "Doesn't Larry mean more to me than that?" And as an afterthought, "I *don't* want it to be so final." His gift which had come that afternoon had not helped the situation either, for it served as a confirmation to the estimated situation. Maybe she should have returned it.

If only he had given her some indication, some sign. Were they on friendly terms, or had this been his way of telling her they were through? Larry had been looking, hoping for just a word from her, also. Had she looked at him, opened her arms to him, he would not have hesitated to come back, but she had not. The risk of hurting him again was too great. The next time the wound would be deeper.

She had unconsciously taken him for granted, so comfortable he was to be with. Now she did not want to lose him, but did she want to spend the rest of her life with him? A lifetime spent with the wrong person could be an eternity.

Amy put her forefinger to her lips and wondered if the whole thing had really happened. His touch had been, even as himself, gentle and undemanding.

For the first time since his departure, Amy recalled the only other time Larry had kissed her, and a shiver went down her spine. But he surely was not the same person now. It was as if another person had taken up residency in the frame called Larry Spencer. Obviously this was why she had objected so emphatically to his references to the past, for she had not considered him in that light for some time. This was the first he had referred to it except for that Sunday school picnic when he, Dan, and the two others had put their little wits together to antagonize her. They would never know what they put her through that day.

Dan – yes, she had gotten over him, and when he occasionally came to mind now it was as if he were in another unfamiliar, unreal world. He was a small part of her past though a very important one since he had been instrumental in her salvation. Her feelings for him had been passing ones, almost as if they had never existed.

So the question of the young man of the evening did not create any conflict with an existing romance, for there was none. She had dated Tim Northrop, the young architect from Dave's office in Massachusetts, almost every time she had visited, but she had no sentimental qualms about him. Her brother and his wife had subtly arranged their first meeting, but the many pleasant evenings they had spent together had spurred little or no romantic inclinations from either of them. Furthermore, they each understood.

What about before New Hope, before her life had undergone such a drastic change? Was there anything there to hinder, to haunt her? She supposed she would tell Larry eventually, tell him what misfortunes had come her way, but he was in no position to criticize. She knew enough about him to know that.

At times, Larry seemed to have a wildness about him, a desire to free himself from any ties that might bind. She had noticed this undercurrent of restlessness even though he had never made the slightest advances toward her. Never before tonight.

Elaine's remarks of the previous evening had visibly startled her. Then, just as quickly she had realized what should have been apparent to her. Larry was the reason for her disapproval. Amy was certain now that she had felt it only when Larry had been with her. But why? Oh, Elaine was probably aware of Larry's philandering and boozing, but surely she could see he had changed. Or did she think that because of it Amy stood above him? Some day maybe she would bring herself to talk to Elaine about it.

Larry was a dear. Why not? But she must not be impulsive. There was nothing she could put her finger on, nothing to prevent their relationship from progressing into something permanent. Nothing but her own uncertainty. The magnitude of her problem required a great deal of consideration. And prayer.

Amy slipped off the sofa and onto her knees. She had been trying to solve her own problems again. How foolish that was, when all one had to do was lay them at the Saviour's feet. He was always ready and willing to listen, to intercede, but one must make the petitions. "Ye receive not because ye ask not." But one must ask, "in His will." Frequently this perplexed her, for sometimes she was not sure she had the right to ask. Other times, it frightened her. It took a great deal of courage to say, "Thy will be done."

"Dear Father in Heaven: I thank Thee that I am Thy child, that Thou hast seen fit to claim me as Thine own, that Thou hast blessed me so bountifully when I am so unworthy. But most of all, I thank Thee for the Lord Jesus who so willingly died for me that I might not have to pay the penalty for my own sin.

"Dear Lord, Thou knowest the problems that face Thy children each day. Help me to bring them to Thee, for I have not the wisdom nor the capacity to untangle the confusion I bring upon myself. Show me Thy will, Father, that I might not hurt Larry any more than I already have."

It was much later when Amy wearily arose from her knees. She had had a long talk with her Lord, not only about the present which so vitally affected her future, but also about the many anxieties, the difficulties which faced her each day. She asked Him to endue her with strength, with the right words to teach her class the next morning, and the ultimate aim, to bring these young lives to a personal acceptance of Christ as Saviour.

She had been helper in the nursery class for about a year, and although the task primarily had been assisting with the use of scissors and glue, it had been a delight to her. She had been as a child herself in the knowledge of the Scriptures. Thus, she had been able to learn with these little children the very fundamentals of the Christian life.

She had been asked to take a class of her own a few weeks ago — a group of ten-year-old girls. This challenge had brought her to her knees in a renewed humble dedication. She spent much time in prayer and preparation and rejoiced as the weeks went by to see the steady spiritual growth of her charges. She took it upon herself to get to know each girl and her particular problem in a real, personal way, and she was amazed to see how it helped as she prepared each lesson, giving it an application to the difficulty of each young life.

Larry *was* a dear. Good, dependable Larry. He was ready and waiting at her beck and call, and she wondered now if she had not relied upon him too much. She had not meant to hurt him. Life was so full of problems.

Karen Winslow was one of her biggest problems, her favorite pastime being the pillage and annihilation of Amy.

"You sure let a nice one get away!" Karen had made this sneering stab at Amy right after Dan left. "But I guess it doesn't matter as long as you-know-who is around, huh, Amy?"

Amy seethed with irritation every time Karen referred to Larry as you-know-who. "Dan and Larry are both good friends, Karen."

"Real *good* friends, huh?"

"Karen," Amy had said, not unkindly, "didn't it ever occur to you that a girl can be friendly with a man without designing to trap him?" It was hard to hold her tongue with this girl.

"No!" she had snapped. It was an unheard of thing in Karen's circle, and she had laughed sarcastically. "You know, he's sure hooked, Amy. He's really gone on you! Why, what other reason could he have possibly had for taking on this religious bit? He knew *you* wouldn't give it up! Larry Spencer, hah!"

Amy cringed under her boisterous acrimonies, but she had learned to quietly ignore her and go back to work. She prayed for Karen every day, and it was not easy.

Larry disliked the girl immensely. "I always feel trapped when she's around," he had told Amy more than once.

"She has a heart and soul, too, Larry."

"Don't you believe it, Amy!" he had returned. "A soul maybe, but a heart? No, not Karen Winslow." But Amy had continued to pray.

As she slowly climbed the stairs, her thoughts were again concentrated on Larry. She knew, in all probability, that she would not receive immediate answers to her petitions. God did not always work in that way. His way was best. He not only planned each step for his loved ones, but also taught them patience, complete dependence upon Him through difficult paths. She would have to be patient for His direction.

As she reached the top of the stairs, she flipped the switch to turn off the hall light. Perhaps the morning light would bring with it a revelation, an affirmation, an open door where there had been nothing but a blank wall.

Chapter 16

THE LAND OF the rising sun was a land of darkness and sin. Its people were hungry for the Word of the living God, but there were not enough messengers to carry the message to all who would hear it. At times Dan was almost overcome with his own inadequacy for the task laid upon him. All about him was sickness, sadness, sin and death.

He had visited Kamakura where stands the seven-hundred-year-old Buddha. He had watched the oriental worshipers bow before the bronze statue as they paid homage to the "Enlightened One," the Hindu prince, Guatama, for whom the statue had been erected.

"Christ is the only way!" he had wanted to shout. "Christ, the Son of the living God! A god of stone cannot wash your sin away, cannot soothe the troubled breast! It cannot hear your prayers! I have a living Saviour, and He loves you too!" But at that time the language barrier had prevented any communication between him and these people he had come to serve.

A wave of evangelism had swept through this country after World War II, and the Christian realm had rejoiced. These people were readily accepting the religious faith of their conquerors. But the land had long lived in subjection and obedience to its rulers, and when it turned out that the victor was not conqueror after all, the people soon drifted back to their Shintoism and Buddhism.

Dan thought the first year in this country was probably the hardest year of his life. The homesickness he suffered was almost more than he could bear, for he had come to the conclusion that the closer the earthly ties, the harder the parting; but by the same token, the happier the reunion. Then the vicious circle would start all over again.

He had scaled one mountain that year, perhaps two. He had been able to conquer this nostalgia, this longing for his dear ones even though there were times when he ached to be with them. This truly had been a mountain to overcome.

He had spent those twelve months learning the Japanese language, a difficult task, and he now wondered which summit had been hardest to attain. He still had a long way to go before he would be able to speak it fluently, but the barrier between himself and the people was greatly minimized.

He had made his home with a Japanese family for those months, a Christian family, and this had proved to be a boon. It had not only speeded his understanding of their language, but it had also given him a wealth of knowledge concerning their daily activities. Then, too, after a steady diet of their food, he had learned to like it, even to enjoy it.

During this time he had also been able to do some missionary work, and it was a real challenge as he tried to make himself understood. Then it came time to leave that place he had called home and spend full time working for his Lord. The field was white unto harvest, and the responsibility was overwhelming. So Dan's loved ones had to be put in the background, and his homesickness became almost entirely a thing of the past.

The work in Kyoto, his new and permanent home, had been most fruitful this past year, but for everyone who responded to the message of salvation, there were thousands who had never heard.

He and his co-workers, Laura and Charles Sherman, had established a little church here, and the new work was growing rapidly. But where the Lord was working, the devil was working doubly hard, and there were times when discouragement would have conquered had it not been for the life line of faith.

"Hello, Josh. How are you today?" Dan asked the eleven-year-old boy in his native tongue.

"I'm happy, Dan. The Lord Jesus has given me a clean heart."

Josh had been in an accident some months ago, in which his mother was killed, and the boy had hovered in the valley of the shadow of death for two weeks after. He had been badly crippled, and the doctors gave little encouragement that he would ever walk again. He had gone through untold physical pain, but the mental anguish over losing his mother had almost taken its toll. His father was an unknown American GI who had left another living memorial to a weak and suffering nation.

Sometimes Dan thought it would have been better if the Lord had taken Josh home too. "Father, forgive me for such thoughts. Our earthly minds fall far short of understanding Thy plans."

Dan's mind had given birth to the idea of some day adopting the little fellow. He had grown very close to the boy this year he had been in Kyoto, and especially so since the boy's accident when Josh had come to live with them at the mission house. Dan had hopes that he would be permitted to finance necessary operations for the boy's complete recovery, but so far the doctors deemed it hopeless.

Dan carried Josh to his own room. He often did when he had letters to write or studying to do so that the boy might be with him.

"You marry pretty lady?"

Amy's picture stood on the desk. He had forgotten to put it away. "Maybe some day, Josh."

He missed Amy. Oh, how he missed her! At least once a day he took out this little colored snapshot he had taken of her the day of the wedding, one that she had not known about nor had anyone else seen it. He looked at the sweet face now with its high cheekbones, slightly turned-up nose, and the curly blonde hair which always smelled so fragrant. He wished he could tell her.

He had wanted to tell her that afternoon in his own living room when he first became conscious of his feeling for her. But he had restrained himself, hoping he would see in her eyes some sign that she felt the same way. He had almost told her the day of Elaine's wedding. It had been such an exciting day, and she had looked so lovely. Perhaps he would have declared his love for her regardless if he had not been aware of her opposition to the mission field. She had made it apparent that she would not go, not in so many words, but he had grasped the message.

Elaine had promised to keep him up to date, but he was unable to obtain any concrete facts from her letters. Amy was seen with Larry a lot, but more often than not, others were with them. Still, she urged him to write to Amy and put it straight on the line. "Stake your claim," was the way she had put it. Strange for her to say it that way. Sounded more like Paul. But could it be there was a message between the lines of her letters?

Dan sat with a clean sheet of stationery before him and drummed his pen on the desk.

"You ask pretty lady to come here with you?"

He was as persistent as Elaine. "I'll ask her, Josh. Sometime." Dan smiled at the boy.

He wanted with all his heart to tell Amy that he loved her, to ask her to share this life with him, for he was certain that in two years' time someone else would claim her love. He had seen how Larry looked at her, had recognized the look since it was the same one he had for her in his own heart. It had rubbed him the wrong way—how he had bristled!—when he had seen the two of them together.

Dearest Amy, I love you. I want you. I need you.

But the words never passed the tip of his pen. Instead he always wrote, Dear Mother, Dear Paul, Dear Elaine, or Dear Somebody Else. Never Amy.

Elaine was getting extremely persistent about the matter. In fact, she was threatening to tell Amy herself if he did not do something about it soon. But Dan knew her better than that. "You know the saying, Danny," she said in her last letter, "absence makes the heart grow fonder—for somebody else." She might harass, lecture, scold till she was blue in the face, but she would never break a confidence. How he longed to see her, his mother, Paul, the dearest family a person could ever wish for. But the longing for Amy, that was getting out of his control. He must write to her soon.

Would the knowledge of his love affect her feeling for Larry? He thought of the disparity in their ages, of how unlikely they were suited to each other, of this reason or another why they should not be interested in each other. But no matter how he tried to rationalize, the fact was that Amy and Larry had grown very close in spite of their previous relationship. Perhaps not in spite of it but because of it. Perhaps Amy and Larry—

Dan immediately put these thoughts from his mind, knowing he must leave it in God's hands. But he could not keep thoughts of Amy from his mind. Her image was etched indellibly upon his heart.

The holidays were over and life went on as usual in New Hope with no consequential changes. The situation between Amy and Larry had not altered as much as she had believed it would, although he was withdrawn and somber most of the time. It was especially in evidence when they were alone.

The weather had remained cold, the snow seemed to be accumulating faster than it was melting, and to all appearances, spring never would break through.

Then one morning it made its appearance. The flowers had not yet emerged, the snow was still visible in small patches, the trees were bare. But nevertheless, spring had arrived. It was in the air.

Within a matter of days, the remainder of the snow had vanished leaving a gold mine of mud for little exploring feet to "waller" in. In place of the snow, the crocus bravely stood having received their signal from the snowdrops, and announced to all the dubious ones that spring honestly and truly had arrived. The white birch stood tall again, relieved of their weight of snow which had bowed them in humble obeisance to the earth.

With the new season came a decided change in Larry. He emerged from the cocoon into which he had crawled, and to Amy's relief, he was himself again. It became apparent the first Sunday after the appearing of the crocus. The Martins were sitting on the porch when Amy and Larry returned from church, and they encouraged him to stay for dinner. He did not need any coaxing, only the suggestion.

Amy was no nearer to an answer, but she was glad to see him so gay. It had disturbed her that she had cut him so deeply, and she felt more at ease with him when he was this way—almost flippant.

After the meal, he took her out for a driving lesson, a chore he thoroughly enjoyed. It gave him a chance to be near her. She had asked him many months ago to teach her how to drive since she wanted to get a small car of her own. He was not anxious for that to take place, but he had willingly taken up the roll of teacher. This, however, was a long delayed lesson. It was the first time since Christmas that he had suggested they resume their studies.

It was a lovely day, and the ride was more a pleasure than a duty. The afternoon had wings, and as they pulled up in front of the house, the older couple was again sitting on the porch, enjoying the day as long as possible. The evening was fast descending, bringing with it a reminder that winter had not been too long gone.

Amy was behind the wheel, and as he reached over to put the car in gear after she turned off the motor and pulled up the brake, he spoke to her. His voice was softer than she had heard it in a long time. "What's new, Amy?" He had not referred to it all afternoon, and she appreciated it, but she wished he would not now. He had not referred to it, in fact, since that memorable evening before Christmas. He spoke softly, and although the car windows were open, had one not known of what he spoke, one would have thought he was but passing the time of day.

She smiled, and her voice was as soft as his own. "Nothing, Larry."

They got out and sat on the porch steps to chat. The conversation was free and easy. Amy felt as if she were loosed of bonds which had been stifling her, choking her life's breath away.

"Do you believe in reincarnation, Amy?" Larry asked. He was in a ridiculous humor.

She laughed. "No. Do you?"

"No, but I used to. There were some people in our town—met right across from my dad's church. They believed in it. See that fuzzy caterpillar down there? Well, when we were kids, whenever we saw one of those, we used to spit on it and say, 'That's not my grandfather!' It made my grandmother furious!

"That reminds me. One Christmas—I was about five, I guess, my dad bought me a tool set. Well, that spring, my mom hollered out one day and asked me what I was doing. You can't imagine what I told her. 'I'm hammering inchworms to watch them bleed!' Only I hadn't got my tools straightened out, and I was really pinching them with my pliers. She got sick when I showed her."

Larry rambled on as if he were reluctant to have his thoughts interrupted. "That same Christmas my brother, Mike, got a pop gun. Boy, did he have a good time untrimming the tree. And from the other side of the dining room table too! He let me try it once or twice, but his aim was much better than mine."

"Larry, your family sounds wonderful," laughed Amy. "I don't know why you ever left them."

"I thought you knew," he said, looking at her in surprise. "I was looking for you." He smiled and winked at her. "Those were lean years though, Amy. Let me tell you they were. But I wouldn't trade my family for all the salt in kingdom come."

"I'd love to meet them."

"I think it's about time you did. But you'll have to marry me first. So you won't change your mind. No, they really are the greatest. But you'll have to have a file cabinet to keep them all straight. My sister, Mary, is having her seventh. Boom, boom, boom. And she was a drippy-nose little kid when I left. Talk about prolificity! Is that a word?"

"I think not," Mr. Martin said with a chuckle.

"Prolificness? Anyway, she's got a houseful."

Amy helped Mrs. Martin bring sandwiches and iced tea out to the porch.

Larry was still talkative while they ate. Life was good again. It was spring.

He insisted the other couple join them for the evening church service. Later that night, as the Martins disappeared into the house, Larry put a detaining hand on Amy's arm, at the same time calling a good night to the older couple.

Amy stood with her hands behind her back and rested against the wall adjacent to the door. Larry leaned heavily on his hands, one on either side of her head. He was terribly close. The distance was lessening each second. Amy ducked under his arm and stood by the railing.

"How long do I have to wait, Amy?" He sat on the railing and looked into her eyes. He was so debonair. He was so adaptable to any situation. He was so lovable.

"I have to be sure, Larry. You know that. Please be patient."

"I'll try." He stood up and put his hands in his pockets. "But I love you." He was so serious. He took her hand as they walked to the top of the steps.

"Good night, Larry. And thanks – for being so nice."

He leaned toward her and kissed her cheek. "Good night, Amy." He pressed her hand tightly and left.

During the ensuing weeks Larry was buoyant, easy-going. But he was so unpredictable! He enjoyed throwing protocol to the winds – if he ever had any. Amy became exasperated.

"Marry me, Amy." It was a stage whisper, and it made the color rise vividly to her cheeks. Larry was a terrific guy, but he was too impetuous. She had liked this in him, too, for it was this trait that had made him so much fun to be with. But now she was in agony. He was enjoying her chagrin much as a little boy enjoys the confusion of a trapped insect searching for a way out of its dilemma.

She could have coped with the situation quite gracefully had it not taken place in the crowded elevator between the second and third floors, crowded with fellow-employees who, had they known of a romance between them, were unaware of the teetering of it.

All eyes were on Amy. She looked at Larry in frustration, pleading with him for help. She cleared her throat and moistened her lips. She shifted from one foot to the other, then exchanged her purse from one hand to the other. But in a matter of seconds she regained her composure and looked him straight in the eye.

"Not today, Larry."

She was most pleased with herself that she had been able to revert the situation to save face. She had said the few words with the same matter-of-fact tone she might have used to the grocer, "No cabbage today, thank you."

It was an explosive moment, and she had recovered quite well, but she was simmering with annoyance for the young man who had put her on the spot. She got out at her floor as did everyone else, without uttering another word to him. Larry was a little too glib about something terribly serious, and she did not like it one bit.

Amy did not see him for several days, and although she was certain it was he calling during the evenings, she went out under one pretext or another. She heard the phone ring after she had retired but kept silence when Mr. Martin knocked on her door. He was not being much help.

Then one morning Larry stepped into the elevator just before the door shut. Amy was miserably uncomfortable. She was near the door, too, and she wondered what he would have made of the situation had she been among the first in.

His eyes were mischievous. "How about today, Amy?"

"I'll be busy all day," she snapped, clenching her teeth. She was not amused. This time Larry knew it.

Late that same afternoon he stopped at her desk. Her fair head was bent over her work as she and Karen went over some typewritten sheets. He stood waiting for several minutes before she realized he was there.

"You!" she exclaimed, completely disgusted.

"I'm sorry, Amy. I guess I got carried away," he said humbly. "It was kinda thoughtless of me."

"To say the least. How could you? How *could* you, Larry?"

"I said I'm sorry, Amy."

She had to smile. "All right, Larry."

His face was sober, his eyes still serious. "How about next week at two o'clock?"

The office was almost empty, but all eyes were on them, wondering why the burst of laughter from the two in Amy's corner. Karen glared at them.

Spring was short. The length of it was actually no different from any other year, but the summer heat was upon them before they realized that winter was gone for certain.

By midsummer Amy was still in a quandary. Life seemed to be increasingly complicated with each turn of the road, and each added problem magnified the previous one. Larry was insistent. Elaine was standoffish and for no apparent reason. Then there was that matter which overshadowed her every waking moment. The matter of Todd Kenyon. That was a page she would like to tear out and obliterate. Larry would understand when she told him. And she would tell him if she accepted his proposal.

She and Larry seemed to go together like bread and butter—except for one major dissension which never reached a solution.

She snapped an unlighted cigarette from his lips and replaced it with a stick of chewing gum. It was not the first time she had done it.

"You're a shrew," he said angrily.

"You're a slave," she retorted.

"To you."

"To these things." She crumpled the item in question and stuffed it into his pocket.

"I'd rather be to you."

"But not to both."

"You drive a hard bargain. I wouldn't mind if it were a sure thing."

"Nothing is sure but death, taxes, and rain on Sunday."

"I chucked the cigars just for you—"

"Then I wish you hadn't bothered."

"Huh?"

"For me. If you did it for me, I wish you hadn't bothered."

"That's gratitude for you. You know I'd do anything for you, Amy."

"Then you'd better go home. It's getting late."

The next day, Amy climbed the back steps of the Sanderford house as Larry turned his car around and started out the drive. She turned to wave to him before he disappeared at the corner of the house.

She entered without knocking and the screen door banged shut behind her. The house was so still and lifeless that her own footsteps as she crossed the kitchen and made her way up the back stairs were as hammer blows announcing her arrival to anyone who might or might not be at home. The latter were in the majority.

The house was filled with the aroma of homemade bread and apple pie, a sure sign that Paul was home for vacation.

How had she ever thought this house pretentious, austere? It was warm and homey; it was love and happiness. Its occupants had made it that. But now it was lonely, and the quietness of it made her uneasy. She thought of Dan's remark, how it had seemed like a tomb after his father's death. It must have been like this.

Aunt Louise would be there in her room, Amy knew. She would be sitting at her sewing machine, or more likely, sitting at the window with a lap full of some lovely garment she was working on, needle and thread in hand, pins, scissors and such close by where she could easily reach them.

They had spent the Saturdays of the last several months in this room. Aunt Louise had been helping Amy with some sewing, and it was often hard to decide who required more patience, the instructor or the instructed. If Amy never learned the art of needle and thread, she had learned much more during these sessions. She loved the older woman dearly, and they had had many heart-to-heart talks during these hours they were together.

"Amy?" She heard her name as she reached the top of the stairs.

"I'm here," she called back cheerfully.

She hesitated as she passed Elaine's room, for inevitably the memory of Elaine's wedding day came back to her as she passed. The recollection of it all – of Dan standing straight and tall in the doorway with his arm around Barbie, of Dan coming down the aisle to give the bride away, of Dan when he took her home at the end of the day –

Amy acknowledged the fact that the man meant nothing to her, but occasionally he appeared in her mental vision just as sharply as if he were present. Then the strangest thing took place. Dan faded from the picture, and in his place was Larry, the impression of his round freckled face just as vivid as Dan's lean handsome one had been. And try as she might, she could not reverse the procedure. Perhaps this was her answer.

"Hi, Aunt Louise. You weren't expecting someone else, were you?"

"No, child, but you were so quiet I wanted to be certain it was you. Why didn't Larry stay for lunch?" He sometimes did.

"He's going over to help Reverend Carlson with the Boys' Club. I'm sorry I didn't call to let you know."

"That's right, they're having that clean-up day today, aren't they? It's good of him to help."

"I'm glad he's interested enough to help. They sure do miss Dan's helping hand."

Amy sat on the window seat and examined the handiwork. She was enthused over the progress but did not feel mentally equipped to cope with such difficulties today.

"Something wrong, Amy?"

"Not really. I go on vacation next week, you know. I guess I'm getting restless."

"How are things with you and Larry?"

"Up and down. More down than up, I suppose. I wish someone could give me some answers. Sometimes it seems all right, but other times it seems all wrong." She got up, walked over to the dresser, and picked up the framed portrait of Jonathan Sanderford. "How did you know Mr. Sanderford was the right one for you?" she wondered if she should have asked, but it was too late for retraction. "How did you know you wanted to spend the rest of your life with him?"

Louise put her work down and looked at the girl, her attention undivided. "I knew I could not live without him." She went on, and Amy wished she had not asked. "Then, after twenty short years, I found I had to live without him. He was all the world to me, to all of us. And a little part of me died with him." There were tears in her voice, but none in her eyes.

It was quiet for a while as the two sat there, each absorbed in her own thoughts.

Elaine and Mark had gone to visit Mark's folks for the weekend. Mark Jr. was six weeks old now, and they were anxious to get the paternal grandparents' approval of their little son. Paul and Judy had gone on a picnic. All too soon they would be returning to college for their final year, and since each was holding down a job for the summer, their well-earned Saturdays were spent in recreation.

"Aunt Louise, how can you give up your boys this way?" queried Amy. "How can you bear to lose Paul now too?"

Mrs. Sanderford knew to what Amy made reference. The previous Sunday evening, Paul and Judy had given their lives for full-time service.

"It's difficult for others to understand, Amy, but I haven't lost anything. I gave my children to the Lord many years ago, to use as He saw fit. Would you like to hear about it?"

"If it's not too much for you. You look tired, Aunt Louise." Amy had noticed this the last few weeks.

"I'll be fine, Amy." She put her sewing down again. Her lovely blue-white diamond flashed with every movement of her hand. "Before I was married, before I met my husband-to-be, the Lord told me, unquestioningly, that I was to go to the mission field. I thought perhaps Africa. Then I met Jonathan, and we fell in love. I still felt led to go to the field, but he didn't. We loved each other so much we were certain the Lord would reveal His will to us after we were married." She paused to regain control of her voice. The warmth of the afternoon was stirred by a gentle refreshing breeze which in turn stirred the fluffy organdy Priscillas at the windows.

"Now mind you," she went on, "he was willing to go, too, but had not felt the Lord's leading in that direction. We did not go. We thought it was just as important to serve the Lord here, and it would have been if He had wanted us here. This may come as a surprise to you, Amy, but the first three years of our marriage were miserable, unhappy ones. We were no longer attentive to His voice, nor did we look for His leading hand." She paused again, and each time she did, Amy wished she knew what to say, a word of comfort, a request that she not go on. It was painful for Louise Sanderford to relate this unhappy episode of her life, but Amy was spellbound.

"We were married about a year and a half when our first baby was born. Jonathan Paul, Jr. Surprised, Amy? And so were we. And heartbroken. Five short days later He took our baby from us." Her voice trembled.

"Aunt Louise, don't punish yourself this way."

"That was our punishment, Amy. The Lord was rebuking us. He took our baby home to be with Him. We could no longer obey His call, for my health was broken. My heart too. I was certain then that our home would remain childless."

"You had a wonderful family."

"Yes, we did. Almost two years later Dan was born. The Lord had broken my spirit so completely I was sure I would lose him, too, in the same way. When we realized our chastening was over, we gave Dan to the Lord, asked Him to use our son to take our place, to go where we should have gone. He was a dear little boy. I miss him, Amy, but I would not, I *could* not have influenced him to do anything but what he is doing right now.

"Then Elaine came along, and I had the little girl I had always wanted. She and Dan are very close in age, just a year's difference between them. Four years later Paul was born. He was the happiest baby I've ever seen. But no matter how close I've wanted to hold them, I've had to remember that they belong to the Lord. For a long while I thought Paul would never settle down, but his call is another answer to my prayers."

"What about Elaine?"

"She was free to go if she had been so led. She knew that."

Louise took up her sewing again, but her hands immediately dropped to her lap. "Amy, be sure you know God's will for your life. If ever you feel led to go to the field – or anywhere else, for that matter, don't do as I did. You'll suffer for it."

"I don't belong on the mission field, Aunt Louise. I'm sure of that."

They had lunch, and the day passed quickly, although not in the way it had been planned. Each had so much to talk over.

When Larry came after dinner, Amy kissed her friend on the cheek and bid her good-by. "Take care of yourself, Aunt Louise, and try to get some rest while I'm away."

"Good-by, Amy. I'll see you tomorrow. But if I shouldn't get a chance to speak to you, remember, I'll be praying for you while you're away from us."

"And I for you, dear friend." Amy squeezed her hand, then left with Larry.

Louise Sanderford stood at the kitchen window as she had so many, many times while watching her children at play in the yard. But now she watched Amy and Larry as they got into Larry's beautiful, showy car.

"Dear Lord," she prayed silently, "don't let that dear girl do anything she will regret. Give her a willingness to serve Thee, to earnestly seek Thy will in all she does. Watch over all of us, Father. My Dan boy so far away from home; Elaine and Mark and the new little life Thou hast entrusted to their care; and Paul and Judy as they prepare themselves for Thy service. Give me grace to accept whatever Thou hast in store for me in the weeks to come – "

Louise's silent prayer was broken off abruptly as her thoughts again turned back many years to the children at play in the yard.

The big old apple tree – it stood exactly as it had when the strong little arms had swung from its branches. Dan and Paul had spent the greater part of their childhood up in that tree. They knew each foothold, the best places to grasp for security, the most comfortable spots to sit for long periods. The tree stood on a knoll some distance from the house, and from its higher branches the boys had been able to view most of the neighborhood. It had impressed her with the widening scope of their horizon.

Then there was that day they coaxed Elaine up with them. She was in no sense of the word a tomboy. But far be it from her to allow her active, muscular brothers to call her a sissy. "Sissy-breeches" was the name they used to raise her dander. So Dan pulled from above while Paul boosted from beneath as far as his little arms could reach. But Elaine was suddenly overcome with panic and writhed herself free from their helpful hands, falling heavily, painfully on top of Paul. It was somewhat of a miracle that he had come through that with nothing more than a broken arm. Elaine had a large bruise. Paul had frantically pushed her off him with one arm and two bare feet, causing her to sit quite abruptly on a large rough stone.

Dan was a great climber. Louise's heart turned over as she recalled the day the roofers came to repair and replace some shingles which had torn loose during a storm. For an hour after the men left, she had searched for her elder son, her big five-year-old.

"Here I am, Mommy," he called to her from his lofty perch beside the chimney. She was frantic. After warning him over and over to sit still, she hurried into the house and called the fire department. During the ten minute interval before they arrived, she hovered like a mother hen under the edge of the roof, hoping to catch her precious cliff-dweller should he fall. After his transportation to safety, and after a ride to the end of the drive in the fire engine, she gradually heard and put together bits of his escapade. He had followed the roofers up the ladder and had hid himself in the corner of a gable until he was sure they had gone away in their truck.

How did mothers survive such ordeals? And the anxieties had increased with the years.

There was the time Dan and Paul had locked Elaine in the butler's pantry. She screamed and fretted for what seemed like hours to Louise who had been required to listen to it while the boys sat smugly on the floor, keeping guard. When silence reigned for some time, Dan's curiosity got the better of him, and he crept mouselike on his haunches to peep into the keyhole. He was unaware that Elaine's silence inferred that she was awaiting just such a move from one of her brothers. Dan did not have a chance to focus his one peeking eye on the scene beyond when it was filled with pepper, a good supply of it which his sister had been patiently holding in the palm of her hand just below the level of the keyhole, her lips pursed, ready to drive the ammunition to its goal. Dan had suffered with a red, swollen eye for weeks. Needless to say, Elaine had not gone unpunished. Nor Paul. Dan had received over and above his due reward.

There were other times, too, when punishment had been unnecessary. At a very tender age her children had learned the meaning of the verse, "Be sure your sin will find you out."

Now, as she looked back, it seemed that the hurts, the happinesses, the punishments, the surprises were all necessary components in the breathtaking picture of a beautiful, satisfying life.

Whatever the future held, Louise could accept it with peace in her heart. Her children were in the Father's keeping. During the years, one by one, these same mischievous children had come to her, knelt by her side, and asked the Lord Jesus Christ to come into their hearts. They belonged to Him, and she must trust them to seek His will in all things.

Paul had been the last to take the step, and he had come ever so close to breaking her heart before yielding to the gentle, pleading voice of the Saviour.

"Dear Lord, take care of them all." Louise resumed her prayer as if it were an unfinished conversation with someone in the room. "If it be Thy will, give Dan a good Christian girl to love. Thank you for giving Elaine such a fine man, and for giving Paul such a lovely girl. Take care of us from day to day, and some day, when we meet at Thy mercy-seat, may we know we have done our best for Thee. Thou hast done so much for us."

Again she terminated her conversation with her Heavenly Father. Paul's car was coming up the drive. It was almost dark, but she could see that Judy was with him. They probably had not had supper yet.

Amy and Larry were soon speeding along the highway toward town. They had not spoken since leaving the Sanderford drive.

"Any place you'd like to go tonight, fair maiden?"

"I'd like to go home, if you don't mind. I have tomorrow's Sunday school lesson to review, and I am rather weary tonight. Thanks anyway."

He reluctantly pulled up to the curb. "I'd be glad to help you," he offered hopefully.

Amy smiled. "Don't bother getting out," she said kindly, not without appreciation. She was not up to conversation with him tonight.

He followed her up the porch steps. "Amy, please – "

She knew what was coming. Larry was impatient and he was persistent. This made – how many times since the elevator incident? Perforce, it had brought her to somewhat of a decision. Not only his persistence had encouraged it, but also her confidential talk with Louise Sanderford, although she could not put her finger on any one aspect of their talk that had wrought the decision.

She was about to say good night and leave him at the door. He was hoping to be invited in. She interrupted before he could finish what he was about to say.

"Larry, be serious for a minute."

"You think I'm not?"

"I know you are, but sometimes it's hard to tell. Larry—" She hesitated. He was not going to like this. "I think we'd better stop seeing each other."

He stared in unbelief. He would not have been more stunned had she slapped his face. He tried to speak, but closed his mouth for fear of saying something he might regret. Instead, he made a fist and slammed it into the door jamb.

Amy winced. "Was that for me?" she asked softly.

"No. No, Amy." His gentleness surprised her. "For me. Thunderation, Amy, I'm always putting my foot in it. Don't say that, Amy. You didn't mean it, did you? Please say you didn't." His disappointment bordered on bitterness.

"For a while, Larry. At least for a while. I think it would be best."

"What possible good would it do? You'd go joy-hopping around with some other crumb, and where would I be? Come off it—"

She was annoyed. "I wouldn't be joy-hopping with anyone at all. But it would give us—me a chance to think—clearly."

He had walked away from her, but he whirled around and quickly came back to where she was standing. "Amy, I'll—" he paused, then started over again. "If I promise to be good and not ask you again, will you change your mind?"

"I don't—"

"Please, Amy? I promise I won't ask you again—ever." He was like a small boy, a far cry from the repulsive man she once hated. "I'll wait until *you* ask *me!*"

She half-smiled in amusement. "I don't know whether to believe you or not."

He pretended to be hurt that she would doubt him and put his left hand up, three fingers pointing skyward. "Scout's honor."

"I never proposed to anyone before either," she mused skeptically.

He smiled. "There's always a first time for everything, you know. Please, Amy?" he pleaded for the umpteenth time.

She nodded her acquiescence, not at all certain she should not have been more firm.

Chapter 17

THE DOORBELL RANG. The Martins were not at home, but Larry would wait. He was probably sitting in the wicker chair on the porch. He was always on time, and he always rang the bell to announce his arrival, then sat down to wait patiently. That was one thing to which he was becoming most accustomed. But he did not like it. The bell rang again, and Amy smiled. My, he was getting impatient! And early, at that.

She hummed a little tune as she snapped her suitcase shut and picked up the assortment of odds and ends she had ready to take. She was enthused over this vacation. Larry, just as full of anticipation, was to take her to Ocean Point.

The bell rang again. Putting her bag on the floor, Amy opened the door with her free hand. "You're – "

She froze. *Todd Kenyon!* Dear God, why? After four years, why? Why, when she had found such happiness without him? Why, why, why? And how had he known where to find her?

She felt weak. The things she held in her hand, her purse, hat, gifts, all fell to the floor in disarray as she stared at the man who was smiling pleasantly at her.

"Hello, Amy." There was a nervous quiver at the corners of his mouth. His eyes flitted to the rug, to the kitchen at the end of the hall, to the faded picture on the wall, then back to Amy. "You're looking well."

She looked with disdain upon this young man she once thought she loved. How *had* he found her? Hatred seethed within her, hatred for him and for everything about him.

"Why did you come?" Her voice was weak.

"That's a fine way to greet an old friend. I thought you wanted me to come."

"*Why* did you come?" She repeated the question through clenched teeth as she stared unmercifully at the clean-cut face of the dapper gentleman.

His mouth twitched. "I wanted to see you."

"The feelings aren't mutual."

"I was hoping you might have a little corner left for me." He fidgeted nervously, wishing she would invite him in, unwelcome though he might be, away from inquisitive neighborly eyes.

"I had more than that four years ago," she snapped. "But did you really expect me to wait four years? I gave up after the first two."

"I was confused, Amy. But I still feel the same way about you. My folks—"

"Hang your folks!" She had found her voice, and her anger reached the boiling point. "You let them talk you into a lot of things, didn't you?"

He was red and uncomfortable. "Mother passed away two months ago, Amy."

That explained it. "Oh." She was unsympathetic. "You're a big boy now, is that it?"

"You're not being fair, Amy. I'm sorry about—"

"Sorry!" She cut him off as she screamed the word. *"Sorry!* Such a convenient word! And as far as being fair, just what gives you the right to accuse *me* of not being fair? I'm sorry, too, and I'll be sorry for the rest of my life! Go home to your apron strings. They must still be there somewhere."

She stooped down to pick up the things she had dropped, dismissing him in the action, but she froze again.

"What's the big idea?" Larry's face was burning with anger, and the veins in his neck stood out as he shouted at the man. He held Todd by the scruff of the neck, and his clenched fist was drawn back, ready for the blow.

"Get your hands off me!" Todd spoke with authority and he swore violently.

Larry's fist reflexed again, ready for action. He was not to be intimidated by either the man's size or his voice.

"Stop it!" Amy screamed. "Stop! Both of you! And get out of here! I don't want to see either of you, ever again!"

Larry reluctantly released his grip, and Todd Kenyon shrugged his shoulders to rearrange his disheveled clothes. He looked at the smaller man with disdain as he slowly, defiantly descended the steps. "We'll settle this another time, Amy," he assured her. "In *private!"*

Amy retreated to the haven of the living room. The shock of seeing Todd had made her forget Larry's coming. Not that she could have done much about it. She sank down on the sofa and covered her face with her hands.

"You rotten scum!" Larry's voice boomed. "Don't let me catch that dirty mug within ten miles of here, or I'll make hamburger out of it!'' He exhumed some choice words of his own.

Amy winced. Larry had a temper that was too close to the surface for comfort. Too close for his own good. She heard him walk to the doorway, as if uncertain where she had fled.

"I told you to go too," she said in a tight voice, not looking at him.

He put his hands on his hips. "Well, if that isn't a fine how-do-you-do!" He gave each word a lingering emphasis. "Come off it, Amy. Who do you think you're kidding? What's with you, anyway? I happened to *hear* what you said to him, and you weren't begging him to stay!"

"Go a-way!" she strained through clenched teeth. She sensed that his irritation was not as much with her as with the scene in which he had just taken part.

"I'm going. Have a nice vacation." He walked slowly to the front door but quickly and quietly retraced his steps when he heard her muffled sobs—quick breaths as she tried to conceal them.

He stood looking at her. "Do I, or don't I?" She shook her head in the negative, and he walked closer to where she was sitting. "Good gravy, Amy, do you think a louse like that could change the way I feel about you?" He motioned a thumb in the direction of the street as he sat next to her.

Larry leaned forward and rested his chin on a hand which encased his other fist. They stared at the floor. The minutes ticked by—five—ten—fifteen. Finally he turned to look at her. "Feel like talking about it?" She shook her head in the negative again and put a tear-dampened hanky to her nose. "It might help," he encouraged softly as he took a clean white hanky from his pocket and handed it to her.

"It's just that—" She stopped and wiped her eyes. "I'm sorry."

He was still looking at her. "Such a convenient word."

Her eyes flashed, but her anger quickly subsided when she saw his dimpled grin. "It's just that—"

His shoulder touched hers as he leaned back. He took her hand. "You said that before."

"I know," she sniffed. "It's just that I was going to tell you about him. But I didn't want you to find out this way."

He dimpled again. "Then this didn't happen. I'll go out and we'll start all over again." He stood up, still holding her hand. "What say we lam out of here?"

She gave him a tearful, grateful smile as she stood up. He turned toward the door. "Larry," she choked. He looked at her, and she hastily planted a kiss on his cheek.

"We-e-ll!" He gave a long, low whistle. "My rating is going

up!" He put his hands on her shoulders and looked into her eyes. "I love you, Amy. Very much."

"I know," softly, as if to reassure him that she had not forgotten.

It was wonderful to be at the shore in August. Amy felt quite fortunate that she had been able to obtain this time for her vacation. New Hope was completely unbearable during this blistering month.

It was lunch time as they pulled up in front of the picturesque white Cape Cod home, and the three-year-old twins came racing out to greet them. Becky reached her aunt first. Her sister was weighted down with their big, yellow tomcat which she had slung over her arm. She carried it as one would carry a fur piece, or perhaps a coat, and the hind legs just barely missed scraping the ground.

Tim Northrop, one of Dave's promising young architects, had given him to the girls when he was still a tiny ball of yellow fur, not too long after their "male" cat had blessed them with a litter of kittens. He had obtained permission from the elder Archers with the warning that he would get it back if the same mistake had been made about this one.

There had been quite a discussion as to a name for the pet. "Yaller cat." That's what Dave called him. "C'mon, yaller cat," he would say, excusing himself as he booted the big tom out of his chair. But the animal was a duplicate of Stevie Hastings' cat, so the twins were insistent that he be called by the same name, Tommy Tucker. No one else agreed, but the twins were adamant. Tim finally settled it. "Why don't you call him Tucker Too?" Tucker Too it was from then on.

Joy was well aware of the cause of her children's excitement and followed close on their heels. She was considerably trimmer than she was on Amy's first visit three years ago, but she had the same roundness of face and form which gave her a jocular appearance.

Amy was hugged by all three of them, then scolded by the two little girls for taking so long.

"Where's my handsome brother?" she asked as they went up the flagstone walk. Larry carried her suitcase and bandbox. Joy was laden down with her purse and packages. Amy's hands were full too. She had a difficult time keeping her balance with a lively miss tugging at either side.

"He'll be along any minute. He had to run down to the office for a couple of hours." Joy glanced down the road and did a double-take as their car came around the curve. "Here he comes now."

They waited until Dave got out, brief case in hand, and greeted them. There was no need for introductions. Joy and Dave had met Larry in New Hope when they had passed through on vacations and business trips. They were very fond of Larry and were anxiously waiting for Amy to make an announcement concerning the two of them. Although she seemed aloof in her manner toward him, there was nothing indifferent in his attitude toward her.

"I thought I'd be back before you got here," he said apologetically.

"You almost made it," laughed Amy. "Oh, it smells good here! You know, I get homesick for that salty air. And just think, Sunshine, I'm going to be here for two whole weeks!" She hugged her niece and kissed her again.

The little girl vigorously rubbed the spot where Amy had kissed her.

"Honey, why are you wiping it off?" Amy exclaimed.

"I'm not wiping it off, Aunt Amy." Rachel looked at her in surprise. "I'm rubbing it in!"

Amy laughed. "I'm sure glad about that! How's Tucker Too? My, he's getting almost as big as you." Amy had often said that when personalities were being handed out, Tucker Too forgot to get in line. He made no protests whatsoever about anything the children did to him.

After lunch they headed for the beach. The first sight of it was overwhelming. The cloudless tissue paper sky reflected itself in the azurite sea, scattering it with a million twinkling peridots.

"Oh, Larry," Amy bubbled excitedly, "isn't it beautiful here?"

"It sure is," he replied without taking his eyes from her.

They spent an hour battling the waves and they were exhausted as they stretched out on the blankets in the sun. The twins stayed close by with their pails and shovels, knowing the water was off limits unless someone big like Mommy or Daddy was with them. Larry helped them construct a giant sand castle. They ran back and forth with their pails, trying to fill the moat before the water seeped into the sand.

It was nearing suppertime when Larry suggested they go for another swim. His coaxing was to no avail.

"I'm all dry," Amy insisted, closing her eyes. The twins took care of that little detail, however, with just a suggestion from the red-haired young man. Two pails of cold ocean water were dumped onto her sunsoaked body. The shock of it took her breath away. Before she recovered enough to resist, Larry picked her up and carried her to the water where he unceremoniously dropped her. The twins were delighted. Larry was pleased. But Amy ran back to the blanket, shivering, and wrapped herself in it.

Larry took two big towels down to the water's edge, and, one at a time, doused the twins up and down, freeing them, to a degree, from the large quantity of sand engulfing them.

"Fatherly type," Dave mumbled when Larry was out of earshot.

He cast a quick look at Amy. "Pretty nice fellow." He was fishing.

"I know." She was uncommunicative.

Larry carried the twins up to the blanket after he had swathed them in the oversized towels. He and Dave each carried one back to the house on his shoulders.

Dave started a fire in the barbecue grill as soon as they returned while Joy scrubbed the potatoes, wrapped them in foil, and put them over the whitening coals to bake.

Amy took the little girls upstairs to bathe them. They were so happy to have her back with them they could scarcely let her out of their sight.

"Time to get out," she said as she pulled the stopper.

"No! No, Aunt Amy!" they screamed as they scrambled to get out of the slippery tub. They were panic-stricken. Amy was beside herself to know what caused the outburst.

Dave popped his head in. He had heard the commotion from his room. "Don't you know, Amy, you should never let the water out while they're still in the tub." He was trying to suppress a laugh. "They'll go right down the drain and come out in the ocean. Didn't you know that."

"David Archer! Did you tell them such a horrible thing?" She was trying to keep from laughing herself, but the girls were still clinging to her, not quite so amused by their near tragedy.

"I certainly did not. They figured it out all by themselves." He was still chuckling. "Hurry up, girls. Daddy has to get cleaned up too."

Amy helped them into their clean play clothes. When they joined their mother, most of the supper preparations had been completed. Amy and the little girls set the table on the patio.

When the potatoes were almost done, Joy summoned Dave who donned a ridiculously high chef's hat and large apron, and performed the art of broiling the steaks. Larry tried to help, but he was only allowed to hand the salt and pepper and long-handled fork to the cook.

"It's been a grand afternoon, Joy," Amy said as she and her sister-in-law picked up salads and other odds and ends to be carried out to the table. Grand, in spite of the way it started, she thought.

"Just perfect," Joy agreed. "Amy, you don't seem quite like yourself," she said as they went back into the kitchen. Amy had confided in her many times, so she felt no hesitancy about inquiring. "Is it Larry?"

"Not entirely." Amy smiled at her, glad the pressure was relieved. "He's just the greatest, Joy."

"We think so, too, Amy."

"I know you do. But I'm not sure how I feel about him. Sometimes it's yes, sometimes it's no, and other times I'm just all mixed up."

"We're all for him, Amy, but if you don't hear bells ringing, then it's just not right."

"Do you hear bells ringing, honey?" Dave appeared at the door just in time to hear her last remark.

"You bet I do," she exclaimed as she put her arms around his neck. Larry was right behind him, but he had not heard the prompting of Dave's question.

"That's 'cause you're punchy!" Dave kissed his wife on the nose, then picked up the large meat platter and started out the screen door.

"You're a meany, David Archer," she scolded as she followed him with a bowl for the potatoes. "You're getting to be an old married man!"

"You know what that makes you," he retorted from his vigil by the grill.

Amy and Larry followed with the remainder of the supplies, and they all sat down to the feast. They were ravenous after the activities of the afternoon.

"This is yummy, Joy," Amy said as she bit into the juicy meat.

"But don't forget who cooked it," scolded her brother.

"You didn't grow it, show-off! And, besides, I picked it out," argued Joy.

No one took their bantering seriously, but Larry tried to settle it. "It's the best, anyway. Let's give credit where credit is due." He stood up to make a speech. "Thank you, Joy, thank you, Dave, and thank you, Bossie." The twins squealed with delight at the thought of his thanking the cow. "And thank you, Amy," he added as an afterthought after he sat down.

"I'm afraid I didn't have a thing to do with it."

"Well, if it weren't for you, I wouldn't know your family. And if I didn't know your family, I wouldn't be here, would I?"

"Well, then, we probably wouldn't be having such good steak either," laughed Dave. His wife gave him a wilting glance which he ignored. "Any chance of your staying over, Larry? We have an empty sofa, you know."

"I surely would like to, but I have commitments for tomorrow. I could have made arrangements, but it's too late now. Thanks just the same."

"Like to go fishing? Next time you come, plan on staying longer and we'll spend the day on the water. You can leave Amy home if you like."

Larry winked at Amy, then turned to Dave. "Sounds great. Anything much biting now?"

"Oh, I caught a few postage stamps last Saturday," Dave said, using his own description of very small fish. "If you'd like to go after some real big stuff, we can go out to the tip of the Cape and take one of those cruises. I hear the tuna are biting real good now."

"I'm with you. Just let me know when."

They finished eating, and Dave began giving orders. He was very adept at it. "Now, we'll help you get this stuff cleaned up. Then while you're doing the dishes, I'll get the twins to bed." He stood up and groaned as he was reminded of the great quantity he had eaten. "Then we can sit out here and pitch a little woo. That suit you, Larry?"

Amy picked up a bowl in each hand and started for the house. She heard his reply before the screen door banged shut.

"Suits me fine. That is if you can get your sister to agree. She's not very co-operative, you know."

Amy looked at Joy in despair. "I'll speak to him," Joy promised.

Amy read a book to the children and unpacked some of her dresses. When she finally appeared, the men were actively engaged in a game of badminton.

Dave handed Joy a racquet. "Let's show these two what a good team we make, honey." He gave one to his sister. The darkness was closing in on them too quickly, however, and they had to abandon their sport. "We'll have to show them another time," he said reluctantly.

"Looks like rain," Amy mused as they sat on the patio.

"Alright, yaller cat," said Dave as he tipped the metal chair forward, "it's my turn to sit down. Yes, I was hoping to get a roof over this, but I guess it will have to wait till next summer." It was one of his projects, and he was proud of it.

"This house is like New York City—nice if it ever gets finished." Joy laughed as she poked him in the ribs. She was in complete accord with his home improvement plans since it kept him nearby on his days off. When the fishing bug bit him, which it often did, nothing could keep him at home. But then she went with him.

They talked for a long time as they listened to the breakers, the peepers in the bayberry bushes close by. The sea breezes stirred the foliage about them.

As the wind shifted, they heard the village clock strike eleven, and all were conscious that Larry should be on his way. He was reluctant to leave and made no motion to go, only mentioned several times that he should. It was almost midnight when he rose, stretched himself noisily and actually made an effort to be on his way. He reached his hand out to Amy.

"Walk to the car with me." He turned to the host and hostess. "Many thanks. I really enjoyed it."

"Come any time, Larry. The pleasure was ours. And don't forget that fishing trip."

Larry and Amy walked in silence, hand in hand, to the car. "I'm going to miss you, Amy." He had tried to get his vacation the same weeks as hers so they would be away from New Hope at the same time. He was leaving the next Friday to spend his vacation with his family. Thus, they would not be seeing each other for three weeks. It seemed like such a long time. Amy wondered if he would stick it out.

"Please try to forget him, Amy." Much as he hated leaving her, he was glad she would be away from New Hope for a while in view of the events of the morning. She had been withdrawn all day. "I wish you were going with me."

"You know I couldn't do that."

"People would talk," he mimicked. "People talk anyway. They have nothing better to do. What you really mean is Karen Winslow will talk, right?" He boiled over at the mention of her name. "She's poison, Amy, a real gossip factory. I don't give a hoot what she says, or anybody else for that matter. Why, she's a regular garbage truck. Picks up dirt one place and leaves it somewhere else. Only she's got it all over a garbage truck. She manufactures her own. She's no good for you, and I wish you'd stay away from her."

Amy did not respond to his tirade for she had heard it all before.

"That fellow's no good for you, either, and he just better not come snooping around again. I'll kill anyone who tries to take you away from me."

She laughed nervously and put her forefinger to his lips. "Hush, Larry. Don't talk so."

He grabbed her hand and kissed the restraining finger. As he pressured her hand, a warm, disturbing thrill ran through her, and involuntarily she moved a little closer to him. His other hand was on her shoulder, and he slowly drew her to him. He gathered her in his arms and held her close as he kissed her.

"I've wanted to do that for a long time, Amy," he whispered with his cheek against hers. He kissed her again, and this time her arms were around him. "Amy?" He looked at her longingly.

She did not answer. She was filled with trepidation, afraid of the sound of her own voice.

"People wouldn't talk if we were married, Amy. Please— " He hesitated as his promise crowded out all other thought against his will. "Never mind," he said, taking her hand as he opened the car door.

"I appreciate the ride," she said softly.

"Not half as much as I did," he said, squeezing her hand before he slid behind the wheel.

"Drive carefully, Larry. I'll miss you too."

The first week went by too quickly, the days not nearly long enough.

"Come on, Amy," Joy would say, "let's go to the beach."

"Good idea. But shouldn't we finish up here first?"

"It'll keep. Let's go."

"I never knew anybody who could drop a scrub bucket and mop as fast as you, Joy."

"I know," she giggled. "I just love work, Amy. I could sit and look at it all day."

Thus they passed the first week of Amy's vacation. She was getting as brown as a berry from her outdoor life. And after the first day or so, she managed to shrug off the feeling of apprehension that had been with her since her encounter with Todd Kenyon.

And she missed Larry. For the first time since she had known him, she missed him. All week she thought about the evening they had spent together, enjoying the quietness, the perfect serenity of the atmosphere.

Larry wanted a home of his own, and he wanted to share it with her. His was an unselfish love, and he was pleading with her to claim it.

By the end of the first week Amy had her answer. As far as the bells ringing, well, she was not at all sure about that. But she knew. She sat at the little desk in her room and tried to properly express the thoughts she wanted to put into words. There seemed to be no way.

Finally she wrote.

Dear Larry,
I'm asking. All my love,
Amy

He would understand. She addressed the envelope to his hometown of Farmingtown, Pennsylvania. She did not have a complete address but it was a small town, and all the residents would know the Spencer family.

It was Friday evening. She would mail it when they went to town the next day.

Chapter 18

AT THE SAME MOMENT, thousands of miles away, another letter was being penned. Although it bore no similarity in construction, there was a resemblance in purpose, conversely so.

"Dear Amy, . . ."

The young man sat for many minutes with a blank sheet of paper before him, blank save for these two words he had written neatly at the top. He was having a difficult time trying to express his sentiments on paper and tried to imagine himself back in his own living room with the late afternoon sun creating a frame for the lovely face amongst the shadows. But he was here in another hemisphere, on the opposite side of the globe, and, after all, that was an important component in this epistle which had not yet been constructed.

His quiet room in this oriental abode had been home to him for almost two years, since he left the linguistic school in Tokyo. Propped up before him on the desk stood a small photograph of a beautiful fair-haired girl in a twilight blue gown, the color that matched her eyes.

Dear Amy. He looked at the little picture and read the brief words over again. Then he began his difficult task.

> Dear Amy,
>
> No doubt my writing to you after almost three years of virtual silence will have a surprising effect on you. I do hope you have kept informed on the work here, however, for I have coveted your prayers. I am certain you have been in receipt of our form letters each month.
>
> As a matter of fact, I, too, stand in awe of myself for being so presumptuous as to approach you through this medium for I find it much easier to express myself when I can see the one to whom I am speaking.

Do you remember that day when you told me how you enjoyed the challenge put forth by serving the Lord? It *was* challenging there in New Hope, but I wish you were able to witness personally some of the experiences I have had in the Master's service here. They have been more than challenging.

If you were here, Amy, I would first introduce you to Josh. This eleven-year-old boy has been living with us for a couple of years since his mother was killed in an automobile accident. As a result of this tragic accident, Josh was badly crippled. The sadness caused by his great loss was deep, only to be made harder to bear when we learned soon after that he would never walk again. He had every reason to give up for his life seemed worthless. But his is a determined spirit, and he has not resigned himself to his fate.

You are probably thinking Joshua is a mighty strange name for an oriental boy, but you see, it is a name we missionaries have given him for the sunshine he brings us. But unlike the Joshua in the Bible who stopped the sun for a day, our Joshua gives us perpetual sunshine! Josh has been accomplishing great things for the Lord, and in some ways much more than we can do. The many friends who come to visit him each day come with despair in their hearts as they wonder what they can do, what they can say to cheer him. But they are the ones who are encouraged, for Josh radiates the love of the Saviour. Many boys and girls, men and women have been born again because of his steadfastness.

Then I would have you meet another dear saint of God, a young woman who endured unbearable, unimaginative cruelty from her family because of her belief. She was rooted in it and stood firm, however, and one by one her adversaries have yielded to the voice of the Holy Spirit. The last one, the "ojiisan" – her withered old grandfather, accepted Christ as his Saviour just two days ago. He and his wife, "obaasan" had clung tenaciously to their ancestral worship, so it was a time of rejoicing for all when they were at last united in the Christian faith.

So you see, Amy, the field is white unto harvest. I could go on and on, but time does not permit.

I've thought about you constantly and must confess, when I left New Hope, I hardly dared believe you would remain unattached until my return. But now that the time is drawing near for my first furlough (another year seems not long in relation to the time I have already spent here) I felt the necessity of writing to you, something I am certain I should have done long ago.

Have you considered the mission field? "The harvest truly is plenteous, but the laborers are few." I am praying that the

Lord of the harvest will lay this upon your heart, for should He give you a burden for the people of Japan, I would consider it a privilege to have you join us here in this labor of love.

In His service,
Dan

Josh had been watching from the bed where Dan had propped him, but now he was fast asleep. He did not look good. His face was too pale and for some reason he had been losing weight. Dan hoped to be able to take him to the States with him next year if the adoption could be arranged in that time. There were so many complications. Perhaps it was not God's will. But surely the doctors there could do something for him. He would take Josh to the best doctors, the best hospital.

How would Amy feel about adopting a Japanese boy, a half-breed at that? He had not considered the possibility of her rejecting the idea. She would love these people as he did.

Elaine had been on his back constantly, and now at last he could tell her he had written to Amy. But it was not his sister's prodding that had finally moved him.

"Dear Son," his mother had written. "We're so thankful for the fruit abounding to your account. The Lord is good. We are with you always in our prayers."

When Louise Sanderford had penned these words to her son, she had been filled with divine love and thanksgiving to think of the fruitful way God had been using him. His spiritual orchard was thriving, and now his fruit was bearing fruit of its own. Her heart was filled to overflowing.

"I do wish He would supply you with an helpmeet though," she had gone on, "for I fear you are so taken up with your duties you have completely neglected your personal life. I would feel better if I knew you had someone to take care of you.

"It looks as if Amy and Larry might be getting ready to take the big step. They make a lovely couple, but I do pray it is right for them. I would not wonder at all except that Amy herself has been wondering."

She had gone on to tell about the activities in New Hope, but he had been conscious of only the first part of her letter.

Had Elaine talked to her? No, giving a confidence to Elaine was like sealing it in cement. Was it merely coincidence that his mother had given him this advice and then, almost in the same breath mentioned Amy? It must be.

He read his own letter to Amy, reread it and put it in the envelope. It was a far cry from what he wanted to say, but those things could not be put on paper. They would have to wait, at least until he knew she was in alliance with him in his calling. But surely this would transmit to her the desperate needs of these people, and more indirectly, the needs of one, Dan Sanderford. He addressed the envelope and was putting the stamp on it when Laura Sherman appeared at the door.

"Telephone call for you, Dan." She tried to sound calm, but the call itself was enough to cause alarm. "From the United States," she added hesitantly.

Dan put the letter in his inside breast pocket, at the same time casting a troubled look at the sleeping boy.

"I'll stay with him, Dan. Go ahead." She could not help noting the picture on the desk, surmising the connection between it and the envelope Dan had put in his pocket.

The home was adjacent to the mission station which housed the church sanctuary, Sunday school rooms and offices. Dan ran to the front office where the telephone was located.

He had not talked to anyone at home since he had been here. Why now? What possible event could have prompted anyone to call just now?

He picked up the receiver and heard the long-distance operator in her formal voice, "I have a long-distance call for Reverend Daniel Sanderford."

"Yes. Yes, this is he, operator," he said impatiently.

"Go ahead, please."

The connection was bad, but he immediately recognized the familiar voice of his sister. He was disturbed by the tremor in her voice.

Louise Sanderford was dead.

The telephone call came from Elaine on Sunday morning as Amy was about to leave for church with Dave and his family.

That Sunday morning had dawned bright and clear. When it came near time to leave for church, however, the usually brisk moving air had turned heavy and humid.

As Amy fastened the belt of her lemon-colored cotton, she was trying to imagine Larry's reaction when he received her note, probably tomorrow morning. There had been moments during the preceding day when she had felt misgivings. Maybe she should not have written it. But didn't every girl feel some foreboding when contemplating the all-important step?

Becky stood beside her with her back toward her aunt, a silent request to have her dress buttoned and her sash tied. Amy wordlessly condescended, then brushed her niece's silky dark tresses. The child scampered away to get her purse and tiny Bible even though she was unable to read. She had to be like Daddy. Rachel came in, and they went through the same procedure.

Amy brushed her own hair, cast an approving glance in the full-length mirror in the hall, then joined her brother in the living room where he was going over his lesson.

Dave taught a class of teen-age boys, and he sometimes expressed the wish that they had been entrusted to the care of someone more capable than he, someone more patient.

"Dave?"

He marked the place with his forefinger and looked up.

"I've made up my mind. I wrote a letter to Larry—"

"I'm glad, Amy. It's about time, I might add. But your happiness overwhelms me!"

She laughed. "I *am* happy about it."

"He's a great guy. I know he'll make you happy. He must be out in Pennsylvania now, isn't he? I'll bet you'll see him back here just as soon as he gets that letter!" He smiled and winked at his sister.

The twins stood before him, each with an outstretched hand, palm upwards. They had learned the blessedness of stewardship at an early age.

Having extinguished the heat under the partially cooked meat and vegetables, Joy breezed in from the kitchen. This was the signal to be on their way.

"Looks like we're going to be preparing for a wedding, honey," Dave exclaimed to his wife.

"Oh, Amy, I'm so glad!" She hugged her as she squealed with delight. "When is it going to be?"

Amy laughed. "I don't know yet. In fact, Larry doesn't know either." Joy gave her a puzzled look. "I just wrote to him," she went on to explain.

Dave was about to close the door behind them when the telephone rang. He paused as if contemplating the possibility of ignoring it. "It's for you, Amy." It was a simple statement.

But Amy's face registered the alarm she felt. What should be frightening about a telephone call? Maybe it was Larry. But he would not have received her letter yet.

"It's from New Hope." It would not be Larry.

"Hello." Amy's voice trembled.

"Amy—" It was Elaine's voice, but it did not seem like Elaine behind it.

Amy could scarcely keep from screaming into the receiver. "Lainey, what is it?"

"Mother — " Elaine's voice broke again.

Amy felt helpless as she heard Mark take the phone from his wife. "Amy," he started. It was no easier for him. "Mother Sanderford has gone to be with the Lord." There was no sound from either end. "Amy, are you there?" Mark finally asked.

She was there, but she was powerless to speak, her visage drained of any color. Her knees gave out from under her, and as she sat down, Dave grabbed the instrument before it fell to the floor. He talked briefly with Mark and hung up.

"No, no, no, no," Amy cried as Dave tried to console her. Joy came in after putting the children in the car, and he gave her a brief explanation.

"I can't go to church." She wiped her eyes, but it did not help. The tears would not stop. "I've got to go back. Dave, please call the station. See what time I can get a train."

The next one was at five after one. That would give them just enough time to get her to the station after church.

"I'll stay with you, Amy," Joy offered.

"I'll be fine, Joy. You go ahead."

The house was unbearably quiet as she went about her packing. She had assured them over and over that she would be all right, but now she wished she had let Joy stay with her. Time was dead weight. She put her suitcase on the front walk near the drive, then busied herself with the breakfast dishes. She set the table for their dinner.

She was standing beside her belongings when they drove up. Joy and the girls got out, said good-by, and she got in. Dave backed out without saying a word as the twins watched sadly. They were heartbroken, but sensing that something was amiss, they kept back their tears.

The ride to New Hope was interminable, and it was almost four o'clock when the train finally pulled into the station. She picked up a discarded newspaper from a vacant bench and turned to the obituary column. As she saw the name of her dear friend in print, the tears came close to spilling over again. It made it so final.

"Friends may call from 2:00 to 4:00 and 7:00 to 9:00 on Sunday and Monday."

Amy gave the name and address of the funeral parlor to the cab driver. It had been discomfiting at first that she had not been able to make it by four o'clock. But surely they would not mind if she stayed only a minute. It would give her a chance to be alone with her sorrow without inquisitive eyes upon her.

Amy put her bag in an inconspicuous spot in the huge entryway and went into the spacious room which the gentleman had indicated.

She was glad she had had foresight to change into the Navy silk dress she now wore. Yellow was much too gay.

Paul was there, his tall form bent over in remorse. Just Paul. As Amy walked with eyes downcast over the thickly carpeted floor, she was glad no one else was there.

The carpet strangely reminded her of placid water, uninterrupted by color, pattern or feeling. The pungent fragrance of the flowers was depressing. The source of their growth had been cut off, and soon they would be dead too.

"Hello, Amy."

She had but a half dozen steps to go when the voice intruded on her meditations and caused her to look up in surprise to see—

"Dan!"

The word was hardly an audible whisper, yet it seemed she had shouted it. She had not considered the remotest possibility of his getting home. Yet she should have known—

He seemed taller, his eyes darker and more serious, his face thinner. "Is it really you?" She found it hard to comprehend what her eyes told her was true.

But the joy of seeing him did not lessen the anguish of losing her friend. She stepped closer to the casket. Uncontrollable sobs shook her.

Dan watched her patiently, understandingly, but there were no tears in his eyes. They were inside. He waited until hers subsided before he spoke. His voice was soft, seasoned with experience. "I think we'd better go now, Amy."

He carried her bag to his sister's car. Amy opened the door before he had time to put it down. It was no time for formality. He got in but made no motion to start the motor.

"It's good to see you, Amy."

"I'm so glad you were able to come home, Dan. I never dreamed you would be able. It wasn't time, was it?"

"No. I'll be going back in two or three weeks. Mother wanted to see me. I couldn't refuse."

Amy registered her surprise as she looked at him. "You mean you were able to talk with her before—" She faltered. "Tell me about it, Dan."

"There's not much to tell. It all happened so fast. Elaine called me Friday evening. I took a jet to Frisco the same night, another jet to New York. Mark was waiting for me at Kennedy Airport, and I was here before noon yesterday. Course there's a time difference there—" But that was irrelevant. "I'm thankful for telephones and jet propulsion. I was able to spend several hours with her."

"I'm glad. Where was it? And what time?"

"At home. Late yesterday afternoon. It was quite an upsetting time. I hope you understand why Lainey didn't call you sooner." The quiet, torrid afternoon, the incomprehensible thing which had so recently taken place made the past seem like a dream, the future unreal. "Why do these things have to happen, Dan? She had so much to live for." She knew he could give her no better explanation than she already knew.

"It's hard to say, but all the more reason we should be ready."

"She meant a great deal to me, you know."

"I know, Amy. But she is in a far better place. It's only for ourselves we grieve."

She thought about this as her eyes filled with tears again. "May I go back to the house with you for a few minutes? I'd like to see Elaine."

He acquiesced by starting the motor. They made no attempt at conversation during the ride, and although Dan remembered the letter in his pocket, he made no allusion to it. He was glad now that he had not mailed it, only because it would be a much simpler matter to express himself verbally. He would have to wait for an opportune time though, and certainly not now when their hearts were so filled with sadness.

Paul was sitting on the edge of a big chair in the living room. He was hunched over with his elbows on his knees, staring into the empty fireplace.

"I'm so sorry, Paul," Amy said softly as she laid her hand on his arm in condolence.

He put his face in his hands and cried like a baby. Paul, the football hero; Paul, the practical joker; Paul, the harlequin. Paul, the grief-stricken little boy. She had never seen him this way. His heart was torn in two.

"Pull yourself together, fella," Dan said, putting his hand on the large, trembling shoulder. Dan, their strength, thought Amy.

Elaine came in, her face strained and red from the endless flow of tears. Amy put her arms around her, and together they poured out their hearts.

"Lainey, if I had only known, I never would have left." It was so difficult to talk.

"I know, Amy. You couldn't have known any more than the rest of us. We would have called you sooner if we had known she had such a short time left."

"I know that, Elaine. It's been a terrible shock."

Elaine went on as if thinking aloud. "She seemed to be content to go after Dan came."

The old house seemed a strange place, for although it had been subject to many a change during the passing years since Amy had come to know it, it would never again be the same. Its loved ones had lost their most precious earthly possession, and the pain was too deep for words to express. But underneath were the everlasting arms.

The next day or so, Amy stood by to help in any way she could. She took care of little Mark most of the time so that the others might be free. There was a steady stream of visitors coming and going intermittently. It was an exhausting ordeal, but so good to have friends at such a time.

During the time before the funeral, Dan watched Amy constantly, watched and hoped for a sign, just a faint indication that she considered him more than a friend. But there was none. When a heart is anxious, seeking, the waiting game is never devoid of the excitement of a furtive glance met unexpectedly or of the nearness of one's secret love without the foreknowledge of that nearness.

His own heart, weighted down with the burden of his loss, needed the soothing balm of her loving hand which, in a measure, could have lifted and eased the deep pain. There was nothing in Amy's expression or action to give him encouragement.

The service was the most heartbreaking event Amy could remember ever having witnessed. But the scene at the grave tore her very heart out. "God Be With You Till We Meet Again," was the song that drifted softly from the little chapel nestled back under the trees. And as the body of this dear one was being lowered into the cold ground, Paul and Judy clung to each other as they tried in vain to remove the void created by the painful loss. Elaine collapsed, and if Mark had not been there to hold her up, she would have been completely helpless. Mark, too, was almost overcome with grief. But Dan stood alone, his head bowed, his shoulders stooped.

Their eyes met briefly. Were his eyes glassy, or was it her own tears distorting her vision? If only he would cry, it would make it so much easier for him.

Amy had a sudden impulse to go stand beside him, to comfort him. But she could not.

Chapter 19

THE DAYS WERE slipping by, and Dan had no opportunity to talk to Amy about the things his letter had been meant to express. He and Paul had tied themselves down with a myriad of legalities so that their sister might be spared the long, drawn-out procedures. He spent a great deal of time on the road, either to see various members of the mission board or to speak at one of the churches nearby. He tried to call her several times to see if she might accompany him on one of the evening trips, but he had been unsuccessful in reaching her, disappointingly so.

His duties were not easy ones, having so recently been through deep waters, but, nevertheless, the tasks were his. Had he not obtained power from on high it would have been a simple matter to excuse himself from the mission he had been called upon to fulfill. On the exterior he was a vessel of strength, a laborer worthy of his hire, a spiritual dynamo – and he *was* all of these. But such qualities were not attainable through personality or learning. In fact, these attributes were unconsciously his. They were gifts bestowed upon him through sweat drops of prayer, untiring hours of meditation in God's Word. His daily devotions were a treasure-trove of unlimited blessing, available through no other source.

Dan was reluctant to leave each day, for it meant that Elaine would have to spend too many hours in the big lonely house, Mark being away most of each day. Little Mark, or Chip, as Dan called him, helped to keep her occupied, but emptiness seemed to fill the place, every room, every drawer, every nook. At times, the silence screamed at them, not wanting them to forget the vacant chair, the quiet sewing machine, the unoccupied slippers still sitting beside the bed. Elaine wanted to prolong the disposal of her mother's possessions, and although Dan did not condone the decision, he was silently agreeable.

"Mark, why don't you take Elaine away for a while?" Dan had

asked his brother-in-law a day or so after the funeral.

"I had thought about it, Dan. Are you sure you wouldn't mind?"

"Certainly not. I'm going to be home very little anyway. I think it would do her a lot of good, even if it's only for a few days."

So Mark, Elaine, and the baby had gone, and when they returned two weeks later, Dan was not as certain it had been the right thing to do. But Elaine was strong, the source of her strength coming from a lifelong dependence upon her Heavenly Father. She had placed herself in the hollow of His hand and had willingly submitted to the leading of His will. Through this time of trial she had come to lean more heavily upon the Lord. Her troubled heart was soothed by His gentle hand.

It was through God's hand they had been saddened, through this same hand they had been strengthened, only to find they had been made more stalwart through their undoing.

Amy wondered why she did not see Dan during those weeks he was to remain at home, why she did not hear of his departure when that time had elapsed, but she felt relieved that he was gone. She was in such a state of confusion that she did not know why she should feel so at his leaving, nor did she recognize it as the same feeling she had experienced the first time he left three years ago. It was strange though, that he had not said good-by. In fact, the only contact she had had with him since the funeral was a note she had received from him several days after. At first she had been puzzled.

"Dear Amy," it said in his neat, mannish scrawl. "It disappoints me no end to have to break our date, but I'm sure you will understand. Of course when we made the date, we had no idea of the circumstances which would bring me home, nor that the first Saturday would be such a sad one. I have not forgotten. With apologies, Dan." She remembered. She had forgotten.

Larry returned to his family the day after the funeral without questioning Amy's brief note which she was certain he would have received before he left his home to come to New Hope. He had been most insistent that she return to Ocean Point for the remainder of her vacation but had finally given up pleading with her when her stubbornness had turned to annoyance. She wanted to be with Elaine, to be near if they needed her. But as it turned out, Mark took Elaine to be with his folks for two weeks. It was good for Elaine, but Amy could not understand her leaving when Dan was to be home for such a short time. Unless, of course, Dan had gone, too.

Amy was lonely. She was glad when it came time to return to work the following Monday.

"I see Dan Sanderford is home," Karen Winslow said to her

the first day she was back. Karen was in one of her better humors.

"Yes. His mother died."

"I heard. That's rough. They were very close, weren't they?"

"Indeed they were. She meant an awful lot to me too." Amy's eyes filled with tears. The wound was still too fresh.

"I didn't know that. I'm sorry. How long will Dan be home?"

"Another week or two, I guess. I haven't seen him since the funeral."

But Karen's rare pleasantries later turned to acidity, and she found some great, peculiar pleasure in adding to Amy's sorrow.

"Two weeks isn't a very long time, Amy," Karen said, working on a long shot. "Better get while the gettin's good. He's some catch, Amy. Better shift into high gear!"

Amy completely ignored her. She had not the endurance for rebuttal. That night she prayed that the Lord would give her relief from the lashing, at least until she might recover her spiritual footing. But they continued, more destructive than ever. Amy found it increasingly difficult to keep patience with the girl. Along with her vicious acerbities, Karen had instigated an office gossip line, and the numerous tales concerning Amy and Larry, although few of them ever reached their ears, had caused the raising of eyebrows and the wagging of tongues.

Larry returned at the end of his two weeks, and the consternation Amy felt from his lack of reference to the letter contributed to her befuddlement.

Four weeks after the posting of the letter, Mrs. Martin handed her the mail, and there, on the top, in her own familiar handwriting was, "Mr. Lawrence Spencer, Farmingtown, Pennsylvania." Across the top of it and partly obscuring the return address was the Post Office stamp with its finger pointing to Amy's name and address and the words, "Return to Sender." There was a list of reasons from which to choose. A check had been made where it said "Insufficient Address." She tore the letter to bits.

That was a Saturday, four weeks after Dan's return.

Then, without warning, he was there.

"Why, I thought you were a million miles away, Dan!" she exclaimed in surprise the next morning before the worship service.

"Not quite so far, Amy," he smiled. "I've been away the last two Sundays. And then I've had a lot of legal ends to get tied up so Lainey and Paul wouldn't have to take care of it all."

"But I thought you were to be home three weeks, at the most."

"Oh, hadn't you heard? The board decided I should take my furlough now. They have plenty of field work for me to take care of—and I mean plenty!" His voice expressed an impatient desire to return to his beloved new home.

Amy was dumbfounded. She also felt a combination of alarm, fear, and strangely enough, happiness. The agitation caused by these mixed emotions resulted in self-inflicted chastisement. She kept her feelings to herself.

The days slipped into weeks, the weeks into months, and Amy slipped into a restlessness which bordered on depression. Such mental disquietude had become unknown in her life since she had become a Christian, and the fact that it was becoming an everyday experience was more than disturbing. It was significant that her lack of enthusiasm for the things once important to her had begun simultaneously with the occurrence of two events: the appearance of Todd Kenyon, and then just a week later, Aunt Louise's death. She attributed her retrogressive state on those two events alone.

"You've got to snap out of it, Amy," Larry said to her one day just after Thanksgiving. He had noticed her change of attitude. She had known he would. "We all thought a lot of Mrs. Sanderford," he said kindly, "but you can't let yourself get run down this way. You've got to look ahead."

"I know you're right, Larry. I'm trying."

"But if it's that bloke who's got you upset – well, don't let him. I'll take care of him if he shows up. I'll tear him to pieces!"

There were times like these when the situation seemed *status quo,* and Amy came close to telling him what she had meant to express in her note, but she bit her tongue. Inevitably, the dissonance which had become an unwelcome component of her inner self flowed over her in sickening waves. She found herself leaning more and more upon Larry even though they were growing consistently apart. No matter how long she kept him waiting, she could not accept his proposal with this eating away inside her. This atrophy was destroying her very purpose of existence – her desire to serve the Lord.

Where she had known peace there was unrest; defeat had taken the place of victory; resignation had replaced challenge; enthusiasm had been overcome by listlessness.

After her one conversation with Dan, Elaine had told her that he was traveling through the south and southwest and would be gone some months. She couldn't care less.

The pain of the great loss produced a hopeless case of "cause and effect" for had she been able to confer with the older woman on the discord of her life, perhaps she could have obtained the stamina she so badly needed to cope with it. But the cause was, in part, the death, and the effect could not be relieved because of it.

Another uprooting element in the overall chain of events was Elaine's sweetness, her submission to God's will, for was not the loss harder on her than it possibly could be on anyone else? Amy knew that she had not experienced the depths of heartbreak that Elaine had gone through. And although the boys' sorrow was deep, they had, in effect, broken the home ties and were much more prepared to live independently from that upon which they had once depended for their very existence.

There had been a bond between Elaine and her mother, the strength of which would have been apparent only to those who knew them well. It was a mother-daughter relationship which in no way interferred with that of husband and wife. Louise Sanderford had often said that her home belonged to Elaine and Mark that they might provide a home for Dan and Paul when they were on furlough. Perhaps she had foreseen that for which the children had been totally unprepared.

One bright spot on Amy's limited horizon was the new baby Joy and Dave were expecting the latter part of May. They had told her the good news as soon as they knew it themselves, and she had immediately put in her bid for the last week in May and the first in June for her vacation. Although it was still months away, she was extremely anxious for the time to come so that she might get away from this place, even for that short a time. But the days dragged into more weeks, and the weeks into more months.

"I wish I hadn't made that promise to you, Amy," Larry commented sadly, knowing he was breaking it in making this statement.

Along with everyone and everything else, he was beginning to irritate her. She tried to be amiable, but of late it seemed she was incapable of bringing anything but misery upon any element with which she came in contact, and this included Larry. Especially Larry.

"I'm sorry." She said it flatly. Just words, that's all they were. A convenient expression.

"Things never seem to get better for me, do they?"

"For me either. I guess it was never meant to be."

"I don't believe that."

"I wish you would go."

She had been cruel, but not intentionally so. He left without a word. He would be back. He always came back.

In due course, Christmas came. And suddenly, when Amy returned from Ocean Point, he was there. Day after day, week after week, though not always in visible form, Dan was there. Her heart sang. It had a disconcerting effect on her, however, for underlying this strange happiness was the same depression she had known since his return from Japan. She only admitted that fact since it was correlated with Aunt Louise's death and the timely appearance of an unwanted suitor. They were the real cause of her trouble, not Dan.

After the holidays she went on a number of local trips with him, short trips which extended to a radius of perhaps a hundred miles of New Hope. Larry was always present, and often Mark and Elaine accompanied him, sometimes other of the young people.

Amy was enjoying these trips. The presence of a certain young man seemed as a solvent to her cold heart. Or was it the fellowship of these fine friends? They construed games to help pass the miles away, each trying to stump the other with a question from the Bible, and when they tired of that, they joined in the singing of hymns, delighting in the beautiful blend of their voices as they joined in four-part harmony.

Or perchance these occasions afforded a respite from the steady pounding she had been enduring as if in defiance to herself. She persistently tried to assure herself that everything was hunky-dory. She had created a front, a retaining wall to conceal her lack of power, but if it were to be removed, she would be revealed as an unhappy, disconsolate creature.

When Dan returned Christmas Eve, Elaine, Mark, and Paul were putting the finishing touches on the tree. He was pleased to see that things were proceeding much as they normally would have. It was good they were all together this first Christmas without their mother. Neither Paul nor Dan would be home for the next four to come.

"I'm glad you're home, Danny. I don't know how I would have survived. And do you know, it's good you and Paul are leaving about the same time. Then your furloughs should fall together, shouldn't they? I'm going to miss you both though." She had been looking forward to their next return, and this last statement brought her close to tears.

She poured coffee and she, Mark, and Dan sat at the kitchen table. Paul was putting on his overcoat.

"Yes, I thought about that too. It'll be good to get together every four years, won't it? Compare the brilliance of our children and all that, huh?"

Paul and Judy were to be married in July, soon after graduation. If all went as scheduled, they would be ready to leave for Ecuador by late fall.

"Aren't you having coffee with us, Paul?" Elaine asked.

"Not this time. Say, Ichabod," he said, turning to Dan, "you wouldn't mind if I skipped out for an hour or so, would you? Have a little business to talk over with Judy."

"Go ahead, Ebenezer. It wouldn't do any good for me to mind anyway, would it, sport?"

Dan knew, as did the others, that in his pocket his brother carried a little circlet of gold highlighted by a large, sparkling stone. Paul was anxious to put it where it belonged that their betrothal might be made official. Paul chuckled as he buttoned his coat.

"Danny," Elaine said as she looked at her husband who was bursting with pride, "we're going to have another baby."

"Say, that's swell!"

"I must admit, that wasn't my first reaction since little Mark is so young. But I will be getting the use out of my maternity clothes!"

"Well, you sure aren't wasting any time! But I think it's just great. Going to name this one after me?"

"No. Jonathan, if it's a boy. We haven't decided on a girl's name."

"We're leaving your name for your first son," Mark said.

"That's a shame. Such a nice name going to waste." His eyes twinkled.

"Well, they'd have to have twins then, so they could name one of them after me!" Paul called as he sailed out the door, slamming it behind him.

"Dan, you haven't talked to Amy, have you?" Elaine plunged into this disturbing subject as if she had been waiting for her younger brother to leave. She did not mince words.

"No."

"Why?"

"I wrote her a letter."

"Well, hallelujah!" she exclaimed, pleased that at last he had made some attempt at courting his love. "And?"

"Lainey, you—" He sighed. "I never mailed it."

"Dan—" She elongated the word, and it held a scolding tone.

"I wrote it the night you called me, Lainey. Carried it all the way home with me too. I tore it up a few days ago."

"I wish I had found it. I would have mailed it," she continued to berate. "And when are you going to talk to her?" She wanted a definite answer.

"When the right time comes."

"Dan, you're going to have to *make* the right time. Something is troubling Amy, and sure as shootin', it's you." She was emphatic.

"You're right about something bothering her, but I'm not so certain I'm the cause."

"Well, I am. I've been watching her these past few months, Danny, and every time your name is mentioned she suddenly loses interest in the conversation. She makes such an effort to show her lack of interest in you, why, Danny, it's as plain as the nose on your face."

He smiled and touched the straight line of his nose with the tips of his fingers. "You'd make a wonderful detective, Elaine."

His implication did not by-pass her eagle eyes. "Meaning I'm nosy? Well, maybe so, but I don't want you to get hurt. Or Amy. Or Larry either. But I fear someone will be before this is over. I guess I am a busybody, but I'd prefer to call my fault sentimentality, if you will."

"Okay, I will," Dan said with a smile of appreciation.

Mark was taking it all in. The topic was not news to him. Amy and Dan had been on their prayer list since his wife first suspected her brother's unspoken love for the girl.

"Dan," Mark said in his deep resonant voice, "to all appearances, Amy was content before you came on the scene. At least she tried to make us think she was. But then you came and upset the applecart!"

"I'm not quite so convinced."

"I am. But I wasn't until a week or so ago."

Dan's dark brown eyes searched Mark's face for an explanation. "And?"

"Amy went upstairs to put the baby in his crib, but she didn't know I was in our room, Dan, and I watched her. She stood by your door, just looking in for a couple of minutes—"

"I hope it was tidy." Dan chuckled.

"She finally went in, and honestly, Dan, you would have thought she was walking on holy ground. She looked around for a while, just touching things, and then picked up your little old Bible from the dresser and sat in your chair leafing through it."

His very first Bible. Mother and Dad had given it to him for his fifth birthday. Dan had a sudden impulse to laugh. He wished he had caught her! How flustered she would have been! And how the color would have rushed to her cheeks!

Mark caught Dan's reaction even though he had suppressed the impulse.

"It wasn't funny, Dan. If you had seen her you wouldn't think it was funny at all. She was still holding the baby, and he began to get restless so she put the Bible aside and rocked him. I thought surely she would see me but she didn't. She was crying, Dan. Not so you could hear her, but the tears just streamed down her face."

"She has missed Mother—"

"Then why didn't she go into your mother's room and cry? No, Dan, I'm convinced. I do believe she would have married Larry by this time though if you hadn't upset things."

"Not if she were meant for me."

"Dan," he chided, "don't you believe that is the reason a lot of Christians are unhappy? They go their own way, follow their own wills, and the sad part of it is, there are so many others hurt by their foolishness. The Lord permits them to do as they want, but a life that's all mixed up with human desires is a hard one to straighten out, especially where marriage is concerned."

"I know you're right, Mark, but I can't force the issue. I'm quite certain it's not me she's avoiding. Her willingness to go to the mission field has to stem from her love for the Lord – not for me."

Elaine had graciously let the men take over the conversation, but she could not be still any longer. "I know that, Danny, but Amy is in a spiritual slump, and I'm afraid she will do something she might regret just to try to get out of it. That miserable Karen Winslow hasn't been doing anything to help either. The witch!"

"Now, now, Elaine, let's be charitable. I've heard about that though. She was giving Amy a rough time before I left the office."

"It's only recently that Amy has allowed Karen to bother her."

Mark voiced his agreement. "She was on the mountaintop for so long that when she fell, she really took a tumble. She needs our prayers."

"Yes. And I do appreciate your prayers. Keep it up, will you?"

This had taken place Christmas Eve, and here it was past the middle of May already. Dan had prayed earnestly that the Lord would open Amy's heart, that she would share his burden for the people of Japan. It was for this reason he had asked her to go on many speaking engagements with him, hoping the repeated message of the great commission would eventually stir her heart, but she seemed further from responding with each telling. Had her cold heart become a stone that it was no longer pliable under the hands of the Potter? Clay that was useless in the molding and making for His use?

Dan was bewildered. But he had left it in God's hands, and he would accept His will, unreasonable though it may seem to his mortal mind. He knew that God would solve his problem – or dissolve it.

He was aware that Amy would be leaving soon for her vacation, and time *was* getting short. By the end of August he would be on his way back to his beloved people, so he must not put this off any longer.

It was late Thursday afternoon. He had to go to Brookdale that evening. In fact, he should be leaving in an hour or so. Without actually forming the idea in his mind, Dan found himself dialing Amy's number. He knew it by heart.

It would be an ideal time; it was such a pleasant ride. If he could just arrange to take her without feeling obligated to ask Larry or any of the others. Elaine and Mark would understand. His sister would rather not ride too much any more, anyway. But how could he gracefully ask Amy without suggesting she invite Larry? This was a problem he would have to work out.

He was about to hang up when he heard Mrs. Martin's cheerful voice at the other end. He thought he detected a chill when he told her who was calling. He waited patiently for Amy to come.

Mrs. Martin did not like this Dan fellow. And she did not like the stranger who had appeared some months ago. He had come one evening when Amy was out, and when she had told Amy about him later, she had learned that he had returned. She did not imagine the worried look she had seen in the girl's eyes. Mrs. Martin did not like anything that might disrupt the romance between her Amy and Larry. She wished she did not have to summon her to the phone.

Chapter 20

SPRING HAD COME. Winter had disappeared, so spring had no alternative but to follow in monotonous succession. Winter's departure had forced its arrival, but it bore a striking contrast to that of the previous year. It did not bring with it the exuberance which had set that one apart from all the others they had known.

Its coming did not delight Amy. She was completely oblivious to the changing of the seasons, to the new songs the birds were singing, to the freshness of the earth. The vacuum in which she was engulfed created a void, a lack of sensitivity to the atmosphere about it.

The situation at the office was unbearable. Karen's lies had increased maliciously until Amy had reached the point where she had no resistance. Up until a few days ago, the attack had been only verbal and Amy had found it relatively easy to ignore. But earlier this week some jewelry and money had been stolen from a purse belonging to one of the other girls. She had not been too much interested in the matter, but since it had happened before and the thief had never been caught, she kept her own purse locked in the bottom drawer of her desk. But later that afternoon, the stolen articles had been found in her own desk.

Amy had been openly annoyed, but Larry had seen red, and his fury had been evidenced to all. And still was, for that matter. The last few days at work had been agony for Amy but she had listlessly gone about her work while he fumed.

Now it was Thursday, and tomorrow she would be on her way to Dave's. Maybe she would have more energy to withstand her trials when she returned. She sat in the chair by the open window where she had flopped. The effort of standing required too much energy, and energy produced heat. More of that she did not need.

The heat was motionless, monotonous, unrelieved by the faintest disturbance in the air. The condition was overpowering since the summer season was yet officially a month away. They had been caught unprepared under this premature blanket of unrelenting heat, both mentally and physically.

Amy had not bothered to remove her clinging clothes from her perspiring body, for that, too, was an effort. Perhaps after she dried out a bit. She put her elbow on the window sill and sat with her chin on her thumb, hungrily waiting to grasp the slightest stir in the air. This had been the unloading zone for untold problems during the five years she had been in New Hope, and during the last four it had been the scene of many an informal talk with her Father in heaven. But she was not finding relief for her troubles any more than she was finding it for the heat. Rather she was mulling them, saturating herself with unpleasantness.

The clouds of the western horizon ranged in hue from purple-blue to black giving the neighboring buildings an unnatural, ominous cast. In them the thunder threatened, bellicose, then retreating, defiant, then cowering. The young lady did not cringe but rather hoped for the impending storm, hoping the rain would overcome the heat and bring it in submission to the earth. An ovenbird with its *teacher-teacher* song called to his feathered friends to tell them not to be

Time could not pass quickly enough for Amy. She wanted to be away from Larry, away from Dan, and away from the questioning glances she was constantly feeling upon her. Her present state was that of perpetual depression, and although just now she attributed it to the heat, the truth of the matter was, things were not going as they should. And try as she might, she could not seem to straighten them out.

In short, Amy's whole Christian experience had lost its vitality; her daily devotions were uninteresting, and the time she spent reading God's Word had consistently grown shorter while the periods between had grown. She tried to pray, but the words went no further than the ceiling, so she gave that up too. Her church attendance had not wavered but her interest had, and she found it increasingly difficult to listen to the messages.

The Sunday school class she had been teaching, once a rewarding experience, had become too much of a drudgery. These young girls' response at one time had thrilled her as they eagerly listened to each lesson, received Spiritual food, and grew in grace even as Amy herself had done. But the preparation was now burdensome, the teaching a chore. The teacher was impatient and the pupils were disrespectful. They were to blame for the slump, not Amy.

There was a knock at her door. Telephone call. She had heard it ring several times. She did not bother to answer Mrs. Martin but went to the door and picked up the extension at the top of the stairs. She hated telephone calls.

"Hello, Amy." It was Dan. "Are you busy?" He did not wait for an answer. "I'm looking for company to drive to Brookdale with me this evening." She was about to refuse, but he did not give her a chance. "I have to leave in about an hour. Can you be ready?"

"I haven't had dinner yet," she said apologetically, glad she had an out.

"Neither have I, but the service is at seven, so I thought we might stop somewhere on the way home. I'd rather not eat before I speak anyway. Is that all right with you?"

His question was answered in hers. "Dan, do me a favor?"

"Name it." He was noncommittal.

"Don't ask Larry—this time." It was quiet on the other end. Amy felt the color rush to her cheeks. She hesitated, wishing he would say something to ease her discomfort. How stupid of her! She hastily went on. "That was a selfish thing to ask, Dan. I—we—" She verbally stumbled over her blunder—his silence. She paused, then started over again. "He's very irritated with me, and I'm sure—well, it might make it unpleasant for everyone."

Dan finally acknowledged his presence at the other end. "I see." That was all.

"But if you've already asked him, Dan, I'll stay—"

"No. No, I haven't, Amy."

"Well, if you'd rather—"

"I'd rather take you." He was being kind, she was sure, easing her embarrassment. "See you in an hour, less if you can make it."

This would be the last time. She should have refused, but she desperately needed to get out of that room, out of the house. She bathed quickly and slipped into a light blue and white silk dress, white linen pumps, and laid a fluffy white sweater on the bed. She zipped up the fitted bodice of her dress and fastened the blue cummerbund into place.

Amy brushed her curls vigorously, then carefully added a soft touch of color to her lips, a dab of powder to her nose and a spot of perfume to her hair, a turn to her hanky. She looked with approval at the image she observed in the mirror, drew her fingers across her forehead to erase the furrows in her brow, and was thankful the glass was unable to reveal the turmoil within.

What would this fine man think of the young man who had come to visit her? It seemed like so long ago that he had been a part of her life. If only she could eradicate that chapter, tear it from the story of her life, just as one would tear a page from a book.

It really did not matter what Dan thought, but the most troublesome aspect of her plight was its origin. It was Dan's return, nothing else, she had since reluctantly admitted. But the responsibility of this state of affairs was not hers, for she had been an unwilling participant in the game of hearts. As far as Larry was concerned she had been willing, but that had been a rough road from the very beginning.

Dan was standing by the door as she came down the stairs. She did not want her heart to start pounding every time she was near him; she tried to keep her eyes from lighting up every time she saw him, her voice from trembling with excitement when she spoke to him. He must never know.

"Lavender?" he asked as he opened the door. She nodded in assent as she called a good-by to the landlady in the kitchen. He was most observant.

She looked up at him in surprise as they went down the stone steps. "Where are the others?"

"Do you mind? Elaine isn't feeling too well, neither is Chip. He's cutting teeth and she didn't want to leave him with a sitter."

She minded. It was too cozy. She got in and her eyes followed him as he went around to the driver's side, then turned away as he opened his door.

Dan swung his car around hers as he pulled out into the street. The car she had been so excited about buying. She had never owned one before. Larry had helped her pick it out. Larry. Unpleasant thoughts. They followed her wherever she went.

"Car running all right?"

"Hmmm? Oh, fine. I haven't used it much, but it will be getting a real workout on Saturday."

"Oh? You're driving to Massachusetts?"

"Yes. I'm a little nervous about it, but I guess the worst part of anything is thinking about it."

"You'll do fine, I'm sure." He turned to give her a hasty smile. "Just take your time and stay in the slow lane."

Amy talked about the heat, about Paul and his graduation, his and Judy's wedding, the beautiful gardens. Dan talked about Japan and the work he had left. "I tried to bring the little fellow over here, but there's such a short time left I guess it's too late to hope for that now. I know the doctors here could have helped him."

She heard, and she talked, but her thoughts went unwillingly to Larry, repeatedly, as if he were forcing her subconsciousness to consider his petitions.

"You made me promise, Amy, but promises are like hearts. They're made to be broken." He had made his ultimatum less than twenty-four hours ago, his lips forming a narrow straight line. "If you won't marry me now, I'm through—calling it quits." The words had come out unnaturally, as if they had been spoken to himself a hundred times before being voiced.

He had taken her by surprise again, but she recovered quickly. She had acquired the habit. "All right, Larry. If that's the way you feel." She chose her words carefully, kindly, for she had unwittingly cut him to the quick when she had not desired to hurt him at all. "I won't be forced into a decision. You know that."

He was bitter. "You know that's not the way I feel, Amy. I'd wait forever for something I really want. But you've been dangling me on a string, and it appears to me now that I should have cut it long ago. How long must I wait, Amy?" His irritation increased the volume of his voice.

"I'm sorry." She was angry, too, to think that he blamed her for his attentiveness. Still, if the break were coming, better not to have the edges any sharper, any more cutting than they already were. Words could be as whiplashes when voiced in retribution. She had a forced humility. "I didn't know that's what I was doing."

He had left in a rage amidst slamming doors, racing motor and screeching tires. This time he would not be back. Amy was sorry it was over, sorry it had ever started. But she had been warned.

Dan was unusually quiet during the ride to Brookdale, his thoughts full of the service to come. Amy liked the quietness.

There were countless people entering the large church when they arrived, but if anyone noticed the lovely young lady with Dan, there was no surprise evidenced. She sat near the back, and he headed for the platform. He stopped midway down the busy aisle to shake hands vigorously with the elderly minister. They sat in the front pew to make final preparations for the service, and after glancing back at the clock on the wall, the two of them arose and mounted the two short steps to the platform.

The church was nearly filled to capacity when the pastor arose to introduce Dan to any who possibly did not know him. A few stragglers hurried in and were ushered to seats.

The congregation joined in singing several hymns after which the elderly man asked Dan to sing a solo. He almost always did, but apparently this had not been planned. Amy had never heard the song before, something about the path of a Christian and letting God choose the way, but she was most absorbed with the voice. The lovely poetry was merely a convenience without which the voice would remain lifeless, unexpressed in its magnificence. How she wished she could store some of it to hear when Dan would be far, far away!

The song was over too soon, and the message was begun. Amy's complacency would have been turned to discomfort, however, had she sensed that Dan's words, though meant for all to hear, were prayerfully directed at her.

He put his glasses on as he read his text, Romans 10:13, 14.

"For whosoever shall call upon the name of the Lord shall be saved. How then shall they call upon him in whom they have not believed? And how shall they believe in him of whom they have not heard? And how shall they hear without a preacher? And how shall they preach except they be sent?"

After he read the two verses and opened his message, although her eyes were on his face, Amy heard nothing of what he said. Oh, she caught a word now and then, but they meant nothing to her as mixed as they were with her turbulent thoughts.

He removed his horn-rimmed glasses as he spoke. "Whosoever. Whosoever," he said softly, as if repeating it to himself. Suddenly his voice was loud, shutting out any alien thought from the people before him. "Whosoever shall call upon the name of the Lord shall be saved!" His voice echoed and re-echoed in the silence that followed, a quietness that lasted for a full minute. When he went on, his voice was soft again. "Need I say more? Have *you* called upon the name of the Lord? I trust all of you here tonight have done just that, but if any has not, I hope you will do so before you leave this place.

"But *this* question is for those who believe, those who have accepted Him as their Saviour." He leaned forward on the podium as he earnestly asked, "What if you had never heard? What if no one had ever told you that God loves you and gave His Son as a sacrifice for your sin? There are many, many people all over the world who have never heard because there is no one to tell them.

"How I wish I could take you all back to Japan with me so that you might meet some of your oriental brothers and sisters and realize the joy we share in the common bond of our slavation! It has been our privilege to lead many of these people to the Lord. I'm sure you all know about the little church that was started just three years ago.

"But if I could take you to Japan with me tonight, I would say, 'Friends of Brookdale, I would like you to meet my friend, Josh!'" Dan turned to an imaginary boy on the platform as he spoke. "'Josh, these are my friends from America. They have been praying for you back there and sending money to help the work here.'" He turned back to the people before him. "And friends in America, do you know what Josh would say? Oh, he would be thankful for all you've done for the Lord. But he would say, 'Why haven't they come, Dan? My people need more missionaries to tell them the stories of Jesus. There aren't enough to go around. Why don't they come?"

Amy's thoughts drifted from Dan to Larry, then to Dave and Joy. She wanted to get to Ocean Point, away from the uncertainty of her state. Dave had said that everything was proceeding normally. The doctor thought the baby would arrive within two or three days of due-date, but it would be good to get there, to know for herself that all was well.

If only Dan would close the service. It was time, anyway. But his voice went on.

"The Lord is using that boy to win other boys and girls, men and women to Him. Josh is a missionary. Is He using you? Are you letting Him use you? There are thousands, yea, tens of thousands of boys like Josh who have *never* heard the gospel story.

"Yes, Brookdale is a mission field. I'm sure the need here is great, just as it is in New Hope. But it is not *your* mission field if it is not the place where God wants you to be. Should you be over there, or perhaps Africa, South America, telling the message of salvation to someone who has never heard?

" 'The harvest truly is plenteous, but the labourers are few; pray ye therefore the Lord of the harvest, that he will send forth labourers into his harvest.' "

With this verse, Dan sat down. Amy stirred restlessly. She really should have stayed home. She had heard the message many times. Besides, the call for reapers did not include her.

The wheels hummed beneath them as the car sped along the concrete pavement, leaving far behind them the darkened church and its homeward bound parishioners.

"Did we come this way, Dan? I don't seem to recall any of these landmarks."

"No, this is the shore road. Can't you smell that salt air?"

"Hmmm. I sure can. Smells good too. Reminds me of my brother's. They live right on the ocean, you know."

"I know. But this is Long Island Sound."

"But the air smells the same."

He chuckled. "Same water, same air! Boy, I'm starved, Amy. How about you?"

"Just a little empty. But that's not unusual for you, is it?"

The inside of the restaurant was rustic and was decorated to resemble a ship. The soft lights with the assistance of the soft music created an atmosphere of relaxation. They were greeted cordially and escorted to a table near a window.

"Listen to the water!" Amy exclaimed. "It *sounds* like we're on a ship, doesn't it? Not that I ever have been," she added, laughing.

"We are, almost. About half of this building is over the water. It comes up pretty high when the tide comes in."

Their order was taken with a minimum of deliberation. Then suddenly there seemed to be nothing to say. It was so wonderful being here with Dan, to sit across the table from him and look at his handsome face, his deep brown eyes. But it was all wrong. He was far out of reach and she could never tell him what was in her heart. She looked away as his eyes met hers.

"Amy, have you ever considered the mission field?"

She toyed with her water glass and wondered why the ice remained in the same place as she turned it. "I've never felt led in that direction," she said without looking at him.

His deep gaze was upon her, but she refused to meet it. His next question was pointed. "Would you be willing to go if you felt led?"

It was hard to be evasive with him for he seemed to have the ability of looking through a person and into the heart. "I suppose," she mumbled.

"You're not being honest, Amy."

She flared. "Don't you think it's between me and the Lord, Dan?" She had a spontaneous reaction for retaliation of late, and it was not conducive to the Christian walk.

He flushed ever so faintly, but his manner was, as always, reserved, straightforward. "You're right," he said apologetically. "If it has been."

The waiter brought their dinner at a most convenient time. It served as an opportunity for a change in the conversation.

"Getting back to scents, Dan, your perception is keen. Not many men would recognize the fragrance of lavender."

"Oh, that kind of scents," he laughed. "I did some research on it once."

"Oh?"

He offered no further explanation. "I like the smell—fragrance," he corrected.

"It's my favorite," she added.

"I know," he said, but his remark was lost in hers.

"That is, next to the salt water. That's the very nicest."

"But you wouldn't want to go around smelling like that all the time," he bantered.

"Especially at low tide!" she exclaimed.

It was quiet for some time while they ate, but finally Dan broke the silence. "I'm sorry if I overstepped my bounds before," he said, trying to get back to the all-important topic. "I didn't realize you would object to my asking you."

Amy knew her objection had done nothing but raise a bigger question in his mind. "It's okay, Dan. Forget it. Are you having dessert?" The waiter had taken their plates and now stood with pad and pencil in hand.

"How about you?" he asked as he scanned the menu.

Always the gentleman, she thought. "I really don't need any. Maybe just a dish of vanilla ice cream." She did not want it, but it was included with the dinner. Dan ordered pie, and after the waiter had turned his attention to another table, Amy scooped her ice cream onto Dan's pie.

"Sure?" he asked, laughing, his fork poised over the dessert. She assured him she was and sipped her second cup of coffee as she watched him devour the delectable dessert.

"That was lovely, Dan," she said as they got back into the car ten minutes later. "Thank you."

They followed the shore line for several miles, but when they decided to head in the general direction of home, they could not locate a direct route. At each intersection they guessed which way would be better, but they seemed to cover a good many more miles on the return trip. Amy disagreed with him a number of times. Later that night she wondered if he had really been looking for the shortest way home.

"You haven't been yourself lately, Amy. Seems hardly a smile crosses that fair face any more. Larry got you down? Or is it something you wouldn't care to talk about? Just tell me to mind my own business again if you want to. Shouldn't let yourself get down in the dumps though."

Her first reaction was to put him in his place in no uncertain terms as she had back in the restaurant, but he had an uncanny way of drawing people out, easing their antagonism. People were his business, and he knew it well.

"It's been this way since your mother—died," she said, hesitating to use the word. It had such an unpleasant sound. "She was such a friend to me, always willing to listen to my problems. I just haven't been able to get on my feet again."

"II Corinthians 12:9. You know the verse, Amy. 'My grace is sufficient for thee: for my strength is made perfect in weakness.'"

"But for some reason He seems so far away." She could have bitten off her tongue for being so openly frank with him.

"He never changes. Perhaps it's you that's far away. Are you sure that's the root of your trouble?"

"Perhaps—" The word hung in mid-air. "Perhaps you *should* mind your own business," she wanted to say, but there was no point. He would be leaving in a few short months, so it was unnecessary to create any antagonism between them. She sat in silence for several minutes until her irritation had subsided. "It's been nice having you home, Dan. I wish you didn't have to go back." This was not true. She would be relieved when he was gone.

"I want to go back, Amy. That's my home now." They rounded

a curve in the road, and the lights of New Hope lay beneath them. "I only wish you were able to go with me." He pulled the car over onto the shoulder, turned off the motor, and switched on the "dimmers."

She was speechless.

"I have a confession to make." He wore a faintly guilty smile as he leaned against his door and rested his right arm on the back of the seat so that he might look directly at her. "I didn't want anyone else to come tonight. You removed the last obstacle."

"Larry." It was a statement. She had no idea Dan would care to be alone with her.

"I know how he feels about you, Amy. It's pretty obvious. But what about you?"

"I'd like to go home."

In the one brief moment she glanced at him, he leaned forward and their eyes met as he spoke. "I love you, Amy." His voice was soft and warm.

The air was stifling. Amy sat motionless and stared at the knobs of the radio as it played soft music. He had never told her what she should have wanted to hear.

"Amy, I've got to know. Amy, dear, look at me." He touched her chin and tried to turn her face toward him. He had never touched her before. "I've got to know," he repeated. "Do you love me, Amy?"

She pulled his hand forcefully from her face.

"Amy?" He wanted an answer.

"No—" she started with finality but her shoulders shook as she broke into sobs. "Yes, yes, yes!" she cried.

His arms went around her and he pressed his face against her hair. He held her close as all her pent-up emotions of the past months were being released in those tears. He gently kissed her hair, her forehead, her cheek. She clung to him as she sobbed.

"Dan," she cried, suddenly pulling away from him. "Oh, Dan, it's no use!" She raised her head to look at him, her voice too loud as she spoke again. "Dan, I *can't—"* she cried vehemently, "I *can't* go to that God-forsaken place with you! I can't go anywhere with you! I can't! I can't!" she cried hysterically.

Dan was behind the wheel again, but he was still looking at her. The only sound was Amy's weeping. Finally he broke the painful quietness. "Amy, I could—" He stopped. "I'm sorry. I had no right—" After a moment he started to speak again, his voice husky with emotion. "Amy, I could never ask you to go anywhere the Lord didn't want you to go."

She thought he was going to start the car, but he turned to her again. She could not bear to look at him so she stared at the white posts of the guard rail on the other side of the road. They stood in militant order, interrupting the panorama of the city below. His words cut their way to her very soul.

"Before I knew I loved you, before I *knew* you, I prayed about this. From the time I felt the call to the mission field, I prayed earnestly that the Lord would spare me the heartbreak of falling in love with someone who could not—" he hesitated again, "*would* not go with me. I don't know why He has let that very thing happen to me, Amy. I'm sure He must have a reason."

She could say nothing to ease the tension. Had she known what to say, she had no voice with which to say it.

"I don't know what to do now," he went on, "except to pray that He will take this love from me. I don't know what else to do," he repeated hopelessly. He started the car. It was so final.

When he pulled up to the curb in front of her house, he turned to look at her before the car had hardly come to a halt. "Amy—"

"It's no use, Dan." She jumped out and ran into the house with the hot tears stinging her cheeks. She heard him drive away as she leaned against the door and sobbed.

There were blinding tears in Dan's eyes, too, as he stepped on the accelerator. He turned down a side street and pulled over to the curb as his large frame shook uncontrollably. His head went down on his arms as they lay across the wheel, and he cried. He cried until there were no more tears. He sat motionless for a long time, then slid down in the seat and rested his head on the back of it.

He had so hoped that things would turn out differently tonight. His whole future had depended upon it. Perhaps he should have waited a little longer. But his hesitancy about approaching Amy had disappeared in the certainty that the Lord wanted him to take her back with him.

Dan's thoughts went back to Josh. The boy had pleaded with him to bring the pretty lady back. "All right, Josh," he had finally promised. And he had been so sure. The promise had satisfied the boy, but now Dan wished with all his heart that he had not made it. These things were not easy to explain to one so young.

"A million miles away." That's what she said once. But he had not known she was so bitter. He was sure now that she loved him as he loved her. His heart ached for her. His arms ached to hold her close. As he thought of her nearness, the softness of her face as he touched it, the intoxicating perfume in her hair, his senses went reeling.

A million miles.

If the Lord did remove this love from him, it would be a slow, painful operation. There was no anesthesia to dull the Surgeon's knife. But if He did not remove it, Dan knew he would be rendered useless, a broken vessel, an invalid servant with a cancer eating away at his very soul.

The house was dark except for the hall light which Elaine always left for him. He turned it off at the top of the stairs, went to his room, and undressed in the dark.

As he knelt down beside his bed to pray, an unexpected peace came over him, for the words of the song he had sung that night returned to him with renewed meaning. "I only know He'll guide my steps if I take them one by one—"

The pain was still very present, but it was far better to let the Lord lead. "Thy will be done."

Sleep came quickly that night.

Chapter 21

THE ROUTINE OF office work was far from mechanical as Amy performed the duties assigned to her. Aside from the disconcerting turn of events of the previous evening, aside from the fact that she was anxious to get away from New Hope, she had finally cried herself to sleep in the wee hours of the morning and it had left her with a splitting headache.

Each cycle of the clock seemed to take longer than the preceding one, but finally, at four o'clock, she put her things away, taking particular care to leave her desk in perfect order. After putting an envelope on Mr. Chapman's desk, she headed for the elevator. Mr. Chapman was at a convention, but no doubt he would return on Monday. That would be soon enough.

"Amy— "

Her heart sank as Larry stepped out of the elevator. She stopped, openly annoyed.

"I was hoping I'd see you before you left," he went on. "I just wanted to tell you I didn't mean what I said— "

"Forget it." She started for the elevator again, but it had disappeared behind the closed door. Her head hurt and she wished he would go. She watched the arrow. How many times had she watched it? This would be the last.

"It's Dan, isn't it, Amy?"

She stiffened. "It's no one, and I wish you'd leave me alone."

He was crushed. She entered the empty cubicle, and the automatic doors separated them as she pushed the button. She had no room for regret. Everyone and everything were working against her. The scars from her own wounds were a reminder of her own hurt, and they left little room for sympathy for anyone else.

She made one stop on the main floor for her pay envelope and waited until she was in the car before she transferred the money to her billfold. As she drew the money out, she might have been surprised to see the yellow slip that came out with it if she had not been in such a state of lassitude. At the office these slips were lightly referred to as *walking papers.* If there was any satisfaction in knowing she had written her resignation before receiving the yellow slip, Amy was beyond feeling it.

She headed the car in the direction of home, but there was no need to go there. She had packed that morning so that nothing would hinder her from getting out of New Hope. "No Hope," that's what it was now.

She stopped in front of the parsonage and sat for a minute, hand poised to open the door, and wondered just what she would say. The church next door seemed to look at her with disapproval, a friend turned stranger.

"Hi, Amy!" Barbie came running. "Aren't you getting out?"

"I didn't see you, Barb. Where were you?"

"On the grass. I was looking for four-leaf clovers."

"Save one for me if you find any."

"Wait a minute." The girl ran to the place where she had been searching and picked up a book from the grass. She brought it to where Amy stood, opened it, and handed her a neatly pressed four-leaf clover. The child was too sincere to recognize the sarcasm in the request.

"Thank you, honey," Amy said, taking it as Reverend Carlson came out. "Can you spare a few minutes?" she asked him. "I'm leaving and I'd like to talk to you."

"Of course, Amy. Faith told me I couldn't leave anyway. Supper is almost ready." He went back into the house, led the way to his study, and closed the door behind them.

"Would you see if you can find someone to take my class?"

"Mary Dalton is taking it, Amy. She's your substitute."

"I mean permanently. Maybe she would be willing."

"Sit down," Roy invited as he sat at his desk. "Why don't you tell me about it?"

She sat on the edge of the chair opposite him and looked at him, trying desperately to hold back the tears. "I'm leaving today, for good."

"What makes you think you can work things out somewhere else if you can't work them out here?" he asked, tapping his finger-tips together.

"Because I'm leaving the problems here. At least I won't have to look at them."

"Do you really think your problem is with any person, Amy? Don't you think it's with yourself – with the Lord?" His voice was kind, understanding, but his next words floored her. "He may never ask you to go to the mission field, just as he never made Abraham sacrifice his son, Isaac. But Abraham was put to the test to determine the extent of his obedience."

"I should have known Dan would come running to you." She was bitter, hateful. She knew Dan had every right to confide in this man, as his pastor and as his friend.

"I haven't seen or talked with Dan for over a week. Don't you think I can see for myself what's been happening to you? In fact, I have never discussed you with him. But I knew how he felt about you before he left here the first time. You see, I know him pretty well."

First Larry, then Reverend Carlson. "That's really quite humorous," she laughed sarcastically. "Everyone knows me and my troubles better than I do myself. And what really makes it funny, I never told them to anyone!" She stared at the worn spot in the rug as the tears slipped down her cheeks unbidden. "But I can't go!"

"Can't, Amy. Or won't?"

She fought to control her voice. "What's the difference, can't or won't? I'm not going—with him. You wouldn't understand."

"I'd be willing to try," he offered. "The great commission is, 'Go ye into all the world and preach the gospel to every creature—' You've heard it many times, haven't you. Or perhaps you haven't let yourself hear it. Is it distasteful to you? But the command is *go.*" His gentle words increased her irritation until she wished she had substituted a note for the visit. "Go, Amy. The command is *go,* not *stay.* Therefore, we should not wait until we are called to go. Rather we should *go* until we are called to *stay.*"

"Then why didn't you go?" she snapped bitterly, wanting to hurt him and all that for which he stood.

"I was going, Amy. I wanted to go," he answered patiently. "I made all the preparations and the board approved my application. Then for no apparent reason, with no warning, the Lord shut the door. A physical infirmity," he went on to explain, meeting her inquiring glance with a steady gaze. "It took me a long time to accept the fact that I was not to be allowed to go, and even longer to realize I could be of use only where God wanted me to be, and nowhere else." He leaned back in his swivel chair. "Where will you go now, Amy?"

"I don't know yet. My brother is expecting me for two weeks. I suppose I have to go there. After that I guess I'll just get lost." She stood up to leave.

"You may be able to hide from us, but you cannot hide from God. We'll be praying for you."

"I'm beginning to think that's a waste of time."

"Time spent with God is never wasted. You know that." He

opened the office door for her. "Count the cost, Amy. Disobedience comes at a high price."

The telephone rudely disrupted further conversation, and as Roy turned to answer it, Amy left. It was almost six o'clock, and barring anything unforeseen, she would arrive at Dave's soon after dark. She did not relish night driving, inexperienced as she was and alone.

She remembered Dan's advice of the previous evening, and in defiance her foot pressed more heavily on the gas pedal as she swung out to pass the car in front of her. She poorly judged the speed of the oncoming car and just barely managed to get back into her own lane to avoid a head-on collision. She drove fast and furiously.

If only she had not had to return for her purse. Why did everything close in on her? Why did life have to get so complicated?

At least she could not be blamed for Elaine's troubles. Larry's, yes. But not Elaine's. But Elaine was her friend, and everyone she knew was unhappy. And she was involved in their unhappiness in one way or another.

Her head pounded with each ridge in the road. She thought of the first trip she made to Ocean Point, the uncertainty of their reception, her reluctance to leave.

"Christ is the answer," she had heard Dan say more than once. "He is the answer to all the world's problems."

Well, maybe Christ *was* the answer, but what could a fine, upright man like Dan know about such a messed-up life! What was the answer to that? Sure, Christ could take away sin, but what about the scars? No amount of purging could remove them.

Heavy, heavy hangs over thy head; what shall this person do to redeem his forfeit?

The game had been fun, the consequences sometimes difficult, but the results? Their childish antics were a far cry from real life with its pain and heartaches. She had forfeited too much, and redemption was far beyond her reach.

A foolish thing she had done, going into Dan's room. Oh, no one had seen her, to be sure. But she had been as an impulsive, foolish child to do such a thing. At first it had been a reckless adventure, but as she sat rocking the baby, a most peculiar feeling crept over her. She had never been so close to Dan. All the times she had been with him, she had never been so close! And she had no right.

And those moments with his Bible, those few stolen moments were precious though a bit frightening. She had leafed through the old Book, reading some of the verses he had marked with a red pencil, scanning some of the notes he had made in his half-print, half-script mannish scrawl. Then, as she leafed through from back to front, she came to the message his mother had written on the inside cover.

Amy immediately recognized Aunt Louise's beautiful flourishing hand. She had inscribed the date and the words, "Happy Birthday to Danny." Then, "Dear Son; Our prayer is that you will seek: pureness of mind that God might freely teach you His way; pureness of heart that you might have a love for the unlovely; and pureness of body that you might be a fit vessel for His service." Amy snapped the little Book shut as the tears blinded her eyes. "Pureness – fit vessel – "

She could never be worthy of a man like Dan, so the best thing to do was stay away from him. He was far too fine to be offered second-hand goods, and that was all she had to offer. He had never lacked for feminine admiration. He would have no trouble finding someone suitable, someone far better for him than she could ever be.

Was I to find myself, only to become a castaway? Was my life to be so fruitful, only to be turned into something so barren?

"Dear God!" she cried aloud. "Don't leave me alone! I don't want to be alone. I'm so afraid!"

But why didn't He hear? Why didn't she feel the closeness of His presence? He had forsaken her, and her depths of despair were far deeper than any she had ever known. The chasm of aloneness was far more abysmal having been claimed and rejected than having never been claimed at all.

The lethargy into which she had slipped took Amy to such depths that no human hands could reach her. Beneath her despair she knew that God would never disclaim a wayward child, but at this moment she wanted to renounce Him. He had left her alone when she needed Him.

Chapter 22

THE BIG HOUSE was quiet as Dan came down the wide, carpeted staircase. He did not like it that way. In his thoughts it had always been warm and vibrant, full of life.

He stepped tall and straight, but inwardly he drooped, for the memory of his terribly brief romance of just last night was too fresh in his mind. "To err is human; to forgive is divine." Who was it that said that? To love is divine; to forget is impossible. He was thankful for the measure of peace God had restored to his heart, but the nearness and dearness of Amy was human, and he could not cast it off as an old, unwanted garment.

"Say, Chip! Where do you think you're going?" "A chip off the old block," Dan had said of Mark's son the first time he had seen him. The name had stuck.

His little nephew, long since navigating himself about on two limbs, had secretly conquered the first five stairs, and seeing his uncle, put his baby arms up to him. Dan picked him up and carried him down the remaining steps just as Elaine came looking for her offspring.

"There you are, little man. I'm going to have to tie a bell on you so I can keep track of you! Time for your supper. Ready to leave so soon?" she asked, turning to her brother as she realized he was dressed to go out, Bible and other material under his arm.

He looked at his watch. Five o'clock. "I know it's early but I may need the extra time if I get lost." He was still holding little Mark and followed his sister into the kitchen.

"Will you stop to eat?" she asked.

"Maybe later. I'll have a cup of coffee now if you have any made." He put the baby in his highchair. "Here, I'll warm it up," he said, taking the pot from her.

"Dan – " Her voice was full of concern as she put a spoonful of food into her son's anxious little mouth.

He was being hounded. He stared at his coffee as he stirred it. Elaine knew he had been with Amy last night, and *he* knew this was coming. "We'll have to leave it in the Lord's hands, Lainey." The hopefulness had left his voice.

"You talked to her?"

"Yes. It's just as I suspected. It's not me but my calling."

"There's not much time, Danny. Three months– " her voice trailed off.

"I know. There's nothing more I can do." He drank his coffee and put the cup and saucer in the sink. "She knows how I feel, and now we both know how she feels. So it's between Amy and the Lord. Somehow though, I got the feeling there's more to it than meets the eye. Did she ever tell you anything?"

"No. She talked to Mother a lot though. They used to talk for hours while they were sewing. Did Mother give you any clue before– "

"No. Only the di– "

"I know," she said as he opened the screen door and turned to say good-by. "Will you be late?"

"Probably. Don't wait up. Bye." Dan waved to the little fellow who was vigorously rotating his arm and laughing at his uncle. Elaine got a shower of pureed applesauce in her face.

Dan slid behind the wheel and reached over to the glove compartment for a road map. He spread it across the steering wheel and studied it for several minutes, tracing his course with his fingertip. Then he folded it into quarters and laid it on the seat beside him, pressed the ignition button, and put the car in reverse. It responded to his touch as he pressed his foot on the gas pedal, giving it much more power than was necessary, for the driveway was so familiar to him he had often said he could back out with his eyes closed.

His eyes were not closed, however, as he glanced in the rearview mirror and slammed on the brakes, at the same time tearing up sand and stone as the wheels bit into the dirt. The vehicle coming toward him did the same thing, and they came to a dusty halt just inches apart.

Dan did not immediately recognize the brand new sports car, and as he got out to determine the identity of the unexpected visitor, he was nothing less than surprised to see Larry rushing toward him.

"Where's Amy?" He was breathing fire, his eyes flashing, his face the color of his hair. He reeked with the disgusting odor of alcohol. Dan was sickened to the pit of his stomach.

Larry did not give him a chance to answer, but his fist, propelled by the fuel of his rage, landed just below Dan's ribs. Doubled over from the impact, Dan raised himself up in amazement as Larry followed through with a staggering right hook to his jaw. Dan lost his balance and fell backward but quickly rolled over and scrambled to his feet as Larry came at him again.

Dan was prepared for him this time, and with his big hands clenched into fists, he pummelled the other man relentlessly until he sensed his weakening. Larry lunged at him again, and Dan grasped the outstretched arm and flipped him to the ground in one swift movement.

Dan knew this man was no match for him. He had no desire to hurt him, but he had been powerless to stop the avalanche of blows from his own fists. Dan held Larry to the ground, face down, with the weight of his own body, and waited until he felt his muscles relax in defeat.

It was while thus poised that he raised his eyes to see Paul's car, laden to the roof with books, cases, lamps—an accumulation of four years at college, at the edge of the drive. His brother, completely amused, leaned against it while he waited to get in the yard, then raised his hand and waved to Dan, as casually as he would greet an acquaintance on the street. Dan was not amused, far from it, but he put his hand to his forehead in salutation. Neither of them saw their sister in the upstairs window as she watched the distressing scene below.

Dan rose to his full height. "Get up!" he bellowed. He was trying to be patient, but occasionally the old nature got the better of good intentions.

Larry sat with his head between his knees. The extent of his defeat overwhelmed him.

"Get up!" Dan repeated, reaching his hand down and pulling him to his feet. "All right, let's have it." He spoke with alarming sternness.

"Amy's gone." Larry was ready to break up.

"She was supposed to go."

"For good. And it's your fault."

Dan withheld comment briefly. He had not expected this. "And you think I spirited her away."

"No. But I think you'd like to."

"I guess I would," he mumbled under his breath.

"I knew it. You're in love with her." Larry's head was spinning, and he was having difficulty standing upright.

"Yes." Dan looked at him, unflinching.

"What about her?"

"You'll have to ask her."

"I don't have to ask her. I saw how she looked today at work. And she was out with you last night."

"The old reliable grapevine."

"Mrs. Martin told me. I stopped to see Amy, but she packed last night and left right from work today. I can't go on without her." Larry drew his bleeding hand across his forehead, then started toward his car.

Dan pitied him. "You'd better get some coffee in you before you try to drive." He took the staggering man's arm and led him to the kitchen, poured a cup of the hot coffee and set it before him, then sat at the opposite side of the table. Paul, who had just come in, leaned against the sink, his face turned serious.

"Dan . . . " The piercing scream was followed by a clamorous, thudding crash. The two brothers sprang to life simultaneously as their already taut nerves reawakened to new calamity. They forgot the man who had claimed their undivided attention when they saw Elaine's inert form at the foot of the stairs.

Larry grasped the opportunity to hasten away from the scene, leaving the black coffee untouched.

"Get an ambulance, Paul! Never mind. I can get her there quicker myself." Dan lifted his sister gently and carried her to the car. She moaned with every step he took.

"Stay here with Chip," Dan ordered. "And see if you can get Mark. He should be home soon," he added loudly as he backed the car out.

His foot went to the floor as he frantically drove the mile and a half to the hospital. No more than fifteen minutes later, Mark arrived, his face ashen and wet with perspiration.

They sat in silence as they waited, listening to the soundless footsteps of the nurses, hearing, yet not hearing the eerie wail of an ambulance as it neared its destination. The two men were scarcely conscious of the activity about them.

Dan left sometime later after being assured that his sister's life no longer hung in the balance. She had lost the baby she had carried for over six months.

"She's going to be all right, Paul," Dan said in answer to his brother's anxious look.

"The baby?"

"Too late. There was nothing they could do."

"Thank God Lainey's safe." Paul spoke for both of them.

Dan was changing when Paul came into his room and sprawled in the chair. He held his nephew on his lap.

"This was all Larry's fault, Dan. The skunk!"

"Don't be too hard on him."

"Well now, look who's talking," Paul sneered good-humoredly, his anxiety lifted for a moment. "He really had you going there, didn't he?"

"Just caught me off guard."

"I was beginning to think I'd have to come help you!"

"That'll be the day!" Dan returned. "Say, Paul, be a good sport and run these down to the cleaners for me before they close." He rolled his soiled suit into a ball and tossed it to his brother. "Tell them I'll pick it up tomorrow afternoon."

"Who won?" Paul asked, wishing he could wring Amy's neck. A few others while he was at it too.

"That remains to be seen." Dan started on his way again. He was going to be very late. "Say, Paul," he called from the front hall, "better give Roy a call. He'll probably want to stop and see Elaine."

It was late when Dan got home. The hall light had not been left on as it usually was, but there was a soft gleam of light from the living room. Mark was slumped in a big chair. He sprang to attention when he realized he was not alone.

"Mark, what's wrong?"

"Oh, Dan, I'm glad you're home."

"Elaine?"

"She's doing fine now. As well as can be expected."

Dan sighed with relief. "What, then?"

"Remember that ambulance we heard while we were waiting at the hospital? Larry was in it. He's pretty bad. Been asking for you." Dan headed for the door. "It's late, Dan. Why don't you call first? He drove into a tree," he explained while Dan dialed. "Ricocheted and hit a utility pole. Car was a total wreck."

Dan put the receiver back into its cradle. "He's under heavy sedation. I have to wait until morning."

"Will he last that long?"

"He's pretty beat up. But apparently . . . "

It was still early morning when, again, Dan entered General Hospital. He opened the heavily-padded, curtained door which the nurse had indicated. The room was semi-dark, quiet, its air heavy and foreboding.

The man in the white bed was still. His head was bound in bandages soaked with his own blood. His left arm was in a cast, and his right one was bandaged from his elbow to his wrist.

It was to his right hand the young lady clung. She sat by the bed, her head bent over her own arm as she dozed, overcome by her long night of vigil. Dan touched her shoulder. Panic crossed her visage as she looked up at him and then cast a furtive glance at the now stirring form in the bed. She took Dan's arm and drew him out into the hall.

"Dan, you must not tell him," she pleaded. "You must not tell anyone." Her eyes were red and swollen.

"Have you been here all night?"

"Most of it."

"Won't your folks be worried?"

"It isn't the first time I've stayed out all night. Dan, I'd like to talk to you."

"You look as if you could use some rest more than anything, Karen."

"Please?"

They walked down the shadowy corridor and onto the vacant sunporch. The hospital was awakening to a new day. Nurses and aides bustled about, a few ambulant patients scuffed down the hall to prepare themselves for the first meal of the day, and the suppressed whispers of the pre-dawn dusk increased to become a part of the restrained noises of daily hospital activity.

Dan's heart was heavy. The weight of his burdens increased with every turn of the road, and each new weight was a dash of salt in the most painful of all wounds. His heart cried out for Amy. If only he could take her in his arms and hold her close, surely these other unpleasant happenings would fall into proportionate place.

Nothing could have surprised him more than Karen's presence in Larry's room. In the dim light he had been certain that it was Amy, and his heart had crashed to a new low. She loved Larry after all. But Karen Winslow? A perplexing situation indeed.

He had no desire to talk with this girl just now. Apparently she was troubled, but wasn't he too? Couldn't he ever be free to nurse his own hurts, to regain his own strength before trying to help others?

Dear Father, I am Thine to do with as Thou wilt see fit. Help me to put my own personal anxieties from my mind when I have a job to do for Thee. If it be Thy will that I witness to this sinful girl, help me to make her understand the way of salvation. Thou hast promised that Thy Word shall not return unto Thee void, so may Thy Holy Spirit use it, and use me, for Thy glory. Give me the strength to accept whatever Thou hast for me.

Karen sat on the edge of a yellow wicker love seat. Dan sat facing her across a small matching table. She twisted the wet handkerchief she held, and although she seemed fairly calm, he sensed that inside she was squirming nervously.

"What's on your mind, Karen?" he asked kindly, trying to put the girl at ease.

She bit her lip until he thought he would see blood dripping from it. "This isn't easy for me, Dan, but I've had a lot of time to think during this long night." She hesitated as if anxious to go on but afraid of being condemned in the eyes of this godly man.

"Sometimes it does us good to have time to think."

"Blazes, Dan, if you really want to know what I've been thinking, I'm just sick to death of the way I've been living."

The tears were still coming down her cheeks, tears which Dan had thought her incapable of—honest tears. This sudden change in Karen was baffling. She had been a troublemaker from way back, and it was strange to think of her in this light. He was ashamed of his thoughts.

"I've had fun—excitement. At least that's what I thought it was. But it doesn't last. I've made a miserable mess of my own life as well as everyone else's." She bit her lip again.

Dan again prayed for guidance. "There's only one thing that really satisfies, Karen, only one Person. That's the Lord Jesus Christ, God's Son. He alone has power to take away your sin and give you a new heart. God gave His Son to be the sacrifice for our sin that we might not have to pay the penalty for it. But unless we accept Him as our personal Saviour, we will have to take the punishment for our own sin. That punishment is an eternity in Hell. 'For God so loved the world that he gave his only begotten Son, that whosoever believeth in him should not perish but have everlasting life.'" Dan spoke softly and slowly.

The hard, bitter girl looked at him, her acridity softened almost to the point of humility through her long night of vigil. Or was it these words Dan was speaking, words which had some supernatural power, words which, if she believed, could change the Godless wretched heart which had beat for nothing but the selfish desires and evil schemings of Karen Winslow?

"But why should a holy God have anything to do with me? I'm not worth—"

"God isn't as much interested in our worth as He is in our needs. None of us could be counted worthy if that were the case." He took a worn New Testament from his pocket and opened to Titus 3:5 and read the verse aloud. "'Not by works of righteousness which we have done but according to his mercy he saved us.'" He handed the Testament to her and pointed out the verse he had read.

She read it and handed it back to him. "You don't know what kind of person I am, Dan. I've been selfish and—oh, rot! I've done everything I could to hurt Amy. It was my fault she got canned yesterday—was it just yesterday? It seems like longer but—"

"Hold on a minute, Karen! Hold the phone! I was under the impression Amy quit her job."

"Maybe I spoke out of turn. She was fired, but it wasn't her fault. Several thefts have taken place during the last month, which honestly, I know nothing about. But during this last week I got Gladys Searles to go along with me on a little joke against Amy. Gladys' purse was supposed to have been robbed, and the things conveniently showed up in Amy's desk. Do you see, Dan? I've done everything I could to hurt her. And now you know why. Not because I didn't like her. I think she's the sweetest thing that ever walked the face of the earth." She motioned toward the room they had just left. "He's the reason. And he hates me. I can't say I blame him," she choked.

"He doesn't hate you. I suppose he couldn't have appreciated the way you treated Amy, but I'm sure he doesn't hate you."

"This was all for Amy, wasn't it? This accident, I mean. I'd give anything to have him care that much about me."

So would I, thought Dan. *One less obstacle.*

"But I can't go on the way I have been. I just can't. I don't know where it will end, and I'm fed up. What must I do, Dan? I can't right the wrongs I've done till I do something about the mess of me first." This was not the voice of the old Karen Winslow. It was the voice of a sinner – a sinner disenchanted with the sin.

Dan turned to Acts 4:12. "'Neither is there salvation in any other: for there is none other name under heaven given among men, whereby we must be saved.'"

"I've heard Amy say that," Karen said with a humility foreign to her nature.

"It's not Amy's word, Karen, nor mine either. It's God's Word."

"But what must I do?"

"Accept Christ as your personal Saviour. Put your faith in Him and let Him take over. He does a much better job of running our lives than we can do ourselves."

"How does one go about this?" Karen asked with a hunger burning in her eyes.

"Believe. It's that simple. 'Believe on the Lord Jesus Christ and thou shalt be saved.'"

"I want to believe, Dan. I *do* believe. But that can't be all there is to it. It's *too* simple." She looked at him dubiously.

"God has made His plan of salvation simple that we might just reach out, in simple faith believing."

A light dawned on the tear-stained face assuring Dan that God's work of salvation had been wrought within. It was a light to assure him that the knowledge had gone beyond the gray matter of her beautiful head to settle in the deepest corners of her contrite heart.

"It's a miracle, Dan."

"That's just what it is," he said smiling. He bowed his head as Karen looked at him in wonder, then bowed hers.

His voice was soft as he prayed. There were few curious eyes to peer in at them as they sat in the corner with their heads bowed close together. "Thank you, Lord, for the eternal life Thou hast given to this searching heart. We know there is rejoicing in heaven over one soul that comes to repentance, and we, too, rejoice, for we are unworthy in Thy sight. We thank Thee for Christ and the salvation Thou hast provided through Him that we might come to Thee. We know there is no other way. We ask that Thou wilt strengthen Karen now as she seeks to serve Thee. Give her the courage she will need through anxious moments and difficult times, for Thou hast not promised the life of a Christian to be a life of ease." Dan hesitated a moment, then went on. "And thank you for Amy's patient witnessing to Karen. Be with Amy now, Lord, too – and keep her – in Thy tender care – and – may she seek Thy will – in all things. In Jesus' name. Amen."

His verbal stumbling had not been from a self-consciousness in Karen's presence, but from a dull ache which seemed to settle in the region of his heart whenever his thoughts turned to Amy.

"Thanks, Dan," Karen said, her eyes misty. He could not mistake the pleading in them. "You won't say anything about this, will you? At least not that I was here. You must promise me, Dan."

"If that's the way you want it, Karen, I surely won't." He stood up to his full six feet three inches. "Would you like to take this, Karen?" He held his little Testament out to her. "I have verses marked which might be of some help to you."

"Thank you again, Dan. I'll return it after I get one of my own." She stood as she spoke. "You really should go see Larry now." He turned to go, but she made no move in that direction. "Dan?" He turned to her again. "Amy did this to me. After all I've tried to do to hurt her, she never did a thing to repay me – just kept telling me about Christ and what He could do for me."

Dan watched her and waited patiently, wondering what she was really driving at.

"You're in love with her, aren't you, Dan?" She smiled at his raised eyebrows. "Oh, I can tell. I had you two all tied up in a pretty pink bow years ago only neither one of you wanted to cooperate. But I also know something is troubling her. I know *who,* Dan, but I don't know *what.* Would it help matters if I told you?"

"How do you know so much about Amy's personal life, Karen? I'm sure she never told you."

"Oh, my, no! But you didn't answer my question. I'll tell you anyway. His name is Todd Kenyon."

Dan made a mental note.

"It was a coincidence, my meeting him like I did. He happened to be at the same resort I went to in Delaware a couple of years ago. That's where Amy is from, you know. I happened to mention I was from Connecticut, and he overheard me. Said he had an old friend who had moved here but he couldn't locate her. Well, I guess you know my ears perked up when I found out who this friend was! It was just the ammunition I needed. It's a long story, Dan, and I won't keep you now, but I knew he had some hold on her. I still don't know what it is. I tried to wheedle it out of him. But now I don't want to know. I finally got him to come here to see her. I told him she *wanted* him to come. I was sure it would break things up between her and Larry, but I think it did more to bring them closer together." Karen sighed. "I hate to tell you all this. I'm not proud of the awful things I've done. Then when you came home – well, I knew who was the real fly in the ointment. Only now I don't want to hurt her, even if it means losing him for good. If I could just undo some of the things I've done." Karen's eyes filled with tears again. "Go ahead, Dan. Larry is probably looking for you if he's conscious. I'll stay here for a few minutes."

"If you'd like to wait I'll give you a ride home."

"I have my own car, thanks. But I would like to talk with you again soon if you can spare the time."

Larry was moaning softly as Dan walked silently to his bedside. His eyes opened and he moaned again. "Amy was here. Where is she? Tell her not to leave me."

"No, Amy wasn't here, Larry."

"I saw her. I know she was here. She held my hand."

"You've been through a lot, Larry. Amy was not here. She's gone, remember?"

"Yeah," he groaned, "I remember. O-oo-oh – " He put his good hand to his head. "Oh, I remember now. I'm a fool."

"What made you think you could drown your troubles?"

Larry closed his eyes, and Dan thought he had slipped into unconsciousness again. It was hard to realize this broken man was the same one who had attacked him so violently the night before. Those lips had touched Amy's. Those arms had held her –

Larry's eyes opened. "After the first one nothing seemed to matter." He was having difficulty getting the words out. "I'm glad you came so quick, Dan. I'm going to die, and I wanted to tell you I'm sorry. I wanted to kill you. I couldn't die with that on my conscience."

"You're not going to die."

"Yes, I am. I don't want to live. I didn't do this purposely though. You've got to believe that," his voice pleaded. With his next words, despair engulfed him again. "I would have done a better job. I can't live without her. Please get her for me. Tell her I'm going to die."

"I can't do that, Larry. Roy Carlson will be up to see you. You can talk to him about it. Maybe he'll get in touch with Amy for you."

"I should have known you wouldn't do that, not when you want her for yourself. But she's mine, Dan. You leave her alone, hear?" Larry's face twisted with pain and he moaned loudly as his eyes shut tightly and his parted lips revealed clenched teeth.

"Take it easy, boy," Dan said compassionately. "I'll send the nurse in." Dan had had a close walk with sickness of the body as well as sickness of the soul during the past few years, so again, his own aches were put in the background. He laid a firm hand on the one that so desperately clung to the edge of the bed.

"A good big dose this time, tell her," Larry cried. "One that'll take care of it for good."

Dan stooped to pick up a wisp of a hanky from the floor and put it on the night table. He stopped at the desk and asked the nurse if she could give him something to make him more comfortable. She immediately went to the white cabinet and fixed his prescribed medicine.

Elaine was also in a private room, so there were no restrictions on visiting hours. Her face was white against the colorless bed linens, but she smiled weakly when she saw Dan. "What are you doing here so early?"

"Visiting you. Feeling better?"

Her eyes filled with tears. "Oh, Danny, I wanted the baby. I really did, Danny."

"See here, Elaine, that's enough of that kind of talk."

"But I said—"

"Never mind what you said," he interrupted brusquely. "No one is going to think anything of what you said, least of all, me. I don't want to hear any more of that. How are you feeling?" he asked again.

"I'm not sure. I'm numb. What was that all about with Larry? I've never seen you so angry."

"I'm not proud of that."

"He must have deserved it."

"He was drunk."

"Oh, no, Dan!"

"He blamed me for Amy's leaving—claims she's never coming back. I guess he must be right too."

"No, Dan. It's Amy's fault."

"If it is, there's a pretty fine dividing line. Who can say who was wrong and who wasn't?"

"I wish you would go find her."

"I can't do that, Lainey. You know I can't." He sat down by the bed. "There's something you don't know."

"Oh?" She was hopeful.

"Larry is here too."

"In the hospital?"

He nodded assent. "He had an accident. I just saw him. That's why I'm here so early."

"Is he hurt badly?"

"Broken arm, several broken ribs, quite a few lacerations. He got quite a gash on the head, and I think I heard the nurse say he had a cracked ankle bone. He's going to pull through though."

"Danny, you should let Amy know. It's only right."

"No, I shouldn't. Maybe someone else will."

The attendant came in with the breakfast tray, and Dan stood up to leave. "Try to eat, Elaine. You'll feel a lot better."

"Come back later?"

"Sure enough. Take care of yourself, and don't worry about anything else. Promise?"

"I'll try, Danny. I promise that," she said, trying to keep the worry from her face.

Dan dragged himself along the lower corridor toward the front entrance of the hospital, his hands jammed in his pockets, his head bent. His feet lagged wearily with one foot preceding the other as if it mattered not in which direction they carried him, just as long as they kept moving.

He raised his head to measure the distance down the long empty hall. His head thumped down on his chest again. He had taken several steps before the picture of a familiar form reached his brain. Could it possibly have been? He quickly looked up, and his eyes searched the echoing corridor, but down went the head again. Why must every gracefully curved form in a fluffy swishing skirt remind him of Amy Archer? He must be taking leave of his senses.

So Dan plodded on, little knowing as he reached the end of the corridor that he had but to turn his head to come face to face with a dear little girl with a broken heart. And it was the same dear girl he had held in his arms such a short time ago.

He heard Paul's voice as he stepped into the living room. "Oh, Amy's brother. Yes, I remember. How are you?" Dan stopped in his tracks. "No, I don't know where Amy is," Paul went on. "I think she left New Hope last night. No, I'm not sure. Just a minute." He put his hand over the mouthpiece. "Dan, when did Amy leave?"

Dan's brow took on a new wrinkle. He took the receiver. "Dan Sanderford speaking. Yes. Hello, Dave. You mean Amy hasn't arrived there yet?"

"I tried Martin's, and I tried Larry's. There was no answer at either place. Then your name popped into my head. Amy has talked about your family so much." David Archer was worried.

"I wish I could help you, but as far as I know she left between five and six last evening. That's about all the information I can give you. She isn't used to driving at night. Maybe she stopped over somewhere. There's hardly any cause for worry." He was doing a poor job of convincing himself.

"Let me know if you hear from her, please!"

"I'll do that. Oh, say, Dave, when Amy gets there, you had better tell her that Larry is in the hospital." He really had not intended to be the deliverer of these tidings. He explained the situation as briefly as he could to this man who was almost a complete stranger to him – Amy's brother.

He was perturbed. Where was Amy? Things had been happening so fast. But he had not considered this possibility.

Exhaustion overtook him as he stretched out on the living room floor with a small pillow from the sofa. Chip, dragging another pillow to where his uncle lay, flopped down beside him.

Dan was a volcano of boiling lava, a troublesome volcano which remained dormant for short periods only. But as each eruption seared over his tired, aching frame, every nerve, every muscle cried out in pain.

"Dear God, help me to know Thy way. Help me to understand it and to accept it," Dan prayed. "And dear Father, please keep Amy safe."

He put his arm around the little lad on the floor beside him. His voice caught in his throat as he patted the thick, crudely-pinned diaper Paul had just installed. "It's a tough life, isn't it, fella?"

Dan closed his eyes and turned his heart toward heaven again. "Dear God, if I can't have her, keep her safe for Larry's sake."

Chapter 23

It was late Saturday night when Amy reached her destination. The house was ablaze of lights as she pulled up in back of Tim's car. Dave's was not there. She hurried up the steps as Tim came rushing out, his sleeves rolled up above the elbows, apron half untied and drooping, towel in hand. He looked awful.

"Amy, where in the world have you been? I'm sure glad you're here."

The twins followed him and threw their arms around her. "Aunt Amy! Mommy and Daddy are in the hospital, and we have a new brother!" They chattered loudly. Amy was not at all certain she had heard them correctly.

"That's right, Amy," Tim said, confirming their report. "You two go finish your ice cream now, and then Aunt Amy will put you to bed."

They scampered back to the kitchen after she promised she would be right in. Tim wanted to talk to her alone, she could see that.

"It doesn't look good, Amy. The baby's going to be fine – eight pound boy. But – "

"Oh, no!" She sank into the nearest chair. "Not this. Please, Lord, not this. Oh, dear God!" Tim stood watching her helplessly, wishing he had not been handed the task of telling her.

The telephone rang. Amy jumped to answer it, but Tim already had reached it. She waited patiently at his side, anxiously watching his face.

"Amy's here, Dave. She just arrived a few minutes ago. Sure." He handed it to her.

"Hello, Amy. We were worried about you. I'm glad you're there with the girls though." He sounded so weary, so dejected. So unlike Dave.

"How is she, Dave?" She asked it fearfully, ignoring his greeting.

"No change yet. I'll call you just as soon as there's any change at all. Pray, Amy," he pleaded.

How could she tell him, at such a time, that her line was disconnected? She went out to the kitchen where Tim was cleaning up the ice cream that had not reached the mouths. She took the girls upstairs and, after washing them and listening to their prayers, tucked them into their beds.

"Aren't you glad we have a brother, Aunt Amy?" asked Becky.

"I want Mommy," pouted Rachel.

"But we have Aunt Amy now, and pretty soon we'll have Mommy, too," reasoned her sister.

Rachel brightened. "And little Davey too!"

"Good night, lassies," said Amy as she kissed them. Under ordinary circumstances she would have been delighted with their chatter, but now it sickened her. How could these innocent babes know the cruelness of a life they had yet to face—perhaps without a mother? How could they know the world was not their big happy playground?

Tim was preparing to leave when Amy came downstairs. "I'm going over to the hospital. Maybe I can give Dave a little moral support. I'll get him some coffee on the way."

"Wait, Tim," she pleaded. "I'd like to know a little more about all this. When did Joy go to the hospital?"

"Dave took her last night. He tried to call you. Nobody seemed to know where you were."

"I gathered that. But what about Joy?"

"The doctor wanted her there so he could keep her under observation. I guess he knew a little more than he was letting on. Anyway, the trouble developed suddenly—toxemia. The baby was born about five this morning, I think. It looked pretty doubtful for him at first, but they're hopeful now. I don't know about Joy—"

For the first time Amy was aware of the difficulty Tim was going through for his boss, for his friends.

"Be sure to have Dave call me, Tim, right away."

He closed the door behind him, but stuck his head back in as Amy was about to go into the living room. "The fireplace is all set to go if you feel cold. Check the damper though."

"That's swell. Thanks."

The house was cool and quiet and most unpleasant. She lit the fire and turned on the radio, wishing at the same time for the company of the two little girls upstairs sound asleep, unconscious of the impending catastrophe.

Amy wandered through the downstairs, automatically tidying up the kitchen, rearranging things which one would hardly expect a man to do right, a bachelor at that. She picked up several toys and listlessly carried them about, not knowing where to put them, forgetting the thing she had started to do. She sat by the fire, but her mounting tensions tugged at her reflexes causing her to jump, keep moving, anything but sit still.

The mantel clock struck midnight as she sank into the wooden rocker, tensely waiting for the phone to ring, wishing it would, yet fearful of its tidings.

The telephone. It had been a symbol of foreboding for as long as she could remember.

She had gone back to the Carlson residence for her purse. The pastor already had left, but Faith had told her about Elaine being rushed to the hospital.

She could not remember much of what took place during the next hours, just the feverish driving—hurry, hurry, get away from that place, away from the people she always hurt.

And then, vaguely, she remembered the traffic circle. She had gone completely around it and had headed back in the direction from which she had come. Elaine was her friend. She had to find out if she were still alive.

At twelve o'clock she had let herself into the Martin house. Just twenty-four hours ago. The old couple had gone away for the weekend, so no one would know she had returned. She went to her room. It was not hers any more. She slept fitfully for several hours, but the morning light impatiently urged her to be on her way again. She stuffed the remainder of her possessions into the car, things she had expected to return for some day. Now she would never have to come back.

As she walked down the corridor of the hospital, she caught a glimpse of a familiar form coming toward her. He had not seen her. That was good. She stepped to the next doorway and, unobserved, she breathlessly watched him pass by. He looked so weary!

She was filled with fear as she looked on the wan face of Elaine. She should not look so. She was supposed to be full of life, bubbling over with vitality.

"Amy! Oh, Amy!" Elaine cried. "I thought you had gone!"

"To all concerned I have. But I just had to see you, Elaine. I had to find out if you were all right. You are, aren't you?"

"I'll be as good as new."

"The baby?"

"No. I lost it."

"I'm sorry."

"Amy, Danny loves you."

"So he said."

"He needs you."

"No."

"Please love him, Amy. Please need him too."

"He'll get over it. He'll be better off."

"He never will. You're the only one. First and last. Amy, won't you tell me why?"

"I can't. Maybe sometime you'll understand."

"Try me now, Amy. Just try me."

"You're too close to the sore spot. You'd tell him."

"I know," she said, choking back the tears. "But do you really think it would make any difference to Dan?"

"It would."

"Then he's more of a man than you think."

"I'm going now. You've been a grand friend, Elaine, and I'm going to miss you."

"Wait, Amy! Please wait. I've got to tell you something."

"There's nothing you could tell me that would change anything."

"Amy, Larry's here too – in the hospital. He was in a bad accident last night."

Amy walked back to the bed. "Lainey, can't you see! Everyone I touch gets hurt! Everything I do is jinxed! That's why I'm clearing out."

"Are you going to see him?"

"Do you think I should?"

"I do. But it's up to you. I can't say I want you to."

"Good-by, Elaine. I hope you'll always be happy. You deserve it more than anyone I know."

"You do too, Amy. Don't go!" Elaine pleaded.

She had gone. It had hurt, but she had gone.

Seeing Larry had hurt too. The nurse told her that he was under a sedative, and all she could do was look at him. She kissed his bruised cheek as her tears moistened his face. "Good-by, Larry." She had wept bitterly.

"Aunt Amy?" The tearful, sleepy voice startled her and brought her back sharply to the present. "I want Mommy."

"Come here, Sunshine." The little girl cuddled in her arms. Amy rocked her niece, trying to offer some consolation in her own nearness. The child was asleep almost instantly, but Amy's arms ached. Her head ached. Her whole body ached.

Things seemed foggy after she left the hospital. She had gone back to her room. Yes, she had been weak and sick. The telephone had jangled incessantly as she unlocked the door and mounted the stairs, but she ignored it. Of course! That must have been Dave. If she had answered that phone she would have saved her brother a lot of anxiety. She did not know what time it was when she left New Hope.

If only Dave would call now. She rested her head on the hard back of the chair, but suddenly every muscle in her body tensed, alerted by the sound of a car in the drive—no, two cars. Dave's and Tim's. But why hadn't they called? And why had Tim come back with her brother? She was nauseous as she waited, her fingernails biting painlessly into the palms of her hands, listening breathlessly as she heard them enter the dark kitchen.

She tried to speak, but no sound came forth. Then she saw him, saw his face as he came through the dining room. She screamed and buried her face in the bundle she held in her arms, crushing the little body to her own.

They loosed her vise-like grip, and Tim carried the terrified child to her bed while Dave tried to calm his hysterical sister. He struck a hard blow across her face leaving it red and stinging, but she reacted as if she were stone. He was shaking her when Tim came hurrying down the stairs.

"Dave, I think you'd better get a doctor for her!"

"Rick. Doctor Richard Hastings—neighbor—" muttered Dave as Tim rushed to the phone. "Number—inside cover—"

He was there in a matter of minutes.

Chapter 24

THE RAIN SPLATTERED almost noiselessly against the shaded windows, but it did not matter. Nothing mattered. Where am I? Perhaps in another world? Perhaps I'll stay here forever.

The return from velvety blackness was slow, an effortless transportation from far away. Amy lay still for some time before she summoned enough energy to open her eyes. There was no connection between her brain and her limbs, and as she looked beneath the counterpane at the hump which should be her toes, it seemed they could not belong to her. But she discovered that by exercising a good bit of determination, she could move them. She tried her fingers, and they moved too. Her arms felt lifeless, but after thinking about it for a few minutes, she managed to raise one of them to her pillow to prop her head on.

But she wished she had stayed in the other world, for suddenly reality swept over her in a sickening wave. *Oh, God, why? Why? Why? Why? Dave and Joy have been faithful. Then why?*

"Oh that I knew where I might find him! Behold, I go forward, but he is not there; and backward, but I cannot perceive Him." The plight of Job, read and pondered so many times, came back to her. She could not understand the Almighty's dealings with this upright man either.

The aroma of coffee and bacon drifted through the open door of the bedroom. Someone must feel like eating, but she would never eat again.

"Dave?"

Her brother stopped, turned to look at her, then came in, perching himself on the edge of the bed. His face was drawn, his eyes red with weariness. But there was no sadness. There was no heartbreak which should have been there.

"You sure went to pieces last night, Amy."

"Did I? I don't remember."

"You didn't even give us a chance to tell you the good news."

Amy sat up straight, her mouth open. "Dave!" she fairly screamed at him. "Dave! Why didn't you call me?"

His hand went to his head, and it was his turn to sit with his mouth agape. "Amy, Amy," he pleaded, "I'm sorry! That's why you thought the worst. Of course! How could I have pulled such a boner! But we were so anxious to get home to tell you – I just never thought of the effect it would have on you."

Amy could not be hard on him and she patted his hand as she lay down again. "You went through plenty yourself yesterday. I guess I'll forgive you. Oh, Dave, I'm so thankful Joy is safe." The tears came to her eyes. "I would have died if anything had happened to her."

He smiled, and his voice was husky. "I guess I would have too." Nobility was overcome by truth.

"I don't remember how I got here. I don't remember a thing after I saw you come in from the dining room."

He was glad. "I carried you up. Rick Hastings came over and gave you something to calm you down. You don't usually fall apart so easily, Amy."

"I had a pretty bad day myself."

"Larry? You may not know. He's in the hospital."

"I know. I saw him. No, not Larry. Not entirely anyway."

"Who?"

"Just myself, I guess. But my troubles didn't seem important when I got here and heard about yours."

"We were worried about you. No one seemed to know where you had disappeared. Where were you?"

"I went back to New Hope. It's a long story. I'll tell you about it some other time. Where are the girls?"

"Eating. But that fellow I talked to said he'd let me know if they heard from you."

"What fellow?"

"Sanderford. Dan, I think was his name."

Amy swallowed the lump that came to her throat. "I didn't see anyone but Elaine."

"And Larry."

"He didn't see me. Did the girls get you up?" He nodded. "I'm sorry, Dave. You needed the rest. You look awful."

"Thanks." He stood up. "I'll catch up later." He walked to the door and slowly drew it closed as he talked. "Feel like getting up? I called the hospital, and they said I could see her in about an hour, but just for a few minutes."

She sat up. Dave went out, closing the door behind him. She

stretched her arms and legs, flexed her joints, and stood up, her circulation not quite completely restored. It was not till she was out of bed that she realized she was fully dressed except for her shoes. She had unbuttoned her wrinkled dress when she remembered her baggage was still in the car. She buttoned it again.

Her brother was coaxing the twins to finish their breakfast when she entered the kitchen. It had a warmth, a cheerfulness which had been so lacking the night before. She looked at the three cups, still on the table with the morning meal.

"Rick joined us."

"You must have had a good laugh," she said, turning the bacon.

"Over what? No one felt like laughing, Amy. We were too full of thanksgiving."

"One or two?" She held an egg in her hand.

"One today. I'm not hungry. I'm sure glad you're here."

"How long will Joy be in the hospital?"

"It's hard to say. Rick said three weeks, at least. I wish you could be here for a month. I guess I'll have to get someone to come in to help after you go."

"I wasn't going to tell you yet, Dave." The change in her voice as she put the plate in front of him caused him to look up at her sharply. "But it does solve a problem – for you. I quit my job."

He pushed his chair back and looked at her in amazement. "You're kidding!" His eyes followed her as she put the bread in the toaster. "In the name of common sense, Amy, why?"

"I – never mind now. I'll be able to stay as long as you need me, anyway."

"And then?"

"Eat your breakfast before it gets cold. I don't know." She wished she had not told him. "I have to think."

"Did you think before you did such a – " he hesitated, "a crazy thing?" He put a forkful in his mouth.

"Please, Dave," she pleaded.

"Okay for now. But we haven't finished this by any means." The big brother had spoken. "Aren't you eating?" he asked as she sat down with a cup of coffee.

"Maybe later. Don't tell Joy. Not yet, Dave."

He finished his coffee, then kissed the twins on the tops of their heads.

"Daddy!" Becky screamed as she raced to the door. He stooped down to her outstretched arms. "Give this to Mommy." She put her little arms around his neck and applied all the pressure she could muster as she kissed him.

"I sure will," he assured her, holding her close and encircling his Sunshine with the other arm. She was not to be outdone. "But I might crush Mommy if I give her such a *big* hug!"

"No, Daddy," Rachel admonished with her forefinger to his lips. "Mommy likes you to hug her tight!"

Dave laughed and pretended to bite her finger. His heart overflowed as the recollection of what might have been swept over him.

"You be good girls for Aunt Amy, and I'll stop and buy a big bouquet for Mommy—just from you!"

"We will!" they shouted in unison as they ran back to the table and started in earnest on their soggy cereal.

Their help in the days to follow, though sincere, served to add chaos to the already hectic business of domestic routine. Amy's lack of amusement at their childish antics only magnified her irritation.

And poor Tucker Too! He took the worst beating of all. Amy was drawn to the second floor window by petrifying screams more than once, for one thing or another. But the most distressing scene of all was that of the poor animal, securely grasped at either end by a determined twin who pulled with all her strength, each as unwilling as the other to let go. Amy scolded for all she was worth, but if they heard they did not hearken, for the cat was making as much commotion as all three of them. He was sure to be torn in two.

Amy was about to head for the stairs to rescue the miserable beast when she saw Dave's car turn into the drive, this also beyond the children's notice. He jumped out and grabbed each girl by an arm as Tucker Too quickly found refuge under the car. Their father soundly spanked each twin. She had had the urge to administer the same hand of chastening many times herself, but now she felt a twinge of sympathy for the child who had to wait her turn. Becky, the first to be released, came running to Amy to seek comfort for the unjust hurt she had just endured. "Daddy spanked me," she cried, "and all 'cause Rachel sqwoze Tucker Too!"

Amy's anxiety over her sister-in-law's condition soon turned to complacency, and she slipped back into her restless depression. Her appreciation for Joy's recovery flooded over her occasionally, but she could not orient herself to her new state of existence, not the present circumstances here, but the future. It was an abyss, a bottomless pit, a separation from the people and purpose she had lived for. She could not return to New Hope. Not while Dan was there.

The premonition that Todd Kenyon would come back was followed by a desperate hope that he would not find his way here to Ocean Point. His presence would be more than she could take. She had made her position plain to him though, and he was not one to pursue his own desires with any momentum. Perhaps some day he would learn.

During the busy weeks she found no time for remorse although there were moments when she would have even welcomed Larry's friendly face. Her feelings for him were ambivolent. Had he suddenly appeared on the scene, she was certain she would have rushed into his waiting arms, forgetting the distressing events of the past weeks. Thoughts of him made her dreadfully uncomfortable. She had hurt him beyond the human power to forgive. If ever he could find forgiveness in his heart—If. But she was too busy for retrospect. The days were too full.

And the nights! How long they were! Sometimes, from her pillow, the room seemed to be closing in on her in the darkness. She had to get up to breathe.

"I love you, Amy." She saw Dan's dear face in her mind's eye as she sat by the open window and listened to the surging of the ocean waves as they sought to wash away her distraught emotions. "Amy, dear, I've got to know."

Her head went down on her arms as she sobbed. "Dan, why did you have to love me?" The breeze stirred the warm air, but it was wasted in its effort to soothe her troubled heart. "I could have borne the pain of not having you had it been confined to my own heart. Oh, Dan, Dan," she cried out in agony, "go back to your wonderful people and leave me alone!"

"I don't know what to do now, Amy, except to pray that He will remove this love from me."

Perhaps He had already done that. It did not ease her burden.

Three weeks she had been here. Tomorrow Joy would be coming home, her recovery far from complete.

Amy climbed back between the cool sheets. She must try and get some rest. Tomorrow would be a busy day. Tomorrow—and tomorrow—and tomorrow—

Morning had a way of coming when she least expected it, when it seemed the night could hardly be over. She lay still for several minutes with her eyes closed before she realized one of her nieces was beside her. "Good morning, dear."

"Hi, Aunt Amy," Becky said, smiling as she touched Amy's hair, poking her fingers into the ringlets about her aunt's face. "Aunt Amy?"

"What is it, honey?" Amy stretched and turned over to look at the child.

"Why don't you laugh any more?" she asked. "Did you forget how?"

Amy closed her eyes tight. "You're up early, aren't you?"

"Mommy's coming home, so I wanted today to hurry up. She's been gone such a long time. Aren't you glad she's coming home?"

"You bet I am."

"It's going to be a fun day." There was wash day, ironing day, shopping day, church day. Each day had its own significance. Very special days could be any of these, but they were called *fun days.* "Mommy has a good laffer."

Amy smiled. "And so do you, sweetie."

"Daddy too."

"I know."

"What happened to your laffer, Aunt Amy?"

They would get back to it sooner or later. "I guess I lost it."

"I'll help you find it," the child offered.

"I was hoping you would, dear. What do you say we get up? There's lots and lots to do 'fore Mommy comes home."

There was an endless supply of chores to be taken care of during the morning hours, and, since it was Saturday, Dave was on hand to lift some of the burden from Amy's shoulders. Finally lunch time came. Then after restoring the kitchen to order, Amy took the girls upstairs to prepare them for the important event of the day.

"I'm on my way, ladies," Dave called to them.

"Oh, Daddy, *please* hurry!" squealed Becky who was finding it impossible to sit still while Amy untied her sneaker. Rachel had disappeared.

"You start the water in the bathtub while I go find your sister."

Becky scampered off to the bathroom, delighted to be free of her clothing, while Amy went downstairs calling Rachel. She had no sooner set foot in the downstairs hall when a piercing scream mixed with the sound of rushing water caused her to hastily retrace her steps. She wearily, frantically hurried to the bathroom.

Becky had obediently started the bath water but had ignored Rachel who had been hiding in the tub, fully clothed. Scarcely able to reach the sides of the tub, she braced her little arms against them, and as the water crept rapidly toward her feet, she walked up the back of the tub in retreat. She posed thus suspended over the steaming water when Amy came to the rescue. Becky jumped up and down, clapping her hands in delight.

"You're a naughty girl, Rebecca!" Amy scolded sternly. But it did not lessen the little girl's pleasure.

Amy tested the water, and Becky climbed in followed by Rachel who had rapidly shed her clothing. Amy went to their room to lay out their clean clothes, but was soon summoned back to the bathroom by another deluge of screams. This time the noise proceeded from Becky, but the sight which greeted her aunt was perplexing, for blood was dripping from Rachel's mouth. She soon perceived that the child's tooth which should have been in her mouth was in her hand.

"What *am* I going to do with you two?"

"Aunt Amy," Rachel squealed with glee, "we had a thug of war, and my thooth came out!"

"Becky, stop crying!" But Becky did not stop until the blood stopped. She feared she had mortally wounded her sister. "Now why did you do such a thing? And pray tell, *how* did you do it!"

"We had a thug of war," the child repeated, "with the wathcloth."

"First you have a tug of war with Tucker Too. Now you have a tug of war with the washcloth. You don't want your teeth to come out yet!"

"Oh, yeth I do," said the happy little girl. "Thtevie Hathingth' thooth came out, and he got ten thenths under hith pillow!"

"You have it all figured out, don't you?" Amy asked as she finished washing them. She was not about to leave the little despots alone again. "Time to get out!" She tried to sound cheerful. "You want to look pretty when Mommy gets here."

They had no sooner seated themselves on the front steps to await the family car when they sighted it coming around the bend. Amy managed to restrain them until it came to a halt, but the little feet were too agitated, the little hearts too anxious.

Dave took his son while they smothered their mother with kisses, and then held little David down at their level for their approval. Amy took the baby while Dave helped Joy into the house.

The homecoming was a jubilant reunion. The three weeks of separation had seemed endless to the children who saw no reason for their mother's long absence.

For Amy it meant double duty, and, although exhausting, it kept her depression from completely overtaking her. The days were not nearly long enough. Joy had been forbidden to undertake any household duties, and although Amy had had complete charge during Joy's confinement, she now had partial care of the new baby and her sister-in-law added to her responsibilities.

But the weeks were passing, – four, five, six. Almost six weeks since her heart-rending experience with Dan. That meant six more and he would be on his way back to Japan. How different those weeks would have been had she been privileged to spend them by his side! But it was not meant to be, and she must not consider what might have been, not even in wishful thinking. It made reality hurt too much. Perhaps some morning she would wake up and it would not hurt any more.

For the past week Joy had been allowed to go up and down stairs, and this relieved Amy's activities somewhat since it meant that Joy's meals could be taken with the family. Joy also began to spend several hours a day amusing the girls and reading to them. During this time Amy was able to accomplish considerably more than she could when she had to constantly check on their whereabouts.

"Go wash your hands for lunch, girls. And tell Mommy it's ready."

Joy came in before she had finished what she was saying.

"I'm sorry we've been such a burden on you, Amy."

"You've been no such thing! I've needed you as much as you've needed me, Joy."

"I know you aren't happy. I wish you'd talk about it."

"Maybe I'll be able to sometime soon – another few weeks or so – when I get it out of my system. If you can put up with me that long!"

"We like having you here. Why don't you plan on staying if you aren't going back to New Hope? I'm sure you could get a job here. Dave knows a lot of people at the bank – "

"No. At least not here with you and Dave. I'd wreck your happy home."

"Don't be silly. We want you, Amy. Please think about it."

"Thanks. It's nice to be wanted."

"Amy," Joy said hesitantly. "Amy, I guess Larry must be part of what you don't want to talk about. But is it all over between you two? I hate to ask, but that was an awful time to leave him, what with the accident and all. So unlike you too."

Amy's eyes filled with tears. "Yes, it's all over. It was over before the accident, Joy, or I wouldn't have left him. I hurt him something awful. For that reason I guess it has to be over."

"A fellow like Larry doesn't give up because he's hurt, Amy." Joy knew she had said enough.

The pleasant kitchen was quiet except for the sounds of silverware at work on china. They were almost finished eating before Amy spoke again.

"Joy, did you and Dave ever consider going to the mission field?"

"Yes, Amy, we considered it," Joy answered, trying to conceal her surprise. She could not have been more unprepared for the question if Amy had asked, "Have you thought about going to the moon?" "We never felt led to go," she added.

"Would you have gone?"

"Oh, yes," she said with finality. "Certainly. Why?"

"Oh – just wondering."

First Aunt Louise who should have gone, but didn't; then Roy Carlson who wanted to go, but couldn't; and now this parallel to add to the maze: Joy and Dave who had no orders to go at all.

But Amy was not going either.

Chapter 25

"THIS FELLOW LOOKS familiar, doesn't he, honey?"

David Archer was sitting on the sofa, reading the newspaper with his wife close beside him, her head resting on his shoulder. "Missionary Speaker," He read the caption aloud before his eyes fell to the article below the picture. "'Reverend Daniel Sanderford, missionary to Japan—' Of course! This is the fellow I spoke to when I was trying to find Amy. You know, the night before the baby was born. I met him once when I stopped in New Hope to visit Amy on my way back from New York. Don't you remember, honey? It was a couple of months after the twins were born. They were getting ready for a wedding—it was his sister's wedding, the one Amy is so friendly with. The one they call Lainey. That's right, and Amy was in it! I'll have to show her this when she comes down."

"You know, Dave, that's strange."

"What's strange about it? It says right here he'll be speaking tonight, tomorrow night, and then at a children's meeting Friday afternoon, one-thirty. Going back to Japan the middle of August."

"Dave!"

He looked at her in surprise. "Honey, I'm right alongside of you," he cautioned as he tapped his ear with the palm of his hand.

"Dave, that's it!" she exclaimed.

"What's it?"

Joy sat on the edge of the sofa and faced her husband. "Today at lunch Amy asked me if ever we had felt led to go to the mission field. When I told her no and asked her why, she wouldn't answer." Dave nodded his head in consideration, not yet assured of the relationship of circumstances. "Then she said maybe she would be able to talk about it pretty soon—after she got it out of her system. In a few weeks, she said. And it's only a matter of weeks before this Daniel Whatsizname leaves. Don't you see, Dave—"

His enthusiasm matched his wife's. "And you know something?

He used to work at the bank with her. In fact," he looked at Joy, impressed with the alertness of his own memory, "it was through him that Amy was saved! Remember her telling about hearing him on the radio? Honey, you're right!" He embraced her in a crushing hug. "I wondered why I married you, and now I know. You're so smart! And you know something else? When I talked to his brother, Paul I think was his name, he didn't seem to know much about Amy. He gave the phone to Dan as if he would be more likely to know something about Amy's whereabouts." He tapped the newspaper with his finger. "Don't say anything to her about this."

"Now, Dave, don't go interfering. She's upset enough already."

He tucked the newspaper under the sofa when he heard his sister's footsteps on the stairs. "Kids in bed?" he asked innocently. "I should have been helping you."

"I don't mind."

"You haven't been out of this house since you came here, Amy. How about going out with me tonight?" he asked casually.

"Where?" she asked with not the remotest trace of interest.

"They're having special services this week out at the conference grounds in Sandy Hook. I'd like to go, but I hate to go alone. And tomorrow night I have to work late. How about it?"

"I'd rather not."

"Please do, Amy," Joy spoke up. "I'd like to, but I really don't feel up to it yet. It would do you both good, and it would make me feel a lot better since I've been such a burden on both of you." She was not sure Dave was doing the right thing.

"Can't you get Tim or someone else. I really don't care to go."

"You'd be doing me a favor, Amy." Dave was not going to give up.

She sighed. "If you put it that way, I guess I owe you a lot of them. I must warn you though, I'm not very good company."

Dave laughed. "Company, nevertheless."

The auditorium was nearly filled to capacity when they entered. It was not until they were seated in the balcony that Amy saw him. In desperation she wanted to get out, but she and Dave were flanked on either side by those who had rapidly filled up the row. The service had started. Amy stared at the program, her heart beating like a triphammer. She could not bear to look at him, far away though he was. She glanced at Dave once or twice out of the corner of her eye, but if he noticed, he concealed it in his interest in the program.

By the end of the song service, Amy had calmed down enough to lift her eyes to the platform. Dan was going to sing. Perhaps he could not see her in the dimly-lighted balcony. The organist was playing the introduction, but she stopped when Dan handed her another book and whispered something to her.

Amy could not take her eyes from him as he sang the familiar melody. Occasionally his eyes sought her out across the vast auditorium.

Once I was drifting aimlessly, I had no port in sight,
There was no sign to lead by day, no gleam to pierce the night.
No captain on board to chart my course, no compass and no goal,
I could not find a ray of hope to guide my fevered soul.

Amy's tears fell silently down her cheeks. She wiped them with the back of her hand and hoped Dave had not noticed.

The Master Pilot took the helm, His blessings never cease,
He took away the stain of sin, He gave me perfect peace.

"'Peace, peace, when there is no peace.' Oh, Dave," Amy murmured to herself, "*why* did you bring me here?"

With her eyes downcast during the remainder of the service, Amy tried not to listen to the dear familiar voice she thought she would never hear again. She tried not to listen to the words he spoke, "Let go and let God," for once again they were prayerfully sent in her direction.

Dan told the story of the Japanese boy, but there was a sadness in his voice that had never been there in its telling. His voice broke as he spoke, for he had anxiously been looking forward to seeing his friend again soon. But Josh had gone to his heavenly home. Dan had received the message that morning.

He closed the message with the same words with which he had opened it. "Let go and let God. Let go and let God have His way."

The congregation stood to sing the closing hymn. Amy excused herself and clumsily made her way out, not stopping to see if Dave were following her.

"I don't thank you for bringing me here," she snapped as soon as Dave started the motor.

"I got that impression." He backed the car out of the parking space. His lips were drawn in a tight line as he guided it along the winding dirt road between the tall pines.

"I don't know how you found out, but don't you think I would have stayed in New Hope if I had wanted to see him again?"

He did not speak until they were speeding along the black surface of the highway. "So he *was* the reason you left."

"Not entirely."

"Maybe he didn't see you."

"He saw me."

"Maybe he'll come out to see you," Dave said hopefully.

"He won't."

"What's holding you back, Amy? You're nuts about the guy. And from the looks of things, he must feel the same way about you."

"Dave, would you mind your own business, and let me take care of mine?" She was angry, and her voice was loud.

"But you're not taking care of it."

"Maybe not the way you think I should."

"Why are you so opposed to the mission field?" Dave's probing was direct and deliberate.

"And what makes you think I am?"

"Well, it certainly couldn't be to *him*. They couldn't come much finer."

"Shut up, Dave! Shut up! Do you hear?" Her voice increased each time she spoke. "I don't want to hear any more!" she screamed.

"I know you want a home of your own, Amy, and that's natural. But what makes you think they don't have vine-covered cottages in Japan?" His voice had reached the same pitch as his sister's. "Why don't you wake up and stop feeling sorry for yourself?"

"Stop!" she screamed at him, fighting to keep back the tears.

"Amy," Dave said, bringing his voice down to a natural pitch, "if you think you can't be happy over there *with* the man you love, what makes you think you can be happy here—*without* him?"

"Dave," she said bitterly, "did it ever occur to you there might be some other reason?"

"No," he said softly, determined to remain calm, "I can't think of any reason for not serving the Lord—where He wants you." He turned the car into the drive. "You've been moping around here for weeks, and I think it's about time you got hold of yourself. Snap out of it, Amy. Wake up! The world's passing you by." He brought the car to a halt near the back door to let her out before putting it into the garage.

"It's good to know how you stand, isn't it? I'll leave in the morning. I hadn't really planned on staying this long anyway, and I can see I've worn out my welcome." She slammed the door and ran into the house.

Dave closed the overhead door and walked the few steps to the back door with his head bent in deep thought. Joy was right. He should not have meddled. Everything he said must have been true, otherwise Amy would not have exploded the way she did. But he would apologize.

All was quiet, however, and Amy had disappeared into her room.

She pulled the suitcase from the closet and angrily threw her belongings into it in such disarray that she dumped them on the floor and started all over again. The tears persistently blinded her until she gave up in frustration and lay across her bed sobbing. "I didn't want to be there, Dan," she cried. "I didn't want to see you again."

Sometime later, she slipped off her bed and onto her knees, not knowing that across the hall, two others, hand in hand, were interceding for her also.

She opened her Bible to the familiar passage in Job, reading thoughtfully the words she had pondered the morning she had thought Joy had been taken from them.

"Oh, that I knew where I might find Him." When she came to the tenth verse she stopped, read it over, then over again. "He knoweth the way that I take; and when he hath tried me I shall come forth as gold." How could anything so worthless and ugly come forth as gold?

It was late when she climbed into bed, but her head throbbed with a dull ache, much as it had the day she left New Hope. She put on her robe and silently slipped through the dark hall and down the stairs. There was a glimmer of light from the living room, and through the open doorway she could see her brother as he sat in the rocker, bent over with his head in his hands.

"Dave," she said softly. He looked up. "Dave, I'm sorry." Her humility sharply contrasted her expressions of early evening. "I don't want to leave."

"We don't want you to leave, Amy. You know that. But it's I who should apologize." He stood up and put his arm around her shoulder, drawing her to the warmth of the fireplace. It was the only source of light in the room.

"For telling me the truth?"

"I wasn't really certain of that, you know."

"What led you to think it then?"

He reached his hand under the sofa and held the newspaper out to her. "This and your remarks to Joy at lunchtime. We put them and a lot of other little items together, and you must admit, we came up with some pretty concrete conclusions."

She looked at the picture of Dan. "Some of them, anyway. Good night, Dave. And thanks." She took the paper with her.

"Good night, Amy." He was not quite satisfied.

Chapter 26

DAN DROVE ALONG the beautiful shore line of the Atlantic Ocean. He never thought of this but what he thought of Amy. She had talked about it so much. But then everything reminded him of Amy.

Ocean Point . . . . Five miles.

He turned his car in the direction indicated. He had looked up the address in the telephone listings back at the conference office and had obtained a general idea of the location from several of the local ministers. He was going to look up an old friend.

He had been asked to take this engagement when the regularly scheduled speaker had become ill. He had reached the point of exhaustion himself, but God alone knew his limits. God had given him a job to do, and he was not about to refuse his services.

When Dan had received the call, he had wondered if there were some significance in the alteration of his plans. He must not get his hopes up again. Such a short distance to where Amy was! About six or eight miles according to the map! By some miracle he just might see her. But then she might be far away. She had told Roy she would be staying at her brother's for only two weeks.

And last night he had seen her. It *did* seem like a miracle. First he caught a glimpse of that dress—the same one she had worn that night—that awful night. And then he saw her sweet face. She looked so thin, so pale. Who was the gentleman? Her brother, of course.

Oh, Amy, his heart had leaped for joy, *God has brought you to me. I hardly dared hope for this. Amy, please hear the message He has for you. The words aren't from me. Please listen, Amy. Please be willing to go.*

But she had disappeared. She had slipped out before the benediction had been pronounced, before he had been able to take his place at the door to greet the worshipers. Apparently she had not come willingly. Or if she had, she must not have known he would be there. But she did not want to see him. It was a bitter pill.

There was no end in sight. "Whom the Lord loveth he chasteneth." Dan did not ask for freedom from the burden. Just the grace to bear it. "My grace is sufficient for thee." It was so easy to quote these words to others, but quite a different matter to apply them to one's own trials.

Dan's thoughts turned to Josh as he rode along. If only he had not had to leave him so hurriedly, he might have been able to cut some of the red tape. But God worked in mysterious ways, and He was omniscient.

Now Josh was gone. Laura's telegram had not given him any of the details. Just the blunt fact. He should be hearing from her in a few days.

Until the time he had received the word from Laura, he had still been hoping that the Lord might make a way for Josh to come to America. If necessary, he thought he might have arranged to stay a few extra weeks so that he might make the trip back to Japan with the boy. And then too, he was hoping to have the extra weeks to remain near Amy—just perchance he might lead her to his way of thinking.

But the river had changed its course. Josh was gone, and Dan's heart ached with a new burden. Had he in some way failed? Could he have done more? Should he have stayed with the boy when he so badly needed him? Perhaps he had failed. But he could not have failed his mother either. He had had no choice in the matter. God knew that. And now he would not be failing in the rash promise he had so foolishly made to the boy.

And now Amy was gone too. Had he cared too much?

Oh, Amy, if there were some way I could bring the joy back to those eyes, the lilt back to that voice, the sparkle back to those smiling lips I would gladly do it. If never seeing you again would do it—

Was it wrong to care so much, so desperately? But his caring had not been a voluntary action that one could put a right or wrong to it. Had there ever been a time when he had known her without loving her? And yet it was as if this love had been a tangible part of him all his life. This burning went back to a long time before he knew her, almost as if the feeling were there all along, tiny yearnings, tiny needs, tiny heartbeats. Tiny seeds that needed only to know her, to love her, to spring into glorious life. How could it be wrong? How could it?

There was only one hard, cold fact tumbling around in Dan's mind that could make it wrong. Only if, before God and man she had made sacred vows to some other, "Till death do us part,"—that alone could make it wrong. But if that were the simple, heartbreaking truth, why would she not have told him? It would have brought his dearest hopes to a shattering shamble, but that would have been easier to take than this. No. It could not be so simple.

How could it be wrong? It could not.

But what about Larry? Perhaps his reasoning was along these same lines. The same hopes had been painfully evident in his eyes. Dan had gone to see him that same afternoon after the accident, aware that his own bruises and swollen eye were an acute reminder to the other man of his rancorous attack of the previous evening. These physical marks of violence made it hard for Dan to keep a restraining hand on his own growing irritation of the situation.

"Dan, I can't live without her," Larry choked. "What am I going to do?" There was a desperate pleading in his words. He was more coherent than he had been earlier in the day.

Dan could offer no prognosis for he was beyond hoping with any real expectation himself. There was with him an undercurrent, an urging to repress the onrushing cataclysm before it would overcome all of them. In the end someone would be hurt. Someone.

Dan took the cigarette lighter from the shaky hand and held it for him. "That's white of you," Larry mumbled, thinking of the many times he had called Amy a shrew for grabbing an unlighted cigarette from his lips and replacing it with a stick of chewing gum. It had been a sore spot between them.

"We may both have to live without her," Dan said it blandly, with an inexorable sense of defeat, almost withdrawal. Larry, in spite of his condition, reflexed to the concise statement and looked at Dan in surprise. "The choice is hers," Dan went on. "Not yours, not mine." He felt the need to move away from the scrutinizing gaze and turned to draw a chair up nearer to the bed. "And she won't be able to make it until she is willing to submit herself to God's will. There would be a lot less heartache now if we all had done that right from the beginning."

"You did?" Larry's voice was weak, but it held a tinge of remote hopefulness.

"I've tried to. But it isn't easy when our own desires are so strong." Dan looked away again, out the window to a world which knew as much of pain and suffering as did the world confined to this side of the glass. His volcano was making speech increasingly difficult. "And it won't be any easier for me to lose her." He brought his gaze back to the heavy-set man in the bed. "I just pray that what I count loss might somehow be gain."

It was Larry's turn to look away. After a minute he said, "Things sure do get mixed up, don't they? But for Pete's sake, Dan, why did Amy leave like that?" He was an humbled man.

Nonplused, Dan met his gaze directly. "I was hoping you could give me some answers to that. Amy has become quite a mystery to me."

"She's had me wondering for four years. What answers could I give you?" He was trying to be vague and succeeding. "And even if Amy had ever confided in me, I wouldn't be likely to talk about it, would I?" He looked steadily, almost defiantly, into the dark brown eyes. "You wouldn't."

"You're right." Dan got up and walked to the window. Without looking at Larry he spoke. "I called your folks."

Larry groaned. "I wish you hadn't." Wishing could not alter it. The damage was done.

"They'll be here this evening."

"Boy, it sure will be good to see them!" he exclaimed in boyish anticipation. "But—how—but—but what did you tell them?" he stammered nervously.

"Only that you were in an accident."

"Great Scott! That's a relief!" He breathed a heavy sigh. "I'm a fool."

"No, you're not." Dan's own attitude had been changing under the pathetic humility borne of repentance. This was not the same man who had struck him with such bitter verve the night before. But it *was* the same man who wanted Amy. "But sometimes we forget that the Lord holds tomorrow in His hands, and His way is best for all of us."

"I know that, Dan. Sometimes I find myself wondering. But down deep I know it. I'm still a fool. I'm a weak-kneed, blundering fool. I haven't touched a drop of that stuff in four years. Then when the pressure is on, I'm weak. No backbone."

"That's not a fact, Larry." Dan was almost surprised to find himself on the defensive. "Remember the story of Peter? He walked on the water, remember? As long as he kept his eyes on the Lord, he was all right. As soon as he took his eyes *off* the Lord he started to sink."

"We're all Peters, aren't we?"

"We're all human, just like Peter. There's a simple lesson in that story—a lesson vital to our spiritual survival. Until we learn it, we can't expect to cope with forces of the devil which seek to destroy that life." His words to Larry were aimed at a much closer personality, a personality which also was struggling for survival. *Not I, but Christ,* pondered Dan.

"You've given me a lot to think about, Dan. You're a great guy. I'm sorry for clobbering you the way I did."

"That goes double."

"Oh, no! I asked for what I got. I had it coming. Boy, did

I have it coming! I appreciate your patience with me though. And thanks for coming."

Larry was getting groggy, and Dan stood up to leave. "Whatever the outcome, Larry, try to remember Peter. It's a good lesson for all of us."

"He and I are going to be great friends from now on." Larry smiled weakly without opening his eyes. Dan left and made his way to Elaine's room, his footsteps heavy on the freshly waxed floor.

He had not called David Archer back that day. His afternoon visit to Elaine had changed matters considerably. It had been quite a jolt to learn of Amy's return.

"She looked just awful, Danny, as if she hadn't slept all night. Oh, I wish you would go find her. She's so mixed up, and I'm so worried about her. Danny, she needs you."

"She knows where I am, Lainey," Dan said with more finality than he had been able to muster during the past forty-eight hours. He went on, as if thinking to himself. "If she were here this morning, then she must be at her brother's by now. Elaine, we've got to face the possibility that maybe she isn't included in God's plan for me."

"I won't buy that."

"Did you tell her about Larry?"

"I didn't want to, but I told her. I wish I knew if she went to see him."

"He didn't mention it. But of course when I left him this morning the nurse was ready to give him something to ease his pain. He probably didn't remember anything after that."

Dan's thoughts made a sharp return to the present when he realized he was nearing his destination. He would not go to see Amy, it would be useless. Call it curiosity, call it peace of mind, call it the faintest glimmer of hope. Call it anything at all or nothing at all, but he just had to see where she was, where she was staying.

He had thought of stopping to see David Archer at his office. That was listed in the book too. But no, he might not understand the situation. He sounded reasonable enough through his anxiety when Dan talked to him on the phone almost six weeks ago. But talking to Amy's brother now would no doubt accomplish very little. Still, he must have been responsible for Amy's being at the service last night.

He would just take a look, then go.

Had it really been six weeks since he had seen Amy? In some ways it seemed longer, as if he were living in some sort of timeless existence. How could one measure eons of uncertainty, of heartache, of volcano eruptions?

If Larry's bones were healed properly, he would be having his casts removed next week. His recovery, aside from the broken bones, had taken much longer than he had anticipated, otherwise he would have been to see Amy long ago. Dan was sure of that. And there was nothing he could do to stop him.

"Sonny, can you tell me where David Archer lives?"

"Last house down that next lane, mister."

Dan thanked the boy, turned down the lane which the dirty finger had pointed out, then drove to the bend in the road. He saw the white house nestled peacefully among the bayberry bushes and long-needled pine, the ocean stretching in its scintillating beauty to the far horizon beyond. It was just as it had been described and left no question in his mind that it was the place.

There was no sign of life. The only evidence of Amy's presence was her car which was parked near the back of the house. It was partially hidden from view by the bushes.

He backed out of the narrow lane and headed back toward Sandy Hook. He had preparations to make for the evening service.

Larry had much to think about, too, and plenty of time in which to do it.

Dan's frequent visits between trips had been a boon in the healing of his weakened spirit. The healing of his body was steady but slow. He had a restlessness borne of his feverish desire to make things right with Amy and the blunt knowledge that he could do nothing but wait until his body was healed.

He had told her he was sorry that last day at the office, but had she actually heard him? He wrote a brief note to confirm his apologies. He supposed she received it. He had not expected an answer.

She was so upset that day. He had the utter gall to open the unsealed envelope she left on Hank Chapman's desk, and he saw red. He had been seeing red all week because of the unjust accusations made against Amy, but this topped everything. And this time when Larry saw red, everyone else did too.

It was while he was on his way home to get his car that he passed the tavern. There was a tug at his senses, a jab at his memories — something that could ease one's tensions, soothe one's pains, minimize one's problems —

And after the second one, nothing mattered. Nothing except the one person who stood in his way. He would take care of him.

He took an awful beating under Dan's stony fists, but it was nothing compared to the beating of his spirit. Then it was as if his mind left him for a short period after that, as if there were no time lapse between that and his waking up in the hospital. He had been so certain that death was near.

Dan visited him faithfully, but many of his visits were cut short by duties which forever called. His friendship had come to mean a great deal to Larry. It was ironical. The one person he thought he would always hate he now considered his best friend. And it had come about through that hate.

"Oh, by the way," Dan said casually a day or so after the accident, "I had quite a talk with Karen Winslow the other day. You might welcome her into the fold when you see her."

"You're kidding, Dan. You can't be talking about the same Karen Winslow *I* know."

"Well, no, it would be hard to believe she's the same one you *knew.* But she's the same one who works at the National Bank of New Hope. I assure you, she's an entirely different person."

"Not that she-devil! I don't believe it! Amy never gave up on her, and after all she had to take from that—"

"I know, Larry. I've known Karen for a long time, and I must admit, I would have considered her pretty hopeless too. But she is a star in Amy's crown, you know."

"If you could have heard Amy talking to her! Boy! She really gave her both barrels. I guess some of it finally penetrated, huh?"

"I think it must have been penetrating for some time, only Karen wasn't one to admit it. You'll find her quite a different person," Dan reiterated. "It's not going to be easy for her though, Larry. She's going to need a good bit of encouragement, and I'm sure you can be of some help to her, especially at work."

"And you think it will be easy for me? I treated that girl like poison. But maybe I'll get used to the idea that she's not."

Dan laughed. "I'm sure you will."

The very next day Karen herself came to see him. She was laden down with a gigantic basket of fruit from his co-workers. Strange that she had been elected to the task when there were so many others he had been friendly with. She was extremely shy and hesitant about coming into his hospital room.

Her apologies were so sincere that, for the first time, Larry found himself ill at ease in her presence. This surely was not the same girl. The awkward moment was somewhat alleviated when Dan strolled in, his face still tense and drawn. Karen left soon after.

The two men chatted about the various happenings of New Hope, each avoiding the subject nearest the tip of his tongue, but Larry was preoccupied. This was mightly peculiar.

"Hey, Dan! Wait a minute! Hold on here!" Mighty peculiar, indeed. "Open that drawer," he ordered. Dan obliged. "You wouldn't know anything about that, would you?"

There was a little wisp of a handkerchief he had picked up off the floor, the little square with the initials KRW embroidered in the corner. Now how did Karen's handkerchief get in there? Dan had forgotten all about it. He quickly closed the drawer and grinned sheepishly, at the same time easing toward the door. "Now why should I know anything about that?" Better keep talking, he thought. "I'll see you later, Larry. I'll be away for about a week, but I'll see you as soon as I get back."

This was one of Dan's brief visits.

Larry spent three weeks in the hospital. At first the time went quickly, probably because of the great lapses he spent in unconsciousness. The last three he had spent in his apartment, his confinement much more restraining than he had hoped. But the steady stream of visitors and the occasional times he was able to get out helped curb his impatience.

Had it been just six weeks since he had seen Amy? Seemed more like an eternity. He stuffed three sticks of chewing gum into his mouth. At last he was to have the casts removed. Next week, Doc said.

And next week he would go to see Amy.

Chapter 27

THE SERVICE WAS already under way when the lone figure in the frosty pink dress entered the auditorium and found a seat in the last row under the balcony. A more obscure place could not be found. She should not have come, but the desire to see him, just once more, was a magnet, a compelling force drawing her back to the scene.

Strange, he was not on the platform yet. Where could he be? Then, without turning to look, she knew he was there. He rushed past her and down the aisle, so close she could have reached out and touched him. But he had not seen her.

"Not My Will," was the title of the poem on the back of the program. Amy read the words over to herself.

My path is ofttimes rough and steep,
The sky above grows dark.
I wish I'd found another way—
One with a clearer mark.
The road that I would like to choose
Is one with the light of the sun,
But taking my cross to the Saviour I say,
"Not my will, but Thine be done."

This road is washed with Christ's own blood
And it's paved with God's own hand.
Why He has given to me this way
I cannot understand.
There's darkness that would cover me
But I'm never left alone,
For I seek the touch of the nail-pierced hand,
And bid Him, "Thy will be done."

He has not promised that my path
Would leave the wilderness,
Or the waters that would compass me

Would part to let me pass.
I only know He'll guide my steps
If I take them one by one,
So, with Him each step I'll boldly take
And whisper, "Thy will be done."

It had a familiarity about it, but she could not pin it down. Then Dan began to sing it, and she knew. It was the same song he had sung that night—

She became oblivious to the messenger as she listened and thrilled to it, for at last her heart was attuned to the message.

Dan was glad he had chosen this song, glad this was the one laid upon his heart to sing tonight. It meant a great deal to him. The words coincided so perfectly with those his mother had inscribed in his first Bible. At the end of the rather lengthy message, she had written inside the flyleaf, "And above all things, Danny boy, keep in step with Him, not letting your footsteps lag behind, not letting them hasten ahead, always remembering He will take each step with you." His mother's words had finally sunk in. It was long before his father's death, long before he had assumed the responsibility of the family, that his mother's words were no longer words, but a living, breathing truth. "Keep in step with Him—"

He must keep in step. No matter what—

He must accept the fact that Amy did not want to see him. It was not right. It was not fair. In all his wildest hopes and dreams she had been his. Now she wanted nothing to do with him. It was not fair.

"Keep in step—"

It was time for the message.

Amy listened intently, dreading the time when it would be over. In her heart she must say good-by.

Dan turned the pulpit over to the director who in turn invited all who would respond to the call to the mission field to stand. Dan left the dais and sat in the front pew with his head bowed in prayer. With head and heart bowed in submission, Amy stood. She hastened out when the closing hymn was announced.

The house was dark. Perhaps Joy was still asleep and Dave had to work extra late. If that were the case, they would not know she had been gone. She walked slowly toward the back door.

"Come sit with us." It was Joy's voice from the patio.

They sat in silence and listened to the night. Dave was the first to speak, and he did so as if he were reluctant to disturb the soft touch of quietness. "How was the service?"

"Lovely. Just lovely. I wish both of you could have gone. I

didn't like to leave you like that, Joy, but you fell asleep. Must have been a good book."

Joy laughed. "I've been living such a life of ease lately, I've really become quite lazy."

"You needed the rest. You're looking a lot better."

"Thanks to you, Amy. I don't know what we would have done without you," Joy declared for the hundredth time.

"Well, I have a feeling things might be a little different around here," Dave said with a quick glance at his wife as he pressured the hand that rested in his. "Seems as if Amy might be getting ready to leave 'fore long."

"Yes," she said pensively, as if she had not yet taken a look at the future. "I suppose I should start thinking about it soon. I wish I knew where I were going though."

They looked at each other and frowned, each supposing the matter to have been settled.

Double headlamps illuminated them briefly as they made an arc and stopped near the end of the drive. They were extinguished, and the darkness seemed darker than before. Amy's fingers tightened on the arms of her chair. She jumped to her feet, prompted by an urgency to flee, delayed only by her unbelief.

Dan stood silently and uncertainly in the shadows at the edge of the patio. Dave rose to greet him, shook hands, then introduced him to Joy. There was a painful lack of small talk. Amy was frozen.

Dan turned to face her. "Hello, Amy." Silence. "It's good to see you."

Her throat was dry. If only she had not gone tonight, Dan never would have come. If only she had made it into the house—

She moistened her lips and opened her mouth to speak, swallowed twice, then opened her mouth again. "I'm ready to go—" She faltered as he took several steps toward her. The moonlight which had shown intermittently through the clouds all evening outlined his handsome face and revealed the trace of a smile on his lips. She took a deep breath and strained through clenched teeth, "—but not with you." She turned away. His smile had quickly faded, and she was unable to bear the look of pain which had taken its place.

Her words were a bolt of lightning. The four of them stood motionless, breathless. The wind and the waves seemed to be holding their breath too. Amy wanted to run.

The tiniest member of the family broke the spell as he exercised his lungs in an urgent call for attention. His mother jumped, ran to the door, then stopped short. She whirled about, ran back to where her husband was standing and grasped him by the hand. He followed her obediently into the house.

Dan shortened the remaining distance between them. He stood behind her, not daring to speak.

"You shouldn't have come," she said in a tight, meaningless voice.

"You knew I would," he said after a moment.

"I was hoping you didn't see me."

"I was watching for you. I saw you drive in." He cleared his throat. "Where will you go?"

"I don't know yet."

"Not Japan?"

"Not Japan."

"You're so sure? The Lord might call you there."

"It's a big place. There's room enough for both of us."

He cleared his throat again. "Amy, I thought—I knew if the Lord wanted me to see you again He would provide the way. Don't you believe there is some significance in our meeting? Don't you think He planned it this way?" Dan was not sure of his own reasoning in the light of events of the past months.

"I have a very meddlesome brother. He planned it."

"The Lord can use them too. I'm glad you're willing to go. I'll be praying for you."

"Thank you. I appreciate that. I really do."

Dan jammed his hands into his pockets. "Is this final, Amy?" She did not turn. "Good-by." He walked slowly to his car, his muscular frame bent in complete dejection. This was the end. He would never see her again. She was willing to go, but she would never be his. Then it was wrong all along, but why hadn't he realized it? Why hadn't he known? It must have been wrong. It couldn't be right.

There was more to it than her opposition to the mission field, after all. So near and yet so far. Dan opened the car door and slid behind the wheel, and for a moment he let his head rest on his hands as they gripped the wheel. But it wasn't so far. Just a million miles.

Amy did not watch him. She sat at the edge of the patio where it formed one step at the front and put her hot cheek against the cool round supporting post of the roof. The car door slammed shut. She waited expectantly for the sound of the motor. The simmering embers of her troublesome life became a holocaust of mixed emotions and she shook with sobs. There were no more tears. The supply had been exhausted.

"I couldn't leave you like that, Amy." The voice beside her was soft. He stood near her and put one foot on the step. He was so close.

Amy's heart pounded against her ribs. "You shouldn't have come back."

"Amy, why are you doing this to me—to us?"

"I didn't ask you to come," she said blandly, never moving.

"I love you, and I know you love me. If I didn't know that, I wouldn't have come. But in view of that fact, don't you think I deserve some sort of explanation?"

"Why must you make it so difficult?" Her voice was hard, bitter. "If you would just go, pretend you never knew me—"

"I can't do that. Nor do I want to."

Amy sat for some minutes, trying to control her voice as she endeavored to arrange some logic from her chaotic thoughts. "All right, Dan," she finally said. "I'll give you some sort of explanation, as you put it. I didn't want to, but maybe if you know a little more about me, you'll go away and leave me alone." She sighed as she leaned against the post again. "I'm not good enough for you. I can't put it any plainer than that."

"Amy, Amy," he pleaded as he sat on the step beside her. "What makes one person better than another?" He waited, not really expecting an answer. "I never asked you to give an account of yourself. And I never will," he said quietly.

"Go away, Dan! You must go!" She was fighting tears again. She had been fighting them for so long.

"No," he said with a sternness she had never known him to possess. "Is there someone else, Amy?"

She supposed he meant Larry. "No," she answered, knowing now that there never could be. "There was once though, before I moved to New Hope." She gave him a quick glance, trying in that moment to determine his reaction.

"I don't want you to tell me."

"I have to. You leave me no choice." Her voice became hard again in her effort to control it. "I want you to leave, so apparently I have to tell you."

"Do you love me, Amy? That's all I want you to tell me."

A silence fell between them. The low eerie tones of a foghorn sounded from far away, and a searchlight sent its beams skyward, here and there piercing the gaps between the low-hanging clouds. The moon had disappeared, now and then showing through to remind them of its presence but making no headway in affirming its reputation as a favorable ingredient in the makings of romance.

"That doesn't matter any more."

"Saying it doesn't make it true."

"His name is Todd Kenyon. We went to a party, a party that ruined my life. I thought I could pick up the pieces but I was fooling myself." It was not easy to tell this sordid story to this man, but for his sake she must go on. "I didn't realize what was going on – oh, I didn't really care until it was too late."

"Did you love him?" Dan asked without looking at her.

"I thought I did. Even that doesn't matter now. But no, I didn't love him."

"Then why?"

"Too much drink. I hate it! It's a tool of the devil! I don't remember much about it. Isn't that enough to sicken you, Dan?" Amy asked disdainfully. "Me, Amy Archer, so drunk I don't remember what happened to me!" She went on in a monotone, as if talking to herself. "He was a nice fellow. We went together in high school, saw each other during college vacations. We were going to get married, but it would have been the end of his education. His parents kicked up a fuss. He said he would come for me when he finished school, but somehow I knew he wouldn't. Oh, I won't say I didn't hope at first. But I didn't tell him where I was. I knew he would find me if he really wanted to. Then *you* told me I couldn't marry him. That afternoon in your living room when I was waiting for your mother to fit my dress. You were telling me about your cousin, Robin – "

"I remember," he murmured. *I remember that day. Every last detail of it –*

"From that time on I prayed that he would never come. Then, last summer he showed up. I wish he hadn't. I never want to see him again." She was bitter. "Disillusioned, Dan? It's a pretty disgusting picture, isn't it?"

He sat with his elbows on his knees, his forehead resting on his hands. Had he expected this? What really mattered, after all? Without moving, he spoke. "He that is without sin among you, let him first cast a stone at her."

"You don't understand."

"No. It's you who doesn't understand, Amy. I love you."

"You can't tell me you don't care, Dan," she said with a short sarcastic laugh. She was trembling. "I know you better than that."

"Do you? I didn't say I didn't care, Amy. I said I love you. How can I say I don't care?"

"Please go!" she cried loudly. She jumped up and ran, the hot tears stinging her face, but he reached the door first and blocked her way. "Go away and leave me alone," she cried in anguish.

"I'm not going."

"You may think it doesn't matter, Dan, but next week, next month, next year you'll say, 'It's too bad, but I certainly am glad Amy was so sensible about it.'"

"If it takes a week, a month, a year, or even the rest of my life, I'll not give up until I knock some sense into that pretty little head." With a sudden awareness Dan realized it was summer. Fall would follow, then winter and spring. Summer would come again in monotonous regularity. He could not face these and the future they held without Amy. "I love you, Amy. That's what matters."

She walked away from him. Her voice was so soft he had to strain to catch her words. "Then I'll have to tell you the rest. That's not the whole story. I was ashamed. I was so ashamed I didn't know how I could go on living. But things got worse. They always seem to for me. Back home they call them shotgun weddings," she said bitterly. "Me, Dan! The one you thought you loved! I was going to have to carry this shame for the rest of the world to see!" There was a hard lump in her throat to keep the tears near the surface, and she swallowed several times before she tried to go on. She felt sick and weak. The shame came over her anew as she stood before this man she loved so dearly and painted for him a picture of the real Amy Archer. "We began making plans to get married. We had talked about it anyway, before this happened. But his parents intervened. I was too scared to fight them and they talked me into it – oh, what's the use! You might as well know the whole truth. I took that life away!" Amy was at the point of hysteria. It did not matter any more what she told him. The damage had to be done so he would go away. "I took away a human life!" She stopped again, and the silence that followed echoed and re-echoed the words.

"I couldn't fight, but I couldn't go through with what they wanted. We quarreled, Todd and I. He was driving so fast and – and I grabbed the wheel from him – " Amy shuddered, then buried her face in her hands. "It was awful. Todd almost died too. His parents sued. Took everything I had. It wasn't much, but it was all my mother left me. You can't know, you can't *possibly* know what it's like to be so near the bottom."

Amy walked to the edge of the patio and stared into the darkness. Without warning, she put her arm against the post, put her head on her arm and cried, "I hate him! I hate him! I hate him!" she sobbed.

Dan stood rooted to the spot. He knew just how she felt. At least a man had his fists when the going got too rough –

"First I thought I was going to die," she went on in the same monotone. "Then I was afraid I wouldn't. Now I wish I had."

Dan walked up behind her and put his hands on her shoulders. "Maybe you'd like to hang a sign around your neck, 'Sinner. I'm a sinner. Don't touch me or you might become defiled.' Do you think that would make you any different from anyone else?" He turned her around gently and took her wrists as she hid her face in her hands. "Amy, look at me. Amy, dear," he said, his voice suddenly gentle again, "if God can forgive you, what right have I not to? Don't you understand, 'once for all.' We don't have to do penance for our sin for the rest of our lives when Christ has already taken care of it."

She did not look up. "Don't *you* understand, Dan. I destroyed a life that God created—"

His hard strong fingers bit into the soft flesh of her arms. There was some strange satisfaction in the pain. She wanted to hurt. She wanted to be beaten until all trace of life was extracted from her aching body.

"That's past, Amy. You can't live in the past. He's given you a new life. Are you going to destroy that too?"

"'Pureness of mind that God might teach you His way; pureness of heart that you might have a love for the unlovely; pureness of body that you might be a fit vessel—'" There was biting sarcasm in her tone.

"But you didn't read the rest, did you? I wish you had. 'May He give you understanding to see the good in others which they fail to see in themselves and grace to overlook that which they think is there but which fails to materialize. And in turn may they do the same for you.' Mother had—Mother *and* Dad had a wisdom given to very few parents. Mother loved you, Amy. I love you." He touched her forehead with his lips.

"No, Dan! No!" She struggled to release his grip. "You can't."

"But I do." The tightness of his grip loosened as he suddenly realized the harshness of it. His deep love bore with it a compassionate understanding for the burden of her load.

She finally lifted her face to look at him, expecting to see in his expression pity, reproach, disappointment. His heart was full of love, and it was only this she saw on his face.

"God only knows how you can."

"He knows I do. Oh, I do love you, Amy." He kissed the palms of her moist hands, then put them to his face. "Please believe me, Amy." He put his arms around her.

She did not remove her hands from his face, but looked at him in bewilderment. "You couldn't, Dan," she choked. "You couldn't. You're so good—"

She was unable to finish for he was kissing her. She put her arms around him as he drew her close, and the tears, so near the surface for so long, refused to stay back. Amy sobbed. Dan waited patiently, content in her nearness, knowing, hoping the tears would wash away any remaining doubts.

"Oh, Dan," she cried with her face buried in his neck, "I love you. Oh, I love you so!" She was trembling again.

Dan drew her closer. "I was afraid I'd never hear you say that,

Amy." He led her to the glider and sat close to her as he kissed her again. "You won't run away again, will you, Amy?" he asked without moving from the tender embrace.

"I have no reason to run any more, Dan," she whispered. "I have nothing to hide now."

They sat close together for a long time without speaking, each deeply moved by the staggering human reaction to a love so divinely created. His arm encircled her tenderly, and her head rested comfortably against his shoulder.

Dan sat up straight and reached into his pocket. "I have something for you."

The clouds had disappeared, and the moonlight beamed upon them in all its glory. The stone sparkled as he put the ring on her finger. "It was Mother's Amy. She wanted you to have it. Of course if you'd rather—"

"Oh, Dan!" she exclaimed. "She knew it all the time!" The joy glistened in her eyes as she looked at him.

"No more tears," he admonished with a smile.

"I can't help it," she said as she held his big hand to her cheek. "They're happy ones this time."

"Then you just cry all you want." He raised her hand to his lips and kissed her fingers. Then he took her in his arms and kissed her, tenderly at first, then hungrily. Dan put his face against the soft curls. It was quiet again, delightfully so, for each was intoxicated by the nearness of the other, hesitant to speak, yet wanting to express the joy that welled up within.

Finally Amy spoke. "I wish your mother could know how happy we are, Dan," she said, looking up at him. "She told me so much, but never that you loved me."

"I didn't know she knew either, Amy. Not until just before she died. Would it have made any difference if she had?"

"I'm afraid not. I would have run sooner." She moved her cheek against his shoulder. "You've both bestowed such honors upon me. I just hope I can live up to your expectations."

Dan sat on the edge of the seat, took her face between his hands and gently shook her head. "Amy, dear, we don't have to 'live up' to anything, not when we're living for the Lord."

She laughed softly. "I guess that's what I've been trying to do, Dan. I couldn't believe my past would ever let me—"

He put his finger on her lips. "Leave the past where it belongs, Amy."

Amy stretched herself, then relaxed again between the cool, crisp sheets and wondered if last night had really been real. She did not know life could be so sweet, so complete again. The memory of Dan's arms around her and the tenderness of his kiss would have been less than perfect had it not been for the restoration of her spiritual fellowship.

"Mr. Archer," Dan had said with mock formality, "I'd like permission to marry your sister."

Dave had been pacing the floor like a distraught father. "Don't tell me she's finally come to her senses!"

Amy laughed and hugged her brother. "Thanks for your help on that score."

"I have a confession to make, Amy. I'm not really sorry for talking to you the way I did last night."

"I forgive you anyway."

"Say, I didn't know I had so many people working for me!" Dan exclaimed, shaking Dave's hand vigorously.

Amy and Dan had talked long after the others had retired. There were so many plans to be made.

"Paul and Judy are getting married on Saturday, Amy. You'll come back with me tomorrow afternoon, won't you?"

"I don't want to miss it, but I can't be ready that soon, Dan."

"Well then, just take what you need. We'll get the rest later. The rehearsal is tomorrow evening and they made me promise I'd get back in time for it. Maybe Dave will take care of your car. There will be a lot of red tape to go through before you'll be able to go back with me. You know, injections, passport. And we've only got six weeks to take care of it all. Besides, Paul and Judy would never forgive you— "

"Dan! You won't go without me!" She looked at him in alarm.

"No, dear. Not a chance."

He was scheduled to fly to the west coast on a Saturday evening and board the ocean liner the next afternoon. They would be married that same Saturday. If Dan could not arrange for her to go that soon, then he would cancel his arrangements, and they would go the next most convenient time.

"It isn't everyone who gets an ocean cruise for a honeymoon trip!"

"I'm glad you're happy, Amy," he said softly. "It won't be easy, you know."

"Anything that's worth-while usually isn't, Dan. You told me that once." He drew her close to him again. "It will be easier than having you go without me. Would you do something for me when we get back to New Hope?"

"Name it." Agreement without commitment.

"Take me to see Larry."

"If you like."

"I hurt him, Dan."

"I know."

"Did you talk to him?"

"Quite a lot. I think he'll recover."

Amy was not sure what time it was when Dan had kissed her good night, but it was very late. He had been reluctant to leave. She had lain awake for a long time after retiring, trying to make herself believe the wonderment of it all.

She reached over to the little table to look at her watch, then jumped out of bed. Could it possibly be ten o'clock, or had she forgotten to wind her watch the night before? She had so much to do, and Dan would be coming for her at three-thirty.

"Well, you're a sleepy head!" Joy teased as Amy poured herself a cup of coffee. "Oh, Amy, tell me your plans! I'm so excited I could hardly wait till you got up! I was going to give you another five minutes, and then I was going to wake you up!"

"I wish you had." Amy gave Joy all the details. "He'll be here at three-thirty—that is if he hasn't changed his mind."

Joy looked at her curiously. "Amy, you're nuts."

"I know," she giggled. "I just can't believe it."

"We're going to miss you. But you look so happy I just think I'll burst!"

Amy grabbed her around the waist and they did several pirouettes around the kitchen table.

The mantel clock struck three as she set her suitcase down in the front hall. The twins followed with an assortment of small articles and put them with the bag. They had shadowed her all morning asking about Dan, her wedding, and why she had to go so far away. They managed to overcome their disappointment, however, when they learned they were going to get "married" with Aunt Amy, and their Daddy was going to give the bride away.

"See, I told you he would change his mind," Amy said as the clock struck three-thirty.

"Just see that you're on time for the wedding or he'll be saying the same thing!" Joy scolded with a twinkle in her eye.

"I have no reason to change my mind."

"And he does? You don't think very much of yourself, do you, Amy?"

"No, I don't," Amy said, her voice too serious. "I'm not worthy of a man like Dan, Joy, and that's why I can't understand why I should be so happy. I know now though, it's only through Christ that we can be on the same plane. Dan finally made me see that last night."

"And you think he'll change his mind! Amy, you *are* nuts!"

Dan wore the same expression of contentment he had worn the evening before. Amy ran to his outstretched arms.

The seemingly endless chatter of the twins abruptly ceased. They stood awe-struck in Dan's presence. Not for long, however, and they soon busied themselves by carrying some of Amy's things out to the car.

Dave came home to see them off. The four of them were standing by the front door, about to go out, when two little voices raised in argument drew them to the kitchen. Rebecca was standing in the middle of the table and Rachel was perched precariously close to the edge of the countertop.

"Aunt Amy," Rachel pleaded, "tell your big man to come over here."

Dan winked at Amy and, smiling, obliged. He stood close to Rachel whose eyes were at the same level as his while she reached over and put her hand on top of his head. "See, Becky," she said triumphantly, "I told you you had to stand up here!"

They all laughed as Dan swung her down to the floor. Rachel looked at him adoringly. "If you're going to be Aunt Amy's Daddy, what should we call you?"

Dan pretended to look puzzled. "Say," he brightened, "why don't you call me Uncle Dan? But you know something? I know a little girl who looks just like you, so I don't know what to call you either!"

She giggled delightedly. "Oh, you're silly. That's easy. That one over there is Becky. She has all her teeth!" The little clown was delighted at their laughter.

"Aunt Amy, Aunt Amy!" Becky screamed. "You found it! You found it! Oh, I'm so glad!" She ran to her aunt.

Amy stooped down and hugged the little girl to her. "Yes, honey, I found it."

"Did he help you?" asked her sister.

"Yes, he did. And so did you."

"Where did you find your laffer, Aunt Amy?"

"Why, darlin', it wasn't lost after all. I just forgot how to use it!"

"You won't forget again, will you?"

"Never again," she promised, hugging them both.

She and Dan drove away midst tears and laughter. The trip home was all too brief as they became absorbed in their plans for the future.

"I'm an idiot, Dan."

"Say, young lady," he said with a frown, "I'll not have anyone talking about my future wife that way!"

She laughed and put her head on his shoulder. "How could I have thought of letting you go? I *must* have been out of my mind."

He wanted to stop the car, take her in his arms and kiss her, but it would not be proper. Not in broad daylight. And on such a well-traveled road. But then he had never been one to stand on convention.

"I wish – "

He never did hear what she wished. "What did you say, Amy?"

"Hmmm? I forgot." He kissed her again.

"Dan, I know you don't want me to talk about it, but I'd give anything if I could tear a few pages from the story of my life."

I *don't* want you to talk about it, Amy. I don't want you to think about it any more, either. But honey, just think for a minute. If that had never happened, where would you be now? The Lord uses different circumstances, sometimes mighty strange ones, to work His plans. Why, you know, you would be Mrs. Somebody Else, and I'd be poor bachelor Dan!"

"I get your point," she said laughing. "And a lot of things have happened since then, things He planned to bring us together. So many things."

"I know, Amy. Hard things, on so many people too." He kissed her again, then started the motor.

The white pavement rounded a curve, and as they reached the crest of a hill, the city of New Hope stretched beneath them.

"New Hope never looked so good, Dan."

"Maybe it's the rose-colored glasses."

"I certainly am looking at it in a different light, if that's what you mean. 'No Hope,' that's what I called it when I left. I said I'd never come back."

It was after seven-thirty when they turned into the Sanderford drive. They walked hand-in-hand to the house and had no sooner stepped inside when they heard Elaine scream. An announcement was unnecessary.

"Amy! Oh, Amy!" Elaine threw her arms around her and cried with joy. "Dan, where did you find her?" she asked, hugging her brother. The rest were there – Mark, Paul and Judy, Roy and Faith.

"Oh, I found her wandering aimlessly along the side of the road." He winked at Amy. Her eyes filled with pride as she looked up at him.

"You didn't!" she shrieked. Elaine was the only one who had not seen the wink.

"Welcome to the family, little sister," said Paul. He put his arms around Amy and kissed her soundly on the lips.

The seriousness of the occasion was not lessened by their levity, for their hearts were filled to overflowing with human, as well as divine, love and happiness.

"Welcome home, Amy." Roy had patiently been waiting to greet her, and his words expressed far more than any of them knew, except for perhaps Dan and Amy themselves.

Chapter 28

SOMETHING OLD, SOMETHING NEW, something borrowed, something blue. Louise Sanderford's wedding veil, the same one Elaine had worn, was the something old. And there were so many pretty new things, but if anyone asked her, she would mention the shiny satin slippers she was wearing. Something borrowed – Elaine's wedding dress, of course, the gown created by loving hands. And something blue? The blue-white gem she had temporarily changed to her right hand, that was a precious something blue.

And the sky was blue, its marshmallow clouds, so startlingly white against it, made it a more vivid hue. It matched her eyes, he had told her once, long ago. And just yesterday he had told her it was all the blue she needed.

His eyes were on her as she moved down the aisle toward him. "I love you, Dan," hers said as she finally raised them to meet his.

"Dearly beloved, we are gathered together in the sight of God and these witnesses to join this man and this woman in holy matrimony." Roy's words, oft repeated of late, had a special significance as these two stood before him.

Had there been any trace of uncertainty remaining for the lovely bride, it disappeared as she put her confidence in Dan's strength. Together they had entrusted their lives to the Heavenly Father's care.

"I, Amy, take thee, Dan – for better, for worse, for richer, for poorer – till death us do part." She looked up at him as she made the promises, and for those moments they were the only two in the sanctuary.

"I, Dan, take thee, Amy – to have and to hold, from this day forward – forsaking all others – as long as we both shall live."

"What God hath joined together let no man put asunder."

The congregation held its breath as Dan kissed his bride, then breathed a contented sigh to see the happy expressions the bride and groom wore.

"Ladies and gentlemen," Roy proudly announced, "I would like you to meet Reverend and Mrs. Daniel Sanderford."

The airport was swarming with people, the travelers far outnumbered by those bidding farewell.

"Oh, Amy, I'm going to miss you so!" It was Karen who had elbowed her way to her new friend's side.

Larry followed close behind, shook Dan's hand warmly and planted a kiss on Amy's cheek. He turned to Karen. "Now don't go crying. Besides, who's going to cheer *me* up!" He laughed good-naturedly.

"Good-by! Good-by!" everyone shouted at once. "Don't forget to write!" The newlyweds boarded the plane as the handkerchiefs waved, just a few of them wet with tears.

The jet-propelled plane whistled down the runway as Amy and Dan strained to catch a last glimpse of loved ones, still waving. In a matter of minutes they were miles away.

"Dan," she almost asked, "why do I hear bells ringing?" She smiled as she moved closer to him and put her hand in his.

The question he was about to ask was answered in her smile.

It was good to be going home.